A DEATH AT FOUNTAINS ABBEY

Also by Antonia Hodgson

The Devil in the Marshalsea
The Last Confession of Thomas Hawkins

A DEATH AT FOUNTAINS ABBEY

Antonia Hodgson

HODDER &
STOUGHTON

First published in Great Britain in 2016 by Hodder & Stoughton
An Hachette UK company

1

A CIP catalogue record for this title is available from the British Library

Hardback ISBN 978 1 473 61509 0
Trade Paperback ISBN 978 1 473 61510 6
eBook ISBN 978 1 473 61508 3

Typeset in Adobe Caslon by Hewer Text UK Ltd, Edinburgh
Printed and bound by Clays Ltd, St Ives plc

Hodder & Stoughton policy is to use papers that are natural, renewable
and recyclable products and made from wood grown in sustainable
forests. The logging and manufacturing processes are expected to conform
to the environmental regulations of the country of origin.

Hodder & Stoughton Ltd
Carmelite House
50 Victoria Embankment
London EC4Y 0DZ

www.hodder.co.uk

For my parents, with love

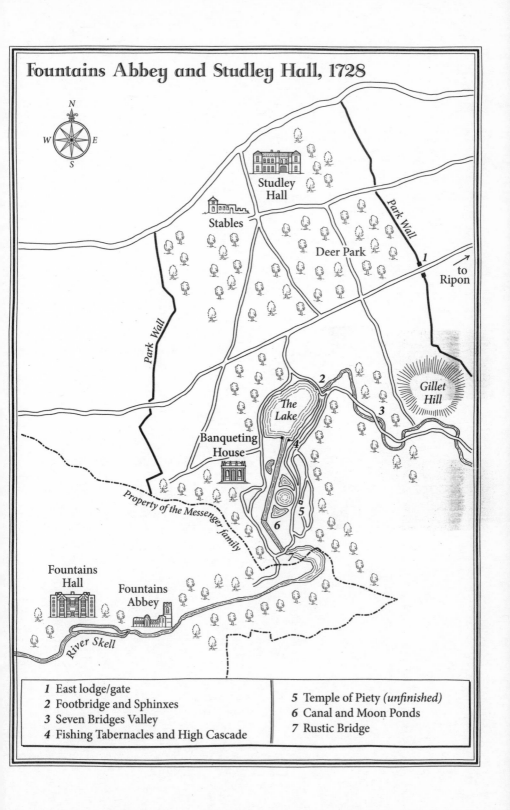

Fountains Abbey and Studley Hall, 1728

N
W E
S

Studley Hall

Stables

Deer Park

Park Wall

Park Wall

1

to Ripon

Gillet Hill

2

The Lake

3

Banqueting House

4

5

6

Property of the Messenger family

Fountains Hall

Fountains Abbey

7

River Skell

1 East lodge/gate	**5** Temple of Piety (*unfinished*)
2 Footbridge and Sphinxes	**6** Canal and Moon Ponds
3 Seven Bridges Valley	**7** Rustic Bridge
4 Fishing Tabernacles and High Cascade	

Was any thing like this ever heard of in any Age
before? Was ever any Englishman us'd in such a
manner?

John Aislabie, 1721

Bonfires were made in the citty the day Mr Aisleby
went to the Tower.

Thomas Brodrick, 1721

Prologue

January, 1701
Red Lion Square, London

She never meant for the fire to spread. It was a distraction, nothing more, a trick to keep them busy while she took what she was owed. She had cried, *'Fire! Fire in the attic!'*, and laughed to herself as the house woke in panic. They pushed past her on the stairs, running to fetch water, to save what they could, coughing as the smoke caught their lungs.

She saw him too, clutching his daughter Mary to his chest as he carried her to safety. John Aislabie. He didn't notice her as he passed, close enough to touch. He hadn't noticed her for a long time.

She joined the flow of servants hurrying downstairs. When they ran out into the square, no one realised that Molly Gaining wasn't with them any more.

She crept down the empty corridor to Mr Aislabie's study, tiptoeing her way in the dark. It was the first duty of a housemaid to be silent. Invisible.

He had called her his treasure. He'd murmured promises to her in the deep night, vows he had never meant to keep. *I will cover you with gold; I will wrap you in silks.* She had believed him.

I

She had given him everything he wanted. And when he was done, he'd tossed her aside, no longer his treasure but some sordid piece of rubbish he would never touch again.

She heard muffled shouts, somewhere high up in the house. Here inside his study, all was still, save for the ticking of the clock. She felt her way to the desk with no need for a lamp: she had swept and polished this room every day for the last five years. She opened a drawer, groping past quills and papers to find a key buried in one corner. Moving swiftly to the hearth, she splayed her fingers, searching for the loose floorboard she'd discovered a few days before. *There.* She lifted the board and reached inside, touching cold metal. A strongbox, so heavy she needed both hands to pull it free.

The key turned with a soft click. A shiver of illicit excitement thrilled through her. She must be quick, before the fire was tamed and she was discovered. She threw back the lid.

He had promised her gold, and diamonds. She would keep him to that promise.

She lifted out a handful of jewels, gold chains dangling between her fingers. Touch and memory showed her what her eyes couldn't see in the dark: long strands of creamy white pearls, gold rings studded with precious stones, a diamond and ruby brooch that she could feel now, cool and heavy in her palm. Bags of gold coins. She tucked them into the wide pocket she had stitched beneath her gown, and reached for more. Enough for the life she had dreamed of. Enough for the life she deserved.

Voices, loud outside the door. She had lingered too long. Cursing under her breath, she threw another fistful of coins into her pocket and straightened her gown just as a young man pushed open the door and strode into the study. His face was handsome in the orange light of his candle, and full of purpose.

'The account books. Hurry!'

Jack Sneaton: Aislabie's clerk. She shrank back, praying he wouldn't see her, while he gathered up books and papers, throwing them into the arms of his apprentice. Trust Jack. Of all the things to save from the fire, he runs for his precious tally books.

He turned for the door.

'Sir?' Sneaton's apprentice nodded towards the hearth.

She was discovered. Fear pressed a fist into her heart.

Sneaton thrust a sheaf of papers into the boy's arms. 'Molly? What are you about down there—' He stopped and stared in dismay at the coins and jewels glinting on the floor where she had spilled them in her haste. He blinked several times, very fast, as if hoping the scene might vanish before his eyes.

'Thief!' his apprentice hissed.

Sneaton winced, as if the accusation caused him physical pain. He took one last, studied look at the empty strongbox. Then he grabbed Molly by the arm and pulled her to her feet.

'No!' she cried, as he dragged her from the room. 'I weren't stealing, I swear. Please, Jack . . . Mr Sneaton, sir – I was saving them from the fire.'

He pressed his hand against the nape of her neck and pushed her through the house out on to the street. She stumbled on the steps and fell to the ground, crying out as a shard of glass pierced the plump flesh beneath her thumb. There was glass everywhere.

She crawled along the cobbles on her hands and knees, sucking in her breath as she pulled the glass free. Blood trickled down her wrist.

And, looking up, she saw what she had done.

The fire was raging from the top of the house, flames tearing across the roof and bursting through broken windows. Thick grey clouds of smoke billowed high above the flames, choking the night sky. A line of servants passed buckets of water up through the building as neighbours hurried to join them, desperate to stop the fire spreading further along the square.

A footman collapsed to his knees at the doorway, his face black with soot. He gulped a few breaths of clear air, grabbed a fresh bucket, and plunged back inside.

'It was only a small fire,' she whispered. She tottered forwards, drawn towards the flames. She could feel the immense heat of them on her face. 'I never meant . . .'

Sneaton pulled her away. 'Mr Aislabie. Mr Aislabie, sir!'

He was standing a few feet from them, closer to the burning house, still holding Mary in his arms. Jane, his younger daughter, was clinging to his leg. Both girls were mute with terror.

'Mr Aislabie,' Sneaton called again, and he turned, and saw them.

'Molly,' he said. 'Thank God you're safe.'

Misery and fury closed her throat. *Now you look at me, John. Now you speak my name.*

'Found her in your room, sir,' Sneaton said. 'She was stealing from your strongbox.'

He stared at her.

'I wasn't thieving,' she stammered. 'I was trying to save them from the fire. You know me, sir . . .'

She saw a flicker of doubt in his eyes. 'We'll settle this later,' he said, distracted by the flames. He lifted Mary to the ground and handed both girls to a neighbour. 'Harry!' he called out to one of his men, limping from the house. 'Where's Mrs Aislabie? Is she safe?'

Harry couldn't speak from the smoke. He bent to the ground, wheezing as he took in the fresh air.

'For heaven's sake, man, where's my son?' Aislabie shouted, in a sudden panic. 'Where's Lizzie? Where's my little girl?'

Harry shook his head.

For a second, Aislabie was too stunned to react. Then he spun about and ran blindly into the blazing house, calling their names. *Anne. William. Lizzie.*

'Damn it!' Sneaton cursed. He pushed Molly into his friend's arms as if she were a bundle of dirty rags. 'Keep a hold of her, Harry. She's a bloody thief.'

Worse than that. She gazed up at the house, the flames rolling across the roof, the smoke pouring from every window. Lizzie, the youngest girl, only just learning to walk. Mrs Aislabie. William, the new baby. What had she done? An emptiness opened up inside her and her body felt light, as if she could drift up into the air and dissolve to nothing . . .

'*Molly!*' Sneaton's voice broke the spell.

'It was such a small thing, Jack. Such a small fire. I never meant . . .'

She never forgot it, the look Jack Sneaton gave her in that long, silent moment. 'You were my jewel, Molly,' he said, quietly.

The cobbles tilted beneath her feet. She never knew. He'd never told her. If she could just go back half an hour. That was all she needed to make things right again – just half an hour. But it was too late.

Sneaton snatched up a bucket and soaked his neckerchief in the water. 'Where are they, Harry?'

Harry pointed to a window on the second floor. 'You won't reach it, Jack. The smoke's terrible.'

Sneaton put the wet cloth to his mouth and ran inside.

Harry pulled her away. She stumbled along with him until they reached a ring of neighbours, clinging to each other in horror as the house burned down in front of them. They watched as Mr Aislabie was dragged out by his servants empty-handed, screaming his wife's name. Saw the last few men beaten back by the smoke and flames.

'Nothing to be done, now, God rest their souls,' one of the neighbours said. 'Just pray it doesn't spread.'

Harry dug his fingers deeper into her shoulder.

Then someone gave a shout and pointed to a window on the second floor. 'There! Look!'

Jack Sneaton stood at the window, clasping a tiny bundle to his chest. He clambered on to the ledge, smoke pouring all about him like a thick grey cloak. No way to clamber down, not from such a height. He gestured fiercely to the men below with his free hand. They gathered beneath him, huddled together. He raised the bundle carefully in both hands, then let go.

They caught it. Safe. A cheer rose up. Someone called to Mr Aislabie. 'Your son! Mr Aislabie! Your son is saved!'

At the same moment a fresh burst of flames swept out through the window, engulfing Jack Sneaton. With a great cry, he dropped from the ledge and fell twenty feet to the ground.

'Jack!' Harry rushed forward to help his friend, forgetting her in his hurry. She couldn't see Jack, but she could see men beating at the flames with their coats, and a man rushing forward with a bucket of water. She could hear screaming.

Molly glanced about her. None of the people standing around her knew what she had done. She was just another servant, caught up in the tragedy. The crowd surged forwards, anxious to see if the night's hero had survived his fall. Mr Aislabie was holding his baby son, and weeping. Amidst the chaos, the shouts for aid, the men running back and forth with more water, Molly stood alone, forgotten.

She took one step away. Dared another.

No one stopped her.

No one even noticed her leave.

Numb, half blind from the smoke, she walked away. Beyond the press of spectators, the street had fallen eerily still. She drifted past the stone watch tower at the end of the square as if in a dream.

Behind Red Lion Square lay a dank alley. It was too narrow for the grander carriages, too muddy and noisome for the better folk to use. This was where the week's coal was delivered, and the night soil was collected. And it was here that Molly Gaining stumbled now, weighed down with a pocket full of jewellery and gold coins. How long before she was missed? How far could she run, and where should she go?

She had reached the back entrance to Mr Aislabie's home, burning as hard as the front. No one had thought to fight the fire from here. Or perhaps there were not men enough to spare. The flames had begun to spread along the roof to the neighbouring house. She thought of the Great Fire, the tales her father had told her of it tearing through the streets for days.

'I never meant to hurt no one,' she whispered, to the flames, to the smoke. The emptiness had returned, a hollow feeling deep in her chest. She didn't know, yet, that it would never leave her.

As she stared at the house she had destroyed, she caught a glimpse of something small and pale shimmering at a window on the ground floor. And Molly knew – she *knew* – what it was.

Redemption.

TWENTY-SEVEN YEARS LATER

The First Day

Chapter One

John Aislabie was in trouble.

'I believe my life is in danger,' he wrote, in a letter to the queen dated the 22nd of February. And then, when he received no reply, again on the 6th of March. He reminded her of the great service he had performed on her behalf, the sacrifices he had made to ensure that the royal family's honour – that the crown itself – had remained intact. He underscored the words *honour* and *crown* with a thick line, making the threat explicit. A determined man, to threaten the royal family. Determined and desperate.

The queen responded a week later. 'We are sending a young gentleman up to Yorkshire to resolve the matter. We do not wish to hear from you again.'

It was a measure of Mr Aislabie's poor standing at court that I was the young gentleman in question.

'Mr Hawkins?' The coachman jumped down from his seat, boots thudding on the cobbles.

I took my hands from my pockets and nodded in greeting. I had arrived in Ripon late the night before, taking a room at the Royal Oak rather than travel the last few miles to Aislabie's house in the dark. After breakfasting this morning

I had sent word of my arrival. The carriage had raced from Studley Hall within the half hour. Clearly my host was anxious to meet me.

I couldn't return the compliment. I had travelled to Yorkshire at the command of Queen Caroline – a command presented as a gift. *It would be pleasant,* non, *a short trip to the country? A chance to recover from your recent misfortunes? Fresh air and long walks?* This from a woman who scarce moved from her sofa. I had declined the offer. The offer was transformed into a threat. So here I was, against my will, preparing to meet one of the most hated men in England.

John Aislabie had been Chancellor of the Exchequer during the great South Sea frenzy eight years before. He'd proposed the scheme in the House of Commons. At his encouragement, thousands had invested heavily in the company's shares. After all, what could be more secure? Mr Aislabie had put his own money into the scheme. He had invested tens of thousands of pounds of *King George's money.*

And for a few giddy months that summer, shares had exploded in value. Overnight, apprentices became as rich as lords. Servants abandoned their masters, owning stock worth more than they could earn in five lifetimes. Thousands more scrambled to join the madness as the price of shares rose hour by hour. In the coffeehouses of Change Alley, trading turned more lunatic by the day. Poets and lawyers, tailors and turnkeys, parsons and brothel women scooped up every last coin they could find and joined in the national madness.

Then the bubble burst, as bubbles do. The lucky few sold out in time, holding on to their fortunes. The rest were ruined, catastrophically so. How many took their own lives in despair, rather than face the consequences of their unimaginable debts? Impossible to say. But the South Sea Scheme had been the

Great Plague of investment – and Mr Aislabie had spread the disease.

The nation shouted for justice. Aislabie was found guilty of corruption and thrown in the Tower. When the public mind had turned to other things, he was allowed to slink away to Studley Royal, his country estate. *Bankrupt*, he insisted. *Scarce able to feed his poor family. Sacrificed to spare more noble-blooded men.*

No one listened and no one cared.

I had been eighteen at the time, studying divinity at Oxford. I am a gambler to my marrow, but I did not have the funds to dabble in stockjobbing, having invested my father's allowance in the more traditional markets of whoring and drinking. I had watched in astonishment and frustration as two of my friends built dizzying fortunes in a matter of weeks. One of them had been wise enough to sell his shares before the final subscription, leaving him with a profit of ten thousand pounds. The other, a young fellow named Christopher d'Arfay, lost everything. He joined the army soon after, and I never saw him again. But I thought of him on the road north. One life destroyed, among tens of thousands.

Mr Aislabie's coachman was a cheerful, robust fellow named Pugh, his cheeks scarred from an ancient attack of smallpox. He must have been near fifty, but he picked up my large portmanteau as if it were empty, and swung it on to the carriage. 'Expected you yesterday, sir.'

I rolled my shoulders, frowning as my spine cracked. My journey had lasted five lamentable days, bumping and jolting along in a series of worn-out coaches until every bone had been thoroughly rattled in its socket. I felt as if I were recovering from a rheumatic fit, I ached so much. 'Bad roads,' I said, though that was not the only reason for the delay.

Pugh grunted in sympathy. 'I've drove Mr Aislabie up and down to London a fair few times. That stretch from Leicester to

Nottingham could kill a man, it's so poor. No better in spring than winter.'

'Yes. Very poor.' It is the nature of long, tedious journeys that – on arrival – they must be lived again, in long, tedious conversation. A simple: 'I travelled. It was dreadful. Here I am,' will not do, apparently.

Pugh tied a box to the back of the chaise. Books, tobacco, playing cards and dice. A brace of pistols. I had worn them at my belt on the road, in case of attack. I hoped I would not need to take them out again.

'A young gentleman fell hard on the Nottingham road a few weeks ago,' Pugh trundled on. 'Broke his arm and his wrist, poor lad. I trust you didn't take a fall along the way, sir?'

'Thank you, no.'

He slotted the last of my boxes into place. 'Glad to hear that, Mr Hawkins. You've suffered enough injury these past weeks, I'd say.'

I raised my hand to my throat on instinct, then dropped it swiftly. A few months ago my neighbour had been stabbed to death in his bed – the day after I had threatened to kill him. At my trial, the jury had judged me not upon the evidence, but upon my character and reputation. I was found guilty, and sentenced to hang. Against all odds I had survived – but only after I had spent ten long, agonising minutes dangling from a rope, suffocating slowly as a hundred thousand spectators cheered me on. Ever since then I had suffered from nightmares: the white hood thrust over my head, the cart pulling away beneath my feet, the rope tightening around my neck. These terrors filled my dreams, and in the day left me with a dull ache in my chest – a feeling of dread that I could not shake.

I was grateful beyond reason to be alive. There were times when the mere fact of my existence could lift me to ecstasy – as if I had knocked back three bowls of punch in one. But I had met with Death that day at the scaffold. I had crossed the border into his kingdom, if only for a few moments. I feared the experience had changed me for ever. I feared, in truth, that Death still kept a hand upon my shoulder.

My hope had been that my story would not have travelled as far as the Yorkshire Dales. In the retelling of that story, I had been transmuted from an idle rogue to a golden hero – a martyr, even. That was what they had been calling me in the London newspapers, when they believed me dead. I didn't want to be a hero. Heroes were sent on secret missions by the Queen of England, when they would much rather sit in a coffeehouse getting drunk and singing ballads.

My dreams of remaining anonymous had been dashed at breakfast, when a serving maid had asked to touch my throat for luck. I'd shooed her from the room, but it had been a gloomy experience.

If she'd asked to touch your cock, you wouldn't feel so gloomy. Kitty, in my head.

'We're ready to leave?'

'We are, sir,' Pugh replied, nodding towards the inn. 'If you would call your wife.'

My wife. By which he meant Kitty, who was neither my wife, nor within calling distance. For the sake of Kitty's good name, and to ensure a civil reception at Studley Hall, I had written in advance to Mr Aislabie, explaining that I would be accompanied on my visit by my wife, Mrs Catherine Hawkins. How wondrously respectable that sounded. Unfortunately I had not had the time nor the heart to write again further along the road to explain that my *wife* and I had quarrelled fearsomely at Newport Pagnell, resulting in Mrs Hawkins' swift return to London.

'Fuck off then, Tom,' she had shouted, in the middle of the inn. 'Fuck off to Yorkshire, and don't blame me if you die in some horrific way, stabbed and burned and throttled and *mangled*. I shall not grieve for you, not for one second. I will jump on your grave and sing *I told you so, Thomas Hawkins, you fucking idiot.* You may count upon it.'

'Mrs Hawkins was called home on urgent business.'

'Sorry to hear that, sir. You're travelling alone, then?'

Not quite. A dark figure slipped out from behind a rag-filled wagon. He was dressed in an ancient pair of mud-brown woollen breeches and a black coat, cuffs covering his knuckles. *My* black coat, in fact, which was several inches too big for him. His black curls were tied in a ribbon beneath a battered three-cornered hat.

'And who's this?' Pugh asked, bending towards Sam as if he were a child. I had made the same mistake, the first time I'd met him. A boy of St Giles, raised in the shadows, smaller than he should be.

Sam's eyes – black and fathomless – fixed upon mine.

'This is Master Samuel Fleet.' Son of a gang captain, nephew of an assassin. And at fourteen years of age, on his way to becoming more deadly than either. 'I'm his guardian.'

Well. Someone had to keep a watch on him.

The town square was packed with stalls for the Thursday market, the air laced with the warm tang of wool and sheepskin. Traders and townsfolk recognised our coach and hurried to clear the way for us: Mr Aislabie's standing was far greater here in his own county. He had been mayor of Ripon, many years ago, and his son was now the town's representative in parliament. Such things command a degree of respect, if not love.

We were soon through the town and riding along a country lane banked with thick hedgerows. Our carriage was a fine, open chaise, pulled by four of the best horses I had ever seen. The sun gleamed upon their bay coats as they raced towards Mr Aislabie's estate of Studley Royal, along a road they knew well and seemed to enjoy. Pugh gave us their names, and the names of their forefathers, and would have continued on if I had not distracted him with a query about the weather. He was the head groom at Studley, and most likely knew the horses' ancestry better than his own. He was a garrulous fellow, and I learned swiftly that a response was neither required nor particularly welcome. He spoke in the way some men whistle, and it was best to leave him to it.

I settled back, enjoying the sunshine. Insects buzzed in the grass, sparrows pecked at the ground with short beaks, a blackbird sang out from the branches above our heads. All about us, left, right and onwards, the fields rose and dipped, seamed with dry-stone walls and hedges. A pleasant, spring green world, spreading out to the horizon.

Sam perched upon the opposite bench, watching it all with a mistrustful eye, as if the land might rise up and swallow him. I had grown up on the Suffolk coast with its quiet villages and endless skies. Sam was born and raised in London, happy in the stink and bustle of its worst slums. He knew every thieves' alley, every poisonous gin shop, every abandoned cellar transformed into a makeshift brothel. He was street vermin, street filth, and proud of it.

A fat bumblebee buzzed between us. Sam froze – a boy who would face down a blade without blinking. 'It won't harm you,' I murmured, so as not to embarrass him in front of Pugh. Sam lifted one shoulder, as if he couldn't care less if it stung him repeatedly in the face, but he looked relieved when it drifted on its way.

Each morning of our journey north, Sam had clambered ahead of me into the carriage and taken the bench closest to the horses, facing backwards. This suited us both well enough: if we had sat side by side we would have rolled into one another at every sharp corner. But it was such a deliberate action that I had begun to suspect a deeper motive; Sam did not do such things upon a whim.

On the day of my hanging, I had been bound in chains and paraded through the streets on an open cart. Condemned prisoners ride backwards to the gallows. The journey had been terrifying: the crowds lining the streets, the mud flung at the cart, the hatred pulsing through the air. My own fear, sharp and solid as a stone in my throat. We must all travel blind to our deaths, but to feel its slow, creeping approach with every turn of the wheel is a horror beyond imagining.

The simple roll and pitch of a carriage could return me to that morning in a heartbeat. Somehow, Sam understood this and took the seat facing backwards in order to spare me. How he had come to guess at such a deep-buried feeling I couldn't say – and there would be no profit in asking. I was lucky to squeeze ten words out of the boy in fifty miles. But we had travelled together four days in succession with no other company, facing one another as the carriage rumbled along. Perhaps he had simply read the truth in my eyes. It was an unsettling thought, that he had been watching me so carefully.

You can't trust him, Tom. Kitty's voice again in my head. *You know what he is.*

We had travelled no more than a quarter hour when I saw a boundary wall ahead, ten feet high and stretching off into the distance. The horses pulled harder with no need for the whip, eager to be home. 'Is this Mr Aislabie's estate?'

Pugh twisted in his seat. 'One corner of it. It's *Aizelbee*, sir.' I'd pronounced it *Ailabee* – the French way.

I hunched lower in my coat. It was a bright morning, but there was a sharp wind blowing in from the east. Sam was sitting on his hands to keep them warm. Feeble city folk, the pair of us.

'Will we pass Fountains Abbey?' Fellow guests at the Oak had mentioned the ancient monastery at supper. According to the – somewhat biased – landlord, they were the largest and the most splendid ruins in the country. And haunted, naturally.

'No, sir,' Pugh replied, and fell silent for once.

We rode through the tiny village of Studley Roger. Sam released his hands and clung to the edge of the carriage, taking in every detail as we passed through the hamlet. The size of the windows, the shape of the chimneys. The doors left open to the fresh air. A couple of muddy lanes. But nothing familiar, not really. *And no tavern*, I noticed, mournfully. *No rowdy coffeehouse, the air clogged with pipe smoke, the latest newspaper laid out upon the table.*

'Second house upon the left. How many geese in the yard?'

Sam blinked. 'Seven.'

This was a game we had played along the road. At least, I had played it and Sam had humoured me. He'd been raised to remain alert to his surroundings. In the city slums, there were threats and opportunities lurking in every doorway. Information could earn a boy his supper, or save his life. But I suspected Sam had a particular talent for it, something he was born with: a precision of mind far beyond my own or anyone else's, for that matter.

We arrived at an iron gate, decorated with a coat of arms and flanked by a pair of stone lodges. An old man hurried out from one of them, waving his hat in greeting as he pulled open the gate. We rode through at a brisk pace, on to an oak-lined avenue. Thick branches reached out across the path, forming a tangle of shadows beneath. The sun, filtered through the leaves, cast a soft green light upon our skin.

I smiled at Sam, thinking of the rookery of St Giles, where planks and ladders criss-crossed the rooftops, creating high pathways through the slums. 'Like home.'

He frowned in disagreement.

'Mr Aislabie plans to chop all these down,' Pugh said, waving at the trees. 'Limes are better for an avenue. They grow straight. Oaks grow gnarly.' As we crested the hill he slowed the horses. 'If you'd look behind you, sir.'

I turned to see a magnificent view, the long avenue of oaks leading straight back towards the gate. From here we could see the valley below and then, rising on a twin hill, the town of Ripon. Through some trick of perspective, it appeared as if one could reach out and steal it. The avenue had been laid out so that the cathedral crowned the view precisely.

Pugh was smiling, waiting for a compliment as if he had knitted the entire thing by hand.

'Wonderful,' I obliged.

He grinned, and moved the horses on. 'Best estate in England. Best in Europe when Mr Aislabie's done with it.'

And how did Mr Aislabie pay for all these improvements, I wondered? Had he not been left *bankrupt*? Perhaps he'd stumbled across a magic lamp.

We turned right on to a gravelled drive already planted with the preferred lime trees. The path grew steep, the horses pulling hard against the harness. As we crested the hill, I craned my neck to catch the first view of the house.

I was expecting grandeur: a majestic heap in the new Palladian style. The views had promised it. The avenue of limes had proclaimed it. But Studley Hall was an indifferent thing, with very little to recommend it. While the front looked out upon a magnificent deer park, the rest of the house was suffocated by dense woodland. The original building, with its great arched porch and tall windows, must have begun its days as a banqueting hall. It looked to be at least three hundred years old and in a poor state of repair. Over time, additional wings had been tacked on to the original frame, with no thought to proportion or symmetry.

It soon became clear why Mr Aislabie had allowed his home to crumble into such a woeful condition. To the left of the house and some thirty yards in front of it, a score of men toiled over a new building. Carts rumbled back and forth, pulled by great workhorses. A large, sweating man stood in the middle of the foundations, swearing loudly at the workers.

Aislabie must be working upon a new home, more in keeping with his vast estate. It was certainly laid out on a grand scale. I frowned at the building works as we passed. Noise, mud, and a ruined view, barely a hundred feet from where we would be sleeping. The foreman caught my frown and scowled in turn, arms folded across his fat belly.

Pugh slowed the horses and the carriage settled to a halt at the front steps. Sam jumped down at once, landing almost soundlessly on the gravel. The house was no more impressive at close quarters. The window sashes needed a fresh coat of paint after a freezing winter, and the roof was in a sorry condition. I searched for something pleasant to say.

'Charming.'

Pugh looked at me, then looked at the house, as if we might be seeing two different buildings.

The doors to the great hall swung open and a man of middling age emerged, one shoulder hunched. 'Good day, sir,' he called down the steps, clutching the edge of the door for balance. As he shuffled out I saw that his right leg was lost, replaced with a wooden peg. I hurried up to meet him, and only just suppressed a gasp of shock. His face had been ruined by fire. The right side had caught the worst of it, leaving behind a thick web of scars. Old burn marks and further scars spread down his neck, disappearing beneath his cravat. His right eye was blind, the iris a cloudy grey. His right hand too, was badly damaged, twisted in upon itself save for the thumb and forefinger.

I did my best not to stare, but it was impossible. It must have been a terrible accident, to inflict such horrifying injuries. He waited, used to the reaction of strangers. When I was recovered enough to give my name, he dipped his head.

'Welcome to Studley Hall.' His voice was damaged, low and rasping. It made him sound villainous, poor fellow.

I followed him into the entrance chamber, an old feasting hall with a patterned ceiling two storeys high above our heads. The latticed windows blocked out the spring sunshine, and the huge stone hearth was unlit. 'Thank you, Mr ...'

'... Sneaton. If you would follow me? Mr Aislabie is waiting.' He was a man of the south, and he pronounced the name differently from Pugh: *Aizlabee* rather than *Aizelbee*. Well really, if the servants couldn't agree on how to say their master's name, what hope did I have?

'Perhaps we might unpack ...' I gestured towards the carriage, hoping to visit my quarters first.

A sullen-faced fellow of about five and thirty strode past us to the carriage, dressed in a green velvet coat and immaculate white stockings, his wig heavily powdered. The butler, I supposed. Two younger footmen trailed eagerly in his wake, dressed in the same livery, though not so fine. Within moments the three men were hurrying back through the hall, bags and boxes hoisted on their shoulders. That is to say, the two footmen carried my belongings, while the butler strode behind them, imperious, as if he could hear a fanfare blaring in his head as he walked.

'West wing, Bagby,' Sneaton called gruffly to this regal creature. 'The oak apartments.' Bagby did not condescend a reply. He strode up the staircase, past a large, faded tapestry, and was gone.

Sam had taken advantage of the bustle to enter the room in his preferred way: unnoticed. He stood with his back to us, staring up at the deer antlers and weapons covering the high stone walls, the swords, muskets and pistols.

Sneaton, spying him for the first time, gave a jolt of surprise. Sam had an unsettling ability to fade into the background, and Sneaton was not the first to be startled by it. 'Your valet?' he asked, in a disbelieving tone. Was it the mismatched clothes that caused suspicion? The black tangle of curls, defiantly kept free of any wig? Or did Sneaton sense something deeper than such surface trifles?

'My ward.'

Sam reached up and traced a finger over the firing mechanism of an old musket. Sneaton frowned, clearly vexed by such an obvious lie but not sure how to confront it. While he struggled with this conundrum, I joined Sam at the wall. 'Find our rooms,' I murmured. 'And have a scout around if you can.'

Sam slipped away up the stairs.

I followed Sneaton through an empty drawing room furnished with sagging red velvet couches and gilded tables. A harpsichord stood in one corner, its inner lid decorated with a classical scene of nymphs dancing by a river. The walls were hung with family portraits down through the ages. The finest of all was set above the white marble fireplace: the painting of a young man in a brown velvet coat. He had a confident, vigorous air, and wore an easy smile, as if he were contented with the world and a little pleased with himself. I stopped in front of him, curious.

'Mr Hawkins,' Sneaton nudged. He was wheezing a little. 'Is that Mr Aislabie?'

'Yes. From thirty years ago.' His damaged hand hovered at my elbow. 'Please, sir. He is impatient to meet you.'

I followed him into a narrow corridor. 'Has something happened, Mr Sneaton?'

He knocked on the door to Aislabie's study. His face was grave, beneath the tangle of scars. One eye blind, the other bright with anger.

'Yes, Mr Hawkins, something has happened. Something devilish.'

Chapter Two

I smelled the blood as soon as I entered the room. The air was thick with it. Some months ago I had woken in a prison cell to find a man murdered in the next bed. Aislabie's study was tainted with the same stink: the unmistakable scent of freshly butchered meat.

'Mr Hawkins. You're late, sir. I needed you here this morning.'

Aislabie stood behind a desk covered in bills and estimates – a tall, neat gentleman with an excellent bearing. He was watching through the open window as his men toiled on the new building. I saw in his profile the handsome young man from the portrait next door, grown older – the same lean face and cleft chin. His jawline had softened and his brows were grey, but at six and fifty, time had treated him well.

A trestle table stood in the centre of the room, in front of the desk. Something lay stretched out upon it, covered in bed sheets. The body of an animal, six feet in length. The sheets were streaked with blood. I slid my gaze across its bulk.

Outside there was a shout of alarm, followed by the low rumble of rocks pouring from a cart. *'You stupid arsehole!'* The words drifted into the room from a hundred feet away. *'Y'almost killed me you fucking idiot!'*

Aislabie breathed heavily through his nose and turned to face me. His eyes were large and dark. With one swift sweep he took me in, from the top of my head to the silver buckle of my shoe. His lips pressed to a thin line. 'How old are you?'

'Does it matter?' Given his own uncivil greeting, I found no reason to be polite in return. I focused my attention on the blood-soaked sheets. A fresh kill. Fresh meat, not yet tainted.

'Five and twenty at most,' Aislabie muttered.

Six and twenty, in fact. I had celebrated my birthday upon the road with a few bottles of claret, amazed that I had survived so long. 'The age you entered parliament, Mr Aislabie.'

I used Sneaton's pronunciation – *Aizlabee* – and placed emphasis upon the word *Mister*, just in spite. Aislabie's public disgrace had ensured that he would never be granted a title. His jaw tightened, at this, or perhaps at the mention of parliament. Old humiliations, old resentments, still raw under the skin.

I tilted my chin to the trestle table, the bloodied sheets. 'What's this?'

His nostrils flared in disgust. 'An *outrage.*'

'It was left on the front steps this morning,' Sneaton explained. He began to roll back the sheets then paused, scarred hand gripping the cloth. 'You're not womanish about blood, Mr Hawkins?'

Womanish. I thought of Kitty, cheering at the edge of a cockpit as the birds slashed each other with silver spurs.

'It's not a pretty sight,' he added. And winced, realising how that must sound coming from one so ravaged.

'When you're ready,' I replied.

Sneaton pulled at the linen to reveal a russet haunch and a dainty black hoof. A deer. I breathed out slowly. I'd been holding my breath without realising it, expecting something much worse. How quickly my mind turned to murder these days.

The blood was much thicker at the animal's middle, and the sheets had become stuck to the wound. Sneaton put his hand under the cloth and tugged it free.

The doe had been slit open from its throat, down along its belly to its hind legs. Its innards had been scraped out, but something was stuffed inside the carcass.

I put a hand to my mouth. It had been carrying a fawn.

I bent down, forcing myself to examine the thing more closely. The fawn had been cut from its mother's womb and then placed back inside the cavity, its tiny head poking out in an obscene parody of birth. Another few weeks left in peace and it would have lived, making its first steps on trembling legs. It must have been alive when it was pulled from its mother's body. Whoever did this must have held it for a moment, warm skin and beating heart. And then wrung its neck.

'Who found this?'

'Sally Shutt. Our youngest maid.'

I rubbed a patch of linen between my thumb and fingers. 'You've ruined some good sheets carrying it here.'

He nodded at the deer. 'She was laid out on 'em when we found her.'

I straightened up. Neither man seemed to appreciate the importance of this fact. I was not sure if Aislabie was even listening. His gaze was riveted upon the dead fawn. 'May I ask your position here, Mr Sneaton?'

'I'm his honour's secretary – and superintendent over the servants. House and gardens.'

I had guessed as much. He could not be head steward, given his broken body. Studley Royal was a huge estate, and one would need to be strong and healthy to walk all its fields and woodlands. But it was plain that Aislabie trusted Sneaton above all others. 'I suggest you ask the housekeeper to count all the linens and see if any are missing.'

Aislabie snapped from his trance. 'You suspect one of the servants?'

I shrugged. Anyone could slip a few bed sheets from a linen cupboard: servant, guest, or family member. 'I'll need the names of everyone living and working on the estate. Mr Sneaton, if you would be kind enough to draw up a list for me, perhaps we might study it together after dinner.'

'Mr Sneaton is busy with estate work,' Aislabie interrupted. 'You must make your own investigations, sir – that is why I sent for you. If you had arrived when you promised, you would know my servants are honest, decent souls. There are no idle rogues at Studley, I do not permit it.' He gave me a scrutinising look, as if I had just ruined that perfect tally.

'Would it not be best, sir, to keep an open mind?'

Aislabie snorted. 'This is clearly the work of a lunatic.'

'Perhaps you are right,' I said, making it clear from my tone that I thought otherwise. 'If so, we are looking for a lunatic who knows how to field dress a deer. Who can carry the weight of it on his shoulders, or wheel it unnoticed to your door. Who can do all this under the cover of night, crossing through your estate without fear of breaking his neck in a fall.'

For the first time, Aislabie looked at me with approval. 'The Gills. Yes! That was my first thought, was it not, Sneaton?'

Sneaton shifted on his hip to ease his bad leg. 'Family of poachers,' he explained. 'Jeb and Annie Gill. They've a smallhold a few miles from here. And nine children, last I counted.'

'Every one raised crooked, no doubt,' Aislabie muttered. He had returned to his desk, searching through his papers for something. 'My old steward hired Jeb Gill to work on the gardens. When was it, Jack – twelve years past? Never again. Thieves and poachers, the lot of them.'

'But the sheets,' I protested. 'Where would they have found them— ?'

'Here. This'll prove it to you.' Aislabie thrust a folded sheaf of papers at my chest. 'Poachers.'

I opened out the papers to discover four letters, two of them spattered with blood. I began to read the top one, the longest of the four. 'That was the first,' Aislabie said, watching me intently. *Dam you Aiselby*, it began,

dam your Pride you son of a hoar You are nort but a Theif.

I squinted at the page. The hand was exceedingly poor and the paper was very thin. The writer must have composed the note in anger – it was torn in several places where the quill had pressed too hard against the paper. I could not make much of it without a closer study – the spelling was eccentric, and the meaning hard to follow. But its ending was plain enough.

If we doe nott here from You be sertain you will die and your Body will be bathed in Blood dam you.

'See this, here,' Aislabie instructed, poking a long finger at one of the more tortuous lines. 'They're demanding free passage on the moors to graze their wretched sheep. *Demanding* it! Damned bloody impudence.'

I picked my way through the sentence.

Sir we ask only free passidge on the Moors theres coneys plenty for all and Growse and graising for our sheep we aske no more than what our Fathers and Grand Fathers was grantid.

'They claim an old right of use.'

Aislabie coloured. 'The land is mine, bought and paid for. I will show you the deeds if you wish it—'

I shook my head vehemently. As a child, during my short visits home from school, my father would often sit me down and force me to read and recite from thick stacks of family deeds covering every parcel of land we had ever bought, every patch of woodland. 'This is your inheritance, Thomas,' he would say when I stumbled over some cramped Latin phrase. 'You must know it all, by heart.' My God, the hours I had wasted in that stifling, dusty room while the sun blazed brightly and the days of summer dwindled. If I gave it but a little thought, I was sure I could remember every damned word of those deeds even now, down to the last inch of land. Which was somewhat ironic given that – following an unfortunate misunderstanding in an Oxford brothel – I had lost my inheritance to my stepbrother.

I examined the second note, written in the same rough hand.

God who is Allmitey Dam your Soul Aiselby why doe you not anser us you Villain.

You nowe that there is no Law for a pore man but If this is not alterd we will Turn Justiss our self. Tell the world the Kirkby moors are free land or Depend upont you Shall not last a Month longer. You will Die and your Carkase will be fed to your Dogs.

'Do you have dogs, Mr Aislabie?'

'Of course I have dogs,' he snapped. 'That is scarcely the point, sir.'

I moved on to the third note. This one was shorter still and again, the writing was poor – but different from the last. An accomplice, then, unless the same man was disguising his hand. There was a great deal of blood staining the back of it, but the paper was also much thicker, leaving the message clear.

'The first two were hammered to the front door,' Sneaton interjected. 'That was left upon the steps, a week ago – wrapped about a sheep's heart.'

Aislabie – your Crimes must be punnished. You have Ruined Good and Honest Familys with your Damn'd Greed. Our mallis is too great to bear we are resolved to burn down your House. We will watch as your flesh and bones burn and melt and your Ashes scatter in the Wind. Nothing will Remain. You have 'scaped Justice too long damn you.

I could not help myself. My eyes flashed to Sneaton, a man so clearly burned by some terrible fire. But it was Aislabie who seemed most affected – and who might blame him? He had lost his wife and daughter in a fire, many years ago. Surely whoever had written those threats had known that, choosing to play upon an old and terrible tragedy. There was something particularly cruel about this note – the gloating tone, devoid of pity, and the determination clear in every word.

'The latest one was pinned to the deer,' Aislabie prompted, in a flat voice.

I shifted the papers, pulling out the final note.

Aislabie you Damned Traitor. This is but the beginning of Sorrows. We will burn you and your daughter in your beds. You are not alone by night or day. We will seek Revenge.

Now I understood Aislabie's urgency this morning and his irritation at my late arrival, even if it was only by a day. His impatience and incivility could be explained by the most natural and tender of causes: the love of a father for his daughter. I considered the doe with fresh eyes, its fawn dragged from the womb and killed. Now its meaning was clear. *Your child. We will murder your child. You will die together.*

'Where are your daughters, sir?'

Aislabie sighed, visibly troubled. 'Jane is at home in Beaconsfield with her husband. Mary is in London visiting her brother.'

'Then they are safe.'

'Quite safe,' he said, distracted.

I glanced at Sneaton, hoping for some explanation. He remained silent, watching his master with a careful eye. I read the note again. 'Is there . . .' I began, then hesitated. How to be delicate? 'Might there be a third daughter, sir?'

A flash of astonishment crossed Aislabie's face, as if I had made a great and unexpected deduction. Then he scowled as he took my meaning. 'A bastard child? No.'

'A daughter through marriage, then? Or a young ward – someone you might consider a daughter, if not by blood?' I waved the note. 'The threat is quite specific.'

Sneaton cleared his throat. 'Your honour . . .'

'In my own time, Sneaton!' Aislabie poured himself a glass of brandy. His hand was shaking.

I took out my watch. Past noon. I could be sitting down to dinner with Kitty at the Cocked Pistol. Better still, chasing her upstairs to bed. I shoved the watch into my pocket. 'Mr Aislabie. I have travelled for five days to reach you. I am tired, sore, and to be frank, sir, I'm not sure what you want of me. What is this matter with your daughter? Will you oblige me with an explanation? Or should I summon another carriage and return home to my wife?'

Aislabie turned in surprise. 'Mrs Hawkins did not accompany you?'

'She was called back to London. The *note*, sir?'

He settled his brandy glass. 'We have a guest staying with us at Studley – a young widow, from Lincolnshire. I had hoped your wife might be company for her. A confidante. You know how ladies are.'

Kitty – a lady? A *confidante*? I had to bite my lip to stop myself from laughing.

'Her name is Mrs Fairwood. Mrs Elizabeth Fairwood. I fear she is in great danger.'

'Indeed? How so?'

Aislabie smiled sadly. 'Because she is my daughter, sir. My youngest girl, returned to me from the grave.'

I stared at him in dismay. His youngest daughter had died in a fire with her mother. Glancing at Sneaton, I saw he had composed his face in that cautious expression practised by all wise servants – that is to say so neutral one might believe he had stopped thinking altogether.

Aislabie reached out, as if possessed, and put his hand upon the dead fawn's head. He gave a shudder, and drew his fingers away.

'Mr Aislabie, forgive me ... I understood your youngest daughter died many years ago.'

'Lizzie?' Aislabie blinked. 'Yes. She died in a fire, with my wife.' For a moment I saw the grief of a young husband, fresh and raw upon his face. Then he pulled the shutters tight across the memory.

'But you believe this visitor to be ...' What, precisely? Mr Aislabie had a reputation for being haughty and obstinate, not unbalanced.

He sensed my confusion. 'I'm a straightforward man,' he said, gruffly. 'I've no time for tales of ghosts and demons. There is this world and – God willing – the next. I do not believe there is a path between these worlds, except in death. And yet ...' He fixed his jaw. 'Mrs Fairwood is my daughter. I cannot explain it easily. And yet I am certain of it.'

The thud of horses' hooves cantering up the avenue took him back to the window. 'Ah!' he exclaimed, 'They are returned.' And then he smiled in such an unaffected way it quite transformed him. He strode to the door, no doubt expecting me to follow.

Sneaton hurried after his master, his wooden peg *putt*ing softly as it hit the oak floorboards. I could see where it had worn a hundred little dents in the wood over the years.

I tucked the letters in my pocket, thinking on a line from the first note – one that neither Sneaton nor Aislabie had chosen to mention.

You robbed England, you rogue.

It was a fair charge. And here he resided at Studley Royal, stranded in splendid exile on his enormous estate. There must be plenty who thought he deserved a harder punishment than that. Could one of them be plotting to burn down his house? Or worse?

To be blunt, it was not my concern, and my interest – in the main – was counterfeit. The queen had not sent me to Yorkshire to protect John Aislabie, or to solve his troubles. He could burn in his bed and she would take the news with exquisite indifference, before reaching for another *macaron*. My true mission was clear and very simple: *Find the green ledger, and bring it to me.*

I might begin now, here in Aislabie's study.

A sharp tap at the window brought me to my senses: Sneaton, beckoning urgently before limping away. I became conscious again of the stink of blood and meat wafting from the deer. If I had arrived yesterday evening as planned, I would have witnessed its discovery this morning. Had this butchery been a warning to me, as much as to Aislabie?

You are not alone by day or night.

I threw the sheets over the deer and its fawn. What a waste. What a damned waste.

Chapter Three

'How's your riding, sir?' Mrs Aislabie asked again.

'Tolerable,' I replied, distracted by the sight of her.

'You are too modest, Mr Hawkins,' she said, patting the thick-muscled neck of her dark bay stallion. Her gaze snagged upon my hips. 'I'm sure you have an excellent seat.'

She must be near fifty, I warned myself, though she didn't look it. We were a small group, gathered upon the gravelled drive: Mr Aislabie, Mr Sneaton leaning upon his walking stick, and the two women on horseback, their faces flushed from their morning ride through the estate. Aislabie had introduced his wife as 'My Lady Judith, daughter of the Right Honourable Sir Thomas Vernon'. Her Ladyship had winked at me, clearly not as impressed by her title as her husband. *Near fifty,* I warned myself again. *Perhaps older.*

Lady Judith was a handsome woman with strong features, as if God had sketched a man's face then changed His mind, adding wide, full lips that curved up at the sides. The silver collar of her riding coat was turned up in the gentleman's style, the effect softened with a froth of lace about her neck. She wore a velvet cap over her pale blond hair, pierced with a white feather that fluttered in the breeze.

All most appealing, but this was not the cause of my distraction. What had confounded me was the fact that she was sitting

35

full astride her horse. That is to say: with one leg upon one side of the beast, and the other leg upon the opposing side.

Naturally this extraordinary position would have been impossible in a gown. In its stead, she wore a pair of close-tailored drawers, stitched in a heavy woollen cloth. No doubt this remarkable garment made for a comfortable ride, but it also meant that, from the waist downwards, Mrs Aislabie's shape was perfectly transparent.

London does not suffer from a lack of women's legs. In my estimation there must be at least two hundred thousand pairs in and about the city. But I had never in my life seen a pair of them parted wide and clamped tight around a horse's flanks. It was a diverting spectacle: so much so that I scarce noticed her companion, dressed in grey and perched stiffly on a fat little pony. She was sitting side-saddle, thank God. One pair of legs was distraction enough.

'You must join me for a tour about the gardens, sir.' Lady Judith leaned forward in her saddle, the leather creaking beneath her. 'I will send for a horse. There is nothing so fine as a good ride before dinner, don't you agree?' She smiled at me.

I glanced nervously at Aislabie, but he was busy helping the woman in grey from her pony. Lady Judith followed my gaze, and her smile faded. 'You have seen the letters?' she murmured. 'We've said nothing of them to the girl, nor this morning's butchery. She is too fragile.' Somehow, in her inflection, Mrs Aislabie conveyed that this was her husband's opinion, and one she did not share.

I watched as the *girl* stepped away from her mount as if it might kick her. She really was tiny – they had given her a training pony to ride, as if she were a child. She was also exquisitely beautiful. This I relay as an objective fact, for it was acknowledged by everyone who spoke of her at Studley, whether they liked her or not: the gloss of her rich brown hair, the high plane of her cheek-bones, the neat little chin, and features so refined and harmoni-ously balanced that they seemed almost a rebuke. *If I am able to achieve such loveliness, cannot the rest of you try a little harder?*

The faint lines about her eyes and mouth suggested she was in her late twenties. Aislabie's London home had burned down in the winter of 1701. If by some miracle his youngest daughter had survived the fire, she would be nearing thirty now.

'Elizabeth?' I ventured quietly, to Lady Judith.

Her wide blue eyes gleamed, but she said nothing.

Aislabie led his charge forward as if he were presenting her at court. She moved gracefully, but her expression was curiously blank, as if she had left her character tidied away in her chamber. Aislabie, in contrast, was almost overcome with feeling. He looked on her as one might expect any father would look upon a lost daughter. With wonder at her return, fear that he might lose her again, and with love: ferocious love.

'Mr Hawkins. May I introduce Mrs Elizabeth Fairwood. My daughter.'

Lady Judith exchanged a glance with Sneaton – frustration and concern, swiftly suppressed.

Aislabie was smiling, tears welling in his eyes. 'My daughter,' he said again, in a whisper. But there was something fragile in his smile, a touch of doubt in his words. Was this *truly* his daugh-ter, lost in a fire so long ago? How could she have escaped? And where had she been, these past twenty-seven years?

Mrs Fairwood lifted her head. Her eyes were as dark and compelling as Aislabie's. And what a fierce, angry look they bestowed upon me! I'd been thrown such a look before by a woman – but at least I had earned it first. One would think – as an abstract example – I'd promised to marry her, then acciden-tally slept with her sister.

I stepped into a low bow, pressing my hand to my heart. 'Madam. I am truly honoured.'

I was mocking her, and she knew it. Her gaze shifted somewhere beyond my right shoulder. 'So the queen has sent *you* to discover who threatens us? Extraordinary. Were there no gentlemen available at court?'

Aislabie looked startled. 'You know of the letters?'

'The servants talk, Mr Aislabie.'

The sun had gone in as we spoke and the sky was heavy with rain clouds, as if summoned by her ill humour. A few light spots of rain spattered upon my face. *Mr Aislabie*. Not, *Father*.

He began to splutter out a reply, but she stopped him with a curt gesture. 'I believe this morning's note contained a threat to my own life?'

'You will come to no harm under my roof, Lizzie,' Aislabie promised.

I had never seen a woman who looked less like a Lizzie.

We had all been ignoring the rain, but with the next gust of wind it began to pour down with a sudden violence. Lady Judith jumped down from her horse, handing the reins to an approaching groom. 'Inside!' she ordered, as if the thought might not have occurred to us. We rushed up the steps into the great hall. Sneaton was the last to arrive, wiping the rain from his coat.

'Well,' Lady Judith said. She stood by the window with her hands on her hips, scowling at the weather. Her plans for a ride about the gardens were ruined. A blinding flash lit up the grey stone walls, followed by a deep roll of thunder. Once it was gone, the room seemed darker still. Bursts of rain blew in through the open doorway, splattering on the flagstones. The butler pushed the great arched doors shut with an echoing thud. It felt as if he were shutting us all together inside a tomb.

'I must change from these wet clothes,' Lady Judith declared. She strode up the great oak stairs, her long legs taking the steps two at a time. Legs, in woollen drawers. Legs, visible, on stairs. I'm sure I paid them very little attention.

I moved to the window, studying the scene that she had been watching moments before. The sudden storm had turned the whole world grey, rain sweeping across the grounds in great squalls. A herd of deer sheltered beneath a beech tree, barely visible through the downpour. The men working on the new building had clustered beneath large waxed canvases that looked like the black sails of a pirate ship. The water poured off the edges in thin streams.

Mrs Fairwood joined me at the window. 'You think me a fraud,' she said, breathing the words on to the glass. 'You are here to expose me.'

I laughed. 'No, indeed. I didn't know of your existence until this morning.'

She frowned, and wiped the mist from the windowpane with a grey gloved hand.

The sky flashed again with lightning. 'Glad I'm not out there,' I said, nodding towards the men sheltering under canvas. 'Hard work in foul weather.'

'Indeed,' she murmured, seemingly surprised that I should consider it. 'And they were not paid last quarter day. Mr Aislabie disputes the bill.'

'They'll be paid.' Mr Sneaton had limped across the room to join us. 'Mr Simpson drinks hard and counts poor. One day I'll catch him sober and we'll make his bill tally. His men are fed and most are quartered on the estate. They won't starve.'

The rain had eased off enough for the men to discard the waxed sheets and take up their tools again. The sound of hammers and chisels rose up once more, ringing against stone.

'They won't starve,' Mrs Fairwood echoed. 'What good fortune they enjoy.'

If Sneaton heard the sarcasm, he chose to ignore it. 'I'll make a list of all the servants for you sir,' he said quietly. 'Mark those who could visit the laundry and the linen cupboards unseen.'

'—Sneaton!' Aislabie was heading towards his study. 'Mr Hawkins, we shall speak further at dinner. And you must visit Mr Hallow, my head keeper. He knows all the poachers hereabouts. See that you ask him about the Gills.'

Sneaton bowed to us and turned upon his good leg, hobbling after his master.

'You have your orders, sir,' Mrs Fairwood said, looking pleased to be rid of me.

'Yes. I'm afraid I'm excessively poor at following orders. If it is not too much trouble, madam, I should like to hear your story. Dinner must be an hour away, at least.'

She drew back. 'It would not be seemly to be alone in your company, sir.'

I had spent so long in London, I had quite forgotten the cramped etiquette found in some parts of the country. I assured her I had no designs upon her virtue. She was a fine-looking woman, without question, but hers was a cold beauty, worn like armour. And she lacked that spark I loved, the wit and play that made seduction so enjoyable. I might as well flirt with a marble statue.

'Well.' Mrs Fairwood remained reluctant. 'I still do not see how it is your business.'

In truth, it wasn't. I had one urgent task at Studley Hall, and it did not involve Mrs Fairwood in the slightest. But that must wait until nightfall. If, in the meantime, I did not investigate the threats made against his family, Mr Aislabie would grow suspicious. And a lost daughter, returned from the grave? I confess – I was intrigued.

I reached into my pocket and drew out the most recent note. Mrs Fairwood read it slowly. '*You are not alone by day or night.*' She shuddered. 'How terrible.'

I found it curious that it was this line that disturbed her the most, more than the threat of being burned alive in her bed. 'It was pinned to a butchered doe. Her fawn had been cut from the womb.'

'Dreadful,' she said, in an absent tone.

I plucked the note from her hands. 'I am under orders from Queen Caroline to investigate these threats. Whoever wrote this letter believes that you are Elizabeth Aislabie, saved from the fire. They would have you burn along with your father. *You are the fawn*, Mrs Fairwood.'

She considered this for a long moment, her lips caught in a deep pout. 'Very well,' she decided. 'Let us be done with it. The library should be empty, unless Metcalfe has taken up residence.'

I had no idea who this was.

She furrowed her brows. 'We should be safe. I doubt he's left his room today.' She drew away from the window and, in an imperious fashion, beckoned for me to follow. I found it wearisome.

'Remind me – what's that fellow's name?' I indicated the head footman, inching silently towards the kitchens.

A flicker of anxiety crossed her face, swiftly buried. 'Bagby.'

'Mr Bagby!' I called.

He gave a start. 'Sir?'

'Obliged if you'd bring a bottle of claret to the library. Wait!' I held up my finger. 'How long is your story, madam?'

She frowned at me. 'I have never timed it, sir.'

'Two bottles, Bagby,' I said. One could never be too careful.

* * *

The library lay at the back of the house. Thick volumes of history and natural philosophy lay open on dark mahogany tables. Terracotta busts of great writers and thinkers stared out blindly from the tops of high shelves. The air smelled of leather and old fires. I rubbed my hands together, and blew on them. The library faced north. Its tall terrace doors helped bring in more light, but the room felt colder than my cell in the Marshalsea.

I kept my eyes sharp for the green ledger – the sole reason I had been sent to Studley Hall. It seemed unlikely that Aislabie would leave something so dangerous and valuable out on view, but one should never underestimate the arrogance of the abominably rich. I would return tonight to hunt in earnest, with Sam.

A young maid arrived to light the fire, carrying fresh kindling in her apron. Mrs Fairwood, perceiving some fault in the preparation, began to direct the girl in a low but insistent tone. I was reminded of my stepmother's meddling in the kitchen, to the despair of our long-suffering cook. This girl was no more than fifteen, but she must have built a thousand fires and surely required no assistance.

I left them to their negotiations, idling my time by examining a handsome desk set in a corner next to the terrace doors. Upon closer inspection, I found it had been somewhat ruined – the green leather top was scratched and torn and spattered with ink stains. A jumble of notes lay abandoned on one side, weighted with a volume of Lucretius' *De Rerum Natura*. I moved the book aside to examine the papers more closely. A gentleman's hand, I thought, heavily blotched and growing wilder as it reached the bottom of the page. It put me in mind of the most recent threats to Mr Aislabie, and the paper was of a similar quality. I slipped the top sheet into my coat pocket.

The desk was covered in little curls of spilled tobacco, that had me reaching for my own pouch. The maid had coaxed a few flames into life, so I stole a piece of kindling to light my pipe, then tossed it back.

Mrs Fairwood had left the fire and stationed herself at the terrace doors, frowning through the glass at the scene beyond. I joined her there, trailing tobacco smoke. She glared at my pipe as if it were an instrument of the devil and reached for the latch, opening the closest door with a hard shove. Damp spring air streamed into the room. Behind us, the maid muttered to herself, shielding the fire with her body.

I leaned against the door post, struck once again by the unfavourable position of Mr Aislabie's house. For a man of his enormous wealth, I would have expected his library to open out on to a tranquil stretch of lawn, or a formal garden with a fountain burbling away at its heart. Instead it looked on to a large and busy yard, servants rushing back and forth to the laundry, the dairy, the water pump. Chickens scratched in the dirt for corn, flapping and squawking as a groom ran through them, heading for the stables. The dogs were barking in their kennels and there were pigs somewhere: I could smell them.

Mrs Fairwood had opened the door to let in the fresh air, but with it had come the warm country stink of sweat and manure, sour milk and wet hay, fresh bread and livestock. These were the smells of my childhood – the happy times when I could escape my father's lectures and roam about the outhouses. The first time I'd fucked a girl the world had smelled the same – a dairymaid with rough hands and a grin that could stir me now, just at the thought of it. In truth she had fucked me, pushing me to the ground and straddling me . . . which made me think again of Lady Judith, and her breeches. *Who must be fifty. At least fifty.*

Our parsonage had remained so close to the outhouses because of my father's miserly tendencies and loathing of disruption, but such proximity was unusual for such a grand estate. I supposed that once Aislabie's new building was finished he would tear down Studley Hall, leaving the working parts of it at a greater remove from the house.

Pugh led a grey mare across the yard, her hooves splashing through silvery puddles. My gaze drifted to the dark woodland beyond, the trees pressed together in dense clusters. It would be easy enough to steal through them at night, torches burning. Or was someone scheming from inside the house? Mr Aislabie seemed determined to trust his servants. A noble sentiment – but if he was wrong, I could burn along with him.

I returned to the fire, settling myself in a high-backed armchair. The seat was well padded in green silk, and – after five days of jolting and bumping along terrible roads – I sank into it with a quiet pleasure. If I must burn, let me burn in comfort. Perhaps I could just stay here for the duration, and let the world come to me? If I might just have a footstool? To my knowledge there was no law stating that a secret and potentially life-threatening mission must be conducted without a footstool.

The maid pushed herself back off her knees. 'Would you like the candles lit, sir?'

'No, that won't be necessary,' Mrs Fairwood replied. She had been toying with a globe set beneath one of the larger bookshelves, turning it slowly east and west across the wide stretch of the Atlantic.

'It's turned dull this afternoon,' I said. 'And I think Mr Aislabie can afford it.' I nodded to the maid, indicating that she should light the candles. She looked quietly thrilled to be acting against Mrs Fairwood's wishes. I asked for her name.

'Sally Shutt, sir,' she replied, in a broad accent. She lit a taper, crossing to each candle in turn. She was a pretty girl, with a plump figure and a fair complexion. A little tired though, about the eyes.

'Do you light the rooms at daybreak, Sally?'

'I do, sir.' She lit the final candle and blew out the taper, tossing it on to the fire.

'You found the deer this morning,' I said. She flinched, which was answer enough. 'Did you see anything? Anyone?'

She shook her head. 'It were barely dawn. Just me and the crows . . .'

A memory, long buried, returned to me – ruined corpses lined up in a prison yard, and the sound of crows cawing in excitement. The cloying stench of death. I could taste it again in my mouth.

'. . . Must've bin a dozen or more, pecking for meat. They made a fine breakfast of it.'

'Enough chatter, Sally.' Bagby had arrived with the wine: two bottles as requested upon a silver tray. 'Cook's been calling for you.' His words were for her, but his disapproval was aimed at me. Perhaps we were not meant to converse with the servants. Some households are tediously fastidious about such matters.

Sally curtsied and hurried from the room, but not before flashing me a look that promised there was more to be said, later. I smiled in acknowledgement, earning myself a scowl from Bagby.

Mrs Fairwood had kept her back to the room throughout this exchange, spinning the globe slowly beneath her gloved fingers. But I could tell from the set of her shoulders, the stiff way she held herself, that she had been listening attentively.

She joined me by the hearth. 'Silly girl never remembers the screen,' she said, moving it in front of the grate. She perched upon the edge of her chair so that her feet might reach the floor, and stared at me, the wine, the butler, with barely concealed distaste. Her eyes were fringed with thick black lashes, and very dark. Despite her ill-humour, they were quite captivating.

Bagby poured me a glass of claret. I wondered how he kept his gloves and stockings so crisp and white. I suspected by giving all the troublesome jobs to his men. Well, it was his prerogative, I supposed.

Mrs Fairwood held a hand over her own glass, and told him to close the terrace doors. 'Then leave us.' Bagby did as he was ordered. 'Ghastly man,' she muttered, without explaining why. But then I'd yet to hear her speak well of anyone. We might all be reduced to a two-word insult by Mrs Fairwood. Silly girl. Ghastly man. Frightful rake.

The sounds of the yard were now muffled, and the pungent stink had been locked outside, leaving only a faint whiff on the air. The clock on the mantelpiece ticked quietly. I gulped down most of the wine, and filled the glass again to the brim.

Mrs Fairwood seemed reluctant to begin, so I prompted her. 'Well then, madam. You believe you are Mr Aislabie's lost daughter?'

She pulled off her gloves and sighed heavily. 'Yes, Mr Hawkins, I do. And may God help me to endure it.'

Chapter Four

Mrs Fairwood was raised in a small village on the Lincolnshire coast, the nearest town a day's ride away. There was money – a good deal of it – and a grand house with servants. She called her childhood 'quiet'– I thought it sounded lonely, trailing the empty rooms, filling the silence with books. She had no siblings, but she was close to her father, who recognised her appetite for knowledge, and encouraged it.

'And your mother?'

'Devout.' Her teeth trapped the last letter. She didn't appreciate the interruption. I drank my wine and settled back, shoulders relaxing in the deep embrace of the armchair. The heat from the fire burned upon my cheek.

'When I was twenty-one, my father decided we should spend the summer in Lincoln with his sister. There was talk of finding a husband. I had dissuaded him many times before. I was content at home.' Her eyes flickered to the shelves behind me. 'My father insisted. He said it was time that I lived in the world, not just in my books.' Her fingers clenched together in her lap.

'When was this?'

'Eight years ago.'

1720. So she was twenty-nine. That would match Elizabeth Aislabie's age, if she survived the fire.

'At the last moment my mother took to her bed: a nervous attack. I thought my father would abandon the trip, but we set off the next day without her. My aunt would act as chaperone once we reached Lincoln.'

She poured herself a thimbleful of wine. 'I do not drink.'

'Evidently.'

Her dark eyes lifted to mine. 'How dull I must seem to you. My drab little story.'

I did not find her dull. Petulant, yes, and chilly, but not dull. In truth her story had drawn me in: the earnest timbre of her voice; the measured way she chose her words. I had grown accustomed to Kitty, who would speak a half dozen sentences in one breath, who spoke not only with words but with her hands, her eyes, her whole body. Mrs Fairwood moved no more than was needed, spoke no more than was needed, her voice clipped and precise.

She sipped the wine. 'Is this a good claret?'

'The best.'

She rolled the stem of the glass between her fingers. 'This glass, too. These chairs.'

Yes, it was all very fine – and hers to enjoy for ever if she could persuade the world she was Aislabie's lost child. This story might be nothing more than a fortune hunter's yarn. I placed my glass on the table. Mrs Fairwood had a closed countenance, but I had made a great deal of money at the gaming tables, reading truth and lies on my opponents' faces.* I leaned forward, watching closely.

'To my surprise, I enjoyed my stay in Lincoln,' she said, returning to her story as if by rote. 'My aunt's circle was small

* And lost it again through debauchery and idleness, but that is another – possibly more agreeable – story.

48

but scrupulously well selected. I had the opportunity to speak with a number of learned men upon a diverse range of topics. The great matters of our age. Theology, metaphysics, affairs of state, the very systems of the universe . . .'

I made a silent note never to visit Lincoln. 'And this is what you study here, in Mr Aislabie's library? That is your copy of Lucretius on the desk?'

She frowned at this fresh interruption. 'It belongs to Metcalfe. You will meet him at dinner, if he can be roused.' She leaned back and stared at the clock on the mantelpiece with the blank expression of an automaton.

I must wind her up, then. 'Pray – continue, madam.'

'Oh.' She feigned surprise. 'Forgive me, sir. I thought you must have grown tired of my story. Would you not rather discuss Lucretius? I take it you have read *De Rerum Natura*.' Her lips curled into a condescending smile.

'I think I fell asleep upon a copy once, at Oxford.' This was not true. I had, in fact, studied the blasted thing at some length as a student. But if Mrs Fairwood wished to cast me as a japing idiot, that suited me perfectly well. Another lesson from the gaming table: better to be thought a fool than a threat. 'Please.'

She dipped her chin in gracious assent. 'That summer in Lincoln was a happy time. Home had become oppressive, though I only realised this once I had left. My mother never strayed far from the village, but in her later years she would not even leave the house, save for church. My father too seemed altered by the trip. He laughed more easily. It is a comfort now to think of those last days.' She looked down. 'He died. My father died. It came without warning. One moment he was well, and the next . . .' A tear slid down her perfect cheek. She trapped it beneath her fingers, brushed it away.

'I'm sorry.'

Eight years had passed, and still the grief lingered. I could see how naturally it fell upon the contours of her face, how familiar and constant a companion it had become. How, in fact, it had shaped her, and turned her beauty into something austere and remote. I had lost my mother when I was a child and understood that ache, that hollow yearning for a beloved parent. This much of her story, at least, was true.

She took another sip of wine. 'I could not bear to return home without him. There was a gentleman. James Fairwood. I didn't love him. He was thirty years my senior and . . . well. I did not love him. But he was kind, and asked nothing of me. I accepted his proposal.' There was a short pause, as she wrapped herself in old, private thoughts of her loveless marriage. 'Mr Fairwood had come recently into a fortune. We bought a large manor house near Horncastle. Five years later my husband fell ill with a fever and died. I was alone.'

I sensed a rich satisfaction in that final sentence. 'That is young to be widowed. You must have been desolate.' I chose the word deliberately – it was too rich an emotion for her, and I wanted to hear her denial.

She gave it at once, with some force. 'Desolate? No indeed! The marriage had been a convenience for both of us.' And then she froze, realising her mistake.

'A convenience? How so?'

She was furious with herself. She had been so careful with her story, reciting her monologue with precision. No wonder she hated my questions. Nothing an actress dislikes more than interruptions from the audience. 'We kept each other company.'

I put my glass to my lips, hardly able to conceal my amusement. Imagined James Fairwood, recently come into a fortune, searching Lincolnshire for the most cheerful companion he could find – and choosing this elegant block of ice. Hogwash. 'There were no children?'

'No!' she declared, before I had even finished the question. And then, recovering, 'No. We were not blessed with children. It is a great sadness to me,' she added, without conviction.

My suspicions were confirmed. Mr Fairwood had been past fifty when he came into his fortune. A man of means must take a wife or else face endless gossip. I would bet every coin in my pocket that Fairwood had no interest in women. A swift marriage to a respectable lady, who wanted nothing from him in return, had been a wise step. It had indeed been a marriage of convenience for both of them. She must have been delighted when he died, poor fellow.

'I sold the house,' she said, 'and set up a new home in Lincoln. Time passed, and I found myself to be . . . content. There were a few suitors, but they were more interested in my fortune than my intellect. Foolish, frivolous boys.' She offered me a sidelong glance. 'I preferred my own company. And then my mother grew sick.'

She rose and crossed to the desk by the window, searching through the drawers. 'I left a letter here,' she explained. 'Metcalfe must have taken it to his quarters. He wanted to study it more closely. He believes I am a cuckoo in the nest.' She closed the final drawer with a smart shove. 'If only that were true. How I wish I could leave this wretched place and go *home*. Sit and read my own books in my own library, and be *myself* again.'

Another truth amidst the lies.

She returned to her chair, fanning her grey gown around her. 'My mother was dying – I knew it the moment I stepped into her bedchamber. She had been ill for months, but ordered the servants not to speak of it. She only called me back when there was no hope.

'She had written a letter, she said – but I must promise not to read it until she was dead, because I would hate her for it. Then she wept, and begged me to pray for her. She was so afraid. She was sure she would burn in hell for what she had done – that she deserved no less than eternal punishment. I couldn't understand her – she'd lived such a cramped and blameless life. I assured her that God was merciful. This calmed her for a while, and she slept. When she woke, she was confused. She didn't know where she was. She didn't recognise me. I told her she was at home, that I was her daughter. She said, "No, no – I have no daughter." And then she died.'

The room fell silent. The air had grown stifling by the fire, and I could feel the sweat upon my back. A father, a husband, a mother – all lost. But only one of them mourned by Mrs Fairwood.

'What did your mother say in her letter?'

She sighed. 'It was addressed to Mr Aislabie. She said that I was his daughter. That her real name was Molly Gaining and that she had rescued me from a house fire and smuggled me away.'

I drew back in surprise. 'She stole you from the family? Why would she do such a terrible thing?'

'She started the fire. Mr Sneaton caught her pocketing coins and jewellery in all the confusion. She couldn't return me without being caught. And I aided her escape. They were hunting for a young maidservant, alone – not a mother and child.'

'But that is . . .' Wicked? Monstrous? The words didn't seem adequate.

'For months, I told myself it was all a nonsense: the ramblings of a sick and frightened woman. I buried my mother, and I told myself I had buried the whole dreadful story with her. But every day I would put on my black crêpe gown and ask myself: was I grieving for my real mother? Or for the woman who had burned down my home and snatched me from my true family? I would lie awake at night, asking myself the same question over and over again, until I feared for my sanity.

'So I hired a lawyer to make enquiries. And it transpired that Mr Aislabie did lose his wife and daughter in a fire. The servant responsible was indeed called Molly Gaining, just as it said in the letter. She had disappeared that same night with a fortune in jewels and was never found.

'Even then, I refused to believe it. I wrote to Mr Aislabie asking for an audience. I placed my mother's letter in his hands with the firm belief that he would dismiss the entire business. But he wept, Mr Hawkins. He broke down at my feet and wept. And I have been trapped here ever since.'

She lowered her gaze, long lashes hiding her eyes.

Now at last I began to understand the anger simmering within her. What a horrifying discovery, if it were true! That the woman she had called Mother all those years had – in fact – ripped her from her real family, leaving her a stranger to her father, her brother, her two sisters. Worse still – Molly Gaining had caused the death of Mrs Fairwood's true mother. And had the husband been complicit? At the very least he would have known that Mrs Fairwood was not his child. Counterfeit parents, living on a stolen fortune. Comfort bought with an innocent woman's life. No wonder she wished it were not true. 'Is it not possible that Mr Aislabie is mistaken? Perhaps in his rush to believe—'

Mrs Fairwood shook her head. 'There was proof contained within the letter. Mr Aislabie and Molly Gaining had ... relations. No one else knew. And there was this.' She reached into her pocket and pulled out a diamond brooch, shaped like a flower with a ruby at its heart. It was small and exquisite. 'Mr Aislabie bought this for his first wife.' She rocked her palm and the diamonds sparkled, catching the light. 'It was the only jewel

Molly kept. She sold the rest. Bought a house near the sea in Lincolnshire. And lied and lied and lied.'

She tucked the brooch back into her pocket and gazed into the hearth. 'I have always been afraid of fire,' she murmured. 'A memory of that night on Red Lion Square, I suppose – though it is all lost to me now. Except in dreams. Sometimes I dream that I am burning.' She waved the thought away with her hand. 'Well, sir, what do you say now? Do you still think me a fraud?'

A hodge-podge of lies and truth, that is what you are, madam. 'I am not here to judge you, Mrs Fairwood.'

'But you must have an opinion, one way or the other.'

I rubbed my jaw. I could see that she would be happier – and safer – if she were not Aislabie's daughter. This suggested she was not dissembling. Then again: one should never forget the lure of money. Mr Aislabie had, purportedly, been stripped of his wealth after the South Sea disaster. But, looking about me, he seemed to have recovered in a swift and quite spectacular fashion. 'I should like to see your mother's letter.'

'Then you shall. I welcome your doubt, Mr Hawkins – it is to your credit. I am aware that my story must seem quite fantastical.'

'Has Mr Aislabie formally recognised you as his daughter?'

'Not yet.'

'Has he spoken with his children on the matter?'

'Not to my knowledge.'

I drained my glass. Poured another. 'They might stand to lose a portion of their inheritance, if you are proven to be their sister. Your brother William, at least.' Both Mary and Jane were long married, and settled with fortunes of their own.

'My *brother* will not lose a farthing. I have no interest in Mr Aislabie's wealth.' She saw my scepticism and laughed, drily. 'Ask Mr Sneaton. I ordered him to draw up a waiver the day I arrived here. I have renounced all rights to a settlement, or any other gifts, in writing and in front of witnesses. I will not take a single coin from Mr Aislabie. Not an inch of land. I want nothing from him.' She propped her chin upon her hand. 'You must know how he came by his fortune.'

'The South Sea Scheme.'

Her dark eyes flashed. 'The greatest fraud ever played upon a nation.'

'Playing with stocks is a gamble. Some won, some lost.'

'You cannot be so naive! It was corruption at the highest level! The enquiry proved that Mr Aislabie was bribed with free shares—'

'—which he denied—'

'—because he is a *liar*!' She dropped back in her chair. 'Well,' she relented, 'I suppose he has convinced himself of his innocence. No man can bear to cast himself as the villain. D'you know, I followed the scandal from the beginning. I read all the pamphlets, and his ridiculous defence in the Lords. I came to Studley Hall expecting to loathe him, but I find that I can't. He has been very kind to me.' She picked up her grey gloves. 'Why are you here, sir? Truly?'

'You know why, madam. Mr Aislabie asked the queen for help.'

Her brow crinkled. There were faint, permanent lines forming upon her forehead, I saw – and deeper ones about her mouth. She frowned a lot, furrowed her brow a lot. She would mar her good looks with her ill-temper. 'Strange,' she observed, 'that he should still have such influence at court.'

It wasn't influence; it was blackmail. A slim green ledger, filled with dangerous secrets.

'Would the queen mind so very much if you failed in your task?'

'She would – most certainly.'

'You should leave, even so. Return to London. There is something evil about this place: I felt it the moment I arrived. Something in the atmosphere, an invisible mist that taints the air. One cannot help but breathe it in, like a poison. Can you not sense it?' She lifted her hand, bending her wrist to show her veins, dark lines vivid against her pale skin. 'If I cut myself now, I think my blood would run black with it.'

I could think of nothing to say.

And then she whispered, so quietly I could scarce hear the words. 'It is not safe here. And I am so afraid, sir. So afraid of him.'

I stared at her in alarm. 'You're afraid of Mr Aislabie?'

'No. No.' She covered her face with her hands. 'I'm sorry. I do not feel well. The wine.'

She had barely touched her glass. 'Mrs Fairwood—'

'Please. I'm not myself. I must retire.' She rose suddenly, and hurried to the door.

'Perhaps *you* should leave, madam,' I called after her. 'Why not go home to Lincoln?'

She paused at the door, a gleam of longing in her eyes. She blinked, and it was gone. 'I can't leave. Not until I know for certain who I am.'

'You doubt it?'

'My head tells me that I am Elizabeth Aislabie. But my heart, Mr Hawkins . . . my heart still dares to hope that I am not.'

Chapter Five

It was past two o'clock when we sat down for dinner. Mrs Fairwood did not join us. Nor did the mysterious Metcalfe. I discovered this much about him – that he was Mr Aislabie's nephew, that he was heir to a baronetcy, and that he kept the most peculiar hours. He had scarce left his room for the last three days.

'Is he unwell?'

'Yes,' Lady Judith replied, at the exact moment her husband said, 'No.'

'I think the weather will hold,' Lady Judith said, after an awkward pause. 'We shall have our ride this afternoon, Mr Hawkins.'

Mr Aislabie frowned, and helped himself to some boiled goose.

There was no servant to attend us, which I preferred. I find the hovering uncomfortable, having not grown up with it. The dining room was in the west wing, behind Mr Aislabie's study. It was long and narrow, and there was a cold draught about my ankles, but the food was very welcome. I was used to frequenting unpredictable chophouses, and had just spent six long weeks in a freezing Newgate cell. Luxury remained a pleasing novelty.

Sneaton was dining with us: another sign of his trusted position within the family. He was drinking soup from a silver porringer, his claw-like right hand struggling with the dainty handle. I had never seen so much silver tableware. I was quite tempted to steal a fork.

'Your boy has been causing trouble,' he said.

'You've brought a servant with you?' Lady Judith called down the table. A strong wind had chased off the clouds and the sun was pouring through the windows to her right. A beam of burning white light caught the lid of the soup tureen.

I blinked, dazzled. 'Master Fleet is a gentleman's son.' Now there was a lie of extraordinary depth. I could almost hear James Fleet pissing himself with laughter from here. 'I'm his guardian.'

'He's moved you to the east wing,' Sneaton said, slurping his soup. 'Insisted.'

'The east wing?' Lady Judith looked irritated. 'It's half-abandoned! Metcalfe has taken the only decent apartments on that side of the house.'

Sneaton shrugged, acknowledging the truth of it.

I took a piece of gammon and a spoonful of pickles. I should probably add a scattering of salad. Kitty was convinced it was an aid to the stomach. She was full of such questionable fancies. She served up so many leaves at our table it was a wonder I hadn't transmogrified into a rabbit. Which reminded me of the fricasseed rabbit by Mr Sneaton's elbow. He pushed it over, at my request.

'I've spoken with Mrs Fairwood,' I said to Aislabie, tucking my napkin into my cravat. 'An extraordinary story.'

Aislabie sawed at his goose. 'It is no story.'

'A figure of speech. Is it true that she has refused any gifts or settlement?'

'Hardly a suitable topic for the table,' he admonished. 'But yes – Mrs Fairwood asked Mr Sneaton to draw up a contract. She sought to prove that she has no designs upon that score. She will not take a single farthing from me, no matter how I press her.'

58

'Your son will inherit Studley, I presume?'

'Of course he will. Why, do you think because *you* are disinherited, that this is the common way of things? Yes, Mr Hawkins – I know your history! And were you not the queen's man, I should not allow you through the door.' He jabbed his knife at me. 'I must say that it is vexing to me that you were left alone in my daughter's company for so long. Pray do not impose upon her again in such an unseemly fashion.'

'*John*,' Lady Judith admonished. 'I'm sure Mrs Fairwood was quite safe.'

'Damn it, Judith – why must you call her that?' Aislabie snapped. 'Why not call her Elizabeth? Why not call her Lizzie?' He looked at his secretary, and then his wife. 'Why do you not believe me? Do you think I am such a fool that I cannot recognise my *own daughter*?'

Lady Judith sighed. Sneaton lowered his soup.

'Can you not see?' Aislabie pressed them. 'This is God's work! She is my gift, for all those years of suffering. All the injustice and cruelty I have faced. *My daughter has come home!* This house should be filled with *joy*. Why would you deny me this? Do I not deserve to be happy?'

'Were we not happy before, John?' Lady Judith asked, softly.

Aislabie did not hear her. He leaned across the table, pointing his knife at Sneaton. 'Jack, you examined Elizabeth's accounts – at her request. Fairwood left her three thousand pounds a year. There are no debts attached to the house in Lincoln. She has no need of my wealth, and no interest in it. You know she has offered many times to leave, rather than cause further discord.'

'Yet here she remains,' Lady Judith muttered into her glass.

'My wife, and my most trusted friend,' Aislabie marvelled, flinging his hands into the air. 'What faith. What loyalty. And you, Hawkins – you have heard her story, you have gazed upon her countenance. Can you not see that she is an Aislabie?'

It was true that Mrs Fairwood's eyes were dark brown, and her complexion a pale cream. But this would describe a goodly portion of the country. 'She is a handsome woman,' I said.

Aislabie grunted, as if that settled the matter.

'I believe you have just recently come into a fortune yourself, Mr Hawkins,' Sneaton said gruffly, with such an obvious urge to change the subject, it was almost comical. I must have looked perplexed, because he added, 'from your wife?'

Ah, yes. The imaginary Mrs Hawkins. Kitty had inherited a large sum from Samuel Fleet, Sam's uncle, and my old cellmate from the Marshalsea, along with his print shop, and an extravagantly broad collection of obscene literature. This fortune was in part the reason we had not yet married. Kitty feared I would gamble it all away which, to be fair, was a distinct possibility. She also feared I would grow bored and abandon her, or – God help us both – turn dull and respectable and never leave. In short, she had very little confidence in my better qualities, and far too much knowledge of my worst.

'John inherited a fortune from me when we married,' Lady Judith said, pouring another glass of wine. 'Fifteen years in April.' She raised her glass, prompting her husband to return the toast.

'True.' He winked at her. 'Fifteen years of quiet, dutiful obedience. On my part.'

Lady Judith snorted with laughter.

I thought of Mrs Fairwood's admission, that she had expected to loathe John Aislabie, but found she could not. He may have abused his power and robbed the nation, and yet ... it was clear that he loved his wife. I worked out the years in my head. Anne had died twenty-seven years ago, leaving him with three young children. It would have been advisable to marry again, and swiftly.

Instead he had waited thirteen years, until he met Judith. Which suggested that he had loved his first wife too – very much.

Sneaton had turned the conversation to the building project next to the house. John Simpson, their master stonemason, had submitted a fresh letter of complaint concerning his bill.

Aislabie rolled his eyes. 'I would have you speak with him again, Sneaton. I will not pay a bill that does not tally. Tell him if he cannot supply us with the proper details, we shall hire Robert Doe to complete the job.' He snatched at his glass and took a long draught. 'I'm mightily tired of the whole wretched business. I'm quite tempted to abandon it.'

'Oh, John – patience!' Lady Judith scolded. 'You know you will love the stables when they are done.'

Stables? The conversation continued about me as I puzzled over her meaning. The foundations for the new building suggested it would be twice the size of Studley Hall. But as Sneaton spoke of the stalls, and the grooms' quarters, I began to realise my mistake. The men labouring outside were not constructing a grand new home for the Aislabies. They were building a grand new home for the Aislabies' *horses*.

'How many do you keep?' I asked, astonished.

'Twenty,' Aislabie replied. 'Have Simpson send in his bill again, Sneaton. The books must tally before the next quarter—'

'*Twenty horses?*'

'Racehorses,' Aislabie corrected. 'The rest will remain in the old stables.'

Twenty racehorses. My God, the cost! 'I thought it was your new home, sir.'

Aislabie was amused. 'No, indeed. I shall build a grand palace down by the lake when the gardens are complete. Or else I shall buy Fountains Hall and the abbey, if I can persuade Mr Messenger to part with it.'

'Mr Messenger is our closest neighbour,' Lady Judith explained. 'Ill-tempered, fat little thing. We are not on friendly terms.'

Aislabie muttered something under his breath. I caught the word *papist*.

The servants were bringing in a fresh course when we heard a commotion at the front of the house, and then a scream – the deep howl of a man in agonising pain. Sneaton rose in alarm, holding on to the table for balance. A moment later Bagby entered the room. There was a distinct lack of concern on his face. 'An accident, your honour,' he drawled. 'One of Simpson's men.'

'Another one,' Aislabie tutted.

'How bad?' Sneaton asked.

'His leg's broken,' Bagby replied, flatly.

Sneaton cursed under his breath. 'Did you see a wound? Was the bone sticking out?'

Bagby looked disgusted. 'I did not enquire, sir.'

Aislabie waved at the servants to set down the dishes. 'Send for Mr Gatteker,' he told Sneaton. 'I'll pay the fee.'

Bagby bowed to me. His features were bland, but counter-weighted by a startlingly expressive face. At rest, it settled upon purse-lipped disapproval. Now he had ratcheted it to bulge-eyed indignation. 'Your boy's put himself in charge, *sir*. Ordering us all about.'

He led me through the house to the great hall, where a small crowd had gathered around the injured man. He had been carried inside on a stretch of oilcloth. His face was grey with shock, but he was sitting upright, which I took to be a good sign.

Sam had fixed a splint around the broken leg from the ankle to just above the knee, and was binding it with strips of linen. One of Simpson's men held the splint in place. The linen was blotched with dried bloodstains, and I realised this was the sheeting used to cover the butchered deer. Better to use ruined sheets than waste fresh ones, I supposed, though it looked somewhat ghoulish.

I knelt down by the injured man's feet and watched Sam work. He must have moved the bone back into alignment before setting the splint. My stomach clenched at the thought. No wonder we'd heard screaming.

Sam had confessed to me once that he should like to be a surgeon one day – not through any particular desire to help the sick, but because of his fascination with the mechanical properties of the body. He would spend hours poring over books of human anatomy, or sketching the connection of bone and muscle, or dissecting rats with a precise flick of his knife. Why Kitty refused to travel with him was a mystery.

'Excellent work, Sam. Very neat.'

'Connie.'

It took me a moment to remember Consuela, the old woman with the cloud of white hair who lived with Sam's family on Phoenix Street. She had brought me back from the brink of death a few weeks ago, after I'd been forced to jump into the freezing Thames. I took from Sam's reply – two syllables! inarguable progress! – that he had watched Connie make a splint, doubtless on more than one occasion. Sam's father was a gang captain and perhaps the most dangerous villain in London. How many times had one of his men stumbled into the den with a black eye, or a broken jaw, or a knife wound? Quite an education for a young boy.

Sally, the young maid I had spoken to earlier, arrived with a blanket. She wrapped it about the man's shoulders, then handed him a bottle of laudanum. 'Here you are, Fred. Borrowed this from Mr Robinson. You'll feel sick at first, but it'll pass.'

He took a long swig, and grimaced. 'Hurts like bloody murder.'

'Lucky,' Sam said. He ran his finger along the injured leg. 'Fibula. Clean break.'

'Fortunate indeed.' Sneaton limped over, wooden peg *putt-putt*ing along the stone floor. 'If the bone breaks through the skin, your only remedy's amputation. Most men die from the shock.'

Fred began to heave.

'Or putrefaction,' Sam added. 'Nasty.'

'Deep breaths, Fred,' Sally said.

Fred opened his mouth, then vomited on the oilcloth.

'That was your fault,' Sally scolded Sam.

Sam blinked, not understanding.

Simpson, the master stonemason, strode across the room to join us, leaving a trail of muddy bootprints in his wake. His face was coated in grey stone dust, streaked with sweat. He was shorter than me by several inches but very solid, with a bull's neck and strong fists, the knuckles grazed and torn from his work. He reminded me of William Acton, the head keeper of the Marshalsea gaol. Not a pleasant thought. 'This is what happens when you don't pay the men, Sneaton,' he snarled.

Sneaton scowled at him, scars puckering. 'For heaven's sake, what possible connection—'

'My men han't seen a farthing since Christmas! They're tired and angry, Jack. Working for nowt – it's bad for the humours. Dangerous bloody way to work.'

Sneaton huffed in exasperation. 'And do your men know you handed in your quarter bill *two weeks late*? And God's truth, to call it a bill would be a jest. A pile of tattered receipts and a scrawl of unreadable names—'

'I'm owed sixty pounds! I *have* to pay my men, my suppliers—'

'Then show me receipts that tally. A clear list of the men you hired and the hours they worked.'

Simpson's eyes popped in outrage. 'Do you call me a liar, Jack? A thief?'

'What is this damned racket?' Aislabie shouted, marching across the hall like a general – the effect somewhat ruined by the napkin tucked into his cravat.

Simpson pulled off his hat and bowed low. 'Your honour, sir.'

Aislabie glanced at Fred, and the pool of vomit. He pulled a face. 'What happened here?'

'An accident, Mr Aislabie, sir,' Simpson answered, still in his bow, clutching his hat in his great fists.

'I can see that. Have you been drinking?'

'No, sir!'

Aislabie narrowed his eyes. He didn't believe Simpson, and to be fair I could smell the liquor on the stonemason's breath from several paces away. The room waited for his honour's decision. 'This will be your last warning, Mr Simpson. If you cannot conduct your business in a respectable manner, I shall hire someone who can.'

Simpson dropped into an even deeper bow, head below his arse. 'Yes, your honour. I'm obliged to you, sir.'

Aislabie gave a sharp nod, concluding business. He leaned towards Sneaton. 'Clear up this mess. And remove these men from my house. They should never have been brought inside.'

He spun upon his heels and left, footsteps fading down the hall. No one mentioned the napkin.

Simpson rose from his bow and shoved his hat on his head. 'Tight-fisted bastard. Ten years I've slaved for him! D'you remember all the mud we had to cart away just to dig out the lake? Who else could have built his precious cascades? Don't you dare say Robert Doe, Jack – don't you dare. What's that soft-pricked Southerner ever built? Follies. Fucking follies.'

'His accounts are very neat.'

Simpson opened his mouth to argue, then realised Sneaton was joking. 'Piss off, Jack.'

Sneaton gestured to Fred, who had sunk heavily against Sally's shoulder. 'Bring the cart around and take him to his quarters. Mr Aislabie will pay the doctor's fees.'

'Aye. He pays when it suits him,' Simpson muttered. 'What's sixty pounds to him? He earns three thousand a quarter from rents alone, or near as makes no matter.'

'That's not true—'

'Yes it is Jack, you bloody liar. You told me yourself five nights ago.'

Sneaton closed his eyes. 'Remind me not to drink with you again, John.'

Simpson gave a triumphant smirk. 'I know all there is to know about you, Jack Sneaton. And Red Lion Square . . . Maybe you should remember that.'

Sneaton stared at him, shocked into silence.

'Ahh, ignore us, Jack,' Simpson sighed. 'I didn't mean nowt by it.' He glanced at me, the only one close enough to have heard the threat. 'How do. Who are you then?'

Now there was a fair, Yorkshire greeting. 'Thomas Hawkins. I'm here to—'

'Half-Hanged Hawkins!' Simpson barked out a laugh. 'Heard you was coming. Bloody hell. Hanged at Tyburn. How's your neck, sir. Still stretched?'

I drew back. 'I've no wish to speak of it.'

'If wishes were fucks, the world would be full o' bastards,' he replied with a shrug.

Sneaton had recovered his tongue. 'Come over to the cottage tonight, John. We'll work through your receipts together.'

'Thanks, Jack,' Simpson grinned. 'I'm grateful to you.' He shoved his hands in his pockets and walked back outside, whistling.

Sally huffed at the fresh trail of muddy footprints.

Fred's chum, who had helped Sam to bind the splint, rose to his feet and stretched. He was a handsome fellow, about twenty years of age, with a dark complexion from working in the sun. 'Begging your pardon, sir,' he addressed Sneaton, 'is it true that Mr Simpson handed in his bill two weeks late?'

Sneaton considered the younger man. 'D'you enjoy working at Studley, Master Wattson?'

'Yes, sir.'

Sneaton drew closer. Annunciated slowly. 'Then remember who you are.'

Wattson nodded rapidly. 'Yes, sir. Sorry, sir.'

Sneaton held Wattson's gaze for a moment to be sure the message had been received. Then he left, following his master's path towards the study. My bones ached to watch him, that mangled walk, the twist of a hip to propel him forwards.

Some brief sound made me glance up at the minstrels' gallery that overlooked the hall like a balcony at the theatre. A gentleman of middling years stood at the balustrade, a pale hand resting upon the rail. Metcalfe Robinson: Mr Aislabie's nephew. He was dressed in his nightgown, head bare. He was staring directly where I stood, but it was as if I wasn't there. His grey eyes were dull, his bristled jaw sagging as if he did not have the strength to lift it.

'Mr Robinson?' I waved a hand to break him from his trance. 'May I speak with you? My name is Thomas Hawkins.'

This jolted him so hard he had to snatch at the rail to steady himself. He stared at me in disbelieving horror, as if I were Hamlet's father come to haunt him. 'Impossible,' he said, hoarsely – and backed away, vanishing into the shadows.

Chapter Six

Lady Judith had been too optimistic about the weather. It was raining again, sweeping across the valley as if God were considering a second flood. No tour of the gardens today. A quiet part of me was relieved. There was something unsettling about Mrs Aislabie, something that sent a pulse through me, half attraction and half warning. She was playful, yes – but then cats play with mice sometimes, before they eat them.

I smoked a pipe, and took a solitary stroll about the ground floor. It was something of a maze, especially the connecting rooms directly behind the great hall. These I named the 'horse rooms', as the walls were covered in pictures of them, from portraits of individual animals to vast hunting scenes. What other purpose they served, I never discovered. I paused in front of a painting of the Ripon races. The riders were all women, wearing breeches. The plaque upon the frame read: Ladies' Race, 1723, Ripon. Racing, gambling, and lady jockeys. I would have jumped into the painting if I could.

The east wing lay abandoned on this floor, although I did stumble across a fellow mending the cornices in one room, so perhaps the Aislabies had plans for it. At the back of the house I found the library again, a little-used music room, and a larger room for billiards.

The west wing appeared to be the favoured aspect. There was a snug little withdrawing room, filled with tempting armchairs and more recent family portraits, and then the long dining room. Mr Aislabie's study sat at the front of the house. He had retired there with Mr Sneaton after dinner, presumably to buy up the rest of the county.

It might appear as though I were drifting aimlessly about the place, and I admit that is one of my preferred occupations. In this case, however, I was drifting with intent. I needed to memorise the rooms while it was still light, so that I could search them more closely in darkness.

Five days ago, I had been tasked by the queen to find a certain green ledger and bring it safely to London. The book had disappeared shortly after the collapse of the South Sea Company. It contained a list of over a hundred illustrious names, and the private details of their stockjobbing – when they had sold their shares and at what price, the exact profit they had made from each transaction. *Hundreds* of thousands of pounds, all neatly recorded.

No scandal there – except that it proved that many of the shares had been given for free, as bribes. In exchange, every person listed in the ledger had supported the South Sea Scheme as it travelled through Parliament and into law. They had encouraged others to invest, inflating the price. And then, mysteriously, these lucky beneficiaries had sold their shares at the ideal moment, just before the bubble burst and the stock value plummeted.

Either they were the cleverest gamblers in history, or they had been passed privileged information – perhaps by Aislabie himself. *Sell now – the entire damned scheme is about to collapse.* Dukes and duchesses, bishops and lawyers, ministers of government, the old king and his mistresses. And the Prince and Princess of Wales

– as they were in 1720. Now their Exalted Majesties King George II and Queen Caroline of Ansbach. All with their snouts in the trough.

The whole world knew that the scheme had been corrupted. But the whole world couldn't prove it, not without the slim green accounts book and its list of names. Questions were asked in the Commons. Offices were ransacked. A government enquiry was set up. Aislabie and his staff were interrogated. Aislabie himself was thrown in the Tower, where he languished for months. The ledger was never found. Aislabie testified that he always destroyed his account books once they were balanced. His secretary burned them – it was all quite routine. The Commons, the Lords, the nation raged, but nothing could be done. The evidence was lost for ever.

The queen knew better. Mr Aislabie hadn't burned the ledger. He'd smuggled it out of London to his country estate, days before his arrest. Aislabie was a politician – and a wily one at that. The book was his security. And now he was using it to demand help from the guilty.

We are all slaves to public opinion, even the King of England. His claim to the throne was tenuous, to say the least. How would his subjects react if they discovered he had helped plunge the nation into catastrophic debt in order to sate his own greed? Violently, I'd wager.

*

'*Have you ever visited Yorkshire, Mr Hawkins? . . . We have a friend, in need of assistance.*' That is what Queen Caroline had asked me just five days before in her private quarters. Aislabie was no friend. He was blackmailing her – demanding her help in exchange for his continued silence. This was insufferable. The ledger must be found.

I held my tongue, and waited.

The queen was standing by the fire, shifting her weight from foot to foot. A touch of gout, I thought. 'How is your little *trull*, sir? Are you still wretchedly in love with her? Of course you are,' she replied for me. 'How charming.'

I lifted the glass of wine to my lips, trying to hide my alarm. The queen had sent for both Kitty and me, but on our arrival at St James's Palace, Kitty had been ordered to wait in the carriage. She was sitting there on her own, furious, rain pattering down upon the roof of the chaise. I hadn't understood why the queen would summon Kitty, only to refuse her an audience. Now I began to suspect the truth.

'Tell me, Mr Hawkins. How does it feel to be in love with a murderess?'

I clutched the glass, and said nothing. Kitty had killed a man. He had been trying to kill me, out on Snows Fields in Southwark. She had shot him in the gut, to save my life. But then she had stood over him, tipped fresh powder into her pistol and shot him again – between the eyes at close range. He would have died from the first shot, eventually. One might even call the second shot an act of mercy. But it wasn't. Kitty had fired in a cold, deliberate rage. I knew that, and so did the one other witness to the shooting. And slowly, inevitably, the story had reached the queen.

She faced me now, one hand gripping the mantelpiece for support. Her rings glinted in the candlelight. This was real power – to threaten without ever speaking the words. 'I am sure you will do your *very* best,' she said sweetly.

And I had agreed that I would, and returned to Kitty, sulking because she had been summoned by the queen and then abandoned in the carriage. The queen had never intended to see her. Kitty's role was to be waiting for me now as I left the palace, beautiful and angry and perfect. *See what you might lose, if you don't do as I command.* It was the first time she had used Kitty's secret to get what she wanted. I feared it would not be the last.

I had promised Kitty that I would stop holding secrets – but I couldn't tell her this. I had lived for weeks under sentence of death and I would not put her through the same torture. I couldn't bear it. So she had complained all the way from London to Newport Pagnell about our ridiculous mission, and how dare the queen send me back into more trouble when I had only just survived a hanging, and why could we not simply refuse and sail for the Continent, as we'd agreed.

Then we'd pulled into the coaching inn and I had discovered Sam, hiding beneath our luggage like a beetle under a rock. Sam Fleet, raised to be a thief and worse, who could tiptoe through a house and never be heard, who could hide in the shadows and never be seen. Who better to find the ledger? I tried to explain this to Kitty, but she had thought it too risky. *You can't trust him, Tom. You know what he is. You know what he's done.*

I couldn't admit to her why it was so vital we succeed, why I must bring Sam with us. So we had argued, and she had accused me of lying to her again, after all my promises to change. Chairs were kicked. The next morning she had refused to leave until I sent Sam back to London. More arguments and more delays. When she saw I would not be persuaded, she arranged a seat on the next coach home. 'I know you love me, Tom – but you love gambling more. This is all another game to you, another chance to test your luck.'

'That's not true, Kitty.'

She took my hands and pulled me closer. 'Then come home with me.'

'I can't. I have to go.'

She shoved me away. 'You don't *have* to do anything. *Fuck* the queen.'

An hour later I was on the road with Sam, heading north with a dark fear in my heart that I had made a terrible mistake. But what choice did I have? I had to find the ledger. I had to save Kitty.

*

And if by some miracle I succeeded, what then? I stood in the great stone-flagged entrance hall at Studley, my hands in my pockets. I had walked all the way around, only to find myself back at the start. How fitting.

I made my way down to the servants' rooms on the lower floor, and found Mrs Mason in her kitchen, hanging a brace of rabbits on a hook. Like most cooks she was somewhat round from tasting her own dishes, and her hands had magical properties, having spent years kneading, pummelling, peeling, cleavering and being plunged into boiling water. She also had the most appealing face. Not that she was a great beauty – it was more that her temperament tended naturally towards laughter and generosity. This had settled happily upon her features after forty years. To put it another way, on meeting her I felt myself to be a small boy again, and longed for a warm hug. Sadly decorum prevented me from asking.

She brewed up a pot of coffee and we talked while she prepared herbs for a stock. She asked me about my trial and hanging, rather as I might ask her the best way to dress a salmon. That is to say, I took no offence from her questions, and recognised a kindred, inquisitive spirit.

She confirmed that two bed sheets were missing: she had checked the laundry herself. Mrs Mason appeared to have an informal role as housekeeper, along with her duties in the kitchen. I suspected that – rather like Sneaton – she was considered part of the extended Aislabie family.

'Must have been a sneaking little devil,' she said. 'There's always someone out in the yard. A woman, I reckon. She could tuck them under her gown.' She pushed a clove into a shallot, and then another.

'Who do you think wrote the notes?'

'The Gills, most likely.'

'The poachers?'

'You might call them that. There's been Gills hunting out on Kirkby moors long as anyone can remember. But his honour bought the moor, so . . . now they're poachers.'

'Bad business with the deer.'

'Died quickly, by the looks of it,' she shrugged, unmoved. She was a cook, after all. 'But now – here's a thing made me wonder. I can't see Jeb or Annie Gill wasting good venison like that. Not in their nature.'

This was a very good point. Surely a poacher would never squander such valuable meat, just for dramatic effect. 'Are they capable of murder, d'you think? Is *that* in their nature? Would they burn the house down for revenge?'

Mrs Mason dropped her shallot in alarm. 'Bloody hell, I hope not. Excuse my language, sir.'

I asked Mrs Mason for directions to my quarters. She insisted on calling Bagby, who'd been napping next door in the servants' hall. He stumbled into the kitchen, rubbing his eyes and grumbling loudly until he saw me sitting at the table, finishing my bowl of coffee. Hiding his scowl behind the thinnest screen of deference, he led me upstairs, back straight, mouth twisted shut. I paused upon the landing to admire the tapestry. In truth it was not a good piece, but it depicted a horse with a splendid mane, rearing up on its hind legs. Horses, I was beginning to understand, were granted an almost divine status at Studley. Even poorly stitched ones.

Bagby made an impatient little noise in the back of his throat. He didn't like me. Why should he? He was not the first servant who resented his low position. Perhaps if I told him I had been tortured in a debtors' prison? Beaten and robbed? Hanged at Tyburn? Ah, but above all that, I was a gentleman – nothing luckier than that.

We turned right on the landing and passed into the east wing, floorboards creaking under our feet. The main body of the house was in reasonable order but this side appeared to be listing, with great cracks in the plaster. There was a smell of damp, and the faded wallpaper was blistered and peeling away, as if the walls were suffering from some awkward rash.

We took a step up into a dark and oddly cramped corridor, scarce wide enough to scrape through in single file. The floor here was uneven, sloping sharply to the right. Low beams ran across the ceiling, as if designed to cause injury. A helpful servant would have said, 'Mind your head, sir.' Bagby remained silent, walking ahead with near-satirical dignity, as if he were escorting me through the Palace of Versailles.

We had reached the back of the house, though with all the twists and turns we'd performed, I did not realise this yet. My apartment was tucked away on a *mezzanino* below the attic rooms. Bagby opened the door with a flourish and gestured for me to enter. A glint in his eye made me pause on the threshold, foot hanging in mid-air. There were three steps down into the room. If I hadn't paused I would have missed them, and stumbled head first to the floor.

I stepped down into the main bedchamber, fighting my disappointment. The bed itself looked inviting, with a scarlet canopy and matching counterpane. But the room had an oppressive feel, even with the fire flickering in the hearth and fresh candles in the sconces. The low ceilings were brought even lower by a series of dark beams, and the mahogany wall panels added to the intense gloom. There was at least a tall double window, but the latticed glass allowed through only a thin light, and was blocked further by a great oak tree growing directly outside.

If Kitty were here ... If Kitty were here it would have felt warm and bright enough. She would have complained loudly about the tree, and the dark panelling, and the fusty smell. Then she would have kicked Bagby from the room and pulled me by my breeches to the bed. She would have kissed me, guided my hand under her gown, my fingers trailing up the heavenly silk of her thighs and—

'Will that be all?' Bagby asked.

I glanced at my luggage. I could insist that he unpack my belongings, but he was a sour addition to the room. The sooner he left the better. I waved him out, crossing to the window. Raindrops were snaking their way down the glass. I pressed my forehead to the pane. My head was pounding from the wine, and my journey, and something deeper.

Kitty. How could I have lost her, and so soon? If I wrote to her now, would she come?

I sighed my frustration out on to the glass. The letter would take at least three days to reach her. Even if she set out the next day, she was more than a week away. My luggage lay a few feet from where I stood, offering another choice. Call for the carriage and return home. Queen Caroline was clever, and manipulative, and excessively good at getting what she wanted. But she wasn't wilfully cruel. Surely she was bluffing. Surely she would not send Kitty to her death.

For five days now, the same argument had circled my mind. And in the end, I would always reach the same conclusion. *Surely* wasn't good enough. This was one gamble I dared not take.

I lifted my head from the glass. No point arguing with myself and dreaming of home.

I crossed to the fire, shovelling fresh coal upon the flames. There was a dark painting hanging above the fireplace – black clouds gathering over a ruined abbey. It was a large picture with a heavy frame, and looked as though it had been painted with a much grander room in mind. I scraped a smudge of coal soot from the plaque. *Storm at Fountains Abbey*. A great tower rose into the blackening sky, looming over the crumbling ruins. Roofs and walls had collapsed, pulled down by time and the violence of men. The fallen stones were scattered all around, covered in a tangle of weeds. The artist had painted the stones in shades of grey and black, their colour muted by the storm clouds. The grass was a steel grey.

I'm not sure how long I stood before that painting. Perhaps it was fatigue, or the trials of recent weeks, or merely the painter's choice of colours – but I felt as though I were not looking at a ruined monastery, but at something more spectral. As if all the souls who had lived and died there were now trapped inside the picture, and were calling for me to join them.

I stepped back, shaking my head to clear it. Fancies and phantasms. I had not come here to indulge in such follies. I must discover the ledger. There was an end to it.

In the meantime I should put the hours of daylight to some use. Mr Aislabie and his family were under threat, and as his guest, my own life could be in peril. It was in my own interest to enquire into the matter more closely.

I perched on the window seat, spreading the four letters out upon the cushion. Who had written them? The more I considered them, the more convinced I became that they were the work of two different men. The first two wavered between bitter resentment and surprising deference, of the kind I'd witnessed from Mr Simpson. Aislabie was addressed several times as 'Your honour'. There was an appeal to his obligations, to his sense of fairness. The accompanying threats of violence were unpleasant, but were swiftly followed by promises of gratitude and obedience, if only his honour would permit the moors to be opened up as common land once more. I would bet my last crown the same arguments had been put to the estate steward and to Mr Sneaton on numerous occasions, without effect. These were notes written in anger and frustration, but with hope for a peaceful resolution.

In contrast, the next two made no demands, reasoned or otherwise. They were short, and cruel. Reading them again, I felt the hairs rise upon my skin.

Aislabie – your Crimes must be punnished. You have Ruined Good and Honest Familys with your Damn'd Greed. Our mallis is too great to bear we are resolved to burn down your House. We will watch as your flesh and bones burn and melt and your Ashes scatter in the Wind. Nothing will Remain. You have 'scaped Justice too long damn you.

Aislabie you Damned Traitor. This is but the beginning of Sorrows. We will burn you and your daughter in your beds. You are not alone by night or day. We will seek Revenge.

These were not threats, but judgements handed down to the accused. Aislabie was a *Damned Traitor*. And the punishment for treason was death by fire.

The scrape of a latch in the far corner of the room made me glance up from my reading. The door was set flush to the mahogany panels – I had noticed it upon entering and dismissed it as a closet space. In fact it opened on to a connecting room for a gentleman's valet. Sam had taken it as his own, occupying it in absolute silence until he had deemed it the proper time to present himself. He stood barefoot in the doorway, his black curls loose about his face.

'There you are,' I said, because I knew it would infuriate him. Any statement of the obvious made him seethe with annoyance.

He stepped aside so that I might enter his domain. It was not much more than a closet after all – smaller than my cell at Newgate – with a narrow bed and two dingy portraits on the wall. It would suit Sam – he preferred cramped spaces. His home in St Giles was filled with noise and people at all times of the day and night, and he had become expert at tucking himself away in forgotten corners.

The room was almost bare: he had brought nothing with him from London save for a handful of coins and two vicious blades, the latter of which I had confiscated from him. To compensate for his loss, and to help him pass the time on our journey, I had given him a pencil and a sheaf of paper – he was an excellent draughtsman – and a copy of *Gulliver's Travels*. This latter – upon learning it was a fictional voyage – he pronounced 'a worthless con', it being 'made of lies'. But he had placed it neatly on a chair with his sketches, his shoes and stockings tucked under the bed.

'What do you make of these?' I handed him the notes.

He read them quickly, unruffled by the content. Then he divided them in half, waving the latest two in his fist. 'Dangerous.'

I took the papers back. 'Aislabie believes that Mrs Fairwood is his daughter—'

'—maid told me.'

'Whoever wrote this latest note knows about Elizabeth Fairwood's claim, and the fire on Red Lion Square.'

Sam shrugged. Sometimes I wondered if he were already five steps ahead of me. He was so close-tongued, how could one know for certain?

I flicked the papers. 'The first two notes were written on old bits of scrap, but this is very fine. I'll wager the second two match Mr Aislabie's best paper.'

'Could've been stolen. It's *Aiselby*,' he added.

'No – the servants call him that. He pronounces it Aizlabee . . .' I paused, then sifted back through the notes. The first two had spelled his name *Aiselby*, capturing the Yorkshire pronunciation. The second two had spelled it *Aislabie*.

Jack Sneaton was from the south, and had corrected my pronunciation to Aizlabee. Aislabie also trusted him to hire all the servants at Studley Hall. That gave him power, and opportunities . . .

Could Sneaton have written the second two notes? He wasn't pleased by Mrs Fairwood's presence – that much was quite evident. Did he want to frighten her from the estate? It would have been easy enough for him to steal the linen and the fine paper. He knew the movements of the household, and when it would be safe to move through the grounds. With his broken body, he could not have killed the deer himself or dragged it to the front steps, but he might have an accomplice. *We will seek Revenge*, the note had promised.

I handed the notes to Sam. 'See if you can find an example of Sneaton's lettering. He must write with his left hand, I suppose. Could you compare it with the second two letters? Even if the hand is disguised?'

Sam looked offended, as if I'd asked him whether he knew his alphabet. He had been counterfeiting papers for his father for years. He'd been doing all sorts of terrible things for his father for years. The first time we'd met, he'd led me down a darkened alleyway so I might be robbed at knifepoint. I was still waiting for an apology.

I poured myself a glass of sherry from a decanter on the dressing table. 'Why did you change our quarters?'

Sam grinned. Opened the window, put his foot on the casement frame—

—and jumped.

I swore, more in surprise than concern. I'd grown used to his acrobatics. I kneeled on the window seat and peered out. He'd jumped into the oak tree and was now sitting on a sturdy branch, bare legs dangling. I peered down at the ground three floors below. There was a path for the carriages, which must lead to the current stables at the back of the house. Beyond the path, a dense cluster of trees. The rain pattered through the leaves.

'An excellent escape route,' I said, raising my glass of sherry in approval. 'If one happens to be a monkey.' Could I leap the distance? Probably, if the need were pressing. If the house were on fire.

Sam crawled along the branch, swung himself on to the window ledge and back into the room. It looked distinctly perilous and much harder than leaping out. 'Family's in the west wing. Won't hear us. Servants,' he added, hoicking a thumb upstairs. Turned his thumb upside down, indicating the three floors below. 'Metcalfe, library, kitchens.' He crossed the room to the connecting door, toe then heel like a dancer, missing every creaking floorboard. 'View,' he called over his shoulder.

The window in his cupboard room looked out on to the servants' courtyard. An older woman hurried from the laundry with a stack of folded sheets up to her chin, shooing chickens away with her boot. I watched for a minute or two as maids and grooms and footmen ran through the yard, and no one looked up at the window. Sam had found us the ideal quarters; quiet, tucked far away from the Aislabies' rooms, and offering an excellent vantage point from which to spy on the servants.

Mr Pugh, our carriage driver, sat on a mounting block, smoking a pipe and talking with an older fellow.

'William Hallow,' Sam said. 'Game keeper. Thinks you're an angel.'

I coughed on my sherry.

'Hanged. Resurrected.' Sam watched me from the corner of his black eyes. 'Touched by God.'

The room fell silent – as it must with Sam standing in it. He never spoke if he could avoid it, kept his words deep in his chest like a miser clutching his coins. And what poor, counterfeit coins they were when he did spend them – a grunt for yes, a strangled sigh for no. In the slums of St Giles, a careless word was as dangerous as a sharpened blade. All his life, he had been taught how to hide in the shadows, to watch and listen and remain invisible. But silence was in his nature too. Sam's father might be the most powerful gang captain in the city, but one could still talk with him over a bowl of punch.

A few months ago I had agreed to take Sam into my household and teach him the manners of a gentleman. To say that I had failed hardly begins to describe the catastrophe that followed. A violent tangle of events had led to murder and my trip to the gallows. Sam had helped save my life. But he had also killed someone in the process.

I had studied Sam closely on our journey from London and could discern no particular change in him – no apparent guilt or remorse for what he had done. His father was a murderer. He was named for his uncle, Samuel Fleet – a highly accomplished assassin, who'd been known in the Marshalsea as the Devil. Such names were not given lightly. I could not ignore the fact that killing was part of the family trade. Nor that – as far as his parents were concerned – Sam had completed his apprenticeship.

For this reason alone, Kitty and I had agreed to dismiss Sam from our home for ever. I'd had no expectation of seeing him again. And yet when I'd helped him down from his hiding place on the carriage, soaked and shivering, I had known at once that I would bring him with me. My damned curiosity again. It's what Fleet had first noticed in me, when I'd stepped into the prison yard. 'Curiosity and a wilful belief that the world is on your side. What an in*tox*icatingly idiotic combination.' Indeed.

I stood before the two portraits, studying them closely. Brothers, I thought – dressed in a style from forty years ago, with huge brown wigs cascading over their shoulders. The younger brother was no more than sixteen, with a soft, soulful countenance. The elder was a few years older, somewhat arrogant-looking. They both reminded me of John Aislabie. They shared the same dark brown eyes and narrow, handsome face. And yet there was something lacking in both portraits. Aislabie was a man of restless vigour. The two brothers seemed languid by comparison, almost lifeless. A failing of the painter, perhaps.

The painting of the younger brother was a little crooked. I reached out and straightened it, noticing a name etched upon the frame. *Mallory Aislabie, died 1685.* My gaze slid to the older brother. *George Aislabie, died 1693.* The year Aislabie had inherited the Studley Estate. These were Aislabie's older brothers, relegated to the east wing while his beloved horses pranced in an endless parade of paintings downstairs.

'They're worried about Metcalfe,' Sam said.

'The servants?'

'Everyone.'

'Why are they worried about him?'

A shrug.

'Should I be worried about Metcalfe?'

Another shrug.

I remembered the note I'd taken from the library, covered in Metcalfe's blotched and frantic scrawl. I pulled it from my jacket to compare it more carefully, but I could see at once that it didn't match. It was too jagged, and he dipped his quill too often, the ink heavy on the page.

'We should go downstairs,' I said. 'The family will be gathering in the drawing room.'

Sam shrank back, as if I'd just threatened him with a blade. Or a bath.

'I've told them you're my ward. A gentleman's son, if you can imagine such a thing. I know it seems unlikely, but we must brazen it out. Everyone will be much too polite to question it.' I pointed at his shoes and stockings. 'Come along. The best houses don't allow you to eat barefoot I'm afraid.'

He frowned. Cards, conversation. *Cutlery.* 'When do we hunt for the ledger?'

'Later. Aislabie thinks I'm here to help him. We must dissemble, a little.'

'But we'll leave, once we've found it? We'll go *home*?'

I hesitated. Home was the Cocked Pistol on Russell Street. A collection of rooms above a disreputable print shop. I couldn't promise him a bed there, not without Kitty's consent. 'We'll go straight back to London.'

Sam's face crumpled. I had side-stepped the promise, and he knew it.

'Put your shoes on,' I said, touching his arm. 'And tie up your hair. You look positively savage.'

Chapter Seven

My arrival at Studley Hall had caused a stir in the neighbourhood, and Mr Aislabie was forced to entertain several unexpected guests that evening. Everyone was eager to meet the celebrated Half-Hanged Hawkins – save for the elusive Metcalfe, sequestered in his rooms. A woman of middling years clasped my hand and told me – tears spilling down her cheeks – that I was a miracle, a *miracle*. I am not sure I ever caught her name, only that she was a neighbour of the Aislabies and had just returned from London herself. 'I'm afraid I missed your hanging. I'd promised to visit my sister in Greenwich and she is most fastidious about her engagements. Can you forgive me?'

'This once, madam.'

'London is a vastly wicked place,' she said, squeezing my hand. 'I miss it dreadfully.'

The vicar of Kirkby Malzeard had ridden several miles on very bad roads to inform me that God had spared my life as a sign of His mercy, and that I must now dedicate myself to His Glory. By coincidence, the church roof at Kirkby was in urgent need of repair. Was it true that I had recently come into a fortune through marriage? I was rescued by Mr Gatteker, the physician, pulling me away by the elbow. He was eager to learn more about the physical effects of my hanging. 'I hear there are certain spontaneous bodily *eruptions*, when the rope tightens.' He leaned closer, and whispered hotly in my ear. 'Venereal spasms.'

I drew back a pace. 'How's your patient, sir?'

'Tolerable. Haven't killed him yet.' Mr Gatteker had been summoned from Ripon to examine Fred's broken leg. He was a genial fellow of near forty, his eyes small but very bright behind a pair of round spectacles. Unlike most doctors I'd met he appeared to be in excellent health, if a little stretched about the middle. He stole two glasses of wine from a passing tray. 'Your brother splinted the leg with commendable proficiency.'

I glanced across the drawing room at Sam, back pressed to the wall as if he might like to sink through it. 'He's not my brother.'

'Is he not? You'd best inform him of that disappointing news, sir. He's been telling the world that you are.' Gatteker took a deep, contented swig of claret, watching me over the rim. His expression was mild, but searching. 'Not brothers. But there's a bond, I think? If that is not too presumptuous of me.'

'Who is that gentleman, speaking with Mr Aislabie?' I asked, gesturing towards a slight, straight-backed man dressed in a sky blue coat, the cuffs and pleats in the latest London style. His left hand and arm hung under the coat sleeve, bandaged and bound tightly in a fine muslin sling.

'Ah, a swift change of subject! I have offended you with my *probings*. Mrs Gatteker oft complains—'

I cut him off before the inevitable and unwanted jest. 'His arm is broken?'

'Fell from his horse. Francis Forster. Decent fellow. Cat-a-*strophically* dull. Mind you don't sit with him at supper.'

Mr Gatteker had a carrying voice. Mr Forster, hearing his name bellowed across the room – though thankfully not the proceeding description – came over and introduced himself with a neat bow. He had the look of a man who had spent long months on the Continent, or aboard ship. The sun had bronzed his skin, and his eyes – a vivid blue – shone out from beneath straight brows, burnished to a white gold. It had been another freezing winter in England, and the rest of the gathering looked pale, one might even say dusty, by comparison.

Forster didn't ask me how it felt to be hanged by the neck in front of one hundred thousand spectators, which by this point in the evening I took to be the height of good manners. I held my pale hand against his. 'I seem a corpse next to you, sir. Are you in the navy?' Aislabie had been Treasurer of the Navy for four years.

'Heavens, no,' Forster laughed. 'Though I have been abroad for some years. I have a great passion for architecture.' He had spent the last three years on a grand tour of Italy, he explained, with two companions. His friends remained abroad, lost in the magnificent, ruined splendour of it all. He had run out of funds over the winter and so sailed home, eager to put his ideas into practice and presumably to find paid work. He had filled countless sketchbooks with his designs, perhaps I might like to see them? I pretended that I would.

'Then I beg you to visit me tomorrow sir, at Fountains Hall,' he beamed. 'Have you viewed the abbey yet?'

'There is a painting—'

'No? Splendid – you must permit me to tour it with you. We must pray for good weather. Now: promise me you will set aside at least three hours, sir! One cannot appreciate all the finer details if one rushes through ...' He then ruined five perfectly decent minutes of my life talking about flying buttresses. Mr Gatteker, the traitor, drifted away. My eyes flickered across Forster's face, which was more interesting than his conversation. A brilliant white scar crossed one golden brow, and another cut into his lip. The lines at the edges of his eyes suggested a man of at least five and thirty, but they might have been formed from squinting at the Italian sun. In fact he mentioned later that evening that he was born in 1700, 'the very cusp of the new century'. It had aged him, that bright sunshine.

'I'm sorry to hear about your arm,' I said, leaping into a momentary lull in his monologuing.

Forster winced. 'Broke the wrist too, would you believe. Damned horse stumbled on the Nottingham road.' The sling kept his arm high upon his chest, his bandaged thumb and fingers pressed to his heart.

'Must have been painful.'

'Screamed like a baby,' he said, laughing at himself in a likeable way – and I forgave him for his lamentable skills in conversation.

But not enough to sit with him at supper.

We were a smaller gathering in the dining room, our party whittled down to eight for a light meal. It was almost nine when we sat down, but the curtains were left open to the black night. It gave a dramatic backdrop to the room, which was bright with candles, flames mirrored in the silverware. Aislabie and Lady Judith sat at either end of the table, our elegant hosts, exchanging affectionate jests at each other's expense. Elizabeth Fairwood sat next to her would-be father in her grey gown, training her displeasure upon her plate. Francis Forster took the chair opposite, eager to speak with Aislabie. They fell swiftly into a discussion about the new stables, to the point that Aislabie called for Bagby, ordering him to bring in the plans for closer scrutiny. Lady Judith overruled her husband, her clear voice cutting above the rest. 'Not at supper, dearest. Poor Mrs Fairwood is drooping with boredom.'

I was seated to her left, Mr Gatteker upon her right. She leaned closer, whispered in my ear. 'Forster is a tedious fellow.

I'm glad that *you* are at my side tonight.' I felt a slim hand on my knee, followed by a gentle squeeze.

Sneaton, placed between Mr Gatteker and Mrs Fairwood, reached for the salted fish, struggling with his damaged hand.

'If you will permit me, sir,' Mrs Fairwood offered, bringing the dish closer.

'Much obliged, madam,' Sneaton replied.

The exchange was brief and excruciatingly polite. They clearly loathed one another.

'How quiet you are, Master Fleet,' Lady Judith scolded Sam, cocooned in silence to my left. 'I believe you have not spoken one word since we sat down.'

To my surprise, Mrs Fairwood spoke up in his defence. 'Is that not refreshing, madam? To speak only when one has something *pertinent* to say?'

Lady Judith was too subtle to acknowledge the insult. 'Now there is a noble ambition! Though I fear under such instruction, the dining rooms of England would fall silent at a stroke. Tell me, Master Fleet, do you enjoy your stay at Studley Hall?'

I sensed Sam's consternation at the question, and his horror at being asked anything at all, to feel the eyes of the table swivel upon him. An honest reply would be no, he was not enjoying his stay at Studley, that – in fact – he hated it and wished more than anything to be gone. I had at least taught him enough manners to know that this was not an acceptable response.

'Yes,' he lied.

I trod on his toe.

'Thank you,' he added, miserable.

Another press of the toe, as if he were a pipe organ.

'Madam.' Half yelped.

'There is much to commend a *quiet* gentleman,' Mrs Fairwood announced to the air, dark ringlets shaking with the force of her feeling. 'It suggests a thoughtful nature. To speak is a common necessity. To listen – a rare virtue.'

'Quite so, well said, madam!' Forster cried. 'Nothing worse than a fellow who cannot keep his mouth closed. I have always felt . . .'

Lady Judith gave me a satirical look.

The supper continued. No one mentioned the threatening notes, or the deer. Talk returned to the stables, and the gardener's extravagant bill for seeds, and then worse: politics. I could sense Sam growing increasingly restless. Eventually, he could bear it no longer.

'Mr Sneaton. How were you burned?'

There was an appalled silence.

'Mr Sneaton—' I began.

He waved away my apology with his damaged hand. He seemed unable to speak. Gatteker poured himself another glass of claret, the wine glugging from the bottle in the silent room.

'There was a fire in my London home,' Aislabie answered at last, in a flat voice. 'Many years ago now. My son William was a baby at the time. I tried to reach him . . .' He swallowed hard. 'I was forced back by the flames. Mr Sneaton ran into the fire and the smoke, and he found my son. I lost my wife, my Anne.' He grabbed Mrs Fairwood's hand. 'But Mr Sneaton saved my son. He almost lost his own life as a consequence. He suffered years of pain. Still suffers now, without complaint. Mr Sneaton is the bravest, most admirable man I have ever met. I owe him every-thing.' He glared down the table. 'Does that answer your ques-tion, Master Fleet?'

'Yes,' Sam said, reaching for the salt. 'Thank you.'

The company rose from the table, subdued by Aislabie's story and his obvious distress. I sent Sam to our rooms, which pleased him very well. He had plans to sketch in his room, using candles he'd tucked beneath his shirt. Sam's instinct was to steal what he needed, rather than to ask and risk refusal. It would not have occurred to him that he could simply demand what he wanted. Not without a blade in his hand.

I suppose I should have reprimanded him for his behaviour, but why waste my breath? I had tried to explain the subtleties of polite conversation. It was like trying to recommend a complicated gavotte to a soldier striding hard across a battlefield. Sam's view was that if one must speak, it should be to a purpose – to discover a useful fact, for example, or to offer a plan of action. Sam had wanted to know how Sneaton had been burned, and now he knew. This, to his mind, was a highly satisfactory conversational exchange.

And how could I argue with him? I now knew how Sneaton had come by his injuries, and why he was treated more as a member of the family than as Aislabie's secretary. After all, servants did not sit down to supper with their masters, in the main. I was certain now that Sneaton had not written the threatening notes. He was loyal, and he was treated with respect – perhaps even affection – by the family. I might not have discovered this if Sam hadn't ignored the constrants of etiquette.

I needed to think, and to restore my nerves. I needed a pipe. As Lady Judith escorted her guests to the drawing room I slipped away, through the great hall and down the front steps. It was a clear night, the waxing moon a brilliant silver. The front of the house was very still now that the work on the stables had ended for the day. Candles glowed softly in the drawing room and I could hear the sound of the harpsichord through an open window.

I stepped on to the drive, feet crunching on the gravel, then moved further out into the deer park beyond, the grass wet around my ankles. Here the darkness found me, and wrapped me in its quiet embrace. In London, night was day for me: I lived in Covent Garden, surrounded by coffeehouses, gin shops and brothels. I had run headlong into that wild and rowdy city, craving its hectic pace – the perfect tempo for my restless spirit.

But the city had turned on me, in the end. I had suffered many nights of agony and despair these past few months. Chained to a wall in the Marshalsea, with the dead festering beside me and the rats crawling across my body. Sweating with gaol fever as a parson prayed over my fading soul. Those endless nights grieving for Kitty, when I believed her dead. The eve of my hanging and the days after, when I would dream it all again. When I would embellish it in my nightmares: trapped in my coffin as they lowered me into the ground. The patter of soil on wood as I was buried alive.

These were the nights the city had bestowed upon me.

Eyes closed, I breathed in the fresh, cool air. There was no city stink here, but grass and mud, and the faintest whiff of cow dung. I could sense the deer close by, awake and alert to threats in the dark. I thought of the butchered doe and its tiny fawn, killed before it could live. Then I pushed the memory away and enjoyed a moment's peace, alone in the night.

A moment was enough. I rolled my shoulders, stretched out my back and neck – still aching from my journey. I packed my pipe and struck a spark from my tinderbox, breathing gently on the embers. The flame burst orange, and a gaunt grey face loomed out of the dark, inches from mine.

I gave a shout of alarm and the tinderbox sailed out of my hands, flame sizzling out in the wet earth. The face vanished, the night a velvet black all around me. I could see nothing, except for my breath clouding in front of me. My heart was pounding so hard I could feel the blood thrumming in my ears. So much for the quiet peace of the country.

'Who's there?' I called out. I had no sword. I'd left my dagger and pistols in my room.

'I watched you die.'

The words drifted through the air, musical and strange.

Metcalfe. I exhaled softly.

Relief turned swiftly to annoyance. What the devil was he doing, creeping about in the dark? I dropped to the ground, hunting for my tinderbox. *I watched you die.* A fine sort of a greeting. He must have witnessed my hanging. Was I meant to thank him for his attendance? My fingers closed around the tinderbox. I stood up and started for the house.

'Mr Hawkins?' he called after me.

I pretended not to hear him, striding back through the grass. He hurried to catch up, breathing hard with the effort.

We had reached the steps, our shoes scuffing on the stone. In the great hall, I plucked a candle free from its sconce and lit my pipe. The first, glorious draw of tobacco sent its soothing message deep into my mind and body. All is safe, all is well. 'You startled me, sir.'

Metcalfe ran a hand across his bare scalp, fingers rasping against the greying stubble. His nails were black with mud. He was dressed in a once-fine waistcoat, ruined by neglect. His stockings were spattered, his shoes scuffed and coated with grass and mud. If I had not known that he was the heir to a baronetcy, I might have taken him for a poacher – and not a successful one, given his thin frame and hollow cheeks.

He peered at my face, standing closer than was comfortable or civil. 'Are you alive?'

'Of course I'm alive,' I snapped, leaning back.

He gave a curious, strangled sound – an almost-laugh. 'You will permit me?' He prodded my chest with a grimy finger, confirming my answer. 'I saw you hang. They put you in a coffin.'

'I was revived. Did you not hear the story?'

'Revived. Of course. Of *course.*' He snorted, disgusted by his own foolishness, and sat down heavily on the oak staircase. 'Forgive me, sir. Sometimes I see things that are not there. At least, there are times when I find it hard to distinguish between truth and fiction.' His soft grey eyes widened in fear at the thought.

I could see now how he suffered – a disorder of the mind, reflected in the body. The poor devil had watched me die, and now here I was looming out of the night in front of him. It would be enough to frighten any man, never mind one caught in the grip of a violent melancholia. I offered him my pipe.

He took a long draw, and breathed the smoke out with a sigh. 'Thank you.'

I sat down next to him, stretching out my legs. He was older than I had expected for Aislabie's nephew. Middling forties, I guessed. He smelled of tobacco and sweat, and his clothes were stained and in need of a wash. Why had he not sent them to be laundered? There were a dozen servants here who could attend him.

He returned my pipe, attempting a smile. His eyes were red-rimmed and bloodshot.

I held out my hand. 'Thomas Hawkins.'

He gave me a rueful smile. 'Metcalfe Robinson.'

We shook hands. 'Do you not remember me from this afternoon, sir? I spied you up there.' I pointed to the minstrels' gallery above us.

Metcalfe looked dazed. He reached a hand beneath his shirt, scratching his shoulder. 'Was that today? What day is it, again?'

I told him it was a Thursday, wondering if he was sure of the month, even the year. He seemed only half awake. Laudanum, I thought, remembering the bottle Sally had borrowed from him.

Metcalfe lit his own pipe. His hands were trembling a little. What a shock I'd given the poor devil. 'You've come to help my uncle, I believe?'

'If I can.'

' "He has done more mischief than any man in the nation." Lord Townshend said that of him, did you know? Although, *He that is without sin among you*, etcetera . . .' He puffed his pipe, eyes narrowed. He was not himself, he was not well. But he was a shrewd man, beneath it all – from a family of politicians and diplomats. 'Walpole sent you?'

I shook my head. I had not met the first minister, nor had any wish to do so. 'The queen.'

'The *queen!*' Metcalfe pulled the pipe from his lips and stared at me, astonished. 'So he yet has influence at court. That is ill news. He's always promised he'd return to power one day. I didn't think it possible.' He yawned, and stretched. 'I have been sleeping. But now I am awake.' He stood up.

Something about those words echoed in my mind. I had heard them before. Not a psalm. A poem, perhaps? 'You dislike your uncle.'

'I despise him.' He gave me his hand, and helped me to my feet. As he pulled me up, he brought his lips to my ear, clutching my hand tightly. 'Something dreadful is going to happen, Mr Hawkins. Can you feel it?' His breath was feverish hot in my ear. 'You were dead. They hanged you and they nailed you in your coffin. And now you are here: the black crow at the window, tapping out its message with its great beak. Death has come. Death is here.'

'Enough!' I snapped, breaking from him.

Metcalfe gave a jolt, as if waking from a dream.

His fingers had left smudges on my coat. I brushed them away. 'I must ask you not to speak of my hanging again, Mr Robinson. It is not a topic I wish to discuss, with anyone.'

Metcalfe wasn't listening. The light that had burned in his eyes was gone, leaving him listless and dazed. He nodded at the trail of muddy footprints we had left from door to stair. 'Poor Sally. See what we've done to her floor. We shall be in trouble! Well, well. Goodnight, sir.'

I stared after him as he headed up the stairs. It was as if he had been possessed, and now had no memory of it. Indeed it was as if I had met three of him within a few minutes: the shrewd politician, the shattered melancholic, and the rambling prophet. That could not be explained by laudanum alone.

They're worried about Metcalfe, Sam had said. Now I saw why.

I stood for a long time on my own in the great hall. I was disturbed by how much Metcalfe's warning had echoed my own fears: that I had become shrouded by death these past few weeks; that it had somehow stalked me back into the living world. And – caught up in such bleak and unhappy thoughts – I missed something important.

Lady Judith had told me that Metcalfe had barely left his room in three days. Now he was wandering through the deer park at night, with mud on his shoes and under his nails. I should have asked myself what he was doing out upon the estate, alone in the dark. I should have asked *him*.

But as I say – I didn't think of it at the time.

Chapter Eight

It was late – much later – and the house was quiet.

Someone had entered the room.

With my eyes closed, feigning sleep, I inched my hand beneath my pillow and found my dagger, curling my fingers around the hilt.

It wasn't Sam. He was downstairs somewhere, hunting for the ledger. And if he wanted to kill me in my bed, I wouldn't hear him coming.

Footsteps, light upon the oak boards. A slight creak. Definitely not Sam. I opened my eyes into pitch-black, shuttered darkness – the very dead of night. Whoever this was, he had walked through the house without a candle. He knew there were steps down into the room. Bagby? Metcalfe? This was the way my friend and cellmate Samuel Fleet had died: alone in his bed, his throat cut. I pulled the blade free.

The intruder had reached the bottom of the bed. I felt a pressure as he crawled on to the mattress. He was close now, almost close enough . . .

I reached out in the dark and grabbed an arm. With a quick snap, I'd thrown him face down on to the bed. I jumped up and straddled him, my arm firm across his back, my blade pressed to his throat. 'Who are you?' I snarled.

'Oh for heaven's sake, Tom!' a familiar voice cried out, muffled by the pillow.

I dropped the blade to the floor. '*Kitty?*'

'Get off me!'

I grinned, confused but happy. I pressed my knees against her side. 'No . . . I believe I shall stay here.'

She giggled, and flipped on to her back beneath me. I could feel her gown against my legs, smell her scent. I ran my hand up her waist in the dark, found the curve of her breast. I squeezed it, gently. 'Is it really you?'

She was laughing now, her chest rising and falling beneath my hand. 'You know it is.'

I leaned down and kissed her neck, her jaw. Where were her lips, confound it? Ah . . . *There*. 'Who brought you here?' I asked between kisses. 'How did you reach—'

She stopped my words with her mouth. 'This first, my love,' she said, wrapping her legs about my hips. 'This first.'

Later, I lit a candle and fell back against the pillow, grinning up at the canopy. Kitty shuffled beneath my arm, resting her head upon my chest. 'I should never have left you,' she murmured. 'But I was so *angry*. I do have a slight temper.'

I didn't refute this.

'I thought you would come galloping after me. All the way from Newport Pagnell I thought, he'll jump on a horse and race back to find me. Only you didn't.' She sighed into my chest. 'And then I began to wonder – because you are not spiteful, Tom, that is one of your better qualities, and you *don't* have a temper, at least not a bad one, and you are also impossibly lazy and never do a single thing unless you absolutely must – so I began to *wonder*, why is Tom determined to go to Yorkshire, when he hates to go anywhere at all if it does not involve drinking or gambling or perhaps a play if there is drinking and gambling afterwards.'

'True.'

She propped herself on her elbow to view me the better, sweeping her long red hair from her face. 'And then I thought, well he has not been himself since he was found guilty of murder and hanged, which is to be expected, I suppose. You know, you have been quite gloomy and mournful and distracted these past few weeks.'

'I'm sorry.'

'I forgive you. And it struck me that perhaps you simply wanted to escape London and all the terrible things that have happened to you. I know you still think of the Marshalsea, Tom, and have nightmares sometimes. And now the hanging as well. And the neighbours calling you a murderer, and speaking out against you at the trial, and then being so fickle and deciding you're a hero once they thought you were dead. *Idiots.* I should want to run away from all of that if I were you, and the queen did order you to go to Yorkshire, so perhaps you simply wanted to leave London, but didn't know how to tell me—'

'I—'

'But *then* I thought, Lord, in which case, why would we not go to Italy, as we'd planned? After all, the queen betrayed you in such a foul and sneaking fashion – she would have let you hang, Tom, you must never forget that – and I couldn't see why in all the heavens you would travel for days to find her stupid ledger unless she had some power over you.' She paused, and put a hand upon my heart. 'She threatened to have me hanged, didn't she?'

I covered her hand with mine.

Kitty's large green eyes filled with tears. 'Why did you not tell me? We made a vow to each other. No more secrets. You *promised.*'

99

I slid from the bed, and poured us both a glass of sherry.

'Walking about naked won't distract me, Tom.'

I smiled, and handed her a glass.

She sipped the sherry, lips curving about the rim. 'Well. Perhaps a little.'

I sat down next to her, and nuzzled her neck.

She pushed me away. 'You broke your promise.'

'Because I love you.'

'Oh, you pig!' She punched my arm. I'd played my ace.

We sat together for a while side by side upon the bed, drinking our sherry.

'I didn't even reach London, you know,' Kitty said, stifling a yawn. 'I paid the driver to turn around at St Albans. I've been chasing you all the way back north.'

'Who let you in so late?'

'The butler. Busby?'

'Bagby. Was he not surprised you travelled alone?'

'He said he was vastly pleased I'd arrived.' She mock preened, poking her nose in the air. 'Are you vastly pleased, Tom?'

'Beyond measure.' But how peculiar of Bagby. Why should it matter to him?

Kitty rested her chin upon my shoulder. 'Let's leave as soon as it's light. It's only a two-day ride to Hull. And then a ship. And then France. And then Italy.'

'I can't leave, not yet. I have to find the ledger.'

She sighed, her breath tickling my skin. 'And what then? Do you think the queen will leave you in peace after that? She will never let you go, Tom. You're too useful. We'll be trapped for ever.'

She was right. I had been mulling over the same problem ever since I'd been given my orders – wondering how I might free myself from the queen's grip. There was one obvious way: a simple if dangerous plan. But I needed Aislabie's accounts book first.

'Where's Sam?' Kitty asked.

'Hunting for the ledger.'

'O-ho!' She pinched me in the ribs. 'Taking all the risk while you lie snoring in bed.'

'I don't snore.'

Kitty raised an eyebrow at that. 'He can't come back to the Pistol with us, Tom. I know he's a sharp and useful boy, and he owns some rare gifts. But I don't trust him, not after what he did that night . . .' She trailed away, as we both thought about that room on Russell Street, the pillow and the forged note. A voice silenced for ever. Kitty had killed a man, but it had been a sudden, unplanned act: one shot to protect me, another to avenge Samuel Fleet, whom she had loved dearly. And while she could not regret it, I knew it troubled her. Was Sam troubled by what he'd done? Had it caused even a ripple to cross his soul? Impossible to know. But the murder had been measured, bloodless, and cunning. Efficient. Fourteen years old – and he had snuffed out a life as if it meant nothing.

I wrapped my arm about Kitty's shoulder. 'I've promised him nothing. He's a born thief – one of the best in London. That's the only reason he's here.'

That wasn't the entire truth. Mr Gatteker had perceived a bond between Sam and me and I felt it too. I couldn't explain it to Kitty. I couldn't explain it to myself.

'I'm freezing,' she said, rubbing her goosebumped arms. So we slipped back under the covers and spoke of other things.

*

Sam took a silent step back from the door, and then another. There was a sharp pain, like a blade in his heart, but he ignored it. It wasn't a real blade and therefore it wasn't a real pain, and it told him nothing.

'He's a born thief. That's the only reason he's here.'

How could he fault the logic?

But I am so much more.

The thought escaped against his wishes, too nimble to be held down. With it came a memory of sitting with Mr Hawkins in Newgate, the day before the hanging. Sam always listened and he always remembered, but that half hour in the prison yard he could conjure up in a heartbeat. He recalled the feel of the wooden bench, rough with splinters. The faint sound of hawkers shouting on the other side of the wall. The underlying stink of unwashed bodies and rotten food. If he chose, he could remember the number of cracks in the cobbles at his feet, the precise colour of the weeds poking through the dirt.

Mr Hawkins had asked, 'If you could do anything in the world, Sam – any occupation you wished. What would you choose?'

And, in that brief moment, Sam had glimpsed another life.

Standing in the damp, sloping corridor of the east wing of Studley Hall, he frowned at his own foolishness. This was what came from dreams and wishes. If he felt disappointed, if he felt betrayed – who could he blame but himself?

As for the pain in his chest, it would pass.

He was a born thief. He would find the ledger. It was a valuable thing, to know a gentleman's secrets and to have him in your debt. Sam's father had taught him that.

He moved silently along the corridor, down the stairs and into the kitchens, then out into the courtyard. The dogs didn't bark as he passed the kennels. He climbed over the courtyard wall and out into the deep wood.

No one saw him. No one heard him. Not a soul. But he saw everything.

The Second Day

Chapter Nine

I woke early, Kitty asleep beside me. I dozed for a time, happy she was there, then slid carefully from the bed. At home Kitty always rose before me, often by several hours. She had spent the last few days in a bone-rattling carriage, leaving at first light each morning in her race to reach me. I let the drapes close again around the bed. Let her rest.

I lifted the latch upon the shutters and drew them back as softly as I could. Dawn had arrived: the sky was growing lighter and the birds were singing in the trees outside the window. A party of tiny goldfinches were lined up along a branch, piping sweetly. I thought of my sister Jane: goldfinches were her favourite. I'd taught her all the bird calls when we were young, holding her hand as we walked through the woods near our home. I must return to Suffolk soon to visit her, and my father. When I'd been found guilty of murder, I'd thought the worry and the shame might kill him. I had known too that I had destroyed any chance Jane might have had of a suitable marriage. Would that change, now I was an *angel*, a *miracle*? Most likely not. The men of that neighbourhood knew me too well to believe in such a transformation.

I tapped my fingertips upon Sam's door and counted to ten. Always best to give a boy of fourteen a moment before entering his bedchamber. But he was awake and dressed, sketching by candlelight.

'Did you find the ledger?' I whispered.

Sam shook his head, keeping his eyes upon the paper.

'Did you search the library? The study?'

He lifted his chin.

'Well, it's a big house, it must be here somewhere. I'd be obliged if you would keep hunting, when it's safe. Kitty's here,' I added.

Sam lowered his pencil and swung his legs off the bed. He stood up. 'We should agree terms for my work.'

'Oh. As you wish.' I'd not considered the question of a fee, and he had never mentioned it before. But it *was* work: there was no denying that. I closed the door behind me, so that we might haggle without waking Kitty. We agreed upon the sum of two guineas. 'And these,' he added, gesturing to his clothes – a black coat and breeches, matched with a fawn waistcoat with embroidered pockets. I'd told Aislabie that Sam had lost his luggage on the road, and asked if we might borrow a suit. Bagby had brought it up last night – with a bill for six pounds. *Borrowing*, it seemed, was not in Mr Aislabie's vocabulary, though *extortion* had slithered its way in.

The clothes had belonged to Aislabie's son William as a boy. He would never need them again, grown up and living in London with his fortune and family. They fitted Sam's slight frame far better than the coat and breeches I'd lent him, which now lay at the bottom of the bed, encrusted with a thick layer of mud.

'What the devil have you done to my clothes?' I picked them up, dismayed – and held them out for inspection. A year ago I would have declared this a tragedy. I'd had no idea how lucky I was to care only for such trifles. I scraped a flake of mud from my coat. 'Where did you go last night? The pigsty?'

'Sally will clean them.'

'Yes, but she won't like you for it.'

A slight blush tinged his cheeks. Not hard to guess the reason. I handed him a shilling. 'Give her this for her trouble. She might forgive you.'

Kitty was still fast asleep, head buried in the pillow. I resisted the urge to wake her, closing the door behind me with the lightest click.

I walked down the sloping corridor, shoes in hand. The wallpaper was tattered in this part of the house and the whole wing had a neglected air. It could not be through lack of funds. Aislabie's interests lay elsewhere, it seemed: in his horses and his gardens, and in other people's land.

I thought I would explore while the house was sleeping. It would be wonderful, would it not, if I opened up an abandoned bedchamber and found a small green ledger lying under a dustsheet. I cracked open a few doors, but most of the rooms were empty even of furniture. I tested floorboards with my toes, searched every cabinet, and found nothing but dust and cobwebs.

I was reaching up into a chimney breast when I felt something cold and pulpy beneath my fingers. As I touched it, it shifted, and with a cloud of dirt a dead pigeon splatted to the hearth. I must have given a cry of surprise because a moment later the door creaked open.

'Mr Hawkins?' Metcalfe stood in the doorway, dressed in the same drab fustian jacket I'd seen him in the night before, patches of dried sweat under the arms. The wrinkles in the fabric suggested he had slept in it. But he looked better this morning, beneath the stale clothes. His eyes were not as dull, and he seemed more conscious of himself and his surroundings.

'Good morrow,' I said, offering my most innocent expression.

'Are you lost?' There was an intensity to his enquiry, a trick of the empty room matched with his deep and resonant voice. It made the question sound somewhat metaphysical.

'I thought I might acquaint myself with the house. I must begin my investigations somewhere.'

'Inarguable. Did the pigeon do it?'

I glanced at the mouldering corpse at my feet. 'He refuses to answer my questions.'

'Would you oblige me, sir?' he asked, then left the room. I picked up my shoes and followed his spindly frame down the narrow corridor, avoiding splinters and loose nails in the warped oak floorboards. He hadn't asked me why I was wandering about in my stockings. *To avoid waking the house*, I would have lied. I doubt he would have believed me.

He opened the door to his quarters and disappeared inside. I crossed the threshold into what I can only describe as his lair. The shutters were still drawn, the room lit by a single candle burned almost to the nub. I caught the pungent stink of a chamber pot in one corner, recently filled. The bed linens were rumpled and smelled of sweat and other fluids. *Venereal spasms*, as Mr Gatteker would have it.

Metcalfe was searching for something. The room was filled with books and papers; I recognised his jagged handwriting, the blotched ink. He plucked his bottle of laudanum from the windowsill, wiggling it so that the liquid sloshed against the glass. 'I have not touched a drop since we spoke last night.' He handed me the bottle. 'I fear I am being poisoned.'

I opened the stopper and sniffed the contents. Sherry and the bitter scent of opium. A strong dose, by the smell of it. 'How much have you been taking, Mr Robinson?'

'Metcalfe, please.'

'Is that a family name?' It seemed unlikely that Metcalfe could be responsible for anything, let alone the threats against the Aislabies, but he clearly disliked his uncle intensely. I might as well learn what I could of him – and he was much less distracted this morning.

'I was named for my great-uncle. And my dead brother.'

I began to splutter out my sympathies.

'Never knew him. Died in infancy. First son. So they had another.' He lifted his hands, presenting himself. 'Dead child, reborn. Metcalfe redux. We both have a touch of the grave about us, Mr Hawkins.'

I frowned at him, and changed the subject. 'Your family seat is close by, I believe?'

He tugged at his earlobe. 'Six miles east, sir. Baldersby. My father has rebuilt it in the style of Palladio. Don't tell Forster; he'll ask me about it. My God that man's dull.'

'May I ask why you're staying here, then?'

'My father's ill. Gout. I unsettle the air about his knee. I don't really, that was a joke. I sensed he needed a rest from me. He worries, and ... grieves. For what I'm not. What I'm unable to be.' He sighed. 'I am the worst son alive.'

'Please, sir. You are not even the worst son in this room.'

He smiled at that, shyly, and looked away.

'Why do you think you are being poisoned?'

'Hmm ...?'

I held up the bottle of laudanum.

'Oh, yes. D'you know I slept almost three days solid. A prelude to the final rest.' An ache of longing seemed to pass through him. He blinked, more of a twitch, really. 'Would you take that blasted thing away for me, sir? Throw it in the lake?'

I slid it into my pocket. The room felt oppressive: the smell, the clothes scattered in disarray, the balls of crumpled paper strewn across the floor. I invited Metcalfe to join me for a pipe out in the deer park. The fresh air and tobacco might help to clear his head.

'I like deer,' he declared, hunting for his pipe under the bedclothes. 'They come right up to the window at Baldersby. Press their noses to the glass.' He pushed the palm of his hand to his nose. Dropped it. 'I'm not sure I'm entirely well, Mr Hawkins.'

'Perhaps we should send for Mr Gatteker. Did he prescribe the laudanum?'

'I brought it with me.'

'So . . . you poisoned yourself?'

He slid a hand under his shirt and scratched his shoulder, as he had done the night before. The hair on his narrow chest was grey and somewhat matted. 'What was I searching for?'

'Your pipe. Here – it's on the desk.' As I handed it over, I noticed a letter written in a very different hand from his: small characters laid out in neat lines, without flourishes. It had been placed on the top of a pile of journals, with a lump of rock to hold it down. I pulled it free and held it up to the flickering candle. Molly Gaining's testimony. Mrs Fairwood had said that Metcalfe had borrowed it for closer study. *He believes I am a cuckoo in the nest.* I read it quickly, struggling in the gloom of the chamber.

November, 1727

—*Mr Aislabie, sir*

I pray you would take heed of this letter, from a Woman I am sure you have curs'd a thoussend times a Day since we last met. It is twenty-six years since I set the fire on Red Lion Square that killed your good wife Anne. It will bring you no Comfort I suppose to hear that I have lived a life since then of the verry gratest Regret and Rimorse and that no Baubles that I stole from you Might ever be enuff to Smother my Shame.

But the Gratest jewell of all what I stole from you is your daughter Lizzie who I tell you now with fear it mite kill you with Happyness and Greif combin'd is alive and the lovvliest Creture in the World. I rescued her from the terrible Flames that night but to my Eternal Shame I took her with me when I mite have sent her to You. The Devil took ahold of me Mr Aislabie and I knew if I ran away with Lizzie people would Think I was her Mother and not the girl who started the Fire, the Murderess.

We have spent our lives quitely in Lincoln I married a verry kind gentleman who knew No Thing of my Past save I had a Child which he brought up as his Own.

Sir I have watch'd your Lizzie grow into a Fine Gentlewoman who loves Books just as you do and I think she has your Eyes and other feetures tho' it is a long time since I saw you I remember you Well, John.

I know you can do Nothing but Hate me for what I did I was a verry Foolish Girl and in Love with you but God will Punnish me soon enuf. I write this in my final Hours knowing I must face Justiss soon tho' I escap'd it these past Several Years – how fast they have Gone.

I send your Lizzie to you now with the Brooch you once Promiss'd me do you Remember it? The Diamond and Ruby flowwer it is the only thing I kept.

I beg your Forgivness Knowing I shall not Have it but Hope you will See that I have Rais'd your Daughter well. If you Can find Forgiveness as the honnest Christian Man that I know you are then I beg you to Pray for your Poor Molly whose Soul quakes as she Prepares for Death but Most of all I ask that you Love my Lizzie as I call her still as I cannot help but Love her as a

Daughter. I send her to You at the End of my Life may God have
mercy upon my Soul.
  I am, sir, your Obedient and Sorrowful servant
  Molly Gaining

'Breaks the heart, doesn't it?' Metcalfe said.

I read the letter through again. Aislabie swore he recognised the hand, and there was an idiosyncratical phrasing to it that must have reminded him of Molly. And then there was his wife's brooch, and the suggestion of an affair. *I was a verry Foolish Girl and in Love with you.* Nor did Mrs Fairwood appear to have anything to gain from forging the note – indeed, she seemed horrified to discover her father was John Aislabie, and not the *kind gentleman* who had brought her up as his own daughter.

Metcalfe had pulled back the shutters and opened a window. He was gazing at the chaos of his room as if some violent storm had ripped through it, tumbling his clothes and possessions into great heaps. 'Let us descend,' he said, mock regally.

I followed him downstairs, pausing on the landing to slip on my shoes. In the great hall, Sally was on her hands and knees by the enormous stone fireplace, sweeping the hearth with a hand brush. The air was gritty with yesterday's ash. She looked up in surprise as we walked down the stairs, then jumped to her feet and curtsied.

I paused to speak with her, while Metcalfe called downstairs for keys to the main doors. Bagby had interrupted our conversation the day before. I asked her if she had more to tell me.

She wiped her hands on her apron. 'I saw someone, sir. When I were shooing away the crows.'

'There was someone in the park?'

She shook her head. 'You know how it is, sir, when you can

feel someone watching you.' She pressed her hand to the back of her neck. 'It were Mrs Fairwood. She were standing at the window on the second-floor landing. I had such a strange feeling . . . like she'd been watching me, all that time.'

'She could see the deer?'

'Yes, sir. The deer, the crows. Everything.'

That explained why she had been so calm when I described the deer to her. But why did she not say she'd seen it? 'Did she seem frightened?'

'I suppose so . . .'

I smiled. 'She is not an easy woman to read.'

Sally's lips twisted. Clearly there were far worse things she would like to say about Mrs Fairwood. 'No, sir.'

'But you thought it odd.'

She hesitated, the natural caution of a servant.

'You can speak freely with me, Sally. I don't work for Mr Aislabie.'

'I was surprised,' she said, carefully. 'I'm up every morning before dawn and I've never seen Mrs Fairwood rise so early. She doesn't like to be disturbed until nine, earliest. Late to bed, late to rise.' She left her disapproval and her envy at such behaviour unspoken, but it was clear upon her face.

'So she was waiting, you think?' The importance of this information struck me hard. 'She knew the deer had been left on the step. She wanted to see its discovery.'

Sally must have had the same thought, or why mention it to me? But she was too frightened for her position to say so. 'I'm sure it was just a coincidence, sir,' she said, hastily. 'She must have woke early for once. You promise you won't say owt?'

A bolt slammed free, making us both jump. Metcalfe, opening the doors. A thin dawn light spread through the hall.

Jackdaws called out to one another, their cries sharp and urgent in the spring air. They were making a tremendous racket.

Sally's brows furrowed. 'The crows . . .' she said, then looked at me in alarm.

'No!' Metcalfe shouted. He was standing in the doorway, sunlight streaming all around him. We rushed over to him, just as he collapsed backwards. Sally grabbed him beneath his arms, staggering back herself as he landed upon her. I took a few steps down and stopped dead.

Three young stags had been laid out in a triangle upon the carriage drive. Their heads had been hacked from their necks, their stomachs slit wide open. Jackdaws strutted along the corpses, cawing loudly and pulling at the meat. They had already plucked out the eyes.

I scared the birds away and circled the stags, my stomach turning. One had a note stuffed in its mouth. I reached between its teeth to pull it out. The tongue was dry and rough against my fingers. There were bloody fingerprints on the paper, red swirls surrounding three words, written in blood.

YOU WILL BURN

I stood up slowly.

Metcalfe was sitting on the top step, his head in his hands. He was trembling hard. 'This is for me,' he said in a hollow voice. 'This is meant for me.'

'I doubt that, sir.'

He dropped his hands. 'Of course it is. It's my coat of arms, for God's sake – the Robinson coat of arms. Three stags, in a triangle. Don't you see? It's a warning. Someone plans to murder me.'

Chapter Ten

Sally guided Metcalfe back to his rooms, leaving me alone with the deer. I lit a pipe to calm my nerves. I'd seen animals butchered – but there was a disturbing, sacrificial quality to this display. I was afraid Metcalfe must be right: this was a warning of worse to come.

Standing about feeling anxious would achieve nothing. I crouched down to study the deer more closely. There were a few patches of blood upon the gravel, but not soaked deep. The stags must have been field dressed somewhere else. The heads had been cut clean, not sawn – with a cleaver, I thought. After death: a small mercy. I reached down to the closest stag, resting my hand upon its stomach. The early morning sun was beginning to warm its hide. The meat would soon be spoiled.

I pushed myself on to my feet. The jackdaws had hopped a short distance into the grass, and were watching me now with their clever, pale grey eyes. I addressed the boldest, waiting a few feet away. 'You saw who did this, didn't you?'

The jackdaw gave a sharp cry. It was standing by a muddy bootprint. I followed it with my eyes to another, and another: a jumbled trail leading from where I stood out into the park, towards the main avenue.

'Talking to crows, Mr Hawkins?' Mr Aislabie had emerged from the house, accompanied by Mr Gatteker. Sneaton shadowed them.

I stepped away, so he might see the stags more clearly, laid out upon his carriage drive.

He grimaced. 'Monstrous. What do you make of this, Gatteker?'

Mr Gatteker pushed his spectacles up his nose, considering the question. 'Venison pasties?'

Aislabie frowned at him.

'They must have been left here within the last four hours,' I said. 'My wife arrived at two o'clock this morning and the drive was clear.'

'Mrs Hawkins has come?' Mr Gatteker exclaimed excitedly. 'Then why are you not abed, sir? Do you not appreciate the priorities of youth?'

I ignored him. 'The kills are recent, but they weren't slaughtered here. Not enough blood. And the noise could have woken the house. They must have been killed out in the woods somewhere, then carried here.'

'A long way to carry one stag, never mind three,' Aislabie said.

'A handcart?' Gatteker suggested, taking a pinch of snuff.

'No wheel tracks.' I pointed to the trail of footprints heading through the grass. 'What lies south of here?'

'The water gardens,' Aislabie replied. 'Then Messenger's land.'

'Could he have done this?'

'If I might answer, as his physician?' Gatteker interrupted, rubbing his nostrils. 'No. Determinedly no. Poor devil is plagued by gout. If he were a horse, I'd shoot him. He's not a horse,' he clarified.

'We are on ill terms,' Aislabie said, after some thought. 'But we argue through our lawyers. This is too foul an act even for him. No – for all his faults, Messenger is a gentleman.' He gestured at one of the stags: its severed head and ripped stomach. 'What do you say, Jack?'

Sneaton limped forward. He was tired and red-eyed, with a film of sweat upon his brow. He'd left for his cottage shortly after supper last night, expecting a visit from John Simpson. Clearly his attempts to help settle the stonemason's bill had descended into a minor debauch, and now he was suffering for it. 'I'd say this was two men, sir. Strong and fit. Poachers, would be my guess.'

'I agree,' Aislabie said. 'It's the Gills. I have been too temperate with them. Too forgiving. Very well – take Hawkins up to Kirkby moors with a half-dozen of Simpson's men. I will have this business fixed upon that damned family today. Beat a confession from them if you must.'

I held up my hands in protest. 'This is not the work of poachers, sir. The notes are the work of two separate parties, I'm sure of it.'

Aislabie's brow furrowed. 'No, I cannot believe that. I am not so misliked.'

There followed an embarrassed silence. I dared a glance at Mr Gatteker. He tweaked an eyebrow, then looked down, prodding the gravel with his boot.

Truly, did Aislabie not understand how much the world hated him? I could mention his name in any tavern or coaching inn from here to Dover and half the room would rain down curses upon his head. Everyone knew someone who'd been ruined by his actions as chancellor – myself included. It was a wonder his house wasn't filled to the rooftops with letters promising fire and death.

It is not easy to persuade a man that he is universally loathed, particularly one so convinced of his innocence. More than that,

Aislabie believed that *he* was the injured party. No matter that he had kept most of his money and all of his estate – his disgrace and the loss of his power still weighed upon him as a gross injustice. He believed himself mistreated, so why should anyone blame him for their own troubles? Why should the idea even flit through his mind? No – it must be the infamous Gills – a *low* sort of people, mistrusted by the neighbourhood.

'This is not about snaring rabbits and grazing sheep,' I said. 'This man is after revenge. He calls you a traitor, who ruined good and honest families.' I paused, hoping that this would be enough, but Aislabie looked blank. Dear God, his self-delusion was extraordinary. '*The South Sea disaster*, sir.'

Mr Aislabie flinched. 'We do not speak of that business.'

'Mr Aislabie, you must see—'

'*We do not speak of it, damn you!*'

I'd had enough – his stubbornness would see him dead, along with the rest of us if the house were put to the torch. I pulled the fresh note from my pocket and held it out to him. 'I found this with the stags. I'd hoped to spare you.'

He snatched the paper from me and read the three words, written in blood. YOU WILL BURN.

'Devil take it,' Sneaton breathed.

Aislabie stared at the note, mute with horror. It was clear that he was thinking of the fire at his London home, all those years ago. His young wife. His lost daughter.

'Would poachers do all this?' I pressed. 'It is too elaborate, surely? Mr Sneaton – would the Gills waste so much good meat? Would they even know the Robinson coat of arms?' I gestured at the stags, laid out in a triangle.

'A coincidence,' Aislabie said. 'Metcalfe is forever seeing patterns where none exist. Conspiracies and dramas . . .'

'But Mr Hawkins speaks fair about the meat, your honour,'

Sneaton said, reluctantly. 'Might it be possible ...' He paused, considering the best way to proceed. 'Might there be some wrong-headed fool who blames you for his ruin? Unjustly, of course,' he added, hastily.

Aislabie shook his head, unable to accept the truth.

'You must see that the first letters were different,' I said. 'For all the threats and rough language, the writer sought a peaceful, reasonable resolution. There is no reason to *this*.' I gestured to the stags.

'Perhaps they grew angry,' Sneaton argued. 'When we ignored their demands.'

'*Precisely*,' Aislabie leaped upon this eagerly. This could not be about his part in the South Sea Scheme. It *would not be*. 'I want the Gills locked up – today. Ride over to the moors, Hawkins. That is an order.'

'This is not the army, sir.' I squinted at the butchered stags, and the grass beyond. In the distance, the rest of the herd grazed under a great beech tree. A doe dropped her head to a water trough and drank.

The sun was rising above the trees. The sky was a pale blue, with no clouds in view. A light breeze riffled through the grass. A day for lifted spirits and gentle strolls. It was hard to believe that we were in danger here. Harder yet to recognise an enemy in such polite company. But someone was plotting revenge upon Aislabie. And, like Metcalfe, I was afraid that this bright, spring day would end in death if we did not discover the truth.

Mr Aislabie had been speaking for some time as I stared out across his estate. Sermonising. I was a clergyman's son; I'd developed a talent for letting them waft over my head. There would be something about duty in there, no doubt, and respect, and obedience. Every sermon is the same, and it is a confounded waste of time to listen to a single word. The trick is to keep one ear half open, so one can be sure when it is over.

'I will ride out and speak with the Gills this afternoon,' I said, when he had spluttered to a close. There would be no peace until I'd agreed to it, and I could at least discount the family from my enquiries. 'Mr Sneaton – would you speak with the servants? Ask them if they saw anything, or suspect anyone?'

Sneaton glanced at his master, expecting refusal, but Aislabie nodded absently. He had been looking up at the house, to a window on the second floor. I followed his gaze and saw Mrs Fairwood looking down at us – precisely where Sally had seen her the day before. She drew back, out of view.

'I must go to my daughter,' Aislabie said, and left us.

Sneaton sighed, a great weary sound. 'Look at these poor creatures.'

The stags smelled of blood and meat. Flies buzzed about the gaping wounds. 'When you speak with the servants, see if any of them know the Robinson coat of arms.'

He nodded, then moaned in pain. 'My head aches consumedly,' he muttered.

'Pot of chocolate,' I offered. 'Helps me when I've drunk too much liquor.'

'A hearty breakfast!' Gatteker piped up. 'Tripe and onions, if you can persuade Mrs Mason.'

'And a fresh bowl of punch,' I added. 'That really is the best remedy.' For anything.

'Gentlemen, please.' Sneaton swayed on his stick. '*Gah* . . . It's my own fault. I should never take a drink with John Simpson, the old sot.'

'Could he have done this? He was angry yesterday – and he's owed a lot of money.'

Sneaton considered this for a moment then dismissed it. 'He

shouts and stamps his foot, but ... this is too sneaking for him. And too *elaborate*, as you say.'

'Did you tally his bill?'

Sneaton shut his eyes. 'In truth? I can't remember.'

I chuckled. 'Sam can help you question the servants. He's a sharp lad.'

Sneaton did not look pleased about that, but he didn't have the strength to argue.

'And what will you do, sir?' Mr Gatteker asked.

I gazed at the trail of bootprints leading across the deer park. 'I think I'll follow those. Once I've had my breakfast.'

There was a note waiting for Mr Gatteker back in the house. Bagby brought it over. I planned to ask him why he had been so pleased by Kitty's arrival, but he had turned upon his heel and left before I could open my mouth. What a queer fellow he was. If he disliked me so much – and I certainly wasn't imagining his seething hostility – why should he be happy to see me reunited with my wife?

'Oh dear,' Mr Gatteker said, reading the note. 'What ill news. Mrs Slingsby has died.'

'A patient?'

'A rich one. I thought she had another ten pounds' worth of bills in her, at least. What a tragedy.'

'Perhaps she remembered you in her will.'

'That is a kind thought, sir,' Mr Gatteker said, rallying. 'I'm obliged to you. Let us console ourselves with a large breakfast.'

'Good morrow,' Kitty called down from the minstrels' gallery. She was wearing her emerald silk gown, with matching ribbons in her cap. She skipped lightly down the stairs and allowed Mr Gatteker to take her hand.

He bowed low over it. 'Mrs Hawkins.'

ANTONIA HODGSON

She smirked at the title. 'Well, then – the stags! What a dreadful mess. I saw them from the window. You were very brave, Tom – examining them so closely. My husband is *incurably* softhearted when it comes to animals, Mr Gatteker, you have never met a more squeamish fellow. Mrs Mason says the stags were laid out to match the Robinson coat of arms. Tom, did you notice the bootprints leading off towards the gardens?' She allowed room for me to nod that I had. 'So I visited Metcalfe's quarters to introduce myself, but he has locked himself in. Can you imagine? He spoke with me through the keyhole. He says he is afraid for his life, and that we should leave at once or else we will be burned in our beds. Or wherever we might happen to be at the time, I suppose. You may let go of my hand now, Mr Gatteker. That is, if you wish to.'

Mr Gatteker, enchanted, bowed again and – with clear reluctance – stepped back.

Kitty smiled at him. 'And *you*, sir. As an expert on the human form. Would you say it's possible for one man to carry a stag of that size on his own? How strong would he have to be? How broad his shoulders? Would he need to be of a particular height, would you say?'

He thought about this for a moment. 'Haven't a clue.'

I liked Mr Gatteker, but he really was quite useless.

'I believe I could carry one,' Kitty decided. 'A small one, wrapped about my shoulders like a scarf.' She demonstrated with an imaginary stag, hefting it around her neck and holding it by its imaginary hooves. 'But for how long? That is the question.'

We took breakfast, the three of us, alone in the dining room. Mr Aislabie had returned to his study, where he was presumably buying up the rest of Yorkshire. Mrs Fairwood had escaped to the library, her sanctuary. Lady Judith had left for her morning ride.

I told Kitty about Lady Judith's breeches. She listened intently. 'Would she lend me a pair do you think?'

'As a physician, I am heartily in favour of them,' Gatteker declared. 'I am persuaded they offer diverse benefits to a lady's health. We must secure them for you, Mrs Hawkins.'

I frowned at him and changed the subject. 'I'm worried about Metcalfe. This business with the stags seems to have thrown him into a fit of despair. You're his physician, I believe?'

'When he's in Yorkshire,' Gatteker said, buttering a roll. 'Excellent man, but a profound melancholic. Prone to fits of paralytic gloom.'

Kitty blinked. 'Is that a medical term?'

Gatteker giggled at the very notion. 'Of course, I tend to see him at his worst. He comes home to Baldersby to rest. Lies there in his bed at odds with the world. Barely eats, barely sleeps. Days go by. Weeks, sometimes. Convinced he's the worst devil ever to have walked the earth. He's threatened to injure himself, you know, on many occasions.'

Kitty shook her head slowly. 'It is a terrible affliction.'

'Yes, poor fellow. He'll rally for a while, but it always comes back. Runs in the blood, I think. Aislabie's brother hanged himself at Oxford, did you know? Seventeen years old. Same age Metcalfe suffered his first attack.'

I thought of the portrait of Mallory Aislabie up in Sam's room, hidden away in the neglected east wing like a shameful secret. Those soulful eyes – very much like Metcalfe's, now I thought of it. 'Would you prescribe laudanum for such an illness?'

'Heavens, no!' Gatteker exclaimed, waving his butter knife at me. 'Fresh air, long walks, and good company. And regular bleedings, naturally.'

I pulled the bottle of laudanum from my coat. 'He's been taking this for a while. He thinks someone's trying to poison him.' I unstoppered the bottle and held it out to him across the table.

Gatteker took a deep sniff. 'Smells regular to me. He does succumb to these fancies . . .'

'He seems most confused and unpredictable. Not sure what's real and what isn't. Is that common for him?'

'Not particularly. Excessive melancholy and self-hatred . . . Disproportionate sense of futility. *What's it all, for? Why is the world so dreadful?* But he knows a hawk from a handsaw.' He sniffed the bottle again. 'Could be a mistake with the dose, I suppose.'

'He said it has kept him asleep these past three days. Could you examine the contents for me, sir?'

'Delighted. I'll try it on one of the little Gattekers. Pray don't be alarmed, Mrs Hawkins!' he grinned. 'I've eight or ten of 'em at home. We won't run out.'

'What a curious fellow,' Kitty called out to me, later. 'He was joking, wasn't he?'

We were on horseback, riding through Mr Aislabie's deer park towards the fabled water gardens. Lady Judith had prom- ised me a tour. Instead I was riding with Kitty, following a set of bootprints that led both to and from the butchered stags. The tracks had disappeared for a time in drier grass, but now we had found them again, heavy prints pushed deep into the mud. Boots sinking under the weight of a deer. The prints were tangled together; it was hard to tell if one man had carried one stag upon three separate occasions, or whether there had been two or even three men working together. Whoever they were, they were strong. I'm not sure I could have carried such a weight upon my shoulders such a great distance.

Kitty rode behind me on a fine chestnut colt marked with a star. She was sitting side-saddle in the usual fashion, and wearing a velvet riding cap. I was riding a dappled grey mare called Athena. There had been some argument among the grooms about whether she should be ridden today. She was set to be covered by Aislabie's best stallion, Blunt. Perhaps Athena had sensed there was something afoot, as she had been 'skittish' all morning, according to Mr Pugh. I must keep a close watch upon her, he warned. She seemed placid enough to me. I patted her flank and nudged her on with my knees down a long, sheltered avenue. A pheasant rustled through a patch of wild garlic, then darted across our path into the woods beyond. Athena plodded on, unperturbed.

Kitty caught up with me and brushed a hand against my leg. It was such a glorious spring day, we might be mistaken for a true husband and wife, taking a quiet tour of the county's finest estate. I nodded to a journeyman trimming the grass along the path, and he touched his hat.

So far our views had been of woods and distant farm land, with the deer park at our backs. As we emerged from the trees, the water gardens were revealed at last. We brought our horses to a halt, speechless with astonishment. Below us, the river had been tamed into a long, straight canal, ending in a dramatic cascade. I could hear its roar even from here, a constant rushing sound. Beneath the cascade, the riverbanks had been widened to form a large fishing lake, smooth as glass. The river travelled on from there through a narrower cascade into a steep valley bristling with pine trees – and out of view.

Kitty was staring out at the lake. Its pristine surface acted as a mirror, reflecting the trees surrounding it and the sky as if there were two worlds, above and below. A pair of swans glided by, the very picture of grace.

'Beautiful,' Kitty murmured.

It was truly a magnificent sight, and for a moment I was left amazed. But we had not come here to admire the view. I leaned down in my saddle to inspect the ground. 'The tracks have disappeared.'

We had reached a fork in the path, the left leading down to the lake, the right taking a steep course up a densely wooded hill. I suspected the men had travelled along one of those paths with the stags across their backs, then moved on to the grass for stealth, to avoid the crunch of gravel beneath their boots.

We turned left, following the path to the lake – and found Lady Judith by the edge of the water, astride her bay stallion. Her horse whinnied at our approach.

'Mr Hawkins. And this must be your wife? Welcome to Studley, Mrs Hawkins.'

'Thank you ...' Kitty stared at Lady Judith's breeches, entranced.

Lady Judith laughed, and rubbed a hand along her thigh. 'Why, I believe you are more astonished than your husband.'

'They are a *wonder*,' Kitty marvelled.

'Are they not? Sadly I can only wear them about the gardens. It would be too great a scandal to present my legs to the world.'

'The world,' Kitty observed, 'is full of idiots.'

Lady Judith laughed again, appraising me anew. Women judge men by their choice of wife, and Mrs Aislabie approved of mine. I edged Athena closer to the lake, curious to see myself reflected in the mirrored surface, but when I peered into the water, all I saw was the silt and mud beneath. A trick of the light and the angle of perspective – but it gave me a hollow feeling, to see nothing of myself.

'Do you like fishing, Mr Hawkins?' Lady Judith pointed to a pair of tiny lodges built on either side of the higher cascade. 'The lake is stocked with carp. One can fish from the window in poor weather.'

I smiled politely.

'Tom is too impatient for fishing,' said Kitty, the least patient woman in the western hemisphere.

'My husband is the same. He must be *doing*. But what do you say, sir, about our little endeavour?'

'I'm lost for words, madam.' And I was truly astounded – at the beauty, and the cost.

'The canal was a nightmare of mud for almost ten years. Thousands upon thousands of cartloads,' she shuddered, as if she had been personally responsible for carrying them all. 'There is much yet to be done, but when it is finished I believe it will be the most embellished estate in England. You must walk the grounds with John tomorrow – he can explain his plans far better than I. This garden is his great passion. At least, it was. He has been distracted these past few weeks. Mrs Fairwood's arrival has affected him profoundly.'

'You wish her gone from Studley, I think?'

Lady Judith looked out across the lake. 'If we may speak in confidence, as friends . . . Yes. I believe it would be for the best. I fear she is dangerous in some odd way. I do not like mysteries and secrets. And Mrs Fairwood is a *great* mystery.'

I explained that we had been following the trail of bootprints from the house, and that they had vanished on the path above. 'Both paths lead into the woods,' she said. 'It's the border between our land and Fountains Hall. Mr Messenger's estate.'

'Mr Forster is a guest at Fountains Hall, I believe? He has invited me to visit him.'

Her lips curved into their familiar smirk. 'How curious, if the trail should lead to him. Perhaps *he* murdered those poor stags.'

'With one arm?'

'He might have bored them to death.'

I grinned, but was not so quick to dismiss Forster. Yes, he was a dull companion at supper, but that did not mean he was incapable of violence, one-handed or otherwise. I had learned not to underestimate anyone, these past few months.

'Have you not explored the higher path yet?' Lady Judith asked. 'We must ride it together.'

We turned our horses away from the lake, following her up the steep path into the woods. We climbed for a short while before Lady Judith pulled upon the reins. 'This is my favourite view.'

The lake was still within sight from here, but now we could also see the vast scale of the work taking place above the highest cascade. On the far side of the canal, three formal ponds had been dug into the riverbank: two neat crescents flanking a perfect circle.

'We call them our moon ponds,' she said.

They were pretty, but the rest of the bank was a hodgepodge of planting and construction. It was clear that the gardens would take years to complete. Behind the precisely laid-out ponds, a dozen labourers were digging foundations for a building. *Mr Doe and one of his fucking follies*, I supposed. Beyond these works stretched a nursery of young trees, which gave the area a bald look. How long before those trees would grow to maturity? Far longer than Mr Aislabie's lifetime, no doubt. But what a mark he would leave upon the land.

There were journeymen *everywhere*. I counted thirty before I gave up: planting borders, carting dung, felling trees, trimming hedges, clearing blown wood from the water. It took an army to overcome nature; countless hours of labour to create serenity. Unfathomable patience and vision. Unfathomable wealth. And I thought – *Thirty more men; thirty more suspects.*

'Could any of those men bear a grudge against your husband?'

Lady Judith blinked in surprise. 'No indeed – why should they? Are you not diverted by the view, Mrs Hawkins?'

Kitty shielded her eyes against the sun. 'Very.'

'We have been working on these gardens for twelve years. It will be another ten at least before they are complete.'

'Can we not see Fountains Abbey from here?' I asked, craning my neck.

Kitty's eyes widened. 'An abbey?'

'A ruined monastery,' I explained. 'There's a picture of it above our fireplace. It sits on the river does it not? Very close to here?'

Lady Judith pursed her lips. 'It is hidden over that hill.' She gestured vaguely at the wooded slopes ahead.

'How frustrating. Well, you must level the hill, I suppose.'

'We have considered it.'

'Indeed?' I had been joking.

Lady Judith huffed. 'We've decided to wait for Mr Messenger to die. Then we shall buy it and open up all the land below.' She urged her stallion up the steep path, beckoning for us to follow. 'We have built something wonderful just up here, let me show you.'

We fell into shadow beneath the trees, the air turning cooler. The top of the hill formed a plateau, the trees cleared away to create a sunken lawn. At the far end of the grass stood a small but handsome stone lodge, backed by a border of elm hedges. It was, in miniature, what I had expected of Mr Aislabie's hall, rather than the groaning, creaking thing we were staying in.

Pheasants scattered into the undergrowth as we approached. Deep in the trees to my left, jackdaws were cawing loudly to one another, in alarm or excitement. I could see where their wings were flapping against the bushes. I shifted in my saddle.

'And here is our banqueting house, newly built this year,' Lady Judith said. Her voice had taken on a knowing tone, as if banqueting were the last thing that happened there. 'We've had some merry times up here.' She jumped down from her horse and looped the reins over a tree, striding over to the door. 'There's a most diverting statue of Venus inside.'

Kitty slid from her horse, but she was watching me closely. 'Tom?'

Two more jackdaws flew low across the sunken lawn and deep into the bushes. Lady Judith's stallion snorted, and shook its head. Athena's ears twitched. I tapped her flanks and rode down into the lawn and up the other side, recognising its shape as I crossed it. A coffin lawn – a memento mori. In the midst of life we are in death. I hated all that nonsense.

I nudged Athena on to a narrow trail amidst the trees and found the bootprints we'd been searching for, pushed deep into the mud. Athena whinnied softly. I stroked her neck and murmured to her, soothingly. She took a few more steps into the woods.

The wind blew down the trail and I caught something ripe and foul in the air. I wrinkled my nose. Burst deer guts. Once smelled, never forgotten. As we approached the bushes the stench became stronger. This was where the stags had been killed, their innards left in piles beneath the bushes. Glistening links of intestine spilled out across the path, covered with a dense swarm of insects. The jackdaws pecked at the offal and snapped insects from the air, as more and more birds joined the feast.

There is nothing worse than the stink of burst deer guts. The stench was unbearable. Athena whinnied, and flared her nostrils in disgust. I jumped down and tried to approach, breathing through my mouth. It was no use. I reeled back and vomited hard, until my stomach was empty and my ribs ached.

'Tom?' Kitty's voice, at the edge of the clearing.

I wiped my mouth. 'Don't come down here, Kitty.'

'Why, what have you found?' I could hear her making her way down the path, gown rustling against the bushes.

'Deer guts. Truly, stay where you are – it is too foul to bear. I won't be a moment.' I wiped my mouth and remembered what Samuel Fleet had taught me. Forget the stink, forget the blood. Step back and *think*. What could I learn from this discovery?

The trees and bushes were thickly tangled in this part of the gardens. It would be easy to kill the stags here undisturbed. The trail itself was well disguised: I would have missed it if I'd not been drawn by the jackdaws. And we were a long way from the house, bordering Messenger's land. Francis Forster's host, and John Aislabie's enemy.

Someone had led the three stags here and slaughtered them. They'd not been hunted out in the woods. They'd been gathered in this hidden place to be killed. But the innards had been abandoned here. That meant there'd been no time to bury them, and no way to discard them elsewhere.

What struck me with the greatest force was the effort of it all. Whoever this was, he had slaughtered three young stags in their prime, ripped out their guts, and carried at least one of them on his shoulders for over a mile, in the dark. He'd found an accomplice or accomplices to help him with the rest. All so that he could lay the bodies out upon Aislabie's front step this morning. *This is but the beginning of sorrows.*

A campaign, then. And if this was how it started – how on earth would it end?

I freed Athena's reins and put my left foot in the stirrup. I needed to speak with Aislabie's keeper, as soon as possible.

I had just swung my right leg over the saddle when the jackdaws rose into the air on a swirl of black wings. Startled, Athena reared up, almost throwing me from her back. I slid in the saddle, my right foot free of the stirrup. As I fought for balance she reared again, then plunged down the trail into the bushes. I gave a shout of alarm, clutching the reins hard.

We whisked through the trees at an impossible speed, branches whipping against my face. I ducked low, searching with my foot for the stirrup. As we raced down a muddy slope I found it, and pulled myself upright.

I pulled upon the reins, trying to regain control, but it was too late. Athena was trapped in a blind panic and there was nothing I could do but to ride it out with her. I held on, terrified, as she tore through the woods, whinnying and snorting as the mud and leaves flew up from her hooves and the jackdaws cawed and circled above us.

If she threw me now, I would break my neck.

A low branch loomed up ahead, forcing me to drop my head. As I raised it again, Athena leaped over a fallen tree, almost throwing me from the saddle. The trees were dense here, with only the narrowest of paths cutting a way through. We scraped through a tunnel of hawthorn bushes, the thorns ripping my hands. I threw up an arm to protect my eyes and in another moment we had burst free from the wood on to a fresh stretch of bright green riverbank. Sunlight dazzled my eyes and the river sparkled.

I pulled again on the reins, but Athena galloped on at a furious pace. The world was a blur of spring grass, glittering river, flanking woods and then, rising up ahead, a vast building of golden stone. We had stumbled upon Fountains Abbey. Athena's hooves clattered on the remnants of ancient floors, thudded through high grass and mud, as we entered the old monastery ruins. Too fast. She leaped over a broken column, faltered, then cantered on down a maze of crumbling walls. The sun disappeared as we galloped through a long, vaulted hall, and then we flew out again into a great roofless space, the sky wide and bright above our heads, birds calling from a great tower, and we were slowing. Thank God, we had stopped.

I swung my leg over the saddle and dropped to the ground, panting hard. Athena moved away as if nothing remarkable had happened, as if we had just enjoyed a pleasant trot through the countryside.

I collapsed, rolling on to my back. The sun warmed my face. Pigeons cooed from nests made high upon the ruined walls. My breath returned to me, and with it came a flood of relief that I had survived. And, now it was over . . . I should rather like to do it again. I put my scratched and bleeding hand to my chest and began to laugh. It came from deep inside me, like drawing water from a well. I had not laughed so freely in a long time.

I didn't hear the footsteps until they were upon me. I sat up, still laughing, to find a stranger standing over me, holding a pistol. He was aiming it at my head.

Chapter Eleven

Mr Messenger's family had lived at Fountains Hall for a hundred years. It was a fine estate, the mysterious abbey ruins a brooding counterweight to the rich farmlands and quarries beyond. The hall itself was built with stone taken from the abbey, binding the two in some ineffable way that some might consider mystical, even holy.

Aislabie coveted Fountains Abbey. He imagined it as the focus of his gardens, the way a chef envisioned a great pyramid of sweetmeats at the centre of a feasting table. He wanted it. He must find a way to have it. Messenger was short of funds. Surely he would give it up, for a fair price?

There had been a time – during the months of the South Sea madness – when Messenger had contemplated the exchange. Boundaries were discussed, and sale prices. Then the agreement had collapsed. Perhaps Messenger had never intended to sell the abbey to Mr Aislabie in the first place. Perhaps it had all been a piece of mischief on his part. But it had soured relations between the two neighbours for good.

Have you forgotten, at this point, that I have a pistol aimed at my head? I have not, I assure you. This particular pistol looked old – older than the man holding it, who appeared to be about fifty. It was a horse pistol, with a long barrel and a plain mahogany grip.

My hope was that it had last been fired some time during the Civil War, and that the internal parts had corroded in the subsequent eighty-odd years. My second, encouraging thought was that, in the main, gentlemen did not shoot other gentlemen in the face. Not without very good reason. Not even in Yorkshire.

'Mr Messenger?' I guessed.

'WHO THE DEVIL ARE YOU?' he yelled. His face was fat and exceedingly red, and there was a bandage tied around his right knee. 'What do you mean by this OUTRAGE! You're TRESPASSING, sir! Are you a SPY? Are you a SPY for that DAMNABLE ROGUE?'

I raised my hands in supplication. 'My name's Thomas Hawkins, sir. I lost control of my horse.'

He narrowed his eyes at Athena, who was munching thoughtfully on a crop of dandelions. 'You came from Studley.' He had a growling but gentlemanly voice, soaked in the local accent.

'Yes, sir.' I kept my eyes upon the barrel of his pistol. 'I'm a guest of Mr Aislabie.'

Messenger's face puckered. 'Aislabie's man are you? Sneaking about my land. A *spy*—'

'Mr Messenger!' Francis Forster hurried across the broken stones as best he could, hampered by his bandaged arm. 'Put down your weapon, sir!' He swept his uninjured arm towards me, as if introducing a celebrated actor to the stage. 'This is Mr Hawkins. I spoke of him last night? Mr *Thomas* Hawkins.' And then, when Messenger still didn't react, '*Half-Hanged Hawkins.*'

'Bloody hell!' Messenger's thick grey brows jerked in surprise. He uncocked his pistol, and lowered it. '*Half-Hanged Hawkins.*'

I stood up, brushing the dirt from my breeches.

Messenger cleared his throat, embarrassed. 'Welcome to Fountains Abbey, sir.'

We bowed to one another as if we were at court. And in truth the monastery did have the air of an ancient palace, built for a forgotten king. Messenger dug a pewter flask from his coat jacket and passed it to me. I took a swig and coughed at its unexpected power. Scotch whisky: a silent signal of Messenger's support for the king across the water. He watched me drink it with a knowing eye, but I have never let politics stand in the way of liquor. And I was half Scots myself. I grinned, and held on to the flask.

'Are you injured, sir?' Forster asked, seeing my scratched and bleeding hands.

'A fight with a hawthorn bush.'

We were standing in the vast nave of the abbey beneath a great arched window, its mullions and stained glass long destroyed. I recognised it from the painting in my chamber: the window, the tower, the thick columns standing firm amidst the devastation. Even in sunlight, the ruins stirred a mixture of awe and melancholy – that something so magnificent should have been brought down with such speed and violence. For four hundred years it had weathered plague and war, until the Reformation claimed it. The abbey was too powerful, too wealthy, too much a symbol of the old ways to be tolerated. King Henry's men had dragged down the roof, taken the glass, smashed down walls, and allowed Nature to do the rest. Fountains Abbey must never rise again.

Now the columns were topped with thick moss, the stone flagging broken and clogged with weeds. An elm tree grew in one corner. The walls were covered in bright orange wallflowers and long trails of ivy. Birds roosted in pairs in the high crevices, as if they had mistaken the abbey for some remote cliff face. Plump pigeons in the main, wings smacking the air as they rose together in sudden waves. Jackdaws commanded the highest walls, tiny black figures lined up like sentinels. There was a constant fluttering and calling in the air, echoing off the ancient stone. A great city of birds, agitated by our presence.

'Magnificent, is it not?' Forster said. 'There is something noble about such ruins, I find. The very act of destruction gives them power. Cromwell and King Henry rot in their graves, but the abbey speaks its story even now, if one knows how to listen.' He pulled out a journal from beneath his sling. It was filled with detailed pencil drawings of the abbey.

'Francis is a most talented architect,' Messenger said.

Oh, God.

'A *right-handed* architect, thank heavens,' Forster amended, waggling his good hand. 'I find the abbey's construction most inspiring – refreshing in its departure from the classical ideal, wouldn't you agree? Where is the balance? Where the symmetry? And yet it has such an exquisite pairing of force and grace, has it not? Every part has a purpose, a spiritual *and* temporal purpose. Is that not the very definition of beauty?' He continued on in this earnest manner for some time, speaking of purpose and power, of ribbed barrel vaults and lancet arches, while I wondered if I could persuade Messenger to shoot me after all.

As Forster spoke, a cloud passed across the sun, and a block of shadow moved slowly through the abbey. It caught us all for a moment: myself, Messenger, and Forster. The heat vanished from the air, enough to make me shiver beneath my thin coat.

'You feel it, eh?' Messenger murmured, below Forster's hearing. 'Old ghosts ...'

I gave a half smile, and the shadow moved on. The world brightened, the abbey walls turning gold again in the sunshine. I took a last swig of whisky and handed the flask back to Messenger.

'Bad for the gout,' he said, which appeared to be a toast, as he then tilted it to his lips and took a great glug. 'What brings you to Yorkshire, Mr Hawkins?'

I hesitated. Aislabie had not given me permission to speak about his troubles; but then I was not one of his men, carting dung and raking gravel from his lawns. 'Someone has been threatening Mr Aislabie. More than one party, I believe.' I described the notes, and the butchered deer.

Messenger shook his head. 'This business with Mrs Fairwood is passing strange. I should say it's connected, wouldn't you?'

'I believe so.'

'It is a wondrous thing,' Forster sighed. 'To have lost a daughter, and grieved for her all these years, and now to have found her again. A great miracle, if it is true. And it does seem to be so . . .'

Messenger snorted. 'If Mrs Fairwood is John Aislabie's daughter, this is my arse,' he said, pointing at his elbow.

'That would be unfortunate,' I said.

Messenger laughed so hard his face purpled. 'You seem a decent lad. Why are you helping that thieving bastard? Leave him to his troubles – he's earned 'em. Come and stay here at Fountains. We'd be glad of your company, eh Forster?'

Forster had been gazing up at the abbey. He wrenched his face away from his beloved bricks and mortar. 'Of course. But are you not under orders from the queen, Mr Hawkins?'

Messenger scowled, his good humour vanishing in an instant. 'Damned gout,' he said, in a clipped voice. 'You'll excuse me, sir.' He gave a curt bow and limped away towards the western entrance.

'Mr Messenger is a papist,' Forster explained, once his patron had left. 'He's not over fond of Hanover George.'

I frowned at him. 'Then was it wise to mention my connection, do you think?'

'Oh! My apologies. I didn't think—'

'Who told you I was sent by the queen? I did not tell you of it. And I don't imagine Mr Aislabie would have offered the information either.'

'Oh!' He floundered for a moment. 'I believe Mrs Fairwood told me at supper.'

'I don't recall that conversation,' I said, coldly. They had scarce spoken two words together, I was sure.

He laughed, nervous. 'You and I were at different ends of the table, sir.'

I studied him for a moment. He was a short, lean fellow – slight, one might call him. Could I imagine him carrying a stag upon his shoulders all the way to Aislabie's door? With a broken wrist and arm? No. But he might have directed someone else.

'I have offended you,' he said, misreading my silence. 'Mr Hawkins – I offer you my most heartfelt apologies. Would you permit me to show you about the abbey?'

'I'm afraid I must return to Studley. I will be missed.' I walked down the sunlit aisle, searching for Athena.

Forster trailed after me. 'At least let me show you the view from the cloister steps,' he begged, pointing through an arched doorway to a square beyond. '*Please*, sir. Let us not part on poor terms.'

'Very well.'

He led me at an eager pace through the cloisters and up a set of worn stone steps. We stood upon an open landing, side by side. I had to admit, it was a fine view: the ruins a grand performance of light and shadow on stone. The tower rose up in front of us, jackdaws circling and settling. The abbey was set upon the riverbank, and we could hear the gentle rush of water below us. No canals and cascades on Mr Messenger's land: the river ran its own winding course, as it pleased.

Forster pointed out the treacherous route Athena had taken – a steep and jagged track down through the woods. Had we

ventured a few paces the other way we would have galloped off
an overhanging rock and broken both our necks. 'Those are not
true paths between the estates,' he explained. 'Mr Messenger and
Mr Aislabie wouldn't stand for it.'

'Poachers' tracks?'

'Foxes, more likely.'

'These hidden trails. They're familiar to you?'

'I've walked them, once or twice.'

I thought about that for a moment, pretending to admire the
view. 'I found the place where the stags were butchered. The
innards had been left beneath some bushes, near the banqueting
house. You know of it?'

His eyes sparked with enthusiasm. 'I do, sir! A splendid
Palladian folly, most neatly done from a design by Colen
Campbell, I'm told—'

'*Forster.*'

'—it has some unusual rustications in an icicle design—'

I glared at him. He fell silent.

'The stags weren't hunted, do you understand? They were
slaughtered on that trail and then carried through Studley Park
to Mr Aislabie's front steps. D'you know the Robinson coat of
arms, sir?'

He blinked at the unexpected question. 'Three stags, is it not?
Two below, one above. Oh ...' His shoulders flinched. 'Is that
how they were found?'

'That is how they were found, Mr Forster. Three stags, slaughtered at the top of a trail that leads directly to the Fountains
estate.'

It took him a moment to understand the accusation, and even
then he mistook it. 'Mr *Messenger*? You believe *he* is responsible?
No, surely not, sir. Well, there's no denying that he detests Mr
Aislabie, but I cannot conceive that he would ...'

'How long have you been a guest at Fountains Hall, Mr Forster?'

He blew out his cheeks. 'A few weeks now. I set off in early February. There was still ice upon the roads.' He lifted up his sling.

'And how did you come by your invitation?'

'I'm a friend of Mr Messenger's cousin, Andrew Benedict. Excellent fellow, has a house on Chancery Lane. Do you know him?'

He was hiding something behind that affectation of nonchalance. A few hundred more questions and I might have the whole story. I settled for a swifter solution. With a sudden lunge, I put my hand upon his collarbone and used my weight to shove him hard against the nearest wall. Forster gave a shout of surprise, fragments of rock and mortar crunching under his back. 'My arm!' he yelped.

I pressed harder. 'Did you send the notes?'

'No! Good God, sir! Let me go!' He was squirming under my weight, his legs flailing beneath him.

'Are you conspiring with Messenger? Do you plan to harm Aislabie? Mrs Fairwood?'

'No!'

I moved my arm higher, leaning against his throat.

He began to choke. 'I swear . . .' He clawed at my arm but he couldn't free himself. 'I'm his spy!' he spat, at last. 'Let me go, damn you – I'm Aislabie's spy.'

It took him a minute or two to recover. He made a great show of rubbing his throat, as if I'd crushed his windpipe. Once he had stopped fussing, and straightened his wig, and brushed the stone dust from his coat, he began his defence. 'I am a man of ambition, Mr Hawkins, I admit. Ambitious for my *work*. The *palazzi* I visited on my tour – such marvellous constructions. I should like to build them here in the green fields of England. But who can afford such an undertaking?' He sighed, and shook his head. 'Did you truly think I wished to burn down Studley Hall?'

'*Someone* wishes it.'

'Well ...' A mischievous tone entered his voice. 'It is *monstrously* old-fashioned. Might be best to burn it down and begin again. Not that I would ever do such a thing,' he added hastily, catching my look.

'You call yourself a spy.'

'So I did. Sounds rather thrilling, does it not? Mr Benedict said I must visit his cousin, see the ruins. He knew I had an interest in architecture.'

Discovered that deep secret, did he? Some sort of wizard, no doubt.

'I was not convinced at first. I'm not a wealthy man. I can't afford to travel all the way to Yorkshire without the hope of some profit ... It is vital I find a patron. Then Benedict mentioned that the Fountains estate bordered Mr Aislabie's land.' He paused. '*John Aislabie!* One of the great champions of the new architecture! A close friend of Lord Burlington! His name appears upon the subscription list for—'

I held up my hand. 'He likes new buildings. I understand.'

'It is not that he *likes* them, Mr Hawkins. He *builds* them. Have you seen the scheme for his stables? The follies for his water gardens? D'you know he intends to build a great mansion by the lake? It will be a *shrine* to the modern style! A building for the ages! If I could be a part of such an endeavour, even on the smallest scale ...'

'The dog kennels, perhaps?'

He frowned. 'You mock me, sir.' He slid his free hand beneath his sling, and pressed it to his heart. 'This is my greatest dream. What is *yours*, I wonder?'

To keep Kitty safe. To return to London. To visit Moll's coffeehouse and drink far too much punch. To carry Kitty through the filthy streets while she sings a ballad, so out of tune I can scarce breathe for laughing. To reach our street, our home, our bed. To be free of all of this.

'I came up to Yorkshire,' Forster continued, 'and I met with Mr Aislabie at the first opportunity. I believe I impressed him. At least, he is prepared to consider my worth. There is a great deal to be done about the estate. It's no secret that Mr Aislabie grows impatient with Mr Simpson. Drunken imbecile. Oh, he's a superb stonemason, I'll grant you, but he should never have been put in charge of such a great project. It is beyond his skills and his temperament. If Mr Doe is brought in to complete the work, then I might take over the building of the follies. And I will be in the perfect position to help with the new hall. Years of work, Mr Hawkins! With a patron who shares my passion, and has the resources to build the greatest estate in Europe.'

'And who asked you to spy on your host.'

'One does what one must.' He shrugged. 'And really, it is no great betrayal. Why, when I come back from Studley Hall, Mr Messenger fires a hundred questions at me. I suppose one could say I was spying for both of them. Perhaps one balances the other.'

'What is it that Aislabie wants from you?'

'Oh, the merest tidbits, I assure you. Land deals, in the main. He's afraid Mr Messenger will sell the abbey to another buyer, out of spite.'

'Is that likely?'

'No. He loves this place – worships it, one might say. You know how these papists are.'

That rankled, but I had learned to hold my tongue at such a common opinion. My mother's family were of the Catholic faith.

She had been forced to abandon both when she married my father, but she had whispered stories and prayers to me when I was a child, and taught me how to genuflect – a gentle secret with no harm intended. It was her gold crucifix I wore beneath my shirt.

'Is it so terrible?' Forster asked. 'Mr Aislabie has it in his power to grant me everything I have ever wanted. This is how he works – making deals and trading information.'

'Using people.'

Forster blinked. 'Yes. But then, he uses you too, sir.'

Him and the Queen of England. 'Are you sure he is the best patron for you, Mr Forster?'

He shrugged. 'I can imagine worse.'

'I'm sorry for throttling you.'

He gave a rueful smile, rubbing his throat again. 'All in the past, sir. All in the past. Shall we begin again?' He held out his good hand.

I smiled, and took it. After all, I had liked him on first meeting. If I could keep him from the subjects of religion and architecture, we would probably muddle along together well enough.

'Who do you think killed the deer, Mr Forster? Please don't say it was poachers,' I added hastily.

He frowned. 'Mr Aislabie is not loved in these parts – though to be fair, I speak only from Mr Messenger's account. He is known for paying his bills late, and his steward drives a hard bargain. He must be the wealthiest man in the county, and that alone breeds resentment among the commonality.' He chewed his lips. 'I'm afraid I have not helped you.'

No, he hadn't. He had just widened my number of suspects to the entire county. Whittling down all of Aislabie's enemies would take a dozen lifetimes. I needed an answer today. I must find another way to reach the truth.

*   *   *

I had a long talk with Athena about her disgraceful behaviour before I returned to the saddle. Her ears drooped as she waited for me to finish. I wasn't the only one with a talent for ignoring sermons. We trotted through the abbey and past Fountains Hall, a splendid sight in the noonday sunshine. As we reached the open road I lit a pipe and let Athena set the pace, anxious not to bring about another skittish frenzy.

It had been a long, brutal winter, and it was good to feel the sun upon my face. Life was returning, spring flowers bright beneath the trees and hedgerows. The countryside wove its spell, too beautiful to feel dangerous. The birds sang, the bees hummed, and I rode on, smoking my pipe.

Chapter Twelve

Kitty sat on the front steps of Studley Hall, arms wrapped about her legs, chin upon her knees. She was pretending to watch the work on the stables, but I knew she had been waiting for me, and worrying.

'Still alive,' I said, cheerfully.

The stags were gone, the blood washed away, and the gravel smoothed across the drive.

I jumped down and kissed her. 'I need a drink.'

'You've scratched your hands. Why did you not wear your gloves?'

We walked Athena around the east side of the house towards the yard, passing the oak tree that stood outside our bedroom window. 'Where's Sam?'

'Lurking.' She tangled her fingers in Athena's creamy white mane. 'I had a nightmare about him last night. I dreamed that I woke up and he was standing over the bed. He pressed a pillow over my face and smothered me.' She looked up at me. 'I know it sounds foolish . . .'

'We'll keep my blade under the pillow.'

She tugged at the jewelled brooch nestled between her breasts. As the brooch slid higher I realised it was the handle of a thin blade tucked inside her stomacher. Sam's mother Gabriela wore a similar device. She'd sliced open my arm with it a few weeks back, leaving a fresh scar to remember her by. She must be wondering where Sam was now. I should send word to settle her fears. But would she blame me for stealing him from her? God knows I had not encouraged him.

'Sam told Mr Gatteker that I was his brother.'

'That would be quite charming,' Kitty said, 'if it were anyone else.'

We found Pugh in the yard, instructing one of the grooms. I told him about Athena's gallop through the woods to Fountains Abbey. 'Best clean up these scratches,' he frowned, showing his man. 'Don't want them turning bad. Poor girl,' he said, stroking Athena's nose. 'You've had a fright, han't you? Let's take you to your stall.'

'Where's my stall and rub down, Mr Pugh? I think I fared the worst out of the two of us.'

He grinned. 'Horses first at Studley. Before servants, before guests, before family.'

'You heard about the stags?'

'Bloody poachers. I'd hang the lot of 'em.'

I didn't bother to correct him. 'I must speak with the game-keeper – I forget his name.'

'William Hallow. He's in the kitchens, taking a mug of beer with Mrs Mason.'

William Hallow was a short, square fellow with russet brows and pale, grey-blue eyes. He wore his own hair, for some eccentric reason, tied at the nape of his neck. His hat was resting on a hook on the kitchen wall while he sat at the table, freckled hands clutching his beer. He had the tired, contented look of a man who had worked hard all night, and was about to go home to bed.

He stood up when Kitty and I came through the door, grabbing his hat so he could shove it on his head and then remove it again. He bowed several times to me without saying a word, overcome with shyness.

Mrs Mason, amused, got up from the table to fetch some more ale. 'Mr Aislabie's asked for an early dinner today,' she said. 'Says you've urgent business this afternoon.'

She waited for me to add to this little nugget of information, but I did not have the heart to talk of the Gills. In truth I had forgotten my promise until now.

'I'm stewing carp,' Mrs Mason continued, not bothering to conceal her disappointment. 'Fresh from the lake this morning. Do you like carp, sir?'

'Delicious.' I hated carp.

'Aye, delicious,' Hallow echoed.

'You hate carp, Tom,' Kitty said.

'. . . I find it can be a little muddy. Sometimes.'

'Very muddy, carp,' Hallow agreed eagerly.

'My carp,' Mrs Mason sniffed, glaring at Hallow, 'is never muddy.'

We sat down. Mrs Mason poured out a mug of ale for Kitty and for me, and freshened her own.

'You must see to those scratches, Tom,' Kitty said. 'They might fester.'

It was true they stung like the devil, but I said nothing, not wishing to appear foppish.

'I have a salve!' Hallow jumped up, groping deep in his breeches pocket. 'I could anoint you, your honour. As the blessed whore Mary Magdalene anointed our Lord Jesus.'

'I don't think—'

'What a kind thought,' Kitty said, in a solemn voice. '*Do* hold out your hands for him, Tom.'

There was nothing for it. Hallow began to slaver a thick paste over the scratches. God knows what was in it, but it smelled pleasant enough. 'I use this on the stags, sir,' he explained. 'Helps when they gore themselves in rutting season.'

Mrs Mason remembered that she needed something from the pantry. I could hear her sniggering behind the door.

'You must be sorry to have lost three stags this morning,' I said. 'They were fine beasts.'

Hallow kept his eyes on mine as he rubbed the salve into my skin. 'Weren't none of mine, sir, praise the Lord for His mercy. Never seen them before.'

'Indeed? Where did they come from?'

'Must ha' been one of the adjoining estates. Fountains would be my guess, sir.'

'No love between Mr Aislabie and Mr Messenger, I hear.'

'No, sir.'

'Did you hear anything on your rounds last night?'

'No sir, your honour. But I weren't on the estate most of the night. Rode up to Studley moor about midnight – weren't back until dawn. Mr Aislabie's orders. Wants us to catch the Gills out poaching. Never trust a Gill,' he added, as if reciting the eleventh commandment.

'Bag of scoundrels,' Mrs Mason said, returning to the table. She took one look at Hallow rubbing my hands, his pale face flushed red with holy reverence, then spun around and headed back to the pantry.

Kitty took a swig of beer. She looked at ease here in the kitchen, and very beautiful with the light at her back. Hallow was oblivious.

I tugged my hands from his grasp. 'Mr Hallow, I must ask something of you. But it must be kept secret, you understand?'

He nodded, thrilled.

'Are you on good terms with Mr Messenger's keeper at Fountains Hall?'

He nodded again.

'I'd like you to speak to him, if you will. Ask if he's lost any of his deer.'

'I'll visit him today, sir.'

We drank our beer. The kitchen fell quiet, save for Mrs Mason, humming to herself as she chopped up a salad. Kitty said something about the weather.

Mr Hallow gulped his beer. 'Mr Hawkins, your honour. May I beg a favour of you, sir?'

'*William,*' Mrs Mason said in a warning tone, without turning around.

I waved at Hallow to continue.

'Begging your pardon, sir,' he stammered, 'but might I touch your neck for luck?'

Oh, God. 'Very well.'

Kitty suppressed a laugh. 'You'd best loosen your cravat, Tom.'

I frowned at her, then untied it, winding the cloth around my hand. My neck felt exposed without it. Hallow reached across the table and cupped his hand around my throat. His palm was warm, and smelled of the salve. His fingers touched the back of my neck, where the hangman had tied the knot.

Hallow closed his eyes, lips moving in silent prayer. Then he sat back, his head bowed.

Kitty wasn't laughing any more. We looked at each other across the table, remembering.

'A miracle,' Hallow said. 'Christ be praised.'

I retied my cravat.

'Thank you, sir,' he said. 'May God protect you.' He smiled at Kitty, as if seeing her for the first time. 'And your wife.'

Four of us sat for dinner that day: myself and Kitty, Aislabie, and Mrs Fairwood. Bagby stood at the window, but had little to do but watch, as we served ourselves. Mrs Fairwood was dressed in another grey gown, this one with a black lace trim. She sat with her back very straight. I had noticed her judging Kitty upon their introduction – unfavourably, I thought. It was more than a mere difference in character. She had narrowed her eyes when Kitty's vowels lurched towards the London gutter, and suppressed a little smirk. I hated her for it.

'Mr Hawkins rides up to Kirkby moors this afternoon,' Aislabie told her. 'He will arrest the Gills in the king's name.'

'I will speak with them,' I corrected, poking the carp about my plate.

Mrs Fairwood lowered her fork. 'You question their guilt?'

'Mr Sneaton wasted the entire morning interrogating the servants,' Aislabie said, frowning at me. 'As expected, they neither heard nor saw a damned thing. It was the Gills.'

Bagby, unnoticed at the window, gave an assertive nod. *Never trust a Gill.*

'Then who took the sheets?' I asked.

'I don't give a damn about the sheets!' Aislabie shouted.

The table fell silent. Kitty, busy crunching a radish, stopped chewing.

Aislabie pressed his fingers against his forehead. 'This wretched business.'

'Perhaps Mrs Fairwood should return home,' I said. 'For a while, at least.'

I'd meant it out of spite, for slighting Kitty. But to my surprise she gave me a surreptitious nod in thanks. 'If you think it best, Mr Aislabie,' she began, carefully.

'No!' Aislabie cried in alarm, as if she might disintegrate in front of him. He snatched hold of her hand, gripping it fiercely. 'We have been parted long enough, Lizzie. You are my daughter and I will not let you go again. *I forbid it.*'

Mrs Fairwood closed her eyes for a moment. 'As you wish, Mr Aislabie.'

'Father,' he corrected. 'Enough of this nonsense. From now on, I would have you call me Father, as I call you Elizabeth.' He waited a moment. 'It would please me more than I can say.'

There followed a moment of excruciating silence.

Mrs Fairwood swallowed. 'As you wish, *Father*.'

Aislabie's face lit up with joy. He gazed at each of us in turn, to ensure we had witnessed this miracle. Kitty, myself, even Bagby. His eyes as they met mine were bright with wonder – and even though I had not warmed to him, I found myself praying that this was all true. That his youngest daughter had in fact come back to him after all these years. For how could he recover if she turned out to be false? He squeezed Mrs Fairwood's hand. 'There, Lizzie! I am your father. You will remain here at Studley, and I shall keep you safe.'

He held her hand for the rest of the meal. Mrs Fairwood didn't speak, didn't eat another morsel.

Kitty and I talked about the carp, and the salad, and the weather. And as soon as we could, we left.

Bagby looked out across the table, and said nothing.

Chapter Thirteen

It was a long ride out to the moors. Aislabie insisted on joining our party, saddling a dark chestnut stallion himself. I had tried – one last time – to persuade him that this was a poor use of our limited time, but he was determined to have the Gills exposed, arrested, and led in chains to Ripon gaol 'before dark'. He was annoyed that I had invited Kitty, thinking it a sign that I did not take his warnings about the Gills seriously. 'This is not a suitable expedition for a lady,' he complained. 'Mrs Hawkins – I think you must turn back.'

Kitty smiled sweetly, and said she was sure that her husband could protect her.

We rode with two of Simpson's men in case of trouble – a silent fellow named Crabbe, and Thomas Wattson, the handsome lad scolded by Sneaton for asking about his master's bill. He looked pleased to have won a rest from breaking stones and digging holes for a few hours.

We passed through the pretty village of Galphay. Aislabie pointed to a raised patch of ground. 'That was a hanging place, long ago. Ah. Sorry, Hawkins.'

Kitty was riding a few paces ahead with Wattson. He was naming the different flowers that had sprouted along the hedgerows. I'd grown up in the country, I could tell her all that sort of nonsense, damn the fellow. I nudged my horse forward. It so happened that the path was narrow at this point, and only left room for two horses to ride abreast. Wattson touched his hat and urged his horse on a pace, joining the silent Crabbe as I settled beside Kitty.

'Bluebells,' I said, nodding at a pile rotting under a hawthorn tree.

'Yes . . . Thank you, Tom.' She sighed, and shifted in her saddle. 'I wish I could have worn Lady Judith's breeches.'

I thought of Kitty's legs astride her horse. And then of Wattson riding alongside her with his clear, healthy complexion, his strong muscles and sharp cheekbones. Closer in age to Kitty, who was not yet nineteen. 'You ride very well in a gown,' I decided. I wondered when she had learned to ride with such ease. As a child, perhaps. Kitty had been working in a coffee-house in the Marshalsea when we first met, but I did know that her early life had been comfortable. Beyond that, most of Kitty's history remained a mystery to me. She had been twelve when her father died, and not much older when she fled her mother's home. She never spoke of how she survived those later years, but I knew this much: she had grown up fearless and sharp-witted, with scant regard for the rules of polite society.

We had just left the hamlet of Laverton when Aislabie called out from behind. 'The Gills live down there,' he said, pointing down a wooded lane. He steered his horse on to the grass bank, coming up alongside Wattson and Crabbe. 'The house is hidden in a copse over in the next field. You won't see it until you're hard upon it.' He handed Wattson his pistol. 'I would have you make the house safe before we arrive – I would not have Mrs Hawkins in any danger. Guard the family until we return.'

'I'm sure I would be safe,' Kitty said, disappointed. She loved a brawl.

Aislabie ignored her. 'The moors are just up here,' he said. 'I should like to show them to you.'

After a good ten minutes' ride we reached the edge of Kirkby moor. At once, it felt as though we had crossed a border into a foreign land. The hills and green valleys vanished, replaced with acre upon acre of open moorland, stretching almost to the horizon in every direction. There were no trees, no dwellings, only tufted grass and heather, and a few rocks lying low upon the ground. We rode on, picking our way through what felt like an empty land, devoid of life. Then the grouse began to call out to one another. We couldn't see them hidden in the chocolate brown heather, but their gurgling cries filled the air, warning of our approach.

'Magnificent, is it not, Mrs Hawkins?' Aislabie prompted Kitty.

'Quite a contrast to your gardens, sir.'

He liked the comparison. 'A pleasing contrast, yes. Here nature is unbound, untroubled by men. I ride here at least once a week when I am at Studley. An indulgence, I suppose ...' He breathed in deep, then out again in a long sigh. And I thought how much more confident and composed he appeared, when he was beyond Mrs Fairwood's reach.

A couple of plump rabbits bounded out from cover to nibble on the spring grass. They kept an eye upon us, hunched ready to hop to safety. 'There's a large warren over there,' Aislabie said, tilting his chin towards a spot close by. 'Excellent meat.'

'Is this the disputed land?'

'There is no dispute, sir. I own the land.'

The idea of owning such a wild, open place felt unnatural to me. No doubt Mr Aislabie, and Mr Aislabie's lawyer, would disagree. 'But it was common land, in the past? The Gills farmed here?'

Aislabie snorted. 'Farmed? A pretty word for it. They snared rabbits and grouse. Grazed a few sheep.'

Then why not let them continue, if their needs were so small? Lord knows, the world was not about to run out of rabbits. And the sheep would help keep the moors cropped close.

I surprised myself with these thoughts. I sounded like my father. He had argued against the enclosure of common land – from the pulpit, at the dinner table. Sermonising. I could have sworn I hadn't taken in a single word, but I must have been listening after all.

I knew better than to debate the matter with Aislabie. As far as he was concerned the land was his, and there was an end to it. And, overnight, with a scrawl of ink, farmers had become poachers.

Crabbe and Wattson had been discovered the moment they stepped on to the Gills' land – by the dogs, or one of the many children roaming about the place. Annie Gill, contrary to her fierce reputation, had invited them in for a bowl of rabbit stew. We found them gathered around a rough table with her husband Jeb, eating the evidence. A tiny Gill was sitting on Wattson's lap. 'Again!' she yelled in delight as we entered the cottage, and Wattson bounced her on his knees, then lifted her high in the air.

'Wattson,' Aislabie snapped.

'Sorry, sir,' he said, the child still raised above his head. 'She clambered.'

'Put her *down*.'

Wattson did as he was ordered. As the girl's bare legs touched the cold stone floor she went very quiet. Then she filled her lungs and began to scream. A baby, asleep in a cot by the fire, woke up and joined in.

'Pick her up,' Aislabie said hastily to Wattson, over the din. 'For God's sake.' His head almost touched the ceiling even at the highest point of the cottage – as did mine.

Annie Gill went over to the cot and took the screaming baby in her arms. She loosened her gown and put it to her breast. 'Mr Aislabie, your lordship. What an honour,' she smirked. The baby suckled contentedly, its tiny hand opening and closing like a starfish.

Aislabie snuffed and averted his gaze. 'You know why we have come, I'm sure. Mr Hawkins has travelled from London at the queen's bidding to discover the culprits. You will answer his questions.' He grabbed me and pulled me to one side. 'Be sure to press them hard, sir.' Then he strode out of the cottage, slamming the door behind him. He might have faced down a knife, or a pistol – but not a bare breast.

Annie Gill grinned. She must have been a striking woman once – tall, with high cheekbones and thick hair now turned an iron grey. Ten years younger than Lady Judith, most likely, but she wore her hard life upon her body. I counted seven children tumbling in and out of the cottage, plus the one at her breast. Her face was etched with deep lines, and most of her teeth were rotten. She walked stiffly too, as though her joints plagued her. Her husband Jeb had fared no better – his back was bowed, his hands gnarly. There was a spirit to them both, though. The Gills' cottage was cramped, and at one point a mouse ran over my foot, but it was a welcome change from the brooding, tense atmosphere at Studley Hall.

'Sit down and have some stew,' Annie Gill said, slapping Wattson from his chair to make space for me at the table. 'And who's this?'

'Kitty Sparks,' Kitty said, then corrected herself swiftly. 'Hawkins now.'

'Just wed – bless you!' Annie exclaimed. Jeb grunted something that might have been congratulations or might have been a withering critique of the very notion of matrimony – it was hard to tell over the noise of eight children.

There were no more chairs, so Kitty sat upon my knee and shared a bowl of stew, while Annie paced about the room with the baby. The food was fresh and very good – much better than Mrs Mason's carp. I started to explain about the threats Aislabie had received, but the Gills knew all about them. 'I hear everything that happens at Studley,' Annie said. 'They're saying we wrote those letters, I suppose.'

'*Never trust a Gill,*' Jeb muttered into his stew. Annie snorted.

'Two of them mention Kirkby moors.' I laid the notes upon the table. 'You claim a right to farm there, I believe?'

Annie wouldn't look at them. 'The moors belong to everyone and no one. There's enough coneys and grouse up there to feed half the county.'

Jeb grunted his agreement.

'But see here.' Kitty held the first note up so that Annie and Jeb could read it. She pointed to a line halfway down the page. 'They threaten to burn the moors to ash. See – this line here.'

Annie and Jeb exchanged an odd, complicit look, then glanced at the note. Annie shook her head, but she seemed hesitant and shifted away at once to nurse the baby. Jeb frowned at the letter for a moment, tracing a finger across the page. 'Bad business, burning moorland,' he said. 'Wouldn't hold with that.'

We talked further, but the convivial mood had faded. Kitty had pinched my leg after the exchange about the notes, but I couldn't understand what she meant by it. Wattson too appeared distracted, the child now half asleep in his arms with her thumb snug in her mouth. Crabbe ate his stew.

The Gills swore they had been at home all night. Raising all these children, they said, aged from three months to seventeen years old, had worn them to the bone. So much so they would collapse into bed at nightfall and know nothing until dawn. Jeb stifled a yawn. More likely he'd spent the night on the moors checking his snares, but I couldn't prove it and had no interest in doing so. A wave of futility passed through me. The visit had been a waste of time and effort, just as I'd expected.

I gave Annie a few coins for the stew, leaving the cottage in an irritable state. It would be dusk soon, and I was no closer to discovering Aislabie's tormentors. I mounted my horse, gathering the reins as the Gills' dogs barked at our feet. Kitty followed a few seconds behind, Wattson holding her horse steady as she settled herself in the saddle. I set off at a trot through the field. The day was ending, and I'd learned nothing.

Kitty drew up beside me. She was grinning.

'Did you see? The *note*, Tom,' she added, handing the first letter to me.

'I've read it a dozen times.'

'Read what it *doesn't* say.'

I glanced at her, catching her meaning. 'There's no mention of burning the moors.'

Kitty beamed. 'I made it up. I pointed to a line about grazing sheep, and they didn't know the difference. D'you see?'

'They can't read.'

'Can't read, can't write.'

The Gills were innocent. Very good. At least now I could focus my investigations upon Studley Hall, as I had wished to do from the start. 'Aislabie will be disappointed. He'd cart all ten of them off to gaol if he could, including the baby.' I reached for Kitty's hand. 'What a cunning woman you are.'

'Hell fire!' Wattson, riding behind us, pulled his horse up short. He poked his fingers into his pocket, growing agitated. 'She's stolen the coins from my pocket!'

'Annie?'

'Little Janey. Gah! You'd best ride on, sir. I'll catch up.' He nudged his horse around and rode back towards the cottage to retrieve his coins.

Kitty watched him go, watched his hips rising up and down against the saddle. I watched Kitty.

Crabbe sucked a piece of meat from between his teeth. 'Never trust a Gill,' he said.

Our ride back to Studley Hall was a brief, happy moment in my trip to Yorkshire. I find my mind often returns to that journey, to that quiet contentment as we trotted through the country lanes. We almost stopped at the inn at Galphay for a bowl of punch, but – worrying over the fading light – continued on.

Crabbe had ridden ahead, so Kitty and I talked of private things, plans for the future, and plans for when we reached our room, and our bed. We talked so well and in such detail that it became necessary to stop, and tie up the horses, and find a clearing away from the path. The ground was too muddy to lie upon, so Kitty leaned against an oak tree, and I pulled her gown about her hips. She guided me into her, grazing her teeth against my neck. I pushed deeper and she cried out in pleasure, so loud the jackdaws cawed and flew off through the clearing.

'We're scaring the crows,' Kitty said, and laughed.

As I said, my mind wanders back to that journey.

We straightened our clothes and stumbled back to the path. Wattson had caught up with the horses and was waiting for us. He didn't ask where we'd been or what we'd been doing; he didn't need to.

'You retrieved your coins?' I asked him, helping Kitty into the saddle.

Wattson nodded. 'I'd best catch up with Crabbe,' he said, and touched his hat before riding off.

Kitty bit her lip in mock dismay. 'He'll tell the servants.'

'Let him. We're married, remember?'

We rode on, casting long shadows upon the path. It was early evening now, the clouds tinged a warm pink. The air smelled of mud and wet leaves. Partridges pecked their way through the undergrowth, and squirrels raced each other around the tree trunks. As we drew close to Studley Royal, I heard a rustle high on a steep bank to my right. I turned in my saddle and saw a stoat, not much bigger than my hand, streaming backwards through the bushes, its body low and lean. It was dragging a rabbit twice its size along the ground, jaws clamped tight around the coney's neck. It stopped for a moment, struggling with its cumbersome prize. Then it began again.

I watched it do this three times, and each time I thought it might give up. It never did. A tiny, determined creature, so much more powerful than it seemed, and full of purpose. It pulled the rabbit deep into the bushes and disappeared.

Chapter Fourteen

Something had changed at Studley Hall. I felt it the moment we rode past Simpson's men. They paused in their work to watch us, clasping chisels and hammers in their strong fists. A tension rippled between us that would have had me reaching for my blade in London.

Simpson was standing on the top of a low wall, legs astride.

'What's happened?' I called out.

He jumped down from the wall and sauntered away.

Bagby was waiting for us in the great hall in his smart green coat and his over-powdered wig. Any last shred of deference had vanished. 'Come with me,' he ordered, swivelling on his heel.

Kitty began to move. I touched her arm to stop her.

It took Bagby a moment to realise we weren't following. He strode back to us. 'Mr Aislabie demands your presence. You must come at once.'

He was stubborn, and so was I. We might have spent the rest of the day scowling at one another, while the fire crackled in the great stone hearth and the housemaids hurried back and forth on their errands.

'Is someone hurt?' Kitty asked.

'Yes, madam,' Bagby replied, making a great show of politeness. 'Your husband's ward. We caught him thieving.'

Damn it.

Bagby caught my dismay, and smirked in triumph. 'He waits for you in the study, with his honour and Mr Sneaton. I can take you to them, sir – if you would be gracious enough to permit me.' He gave me a sardonic bow.

'I know the way. Leave us.' I put my hand on Kitty's back and guided her from the hall.

'What has he done?' Kitty asked from the corner of her mouth. I had no answer.

We hurried through the drawing room. Lady Judith was perched on a plump red sofa, pretending to read a book. She threw me a disappointed look, then rose and followed us into her husband's study without a word.

Aislabie was at the window. He kept his back to the room as we entered.

Sam stood by the unlit hearth, guarded by two of Aislabie's footmen. He looked terrible. There was a cut upon his lip, and his nose was red and swollen. A thick stream of blood had poured from his nostrils, running down his neck and staining his shirt. His guards held an arm each, so tight he was forced on to tiptoes. Sneaton stood beside them, grim and angry, leaning heavily on his stick.

Most boys would have been dazed and frightened. Sam was not.

'What the devil is this?' I glared at the closest footman. 'Let him go.'

The footman glanced at Sneaton, who shook his head.

Kitty approached them. If I'd done the same there would have been a fight, but they would not strike a woman. She put a hand to Sam's chin and tilted his head. He'd lost the ribbon for his hair, and his black curls hung loose about his face, falling over his eyes. She brushed his hair away gently. There was a small cut on the bridge of his nose. 'This will hurt,' she warned, and pressed her finger and thumb on either side. Sam winced, but didn't cry out. 'Do you feel something inside it?' she asked. 'Any more blood?'

'No.'

She moved her finger and thumb down the nose. 'Ooh. Something crunched there.' She dropped her hand. 'Your nose is broken.'

'He's lucky it's not his neck.' Aislabie said, turning to the room.

I strode to the door and wrenched it open. As I'd half-expected, a cluster of servants had gathered to listen, including Sally. They began to back away. 'I need a bowl of hot water and clean cloths. At once! And someone run to the ice house.' I slammed the door on them. 'Who did this?'

'I did,' Sneaton replied, calmly. He held up his stick, to show how he'd used it as a cosh. 'I've had my eye on him since you arrived. I know a gutter thief when I see one.'

Sam smiled a wolf's smile. His teeth were red with blood from the cut upon his lip.

Sneaton didn't see the quiet menace in his eyes; the unspoken threat. 'I caught him in here, hunting through the desk.'

'I won't tolerate thieves,' Aislabie said. 'I'll have him flogged for this.'

Lady Judith had listened to this exchange in silence, sitting in a chair by the door, her fingers linked together in her lap. 'What were you searching for, Master Fleet?' she asked.

Sam shifted his gaze. 'A green ledger. South Sea accounts.'

Lady Judith looked startled. She glanced at her husband, and then at me. 'I see.'

I think – at least Kitty told me later – that I managed to keep an even countenance.

Aislabie ordered the guards from the room. He stood over Sam, legs wide, hands upon his hips as if he were King Henry VIII, about to order a fresh beheading. No doubt this would have intimidated the workers on his estate, who relied upon his good favour. Sam had no such concerns. He had grown up among thieves and murderers: villains who would slit a man's throat then sit back down and finish their supper. Aislabie didn't frighten him. He kept his eyes upon Sneaton, the man who had dared to strike him.

'Look at me,' Aislabie commanded.

Sam ignored him.

There is nothing more foolish-seeming than a weak man posturing his strength. Worst of all to a small, slight boy of four-teen with a tangled mop of curls. 'Insolent boy,' he snarled. And in his rage, and embarrassment, he snatched Sam's shirt in his fist.

My first instinct was to draw my blade. But Sam caught my eye and without a word, without a gesture, warned me to stand back. This was his game.

There was a knock at the door. Sally entered with a bowl of hot water and a stack of fresh cloths draped over her arm. She gave a short gasp. Aislabie, suddenly seeing himself through her eyes, let go of Sam's shirt.

I used the distraction to drag a chair to the hearth and settle Sam upon it. Kitty soaked a cloth and began cleaning away the blood from his face and neck. It struck me that Sam was using his injuries to appear vulnerable. He couldn't have expected or wanted a broken nose, but he added it at once to his arsenal.

When she had cleaned up the worst of it, Kitty dropped the cloth into the bowl. 'You should be ashamed of yourself,' she scolded Sneaton. 'He's just a boy.'

She knew very well he was far more than that.

'Why do you search for the ledger?' Lady Judith asked him.

A plain question: the sort Sam appreciated. It deserved a plain answer. 'Queen wants it.'

I gritted my teeth. He wouldn't spill our secrets without a plan – I just wished he'd shared it with me first.

Aislabie's mouth had dropped open. 'The queen? *This* is why she sent you?' He spun to face me. 'You ordered him to do this. You knew I would be on the moors.'

I didn't contradict him. Might as well appear more cunning than I was.

'You have lied to me from the start. I trusted you. I welcomed you into my *home*.'

'You threatened the royal family, sir! What did you expect?'

'*What I was owed!*' Aislabie thundered 'I could have used that ledger to defend myself, but I held my tongue, even when they threw me in the Tower. And through all my suffering, I never spoke out. *Because I love my country.* If the names in that book were revealed there would be riots in every town in England. The government would fall. I doubt the king himself could survive the scandal. He'd be kicked back to Hanover if he was lucky, along with your *mistress*,' he sneered. 'We'd be kneeling to Rome by the end of the year.'

'You love your country. But you would blackmail the queen?'

Aislabie scowled. 'I will not be judged by *you*, sir. You were a damnable disgrace long before you were sentenced to hang. And yet how swiftly you are forgiven. I hear my keeper touched your neck for luck, as if you were some popish saint.' He snorted. 'See what passes for a hero in these corrupted days! An infamous rake, stewing in his own vice and idleness – and I would say worse, if your wife were not present.'

'At least Tom owns his faults,' Kitty said. 'And he is ten times the better man for it.'

'Your loyalty is touching, madam,' Aislabie acknowledged, gracing her with a patronising smile. 'But your husband knows his true worth, or lack thereof. Tell me, Hawkins – what great services have you performed for your country?'

'Well,' I shrugged. 'I didn't bankrupt it.'

He glared at me, his lips pressed into a thin line.

'Mr Aislabie is an honourable man,' Sneaton answered in his place. 'And this is his home. He has no need to defend himself to you.'

'Thank you, Jack,' Aislabie said. He shook his head. 'See what I endure. Do you see, Judith? Would this scoundrel have dared speak to me in such a fashion, when I was chancellor? No indeed – he would have bowed and scraped with the rest of them. Has ever a man been so ill-treated? I sacrificed my own good name to save my country. I took the blame upon my own shoulders while the guilty prospered. But I was promised, I was *assured*, that once a decent time had passed, I would be raised up again. *Eight years* I have waited. And this is my reward. The first time I ask for aid, to save my family, the queen sends a villain and a thief to steal from me. Do you see how I am betrayed? Because I dared ask for help?'

'You didn't ask, Mr Aislabie. You threatened.'

Aislabie was silent for a moment. He looked at me, and then at Sam, sitting by the hearth with his swollen nose and bloody shirt. His shoulders sank. 'Oh, just go, damn you,' he said, wearily. 'Pack your belongings and leave.'

Sam had been waiting for this. He pushed himself up from his chair. 'No.'

Everyone stared at him.

'You must give us the ledger first.'

Lady Judith, still seated in the corner, began to laugh. 'And why would we do that, Master Fleet?'

'A trade.'

'Oh, a *trade*. I see.' Lady Judith was amused. 'Well, sir – let us negotiate. What great treasure do you have for us?'

'Information.'

Here was the nub of it. Sam had watched his father negotiate such deals all his life. He would not have started down this path if he did not have something with which to trade. And there was only one thing of greater value to John Aislabie than his wretched accounts book. Now I thought of it, why *would* Sam hunt for the ledger in daylight? Why would he let himself be caught? He must have planned the entire business – save for the broken nose. He hadn't anticipated Sneaton's violent loyalty to his master, or the savage crack of the walking stick. A lesson he would remember for next time.

'I know who killed the deer.'

A moment's silence.

'Well? Who was it?' Aislabie spluttered.

Sam put his hands in his pockets.

'Damn you, boy,' Sneaton shouted, lunging for him, but Sam darted out of reach, hands still in his pockets.

Aislabie rushed forwards, but Kitty stepped in front of him, stretching out her arms to block the way. Sam, shielded behind Kitty, allowed himself a brief grin. Such foolish etiquette, these gents. In Sam's world, women fought along-side the rest of the company. Children too, once they were strong enough.

'It would seem there's a deal to be struck,' I said.

Aislabie rounded on me. 'Now we see your colours, sir. You would trade over such a matter? You would risk our lives, my *daughter*'s life for this?'

'If you love your family, hand over the ledger and we will leave your house at once.'

Aislabie's jaw tightened, his chest rising and falling as he fought his temper. He thought for a moment, dark eyes shrewd and narrow. 'How much does the queen pay you?'

I shook my head.

'Come sir, let us not be delicate about such things. What will be your reward, if you hand over the ledger? Whatever she pays you, I will double it.'

'That is not possible, Mr Aislabie.'

'Why, do you think I cannot afford it?' he gestured about his room, the rich furnishings and the work continuing outside in the dusk.

'It's not in your power.'

'An elevation at court, is that it?' he jumped in, eagerly. 'But think, sir – *money buys influence.* I know the worth of every position, believe me. And I have friends at court, in government – even now. My son has many useful contacts. My brother-in-law, Sir William Robinson, is one of the most influential men in the country. I may have been cast into the wilderness, but I have men in my pocket even now. The queen is not the only power in the land, sir. There is a great web of connections—'

'John!' Lady Judith interrupted.

'—clubs and organisations,' Aislabie continued, oblivious. 'You have heard of these new gatherings in London – the freemasons? I could offer introductions—'

'*John.* I don't believe Mr Hawkins has been offered payment or position.'

Aislabie's brow furrowed.

Lady Judith turned to me, her expression soft. 'She has some hold upon you. Something private.'

I gave her a half bow in acknowledgement.

Aislabie's shoulders sank. He had quite transported himself with all his promises. I think I had just witnessed something of the man he once was. Mayor of Ripon. Lord of the Admiralty. Chancellor of the Exchequer. A man of national consequence. 'I did not think . . .' He turned a little pink. 'I see I have misjudged you.'

'Clearly.' Kitty glared at him. 'You thought him nothing more than a worthless rake.'

I cleared my throat. 'To be fair, sweetheart . . .'

'You are much more than that, Tom. I see it, even if you do not.'

'That is the secret of a good marriage, my dear,' Lady Judith said, smiling sadly at her husband. 'To see the best in them, and stay loyal through the worst.'

'The *deal*,' Sam prompted, bored and somewhat disgusted by this talk of love and loyalty.

Aislabie sat down at his desk, his politician's mind examining every angle. At last, with a sharp nod, he came to a decision. 'Very well.'

My heart lifted in astonishment. *We had won.* It didn't seem possible. I imagined myself, ledger in hand, riding away from Studley Royal with Kitty and Sam. Home to London. 'Excellent!' I said, trying and failing to hide my relief. 'Pray send for the ledger at once, so we might be sure it is genuine. If we're satisfied, Sam will tell you everything he has discovered. Assuming his story tallies,' I glanced at Sam, who nodded once, 'we shall take the ledger and leave immediately.' I had no wish to spend another night at Studley Hall. We would have to risk the journey in darkness and hope there would be rooms free in town. 'Are we agreed?'

'We are,' Aislabie said. 'With a heavy heart, we are. Mr Sneaton, pray fetch the ledger.'

Sneaton had remained silent throughout these negotiations. Now he bowed, as best he could. 'Forgive me, your honour. But I cannot.'

Aislabie sat forward in his chair. 'Nonsense. Do as I ask – at once.'

Sneaton bowed again, but didn't leave.

'For God's sake,' I said, losing patience. 'If he cannot go, send one of the servants. I'll fetch it myself if you wish.'

'Sneaton,' Aislabie said, exasperated. 'Where is it?'

Sneaton straightened himself as best he could, his stick grinding into the floor. 'Your honour, you know that I am your obedient servant. You made me promise never to speak to you of its hiding place. You entrusted it to me for this very reason. Hold firm, Mr Aislabie! You were promised a restoration of all your powers. If you lose the ledger, you will remain in exile for ever. It is your dream, sir. I will not let you give it up, after all you've suffered.'

There were tears in Aislabie's eyes. 'Thank you, Jack. With all my heart – thank you. But I have no choice.'

'You do, sir!' Sneaton insisted. 'There's always another way.' He glowered at Sam. 'I am sure I could beat the truth out of the boy.'

'I will break your jaw if you try,' I snapped.

Aislabie had risen from his chair, his expression sombre. He stood in front of Sneaton, and put a hand upon his shoulder. 'I release you from your promise. Please. Fetch the ledger.'

The two men faced each other. I held my breath, praying for Sneaton to see sense. But he only shook his head. Aislabie lost patience. He grabbed his secretary by both shoulders and shook him. 'Do you not understand the danger? My family. My *family*. You know I would give anything to protect them. Every brick of this house, every inch of land. It is all that matters in the end. It is everything.'

'Mr Aislabie, sir. I cannot.'

Aislabie gripped harder. 'For Elizabeth. For God's sake, Jack. I can't lose my Lizzie. Not again. *Not again.*'

Sneaton took a deep breath. 'That woman is not your daughter, sir.'

Aislabie stepped back, as if struck.

'It is true, sir, upon my soul. Mrs Fairwood is not your daughter.'

'And how do you know this?' Aislabie asked, in a cold voice. 'What proof do you have?'

Grief shadowed Sneaton's face – but he wouldn't answer. 'Your honour, I have served you faithfully for over thirty years. I ask that you trust me now.'

Aislabie covered his face with his hands. 'Do not ask me this,' he groaned. 'Do not ask me to choose between you and my daughter.'

Sneaton bowed his head. 'I'm sorry, sir.'

Aislabie's hands dropped to his sides. 'So be it. Mr Sneaton, you are dismissed from my service, without references. Mr Bagby will take up your duties until I can find a new secretary. In the meantime, you will of course be evicted from your cottage. It is almost night, so in recognition of your injuries, you may leave tomorrow at dawn.'

'John!' Lady Judith cried. 'Husband! Let us all be calm, and think for a moment—'

Aislabie ignored her. 'Bring the ledger to me within the hour and I might reconsider. Now get out.'

Sneaton sagged, and would have fallen were it not for his wooden stick. Somehow he found the strength to bow, holding his head low. Then – ever the faithful servant – he limped towards the door.

'Jack!' Lady Judith cried in anguish.

I blocked his path. 'For God's sake, sir – think again for all our sakes.'

He glared at me, one eye burning with defiance, the other

blind, milk-white. His raw, scarred face was inches from mine. 'The queen will never get her claws on that book. *Never*.'

He closed the door quietly behind him. Aislabie slumped into his chair, staring at nothing. Lady Judith had covered her mouth with her hands, as if afraid of what she might say.

'He'll come back,' Aislabie said. 'He's not a fool.'

But the hour passed, and Sneaton did not return. The sun set as the servants moved through the house, lighting candles. Stunned, we allowed ourselves to be led up to our rooms, no longer guests, not quite prisoners.

Kitty flung herself upon the bed, face down. 'What fun we shall have at supper,' she said, her voice muffled through the pillow.

Sam was peering at himself in the mirror. There were bruises forming under his eyes, and his eyelids were swollen.

I put my hand on his shoulder and looked at him in the glass. 'You did well. So – who is it threatens Aislabie?'

He put a finger to his lips.

'What – d'you think I'll give up their names in some fit of conscience?'

A nod. 'Or . . .' He mimed knocking back a drink.

Well that was insulting. I can hold my tongue. And my liquor. 'I could shake the truth out of you.'

He considered this for a moment. Pointed at his swollen nose, and shrank his shoulders, acting the meek little mouse.

There would be no profit in pressing him. He had his own plans and would not be swayed from them. Even if I did beat him – and of course I would not – he wouldn't give me the names. I had brought a thief with me to Studley Hall, but I had also brought a Fleet: secretive, sly and independent of mind. So I let him slink away to his room, back to his sketchpad and his devious schemes.

I sat down on the bed, next to Kitty. 'I thought we'd won.'

She touched my arm. 'Be patient. Sneaton will have a change of heart. He won't lose his position over this.'

I didn't agree with her. Jack Sneaton would not be turned from his path, not willingly. I sighed. God spare us from men of principle: stubborn bastards, every one. I had no wish to hurt him, but I must have the ledger. I must keep Kitty safe.

I had brought a brace of pistols with me to Yorkshire. I did not wish to use them, but I would, if I must.

The sun had set, the sky a deep blue. Soon it would grow darker still.

Chapter Fifteen

'The boy must remain locked in his quarters – upon Mr Aislabie's orders.'

Bagby stepped away from the door to allow Sally through. She was carrying a supper tray for Sam, decorated with a vase of purple crocuses. Seeing that the fire had burned low, she tended to the flames, adding a shovelful of coal. Sam watched her from the doorway of his cupboard room, rubbing the back of his neck.

'You're to be locked in,' I told him.

Sally clapped the black dust from her hands and gestured to the tray on the windowsill. 'Your supper, Master Fleet. The salmon is very good, sir, and there is some cream for the apple pie.'

'He's not a gentleman, Sally,' Bagby scolded her from the door. 'He's a thief.'

Sam hurried to the window and picked up his slice of pie. It was only after he'd crammed half of it in his mouth that he remembered his manners. He pointed to his full cheeks and grinned his appreciation.

'You're welcome, *sir,*' Sally replied.

Sam lifted himself on to the window seat and toyed with the casement latch. The others didn't notice the gesture, not even Kitty, but I had spent a long time in Sam's company. He was sending me a message in his own silent language, one in which I was becoming fluent. *Once you are gone, I will open this window and jump into the oak tree. And then I shall pay Mr Sneaton a visit.*

I gave the briefest shake of the head, tapped my finger against my collarbone. *I shall go myself.*

His response did not even require a gesture, only a subtle shift in his eyes. *Better this way.* And, *You cannot stop me.*

Bagby escorted Kitty and me through the house to the library, more prison guard than footman.

'Mr Aislabie and my Lady Judith have not yet descended,' he said, as if he expected them to float down to supper from a celestial cloud. 'You will remain here until his honour sends for you.'

He ushered us through the door. Metcalfe was sitting at the desk in the corner by the window, hunched over his books. He reached out a hand and dipped his quill three times, clotting it thoroughly before scraping a line or two on to the paper. He held his pipe clamped between his teeth, the air thick with tobacco smoke.

Bagby cleared his throat, but Metcalfe scribbled on, seemingly oblivious, though more likely ignoring him. 'Mr Robinson,' Bagby tried, at last. 'Sir?'

'Writing. Sit them down, Bagby. Sit them down and go.'

'Begging your pardon, sir. Mr and Mrs Hawkins must be watched at all times – upon your uncle's orders.'

Metcalfe sighed, and flung down his quill. He twisted in his chair, resting his arm along the back. His hands were covered with ink, and there was a dark smudge on his forehead. 'And if they attempt an escape? What would you have me do, Bagby? Fling Lucretius at Mr Hawkins' head?' He picked up his copy of *De Rerum Natura* and tested its weight against his hand. His eyes were red and watery and he looked tired, but there was a spirit to him I'd not seen before. He rose to his feet and offered Kitty an elegant bow, pipe dangling from his lips. 'Mrs Hawkins.'

Kitty curtsied. 'Sir. We spoke this morning, through the keyhole.'

'Such wonderful hair,' he marvelled, dismissing Bagby with a well-practised baronial wave. 'Like Bachiacca's Sybil! How you remind me of her! Remarkable likeness. Have you seen it? There's an etching of it here, somewhere. Let me find it . . .' He wandered to the shelves, trailing smoke. 'Bachiacca . . . Always painting redheads – and why shouldn't he? Wonderful creatures.' He plucked a heavy volume from a shelf and brought it over to the table to show us, ink-stained fingers flicking through the pages until he found an etching of a woman who looked nothing like Kitty, but whose breasts spilled over a tight corset, nipples pressing urgently through a gauzy cloth. 'Look at the hair,' Metcalfe said, not looking at the hair. 'In the painting it's red as fire.'

'Are you recovered from this morning?' Kitty asked.

'How kind. Yes, I believe I am. Recovered as an old sofa. New fabric stretched over sagging old cushions.' He tugged at his clean coat, beaming at her.

'I only meant . . .' Kitty gave up. 'You have ink on your forehead.'

Metcalfe moved towards the door, rubbing at his forehead and smudging the ink deeper into his skin. He poked his head out into the corridor. 'Gone!' he exclaimed.

'Who . . .'

'Spies. Agents of Aislabie.' He crossed to the terrace doors, cupping his hand so he might peer into the night. Satisfied, he sprang towards me and seized my hand. His palm was hot and sweaty. 'Sir. My dear sir,' he exclaimed, shaking my hand so vigorously my arm was half pulled from its socket. 'Is it true? Are you here to destroy my uncle?' He grinned, revealing a jumble of teeth.

'Mr Robinson—'

'*Metcalfe!* He let go of my hand, only to clap my arms and pull me into a brief hug. He smelled strongly of sweat, despite his clean clothes. 'I must apologise, sir, for my previous uncivil behaviour.'

'You have been perfectly decent, sir.'

'Have I?' Metcalfe looked doubtful. 'I thought you were his creature, you see. Part of his great scheme to return to power.' He held up a finger. 'It must never happen. Uncle Aislabie is a . . .' he glanced at Kitty and trailed away.

'An arsehole?' she offered.

Metcalfe giggled. 'A thief. A veritable Mackheath. Robbed the country till it bled and pretended he bled the most of all. *Oh, sirs – how can you command me to pay reparation, when I have nothing left? How will my poor family eat?*

'You want to see your uncle ruined?' Kitty asked.

'Yes. No!' He puffed on his pipe. 'Not ruined. Diminished. Chastened. Humbled. I would have him peer into the mirror of his soul and count every dark, festering stain upon it. Let us have some sherry.' He poured three glasses, handed them around.

We drank together in silence, the clock ticking on the mantelpiece. Almost eight. I could see why Mrs Fairwood, with her love of quiet study, preferred not to share this room with Metcalfe. He was a distracting and fidgety presence in a library, if a likeable one.

'How pleasant this is,' Metcalfe said, in a sombrous voice. I found it difficult to follow his moods. He collapsed into a chair by the fire. 'Sneaton will never give up the ledger, you know. He's a man of honour. A man of honour, shielding a scoundrel.' He yawned very hard behind his hand, and wiped his eyes. 'Apologies, my friends. It's the laudanum, at least the lack of it. A plague upon the wretched stuff. Probably shouldn't drink this.' He knocked back his sherry in one.

'I gave the laudanum to Mr Gatteker.'

'Did you?' Metcalfe looked surprised. 'Was he in need of it?'

'I asked him to examine it. You believed you were being poisoned.'

'Oh. So I did.' He rubbed his eyes. 'I am but a shadow of a shadow. You must think me a ridiculous figure, Mrs Hawkins.'

'Not at all, sir.' She sat down opposite him, and sipped her sherry.

He fixed his gaze upon her for a long time, steadying himself again. It was as if his essence was all in flux, no fixed state where he might rest. Kitty did not seem to mind. I sensed this was not the first time she had seen this affliction – a wavering on the fragile border between madness and sanity.

'I like you both very much,' Metcalfe decided. 'I shall help you, if I can.'

And I thought: *Mr Robinson, you poor devil. You can barely help yourself.*

He fixed himself another pipe. 'I hear you have discovered who threatens the house. Would you whisper his name to me, in confidence? I would consider it a favour, as the wretched fellow plans to murder me.'

'I'm afraid I can't help you, sir. Master Fleet will not give up his secret.'

He coughed out a laugh. 'And nor will Sneaton. But come – you must have some inkling.'

'It's a large estate, and your uncle is not loved. I can think of a dozen suspects within the household alone.'

'Including me?' He laughed at my discomfort. 'Come – I should be offended if I were not suspected, sir.'

It was true, I had considered Metcalfe – and then dismissed him. It was something I had realised from my conversation with Mr Forster: it would do no good rounding up all of Mr

Aislabie's enemies and discounting them one by one. Men who had never once met my host might bear him a grudge for his wealth, or his infamous part in the South Sea disaster. To discover the truth, one should not seek out those with cause to hate John Aislabie. One should ask this, instead: what sort of a man would conduct such a violent and carefully executed campaign against him? Not Metcalfe, I was sure of it. He was too chaotic and confused.

We were hunting for a most singular person, that much seemed clear. But, in any case, we would learn the truth from Sam soon enough. Unless he had been conning us all, of course. That was a distinct possibility, and one I chose not to think about too closely.

'I fancy Mr Forster for it, myself,' Metcalfe said. 'No one can be that dull, surely? It is an act – it must be. And the stags were from Messenger's park, I believe?'

'That is not certain.' I had not yet heard from William Hallow. 'I've already questioned Forster. He confessed that he's spying on Messenger for your uncle in exchange for his patronage. His entire future rests upon Mr Aislabie's goodwill.'

'Oh, that is a pity.' Metcalfe lamented. 'I had placed all my hopes on Forster. But do you see how I am proved right about the spies? My uncle is the most shameless devil, truly.'

We all agreed upon that. Kitty and Metcalfe fell into a discussion about London, and the theatre. They had both seen *The Beggar's Opera*, so they sang one of the ballads together, and Metcalfe declared that Kitty could play Polly Peachum upon the stage, which proved he must be deaf, as well as a little mad.

I crossed the room to study the globe standing in one corner, thinking of Kitty's dream of visiting Italy. It rested where Mrs Fairwood had left it, upon the eastern coast of the Americas, and the wide stretch of the Atlantic.

The door opened and Mr Forster entered the room. I introduced Kitty, who rose and curtsied.

'Does she not remind you of Bacchiacca's *Sybil*?' Metcalfe
prompted Forster from his chair without preamble.

'I regret I have not seen, sir.'

'No? Did you not visit it on your travels? Come then Forster,
a game – what great work of art most reflects Mrs Hawkins'
timeless beauty?'

Kitty snorted into her sherry.

Forster tugged at the deep cuffs of his coat, flustered. 'I am
not sure that I recall . . . I do not have a clear memory of such
things. I am more interested in architecture than
paintings . . .'

'Please do not trouble yourself, Mr Forster,' Kitty laughed.

'See! My point is made!' Metcalfe thrust an arm towards
Forster. 'All those months upon his grand tour, and he cannot
remember a single painting.'

'I did not say—' Forster stammered.

'Clearly you are not who you seem,' Metcalfe decided. He
seemed to speak in jest, but his behaviour was so unpredictable,
it was hard to be sure. 'Tell us sir – are you an impostor? Were
you out upon the estate last night, murdering stags? Did you
chop off their heads and drag them to the front steps for me to
discover?'

Mr Forster was stunned by the accusation – naturally enough.
But before we could explain, or he could reply, we were called to
the dining room.

As Kitty had predicted, the atmosphere at supper was strained. I
had hoped to eat and retire as swiftly as possible – smuggling out
a bottle of claret or two – but Mr Aislabie had other plans. He
was convinced I knew the identities of the conspirators, and

spent the meal attempting to coax the truth from me. He appealed to my compassion, my sense of decency. He pointed out that if I stayed at Studley Hall – 'and damn it Hawkins, you *will* stay until I'm satisfied' – that my own life was at risk. 'Do you not care for your wife's safety?' he asked, glowering at me down the table.

'*John.*' Lady Judith put a hand on Kitty's arm. 'You are perfectly safe, my dear, I assure you. There will be twenty men guarding the house and grounds tonight. All the male servants will stay up, and Mr Simpson's men will take turns at watch.'

Kitty smiled. She was, I'm sure, thinking of the dagger nestled inside her gown, the handle disguised as a brooch at her breast. And of the brace of pistols under the bed, and the dagger beneath our pillow.

'I will visit Mr Sneaton in the morning and reason with him,' Lady Judith said. 'He will hand over the ledger, and Master Fleet will give up his information. Good will prevail. Now please, let us speak no more on the matter. I think Mrs Fairwood might faint.'

We all turned to look at Elizabeth Fairwood, who had not spoken once since we had sat down. She was indeed very pale, her face frozen in its customary mask. She was wearing the same grey fustian gown she had worn at dinner, a dress more suited to a governess than a gentlewoman. Only the jewel at her throat gave a hint of her wealth and status: the glittering diamond flower with the ruby at its heart. Her true mother's brooch, if she was who she claimed to be. 'It is a terrible business,' she said, in a flat voice. 'Those poor animals.'

Kitty narrowed her eyes at this. Mrs Fairwood's compassion rang hollow, to be sure. I had seen her gazing at the stags from the window this morning. I'd seen no pity in her gaze. If anything, she had looked rather peevish.

Mr Forster, seated to her left, did his best to rouse the table to more cheerful matters. Even his clothes brightened the room, the gold buttons on his scarlet waistcoat gleaming in the candlelight. For once he did not speak of architecture, but entertained us with stories of his two friends, who had now reached Rome and had both sent letters. Each was in love with the same woman, he explained, without the other's knowledge. The lady, meanwhile, was being showered with gifts from both suitors and presumably laughing behind her hand at the ridiculous Englishmen.

'Tom and I have plans to visit Rome,' Kitty said. 'I should like to travel all across the world, to the very ends of the earth.' She laughed at her own eagerness, and the rest of the table joined her, save for Mrs Fairwood. 'Tom has a friend who lives in the colonies.'

'New York. He's set up a trading company.'

Forster leaned forward. 'There are vast fortunes to be made out there, no doubt – in the south most of all. A whole great continent to exploit – and the cheapest of labour. Slaves and criminals – they must be the hardest working souls in the world. D'you know, I have always wondered – why do we waste so much abundant, free labour on the colonies? Just think, Mr Aislabie, if you could whip your men when required? Your stables would be built in a matter of weeks. You'd need a good slave master, some pitiless brute—'

'No!' Mrs Fairwood cried, and dropped her fork to her plate. She drew a steadying breath. 'Please, sir. I beg you. Do not speak of such dreadful things.'

'Dreadful?' Forster seemed puzzled. 'But I'm afraid it's how the world turns, madam.' He tried to catch her eyes, but she kept her gaze upon her plate. Her shoulders were trembling with suppressed emotion, her slim hands gripping the table. Forster appealed to Aislabie. 'Sir, I'm sure you would agree—'

Mrs Fairwood scraped back her chair with a violent movement. 'I pray you would excuse me,' she said, and hurried from the room.

Mr Aislabie rose to follow her, then thought better of it. He sat back down, and gave Forster a critical look. 'England is not a country of slaves, sir.'

'No indeed, sir,' Forster agreed hastily with his would-be patron, smiling about the table. 'We are all free men here, thank God.'

Lady Judith signalled to Bagby to refill her glass.

Metcalfe roused himself. 'Think I'll take a walk about the gardens.'

'For heaven's sake, Metcalfe, it's long past nine o'clock. It'll be pitch black out there,' Aislabie grumbled.

'We carry our darkness with us, Uncle,' Metcalfe said, then bowed and excused himself.

'Does anyone in this house,' Lady Judith asked, 'know how to conduct an *agreeable* conversation?'

We retired to the drawing room and did our best to pretend this was a perfectly regular evening. To my surprise Mrs Fairwood joined us there, though she crossed at once to the harpsichord and began to play. Aislabie watched her for a while, with a quiet pride, before suggesting a game or two of cards. Fortune favoured me at last.

I am excessively good at cards. I played every day at school, and every night at Oxford. I survived for three years in London almost entirely upon my winnings. I have an exceptional talent for remembering what has been played, and for judging the meaning of each decision, based upon my opponent's character and behaviour. There is an alchemy to it that I cannot put down in words – a hundred subtle ingredients I must draw upon in the few moments before I make my own play. One must understand the risks each player is prepared to take, and read the expression in every eye, no matter how fleeting. From these reactions, and the cards left to play, I am able to make swift calculations on the best use of my own hand. Not only that, I can do it tired, or sick, or drunk.

I wish this much-honed skill extended beyond the gaming tables, that this were all some great metaphor for how I conduct my life. True, cards have taught me how to read minute expressions of the face very well, if I bother to concentrate. But away from the table there are too many distinctions and distractions to make precise predictions. Life is not like a game of cards; life is like nothing but itself. That is why it is so precious.

Kitty preferred cockpits and wrestling to playing cards, and tended to grow restless sitting too long at the gaming table. But she made an exception that strange, unsettled night at Studley Hall. It was as if we had all decided to ignore the encroaching danger – as there was so little we might do about it. Aislabie and Lady Judith were both experienced players, but they were too confident and too focused upon each other's game. I had plucked almost twenty pounds from Aislabie before the end of the night.

As we played, Lady Judith did her best to counsel her husband on Sneaton's behalf, in her subtle way. A passing reference to some work that needed doing about the hall, and how Sneaton would be best placed to arrange it. A reminder of how he had ordered the wallpaper and much of the furniture in the room, obtaining the very best price for each item. Aislabie gritted his teeth through each hint and said at last, when his patience grew thin, 'Enough, madam. Sneaton has put my family at risk with his stubbornness. I will not change my mind on the matter.'

'You have always loved him for his integrity,' Lady Judith said, behind her cards. 'And now you punish him for it.'

Aislabie frowned at her over his cards, and lost the game.

Forster did not join us at the card table. He spent the time speaking to Elizabeth Fairwood while she sat at the harpsichord. I cannot remember what she played, though she played it well. The rest of the world disappears when I play cards. I didn't pay attention to their conversation, spoken softly beneath the music. I didn't notice whether Bagby stayed in the drawing room, or if he came back and forth to refill our glasses and bring fresh candles. And I don't recall when Metcalfe returned from his solitary walk around the water gardens. I noticed him only when we rose from the table at last and saw him slumped alone by the fire, rubbing his forehead with the tips of his fingers, as if suffering from a headache. His fingernails were black with grime.

'Good heavens, it is past eleven,' Mr Forster exclaimed.

And with that, our party broke up.

Bagby escorted us to our chamber, with two footmen following close behind. I had been inside two gaols in the last few months, I knew how it felt to be led back to a cell. 'I will not be locked in like some damned criminal,' I said, as we reached the door. 'I would rather stay up all night on watch.'

'As would I,' Kitty said.

Bagby considered her for a moment, not unkindly. 'Mr Aislabie has twenty men on guard, with dogs. It would be no place for a lady.' He glanced at me, and added in a knowing tone: 'If you wish to stand watch, mistress, I should keep an eye upon your husband.'

'What do you mean? What does he mean, Tom?'

'I don't know.' But I'd had my fill of his insolence. I grabbed him by the throat and shoved him against the wall, squeezing hard. 'Pray tell us. What do you mean, Bagby?'

His eyes bulged, and he began to choke.

The two footmen pulled me away, with Kitty's help. Bagby fell to the ground, pulling at his cravat to loosen it. Kitty took my hand and dragged me into our chamber as he lurched to his feet, wig askew. When he had regained his composure, and fixed his wig, he took the key from the lock.

'What if there is a fire?' Kitty asked, as he closed the door on us.

'I'm to stand guard here,' Bagby replied. 'All night.' The key turned in the lock.

The sound of it sent a wave of rage through me. I rushed to the door and kicked it as hard as I could. 'I'm not your prisoner, damn you!' I kicked the door again for good measure, splintering the bottom panel. I think I might have torn the door from its hinges had I not turned, and seen Kitty's face.

'Tom. Peace. This won't help.'

'Fucking Aislabie,' I snapped, and snatching the nearest thing to hand I threw it against the wall. A sherry glass, as it transpired, still half full. I began to pace the room, kicking at the walls. 'I am *not* his fucking prisoner.' Except I was. Locked up again. Pacing my cell again.

Kitty understood rage. I'd watched her kick and punch and curse at the world, and now she watched me do the same, until my anger was spent. She understood my hatred at being trapped, after my time in the Marshalsea and Newgate. She knew what had happened to me in the Marshalsea strongroom that night, and how it still haunted me. She poured some sherry into our remaining glass and proffered it, more as a tonic than as liquor.

I knocked it back in one gulp and offered her a weak smile. 'I'm sorry.'

She stepped into my arms.

'When I was in Newgate,' I said, closing my eyes, 'I used to dream of holding you like this.'

She sighed into my neck.

I broke free, after a time. Sam had not yet returned – the casement window was open, and his room was empty.

Kitty squeezed into the room with me. 'Look at these,' she murmured, flicking through a sheaf of sketches he had left upon his bed. 'How well he draws. See, he's captured those strange icicle shapes on the banqueting house.'

'What was he doing up there?' I wondered, taking some of the pages from her. Perhaps there was some clue within them, something that had helped him discover the identity of Aislabie's foes. There were architectural studies of the canal and the moon ponds, and details of the new folly under construction – but that meant little. He liked to puzzle out the workings of things through his sketches, whether he was drawing some mechanical device or the skeleton of a bird. The cascades and the canal would have interested him in themselves, and might have no other meaning.

The subsequent pages were filled with character studies of the Aislabies and their guests, Mrs Fairwood with her eyes lowered, next to a portrait of Forster in his smart coat and bandaged arm. His mouth was open, which was characteristic, to be sure. Sam had made several attempts at Sneaton, with separate details of his scars, his wooden leg, and ruined eye. I had grown used to the way Sam witnessed the world and recorded it in his drawings, though I never liked to see my own face in there. But here I was – a portrait from our journey into Yorkshire, when he'd had hour upon hour to study me. I was leaning back into a corner of the carriage, away from the window. He had filled in part of the carriage interior behind me, shading heavily with his pencil. It looked as though a great charcoal shadow had gathered about my shoulders.

Kitty had found another set of portraits. She held up the page for me: four sketches of Sally Shutt. They were the most well observed and finished of all the pictures.

'Is he sweet on her?' Kitty asked.

'Either that or he suspects her of something dreadful.'

'Or both. Well, there is no shame in falling for a maidservant, is there, Tom?'

I smiled at her.

'Has he gone to visit Sneaton, do you think?'

'I expect so. I'd hoped he would have returned by now.' I dropped the pictures back upon the bed.

'He knows how to take care of himself.'

I wandered back into our chamber. 'We must leave the window open for him.' I peered out, and saw one of Simpson's men standing beneath the oak tree holding a lantern. 'Damn it.' I craned my neck further out of the window and saw more lanterns, left and right. The men had formed a boundary all the way around the house. I hadn't really thought I could take Sam's route out of the window and along the oak tree – I valued my neck too well for that. But this confirmed it. There was no way I could leave the room tonight, which meant that my earlier thought to visit Sneaton and persuade him to talk at pistol point was now impossible.

'Sam had the same idea, most likely,' Kitty said. 'No doubt Mr Sneaton is bound to a chair at this very moment, begging for his life.'

I hunted through my belongings. My pistols were still in their box beneath the bed, but Sam had retrieved his blade. I began to pace again, worried for Sam and worried for Sneaton.

'He won't risk sneaking past the men,' Kitty said. 'He'll find shelter overnight, wait until he can slip back unseen. You know how he is.'

I nodded, absently.

'Tom.' She stroked my arm. 'Sam has survived fourteen years in the worst slums in London. He's a Fleet. I don't think it's his fate to die in a deer park.'

I frowned, and touched my mother's cross for luck.

We undressed and slipped into bed, shivering from the draught blowing through the open window. I snuffed out the candle and lay in the dark, worrying.

'He'll be back by morning,' Kitty whispered, running a hand beneath my shirt. 'Most likely with the ledger tucked in his breeches.'

We laughed at this, then fell silent.

Kitty curled into me and kissed my jaw. 'You're not responsible for him, Tom.'

The silence fell heavy around the bed.

*

There is a body lying on the riverbank.

Sam spends two hours hunting for the ledger in Sneaton's cottage, while the old bastard sits snoring in his chair. Two hours of nimble fingers – the quiet pulling of drawers, riffling through neat stacks of ledgers. Senses alert to any sound or movement, to the very density of the air. All the skills his father taught him and a few he'd taught himself, roving through St Giles at night.

He finds nothing.

He returns to the hearth and slides the dagger from his pocket. He holds the blade an inch from Sneaton's neck, keeping his breath steady. No pleasure in this, and no fear. He lets the scene unfurl in his mind, testing it for flaws. First, he would press the blade deeper. Sneaton would wake with a start, and feel the bite of steel. Sam imagines the terror in the old man's good eye. No pleasure in this, no pleasure. Sam would ask his questions. Would the old man answer him? Maybe. Maybe not. He was stubborn, and loyal to his master. He might refuse, even under the threat of death. And then what?

Never make a threat you can't keep. His father's rule and one that Sam respects. A man's only as good as his word.

He can't kill Sneaton. Everyone would know he'd done it.

Sam lowers his blade. No pleasure, no fear. No disappointment. Well, perhaps a twinge.

There is nothing more he can do tonight. Tomorrow will bring new opportunities. This is the first rule of the Fleets: Stay alive till morning.

He leaves the cottage. Mr Sneaton, oblivious, sleeps on.

Sam crosses the estate towards Studley Hall, hurrying through the deer park. He is very quiet, but the deer scent him in the air and rise up from their half slumber. A stag bellows, and the herd moves away across the grass.

And here Sam's luck runs out. Five minutes one way, five minutes another and no one would have discovered him. But two figures have stepped away from the house to talk urgently, and now, as if conjured by magic, their problem is walking towards them across the grass.

They grab him before he has a chance to pull out his blade. He fights hard but they are stronger than him, much stronger than he expected.

'What should we do with him?'

He's frightened now. 'Please, sirs – I won't say nothing. I'll say I was telling stories.'

They don't believe him.

A decision is made.

Sam isn't struggling any more, he's too afraid. He thinks of his mother. He is, after all, still a boy.

'Please,' he whispers.
He feels a sharp crack to his skull.
He feels nothing.

There is a body lying on the riverbank. It is perfectly still.

The Third Day

Chapter Sixteen

I woke to shouts of alarm and the sound of people running.

Kitty swung her legs from the bed and hopped to the floor. She always woke faster than I did. I struggled out of the sheets, half asleep, and groped my way through a gap in the bed curtains. The shutters lay open still, and the room was grey in the thin light before dawn.

'Fire!' someone called, far away on another floor.

Kitty twisted and tugged at the door handle. 'Mr Bagby!' There was no reply. She turned to me, fear in her voice. 'He left us!'

'Wake Sam.' He could pick a lock in moments. I took her place at the door, throwing my shoulder at it. When that didn't work I thrust on my shoe and kicked hard, the wood splintering and cracking under my heel. Even amidst the danger, this was deeply satisfying. I had been wanting to kick something this hard ever since I'd arrived at this bloody place.

'He's not there,' Kitty said, hurrying back into the room.

There was no time to consider the weight of this discovery. I glanced at the window. It was open as we'd left it.

Kitty followed my gaze. 'We can't.'

That wasn't quite true – she could jump to the branch and wait for rescue. It would not, however, take our combined weight.

Kitty shoved on one of my boots and began to kick the door. We worked together, matching our attack, and at last the wood splintered around the lock. Kitty snatched up my spare coat to throw around her wrapping gown and we hurried down the labyrinth of sloping corridors and creaking steps, abandoning one boot and one shoe along the way.

On the landing above the great hall, we watched as servants spilled up from the lower ground, clutching buckets of water. A footman rushed up the stairs towards us – one of the men who'd guarded Sam the day before. 'Where's the fire?' I called.

'West wing, sir.'

'Wait.' I snatched at his arm. 'Have you seen Sam – Master Fleet?'

He shook his head and pressed on.

We followed in his wake, passing servants heading the other way with empty buckets. I could smell smoke, growing stronger as we moved up the stairs towards the back of the house.

Two chambermaids squeezed past me in the narrow corridor. They didn't seem concerned by the fire, and took a singular interest in my shirt, untied and loose across my chest. The bolder of the two smiled at me. 'No need for panic, sir – it's out.'

'Where did it start?'

'Mrs Fairwood's rooms, sir.'

Bagby appeared at the bottom of the corridor. Seeing him, the maids hurried to leave. 'Mistress,' they said, bobbing a swift curtsey to Kitty as they passed. We heard them giggling to each other on the stairs.

Kitty glanced at my chest, and rolled her eyes.

Bagby approached us, stretching out his arms to block our path. 'Go back to your chamber, please.'

'You left us,' Kitty glared at him. 'We might have burned to death.'

He had the decency to look ashamed. 'It was a small fire, madam – you were in no danger.'

Kitty slapped him, hard. '*We* didn't know that.'

Bagby clutched his cheek, more in shock than pain. 'I'm very sorry, madam,' he stammered.

'No matter,' Kitty said, her temper violent but brief. 'We kicked the door down.'

We shoved past him.

Alone for a moment, Kitty stopped me, fingers spread against my chest. 'Did Sam do this?'

I shook my head.

'Can you be *sure,* Tom?'

'Why would he hurt Mrs Fairwood?'

'To hurt Aislabie. To force Sneaton to give up the book.'

'It's possible,' I admitted.

This was the same argument that had driven Kitty to abandon me on the London road. Perhaps Sam had started the fire, or perhaps not. He did what he must – with reason, but without scruple.

A small crowd had gathered in the doorway of Mrs Fairwood's quarters: two footmen acting as guards; Mrs Mason, grey hair hanging loose beneath her cap, peering over their shoulders at the devastation within; Lady Judith just inside the door, dressed in her night robe.

'The drama is over,' she said. 'The wallpaper is ruined.'

'Mrs Fairwood?'

'Unharmed.'

Clearly she wished it had been the other way about.

We squeezed past them all. It was one of the finest rooms in the house, or at least it had been – only the best for Mr Aislabie's maybe-daughter. A grand canopy bed took up much of the space and this was where the fire had started. The silk drapes were burned to blackened rags, pulled to the floor and sodden with water. The bedlinen was also ruined, and the wallpaper behind the bed was scorched. The rest of the room had survived almost intact – Mrs Fairwood's books stacked upon her desk next to a vase of orange wallflowers.

Mrs Fairwood stood in the far corner, weeping in Mr Aislabie's arms. He looked up as we entered, his face grim.

It was only then that I saw Sally, collapsed on the floor between the bed and the window, her palms upturned. They were bright red, the top skin burned away and starting to blister.

Kitty gave a cry of dismay and rushed to her aid.

'What's this?' Mrs Mason pushed her way into the room. 'Bless us, Sally – I never saw you down there. Oh, love – whatever have you done?'

'She saved my life,' Mrs Fairwood said, breaking free from Aislabie. 'I woke and the bed was on fire all around me. She tore down the drapes with her bare hands.'

Sally swayed and leaned heavily against Kitty. Her face was grey, hair stuck to her skin with sweat. 'It hurts,' she whispered. 'It hurts so much.'

Kitty and Mrs Mason helped her to her feet. 'We must take her to the courtyard pump,' Kitty said. 'The cold water will help with the pain.'

'Wait!' Aislabie ordered, stepping in front of the three women. 'Why were you so close to Mrs Fairwood's room in the middle of the night?'

Sally was breathing so hard with the pain, she could scarce answer. 'Weren't middle o' night for me, your honour. I were up lighting fires.'

Aislabie snatched at her chin. 'Did you start this one?'

'No sir!' Sally cried. 'I'd never do such a thing!'

'John!' Lady Judith gasped.

Kitty, without a word, knocked Aislabie's wrist away.

'*Did you start the fire*, girl?' he pressed. 'Answer me!'

'No, sir,' Sally sobbed, sagging between Kitty and Mrs Mason. 'I came to help, I swear it! Oh please sir, my hands.'

'Father,' Mrs Fairwood said, softly.

Aislabie turned to her at once.

'She's hurt. Please – let her go. For me.'

Aislabie glared at Sally for a moment, trying to read the truth in her face. Then he sighed. 'Very well. For you, Lizzie. But she must be locked in the cellar once you are done with her, Mrs Mason. I would speak with her again.'

Kitty and Mrs Mason guided Sally from the room. We could hear her sobs all the way down the corridor.

Lady Judith ordered the footmen from the room. 'For heaven's sake, John,' she said, when they were beyond hearing. 'Sally Shutt has served our family since she was eleven years old. If it weren't for her, the whole house would be ablaze. What is the *matter* with you, husband?'

Aislabie rubbed his scalp. He looked older without his wig, and very tired. 'You suspected the servants from the start, Hawkins. I should have listened to you. I have put too much faith in them. *Again.*'

'I don't think that Sally—'

'Who else could have started the fire?'

Sam. Sam could have started it. But I could hardly confess that. I looked at Mrs Fairwood with a fresh eye. She was uninjured, and her shock seemed counterfeit to my eyes. Could she have started the fire herself? Was it a coincidence that the wallpaper and bed were burned, but her beloved books lay safe a few feet away? I had no proof, and if I did Aislabie would never believe it. So I held my tongue.

'Don't you see, Judith?' Aislabie said. 'There is no other answer.

Hawkins was locked in his room. Damn it! All those men standing guard outside, and the trouble is here – *inside my house*. It is all happening again – at the very moment Lizzie is returned to me.' He covered his face for a moment, then rallied. 'I want that girl guarded at all times until she's recovered enough to stand before a magistrate.'

'John—'

'Fetch your ward, Hawkins. I will send for Sneaton. We will shake answers from them both.'

I hesitated, and in that moment, Bagby slid into the room.

'The boy is missing, Mr Aislabie, sir,' he said.

Aislabie glared at me. 'Where is he?'

'He must have followed us out,' I lied. 'We thought the house was burning down.'

'The window was open,' Bagby said, shoulders back, chin high. 'He might have escaped at any time last night.'

'Really, Bagby,' Lady Judith *tsk*ed. 'They are on the second landing, are they not? In the *mezzanino*?'

'There's an oak tree next to the window, your ladyship,' Bagby replied, throwing me a triumphant look. 'Easy enough for a boy to clamber out, as he pleased.'

'Nonsense,' I said. 'We opened the window when we heard there was a fire.' I turned to Lady Judith. 'Your butler left us locked up in our chamber. We had to kick the door down.'

'So the boy is missing,' Aislabie said, glaring at me. He gestured about the room. 'He could have done this!'

'No, sir.'

He prodded a finger at me. 'On *your* orders!'

'*No*,' I said, with more vehemence.

Lady Judith heard the difference and understood it, even if her husband did not. 'I think we should send out a search party for Master Fleet.'

Aislabie nodded, his eyes on me. 'Aye. I think we should.'

'I believe it best I return to Lincoln,' Mrs Fairwood said, quietly. 'Would you not agree, sir?'

Here was one good reason to start a fire. If she wanted to leave Studley without anyone questioning such a hasty departure . . .

Aislabie reached for her hand, pressing it to his chest. 'No, my dear. You shall stay here. This will all be resolved within the hour, you shall see. We'll find this boy and squeeze the truth from him.'

Mrs Fairwood looked stricken. 'But I *must* leave. Please, Father—'

He smiled at her fondly, eyes shining with love. 'You are safest here, with your family.'

'*Please.* I *must* go home.'

His smile faded. 'This is your home. And I will not part with you again. No – I am decided. You will wait in my wife's apartment until this matter is settled. I'll send men to guard the door. Do not look so frightened, Lizzie! You are quite safe, my dear.'

'Well, Mrs Fairwood.' Lady Judith arched an eyebrow. 'We shall be prisoners together.' She put a hand on Mrs Fairwood's narrow shoulder and led her away.

'My books . . .'

'I have a fascinating volume on horse breeding somewhere,' Lady Judith said, pushing her out of the room. 'You will be most diverted, I promise you.'

I stifled a smile.

'Let's find this boy of yours, Hawkins,' Aislabie said.

Simpson was in the kitchen with a handful of his men, drinking beer and breakfasting after their night's vigil watching the house. A wasted night as it transpired. They had seen nothing, heard nothing.

'Save for Mr Robinson,' Simpson shrugged, as if Metcalfe's comings and goings were of no consequence.

'What time did he return?' I asked.

'He took a walk after supper and another in the dead of night. Four o'clock, I'd say.' He glanced around the table at his men, who nodded in agreement. 'Came back half an hour ago.'

'Did you ask what he was about?'

Simpson slurped his ale. 'Not my place to question a gentleman.'

'Quite right,' Aislabie murmured. 'Thank you, Simpson, for your help tonight. I fear I am in need of your assistance once more. Mr Hawkins' ward has run off somewhere. He's a troublesome boy but we must bring him back safely. I would have you send a few of your men out on to the estate to search for him. Mr Pugh and Mr Hallow will help them. Where would he be hiding, Hawkins, most likely?'

'Somewhere warm and dry,' I said, feeling traitorous. But I was beginning to worry about Sam – and I agreed with Aislabie that it was time to put an end to this business. In this, I shared some sympathy with Mrs Fairwood: I wished to go home.

I returned to my apartment and dressed quickly, pulling on an old pair of boots. I'd hoped to find Sam there, having used the fire as a distraction, but his chamber was empty, the bed untouched. My instincts whispered that something was wrong, but I pushed such thoughts from my mind. Sam's great trick was to vanish when he was in trouble. No doubt he would emerge when he wished to be found, and not before. Either that or one of Aislabie's men would winkle him out. Meanwhile, I would pay a visit on Mr Sneaton.

I reached under the bed, and pulled out my pistols.

* * *

Sneaton's cottage lay on the edge of the deer park, a short walk from Studley Hall. It was very neat, with a vegetable patch and a few chickens still locked in their coop. It was also deserted. There was one room upstairs, and two down. The room upstairs was bare, save for stacks of old accounts books for the estate. That puzzled me, until I recalled Sneaton's wooden leg. Stairs would be troublesome, and dangerous for a man with his injuries, living alone.

I took a moment to search through the books in the hope of finding the green ledger, but I soon realised that they were stored by order of date, the earliest beginning with the quarterly accounts for Michaelmas, 1723 – a good three years after the South Sea crisis.

I came back down the stairs, bowing my head to avoid smacking it upon a low beam. A sudden melancholia seized me as I explored the ground floor. The furniture was of a good quality, the floorboards swept clean, and the windows polished. But I sensed a solitary life, where surely Sneaton must have once hoped for more. I wondered why he had never married. Even with his disfigurements, his position as Aislabie's trusted secretary would have made him a respectable proposition.

I searched the rooms, the chimney, even the chicken coop, but found nothing. Frustrated, I sat down in his chair by the empty hearth and lit a pipe, wondering to myself. Where the devil was he? Had he taken Aislabie at his word, and left before dawn? If so, he'd abandoned all his belongings. And he would have let the chickens out first, I was sure. He was that sort of a man.

'Sam,' I murmured, as if invoking his spirit. A shiver of dread passed through me. Sam had crept out last night, and now both he and Sneaton were missing. I knew that he was capable of murder – more than capable. I put my head in my hands, praying that I was mistaken. If Sam had killed Sneaton, the murder would be upon my head. I had brought Sam with me, refusing to hear Kitty's warning. If a man is shot, one does not blame the pistol. One blames the fellow who carried it.

A tap at the window made me jump, but it was only Wattson. He peered through the glass, hand cupping his eyes. 'Mr Hawkins?' he called, his voice muffled.

The chair I had settled in sat low to the floor. I had to use one hand to push myself up, which had me wondering how Sneaton ever struggled to his feet. Then I spied his walking stick lying between the chair and the hearth. He must lever himself up with it.

I'd never seen Sneaton without his stick.

I picked it up just as Wattson entered the room. He paused at the threshold, alarmed. I must have looked quite the devil, with a brace of pistols at my belt, and a heavy stick in my hand.

I bid him a good morning, and asked why he had come to the cottage.

Wattson looked about the room. The first of the sun's rays gleamed on the polished furniture. 'I've a message for Mr Sneaton, sir.'

That struck me as odd. Wattson was Simpson's man. He worked on the estate, not at the hall. 'He's not here.'

Wattson ducked his head as he inspected the other room. 'You've looked upstairs?'

'Naturally.'

He stood in the centre of the room, his head almost touching the beams. 'But he must be here. The chickens are free.'

'I let them out.'

'Then he's in trouble.' He nodded at the stick in my hands. 'He'd never leave the cottage without his cane.' He pushed past me, heading for the door.

I grabbed his arm. 'Wattson, speak truly – why are you here?'

He hesitated before replying. 'I come at dawn every morning. I help Mr Sneaton over to the house, and then back again at night.'

I thought of the walk I had taken so easily, then imagined Sneaton, struggling to drag his ruined body over the fields. 'You carry him?'

Another pause. 'If the ground's bad. He's not as strong as he pretends. Please sir – you won't tell the family? Mr Sneaton wouldn't want his honour to know.'

'You're fond of him.'

'He's been kind to me. Helped me with my letters. He says I can tally better than Mr Simpson.'

'You brought him home last night?'

Wattson shook his head, miserable. 'Mr Aislabie dismissed him before I'd finished for the day. Must have been hard for him, walking back on his own.'

Hard on his body and his spirit, I thought, resting Sneaton's walking stick against the hearth. The sun was streaming through the windows now: the start of a glorious spring morning. And what had been hidden in the shadows was now picked out in golden light.

There was a dark stain on the rough mat by the fireside, no more than a step away from the chair where I had been sitting. In fact I had walked through it, my boot smearing marks across the floor. I kneeled down for a closer study.

'What is it?' Wattson asked, in a strained voice. But he knew. We both knew.

Blood.

We walked back towards Studley House in silence, lost in our separate fears. And I wondered – *Where was Sam?*

I thought the work on the stables would have been

abandoned for the day, given that the men had spent the night on watch – and that half were out now searching for Sam. But Simpson was already ranging across the site, shouting orders. Wattson hesitated as we drew closer, and we both stopped for a moment, staring out across the park. The deer were scattered way off in the distance, almost out of view.

A dun-coloured stallion was racing along the east drive, half-obscured by the line of oaks. I shielded my eyes, trying to identify the rider. His feather-trimmed hat, and then his head, crested the hill. Francis Forster, his cloak streaming out behind him, showing flashes of purple lining. A few moments later he had galloped up to meet us. I would not have ridden so fast, with one arm bound.

'Hawkins!' he shouted. 'Is it true? There was a fire?'

'A small one, in Mrs Fairwood's chamber. She is unharmed. One of the maids was—'

'Mrs Fairwood!' he exclaimed, jumping down from the saddle and pulling at the silver clasp on his cloak. 'I must go to her.' He threw the reins at Wattson and rushed towards the house. 'Take him to the stables,' he shouted over his shoulder.

Wattson bit back a scowl. 'Mr Sneaton is missing,' he called.

Forster bronzed paused upon the steps. 'Sneaton?' He chuckled. 'Well, I don't suppose he's got very far.'

'Did you see him, sir?' Wattson asked, fiercely. His hands were bunched into fists. 'On your ride from Fountains?'

Forster's face puckered with annoyance. 'This your servant, Hawkins?'

'I'm no one's servant,' Wattson said. His voice was quiet, but there was a boldness to him that surprised me.

Forster glared at him. 'How dare you speak to me in such an insolent fashion! I shall speak to your master of this. What is your name? Well?'

Wattson reddened, and said nothing.

'You did not see Mr Sneaton upon the road?' I said, stepping in swiftly.

Forster tore his gaze from Wattson. 'Was he not dismissed from service yesterday?'

'We found bloodstains upon the floor of his cottage. I fear he may have been attacked.'

'Heavens! That is troubling. Forgive me for speaking lightly before. I pray you find him well. If you would excuse me.' He bowed and bounded up the steps.

Wattson pivoted sharply on his boot heel and led Forster's horse to the stables. I couldn't see his face, but I could tell from the set of his shoulders that he was angry.

I followed him to the courtyard where I found Kitty, sitting on the mounting block with her face turned to the sunshine. She waved and jumped down as we approached.

I asked after Sally.

Wattson halted. 'She's been hurt?'

'She burned her hands, saving Mrs Fairwood,' Kitty explained. 'They'll take weeks to heal, poor girl. Aislabie has her locked in the cellar. He thinks she started the fire.'

Wattson bit his lip, furious.

I touched Kitty's arm. 'Mr Sneaton is missing. We found blood in his cottage.'

'Sam is not returned.'

We looked at one another – afraid for Sam, and afraid for what he might have done. 'We'd best find him.'

'Let me join you sir,' Wattson said. 'I know the land better than most. And we might look for Mr Sneaton, too.'

There were only two horses left in the stables, so I borrowed Forster's stallion, hoping it was not the one that had thrown him off its back. Wattson led Kitty and me to the edge of the water gardens. We paused at the base of the lake, where it narrowed again into a river. There was a wooden footbridge here over a smaller cascade, and a stone sphinx guarding either side of the bank. They stared at each other across the river, front paws stretched towards the water. The one upon this side of the bridge had the face of a woman of middling age. Her hair streamed across her lion's back, and a string of pearls rested on her plump bosom. I leaned down, peering into her face. The expression was cool and commanding, as if she ruled over the waters below.

'When did the search party set out?' Wattson asked.

I sat up straight in the saddle. 'Almost an hour ago.'

'Then he's not here.' Wattson indicated the party of men picking their way through the gardens, hunting under the tangle of bushes and tree roots. He gathered the reins, turning his horse about. 'They'd've found him by now.'

I wasn't sure if he was speaking of Sneaton or Sam. 'Where do you propose we look?'

'Wherever's left.' Wattson rode away from the cascade, following the river downstream.

I urged my horse forward, and followed.

Aislabie had shaped the River Skell into straight canals and moon ponds, mirror lakes and cascades. But as we left the water gardens behind, the river was released back to its natural flow, winding down a steep valley bristling with Scots pines. We had to ford our way across several times, drifting further and further from the water gardens and from the house.

There was no one out here.

'We've gone too far,' I called out, as we reached another bend in the river.

Kitty drew up next to me. 'Let us see what lies up ahead,' she said, lifting her voice over the rush of water.

We had said that at the last turn, and the one before that. We could follow the river to its end, tantalised by the hope of discovery. There was something eerie about this valley, with its narrow banks and silent woods. Some antique memory, some ancestor's ghost whispered through my blood: *This would be the ideal place for an ambush.*

But there was no ambush waiting for us at the next bend, only a wide and sunlit riverbank, dotted with dandelions and daisies. Tiny white butterflies drifted in the air. Red damselflies hovered by the water.

A small, dark figure lay upon the grass.

'Sam!' I heard myself cry out. 'It's Sam!'

The sun beat down upon our heads. The wind pushed wisps of cloud across the sky. The river rushed on down the valley.

Sam didn't move. He lay perfectly still.

Chapter Seventeen

He was death cold.

'Blankets. Fetch blankets!' Kitty, pushing open the great doors of Studley and shouting at the nearest footman.

'Bring him down to the kitchen.' Wattson was waiting for us in the great hall. He'd galloped ahead to prepare the servants. *The boy was found, lying frozen on the river path below Gillet Hill, the back of his skull all bloody.* Mrs Mason had stoked the fire and called for blankets long before we arrived. Rumours spread through the house. *The boy's dead. The boy's alive.*

The boy was dying. He hadn't stirred, not when I carried him in my arms from the riverbank, as I hefted him up on to the saddle. I'd held him in front of me on that frantic ride back from the river, clutching him to my chest and praying that my own heat could warm him. How long had he lain there, all alone? I could feel my heart pounding hard against his back, life thrumming through my veins. Why did he not stir?

The back of his head was sticky with blood. I thought of the blood in Sneaton's cottage and rode on, fury burning through me like a forest fire. When I found who did this . . . God help them.

We stripped off his damp coat and breeches and cocooned him in blankets by the fire. Kitty laid her head to his chest and found a heartbeat, very slow. His face was swollen from yesterday's beating, but it was the blow to his head that worried me, and the fact we could not rouse him. There was a lump at the base of his skull, and blood in his ear. Kitty washed the wound clean, rinsing it with hot water and a few drops of brandy.

I sat down behind Sam on the kitchen floor just as I had sat with him on the ride back, propping his head against my chest. He was so cold. Kitty tucked the blankets around him and settled down with us by the fire.

I closed my eyes, bone weary. I had been prepared to think the very worst of him. Whereas in fact, he had stolen out into the night, risking his life to help me. Someone had attacked him, and abandoned him by the river to die alone. I thought of the deer, slaughtered and carried through the estate. It was the same person, I was sure of it – treating Sam as if he were an animal.

Kitty reached out and cupped a hand to my face. Saying, without words: *This is not your fault.*

I looked away into the fire. Of course it was my fault.

Mr Gatteker was called from Ripon. He flapped his arms against his side, declared it an outrage, and accepted a plate of fresh bread and jam from Mrs Mason. He sat at the table and asked about the night's events. He had not seen Sneaton on the estate, in town, nor upon the road.

'I tested Metcalfe's laudanum on the cat,' he said, sucking jam from his fingers. 'I believe someone may have tampered with the mixture – more opium and less sherry. Can't prove it, but the effects on Marigold were *unfortunate.*' He added a dollop of cream to his bread and took a large bite.

'Tom!' Kitty inched closer, and took Sam's hand. 'His eyes fluttered.' She put her fingers to his wrist, then frowned.

'Rest and warmth,' Gatteker pronounced.

'And prayer,' Mrs Mason added.

Gatteker shrugged, munching away. 'Worth a try. Didn't work for Marigold, I'm afraid.'

I carried Sam to our chamber and tucked him into our bed, small and vulnerable beneath the blankets. We had fashioned a bandage for his head, his black curls spilling over the top on to the pillow. I sat upon the bed and watched for each breath.

Kitty lit a fire before joining me, sitting upon the opposite side of the mattress. We watched him for a long time. I began to worry that if I turned away even for one second, he would slip away. Lady Judith paid a visit. Bagby brought a pot of coffee, some bread and cheese, and a slice of apple pie. 'In case he's hungry, when he wakes,' he stumbled, then bowed and left the room.

Some time later Sam's eyes opened a fraction. I took his hand, and told him he was safe, that he must rest. He couldn't seem to focus, and his hand was a dead weight in mine. His eyes closed again.

Kitty looked at me with tears in her eyes. 'Tom—'

'Don't say it, Kitty. Please.'

I put my head in my hands and I prayed with a force and a fear I had not felt in a long time. I'd prayed for myself that terrible night in the Marshalsea, chained in the corpse room. I'd prayed on the eve of my trial for murder, and on the cart to my hanging. But I had prayed knowing all my sins, knowing in my heart and soul what I had done right and wrong.

Now I prayed for a boy whose soul lay within the Devil's grasp. Fourteen years old and already he had killed someone, without once expressing pity or remorse. I couldn't let him die in such a perilous state. Death for Sam would lead only to damnation. So I begged God: *Let him live. Give him time.*

There was a tap at the door and Mrs Fairwood entered, escorted by one of the footmen. She'd brought the vase of orange wallflowers from her chamber. She stood at the end of the bed, remote and unreadable. 'How does he fare? Has he spoken?'

I didn't have the strength to answer.

'Will he live?' she pressed.

Kitty rose, and ushered her from the room. She was gone for a while. When she returned she stood behind me, wrapping her arms about my chest. 'Sneaton is still missing.' She kissed the back of my neck, and fell silent.

It was not like Kitty to be so quiet. I turned and saw that there were tears streaming down her freckled cheeks. 'Sweetheart.'

'This is my fault.'

'No – by God! What makes you say such a thing?'

She brushed her cheek with the back of her hand. 'You only came here to protect me. Because of what I did ... He's just a boy, Tom. For all he's done, he's only a boy. I will never forgive myself.'

I rose, and held her close. Sam slept on, never stirring, his secrets trapped inside his broken body.

I grow restless in confined spaces. Eventually, when I had paced the room a thousand times, Kitty ordered me outside. Sam was no better and no worse, and there was no sense in us both staying with him – not when his attacker remained uncaught. I walked down to the great hall and out on to the steps, building myself a pipe. The sound of hammer and chisel on stone echoed from the stable works. I counted a half-dozen carts rolling up to the foundations, filled with rocks and pulled by great workhorses. The day was mild for mid-April, the heat closer to summer than spring. Looking out across the deer park, I had to shield my eyes to protect them from the sun. The deer were still far down in the south-west corner of the park, a long way from the house. I frowned, and took a long draw from my pipe.

I heard the crunch of gravel from my left. Mr Hallow, Aislabie's gamekeeper, was walking up the avenue. He hurried to join me, snatching off his hat and performing a low bow. His thin red hair was tied at the nape of his neck, the top of his head near bald and freckled by the sun. 'Beg leave to ask after your young friend, sir? I'm told he was attacked.'

'Yes, some time in the night.'

'Found by Gillet's hill? There's an old poacher's track down there, sir. Steep path, hidden from view . . .'

'It wasn't the Gills,' I said, before he could suggest it.

I waited for the inevitable 'never trust a Gill', but to my surprise, Hallow nodded his agreement. 'Yes, sir. I have news.' He ventured closer, lowering his voice though there was no one else about to hear. 'Spoke with Mr Messenger's keeper last night, sir. He says he's not made a full count of his deer these past few days. Some of the does head into the upper woods to foal. Bugger to find them, pardon my language, your honour. But the stags – he says they're all accounted for. Sir, I showed him one o' the heads. He swears blind it weren't a Fountains stag.'

I frowned. The stags had been butchered on the boundary between Fountains Hall and Studley Royal. If they did not belong to either estate, where the devil had they come from?

But Hallow grinned. 'So I rode further afield this morning, sir. Only a handful of deer parks close to Studley, and I had a notion . . . The stags came from Baldersby. The Robinson's estate.'

I pulled the pipe from my lips. *Metcalfe.*

'I spoke with the keeper, sir. He said Mr Robinson sent an order for three young stags – a gift for his uncle. Not for meat – to join the herd.'

'A strange request.'

'Oh aye, sir. But – begging your pardon – it's not the keeper's place to question a gentleman's order. And Mr Robinson's known to be a little *odd*, sir.'

'So the keeper sent three stags over to Studley?'

'No, sir. The fellow what brought the message came with a cart. Rode them back the same day, bound and tethered.'

'And this *fellow* – what did he look like?'

Hallow, who had until this point been mightily pleased with himself, faltered. 'I— I didn't think to ask, sir.' He slapped a pale hand to his head. 'Oh William Hallow, you almighty fool. I shall ride back and ask, sir.'

'Could you go at once?'

Hallow grimaced. 'Wish I could, sir – but I can't find leave until this evening. I've spent too long abroad today already. Might someone go in my place, Mr Hawkins? It's no more than an hour's ride . . .'

I held out my hand. 'Not to worry.' I could ride there myself, if needed.

'I'm very sorry, sir.'

'Not at all. I'm obliged to you, Mr Hallow.' I put my hand upon his shoulder. 'I would ask that you keep this to yourself – at least for now.'

'Of course, your honour.'

'I'm really not an *honour*, you know.' Barely a sir, given my reputation.

'You are God's anointed, my lord,' Hallow declared, elevating me to the peerage and potential sainthood in one breath. 'Restored from the dead to reveal the mercy of the resurrected Christ our redeemer praise Him.' This said in a second breath, without pause.

I honestly could not think how to address that grave misapprehension. So I thanked him, and took the last draw on my pipe.

'Now, what are those deer about?' Hallow muttered, squinting at the herd grazing way off in the distance.

'I wondered the same. Do they not spend most of the day nearer the house, by the beech tree?'

'Well they wander about as they please. But it's a warm day, sir – best of the season. I'd expect them to stay close to the water trough in this heat.'

A dry day, and yet the deer were grazing a good quarter mile from the water trough. 'Mr Hallow.' I paused, as a thought sent a shiver down my spine. 'Would you walk with me, for a moment?'

I walked through the park towards the beech tree, the sun warm upon my neck. My legs felt heavy. I seemed to see myself as if from above, with Mr Hallow at my side. As if I were watching myself from a high window in the house. *Let me be wrong.*

We had reached the beech tree, its branches spread out as if in welcome. *Come and see. Come and see what lies here.* The stone water trough stood on a higher patch of ground, raised enough that I could not look inside without approaching the rim. It was a heavy, roughly hewn thing, made to sustain the bitter Yorkshire winters. Lichen clung to the sides.

It looked like a stone coffin.

Hallow had caught my darkening mood. He stopped at my side, and waited.

I took a deep breath. In this final moment, there was still a chance I was mistaken – that I would peer over the edge and see nothing but water. I'd been seeing death everywhere these past few days.

But the deer had crossed to the other side of the park in the heat of the day. I saw the great stag in the distance, its head raised, watching.

I stepped up to the trough and looked down. Put a hand to my mouth.

Jack Sneaton's body lay at the bottom of the trough. His mottled face was grey white, both eyes now staring blind through the water. There was a deep gash running across his temple, and the water was dark and clogged with blood. Floating all around him were the ruined pages of an accounts book.

'Oh no,' Hallow whispered. 'Oh no.'

I turned and walked away, back towards the house. I watched my feet taking one step and then another. I moved but felt nothing, not until I reached the front door and leaned my head against the wood. Here was the death I had brought with me from London. Here it was, spreading its cloak across the estate. And I knew, as I pushed open the door, that it was not done with me yet.

Chapter Eighteen

I had not cared much for Jack Sneaton in life. In death, I discovered him anew through the grief of others. He had been loved at Studley Hall, by the family and by the servants. I've heard it said that the spirits of the dead linger for a time before passing on to heaven or hell – especially when a life is taken in violence. If Sneaton's ghost drifted through the estate, it might have drawn comfort from the affection and sorrow it witnessed.

Here was Mrs Mason, inconsolable in the kitchen, weeping in Mr Hallow's arms. Sally Shutt, silent in her shock, sliding down the dank wall of her storeroom prison, legs collapsed beneath her. Up the backstairs to the great hall, where a footman bowed his head in prayer for the man who had granted him his first position. Through the empty drawing room to Mr Aislabie's study, the door closed. I had brought him the news first. He had covered his face and asked if I would leave the room. Now he sat alone, thinking about the man who had saved his son's life.

Up in her apartment, Lady Judith took my message with equal dignity. There had been one deep gasp of shock, breathed out slowly; a shiver as she crossed to the window, arms wrapped about her chest. She put her hands to the window and lowered her head, graceful in her grief. When she turned back she was a queen, cool and determined.

'You will help us find the killer.'

'I'll find him.' This was the man who had left Sam to die. *I would find him.*

Lady Judith heard the anger in my voice. 'And we will have justice,' she said, carefully.

Let her seek justice. I would have revenge.

Mrs Fairwood was sitting alone in the adjoining room, a pot of tea at her side. Her dainty feet did not touch the ground she was so tiny – so she rested them upon an ottoman. Her shoes were grey, like her dress, with dark red soles. I remembered Sneaton's face, grey-white in the water. The jagged red wound on his brow. The floor tilted beneath my feet.

'What is it that you want here, madam?' I asked.

She coloured at the abrupt question, but, glancing at Lady Judith, saw that something was amiss. She lowered her feet to the floor, watching me carefully. 'Nothing. All I want, *sir*, is to go home.'

'You are most anxious to leave Studley.'

She stood up. She held herself rigid, her dark eyes heavy with resentment. 'Of course I am anxious to leave. Someone set fire to my chamber this morning.'

'And yet you are still here.'

She gestured towards the adjacent room, where two footmen stood guard at the door. 'I have no choice in the matter.'

'Mrs Fairwood: you are not a mouse. If you truly wished to leave, you would be gone.'

'Do not presume to tell me what I would or would not do, sir. You know *nothing* of me.'

'None of us do,' Lady Judith murmured.

Mrs Fairwood, sensing she was outnumbered, softened her voice. 'I shall forgive your rough manner, sir. You must be concerned about Master Fleet. Does he rally? Has he named his attackers?'

'No. He is grievously ill.'

I thought I detected a flicker of relief in her eye. 'I am sorry to hear that.'

'What makes you certain there was more than one man?'

'What do you mean?'

'You said: *attackers.*'

Her cheeks coloured. 'I have no idea,' she said, taking a moment to recover. 'What – is my every word to be questioned? This is insufferable! I shall not be treated in this fashion.'

I let her fluster.

'Where is my father?' she snapped. 'He would never permit this interrogation.'

'Enough!' Lady Judith cried. 'You are not his daughter, you wicked girl. You may have bewitched him, but I know what you are. You want a slice of his fortune—'

'I want nothing from him! Do you think I would touch a fortune so tainted? What must I do, to prove it to you? Must I sign another waiver? Send for Mr Sneaton – I will sign a thousand of them.'

'Mr Sneaton is dead,' I said, not bothering to soften my words.

She stared at me, the blood draining from her face.

'He was murdered.'

She clutched her chair with a gloved hand. 'No.'

Nothing else. Just that one word: *no*, spoken in a hollow voice. Everyone else had asked questions. Where was he found? How was he killed? Was I *sure* he was dead? Mrs Fairwood asked nothing. She didn't speak and she didn't move, her hand wrapped tightly around her chair.

'Be assured, madam,' Lady Judith said, cool as an ice house. 'We shall discover his *attackers*. Meanwhile, I am sure you understand that we must ask all our guests to remain here at Studley.'

Mrs Fairwood opened her mouth to protest, then stopped herself. Her shoulders sagged. 'As you wish,' she mumbled, defeated.

Lady Judith followed me from the room, closing the connecting door with a soft click. She motioned for me to join her in the corridor outside her chambers, where we might speak without being overheard. It was a narrow space, and we were forced to stand very close to one another.

'*Damn* her,' Lady Judith cursed. She banged her fist against the wall in frustration. 'I should have stopped this nonsense the moment she arrived. But I was afraid. It is the one chamber of his heart he keeps closed from me, you understand? He spent so many years alone there, lost in his grief for Anne, and for Lizzie.' Tears welled in her eyes. 'That wicked, *wicked* girl. The damage she inflicts, just by her presence! She is like a climbing plant – like those horrid wallflowers she keeps in her room. She has spread her tendrils over him, she has wrapped them about his heart. What would happen now, if I tore her from him? Now that she has weakened him? I fear he would die,' she said, her voice breaking. 'Oh, God. I fear it would kill him.'

I put a hand upon her shoulder. 'Your husband is a strong man.'

She shook her head. 'In all but this. It is so cruel . . .'

I hesitated, not wishing to cause more distress. 'You are quite *sure* she is not his daughter?'

She laughed in disbelief, brushing the tears from her cheek. 'You cannot think her story credible?'

'There are some proofs, are there not? The ruby brooch? Molly Gaining's letter?'

She waved this away. 'The day she arrived, Mr Sneaton spoke to me privately. Her story was impossible. *Impossible*. He wouldn't explain why. He told me it would break John's heart. It had broken *his*.' She paused, upset. 'We came to an understanding. He would offer his proof only if John decided to acknowledge Mrs Fairwood in law, or introduce her to the children. We were sure he would come to his senses before then.' She sighed. 'I should have known better. How could he resist bringing his daughter back from the dead? In the very face of reason – show me a father who could.'

'What was this evidence, do you think?'

'I have no idea. And now it is lost, along with the ledger.'

'No – that has been destroyed. Whoever murdered Mr Sneaton ripped up the pages and threw them in the water trough with his body.'

I should have been more delicate. Lady Judith gave a cry of horror, flinging her hands in front of her face as if to defend herself from the image. 'Oh, God – poor Jack. Oh! You did not see the best of him, Mr Hawkins. I cannot bear to think of him dying alone and afraid. I shall never forget his face, when John dismissed him. So hurt, so proud.'

She began to weep again. I pulled her against my shoulder and did my best to comfort her. It was an honest grief and deeper than I had realised. Beyond the constraints of position and the niceties of society, lay a simple truth. Jack Sneaton had been her friend.

She broke away, rubbing her cheeks and offering me a rueful half smile. 'So the ledger is destroyed. John will be furious.'

And the queen would be delighted. Here was an unexpected consequence of Sneaton's death – I had accomplished my mission, without lifting a finger. The ledger was destroyed. John Aislabie could never again blackmail the royal family with its scandalous contents. The trouble was, I had planned to use the ledger to strike a bargain with the queen myself. Now my dreams of freedom lay sodden and ruined, floating in an old water trough. Sneaton's last vow had come to pass. *The queen will never get her claws on that book.*

'I fear I must go,' I said. 'I've been too long from Sam.'

Lady Judith rubbed my arm. 'You must let me know if you need anything. I confess I have grown rather fond of Master Fleet. Unaccountably so.'

We smiled at each other – affection born from a shared purpose, and a shared enemy.

We did not realise that we were being watched. Bagby was an experienced servant, trained to be discreet. We didn't hear him pause at the far end of the corridor, just as Lady Judith touched my arm. We didn't know that he saw our shared smile – an innocent moment that became something altogether more sinful in his eye.

It is from such small, silly misunderstandings that tragedies are born.

Kitty had already heard the news of Sneaton's murder from one of the servants. She knew very little of him, save that he had broken Sam's nose, and prevented us from leaving. She was shocked, then, and sorry to a degree – but she was not about to don a mourning gown.

Sam lay tucked under layers of blankets, just as I had left him an hour before. Kitty said he had stirred once or twice, and muttered something she couldn't catch. He was not sleeping, it seemed, nor was he awake, but caught somewhere in between.

I waited at his bedside, thinking about the stags ordered by Metcalfe from his family estate. I thought of his reaction upon finding them on the front steps, laid out to form the Robinson coat of arms. Had this all been a ruse, to throw suspicion elsewhere? Could he have attacked Sam, and Sneaton? Could he have sent those notes to his uncle, disguising his hand so well? None of it seemed possible. But then again – how well did I know Metcalfe Robinson? I must have met at least three or four versions of him in the last twenty-four hours.

Sam shifted under the blankets, and moaned quietly.

I took his hand. 'Sam. Can you hear me? You're safe.'

His lips moved, silently.

'Thirsty,' Kitty said.

I reached for the pitcher of small beer standing close by and poured him a cup. He managed a few sips before collapsing against the pillow. His eyes were half open, twin pools of black beneath thick lashes.

'Brother,' he whispered.

I squeezed his hand. 'Who did this to you? Can you remember?'

He winced, and swallowed. 'Picture.'

His eyes fluttered, then closed.

I glanced at the picture directly in front of him, over the hearth. 'The abbey?'

He frowned, and swallowed. 'Picture. Brother.'

Kitty had left the bedside, slipping into Sam's cupboard room. When she came back, she was clutching a piece of paper. It was the portrait Sam had sketched of me on the journey from London, dark charcoal shadows dense about my shoulders. 'I think he wanted this, Tom,' she said. She placed it on the table by the bed, then leaned down and brushed her lips to Sam's forehead. 'Rest, now,' she whispered.

*   *   *

It seemed to me, walking through the east wing's dank corridors, that one person sat at the heart of all this violence and confusion. I knocked hard upon his door.

'Metcalfe!'

There was no reply. I tried the handle and the door swung free. A gust of stale air assaulted me: the stink of sweat and dirty sheets. I stood alone in the chamber, observing the chaos of his room. It told me nothing.

And so I left, brooding, silently and with a wrong turning found myself upon the minstrels' gallery, looking down upon the great hall. Aislabie had gathered the household together, and the room was packed tight with people. The servants were there, and the family, and the estate workers from the gardens and the stables. John Simpson stood with his arms folded, surrounded by his men. Mrs Mason was leaning on Mr Gatteker. Francis Forster was there in the crowd too, holding his feather-trimmed hat to his chest.

Mr Aislabie was addressing them all from the landing, standing in front of the faded horse tapestry with Lady Judith at his side. For a moment, I didn't recognise the gentleman standing with them in his black suit, hands clasped behind his back. And then my lips parted in astonishment. Metcalfe Robinson: looking every inch the baronet's son and heir, from the black ribbon of his pigtail wig, to the diamond-studded buckle of his shoe. He stood with his chin high, gazing down his nose at the crowd below, his expression grave.

'Jack Sneaton was the best, most Christianlike of men,' Aislabie said, his voice fractured by grief. 'We may all take comfort, knowing that he is now at peace. But I promise you, I will not rest until I have found the murderous cowards who took his life. I will see them hanged for what they have done – you may count upon that. And I would ask that if anyone has information, that they come forward in good conscience and speak of it. My nephew has offered to conduct enquiries on behalf of the family. He will speak with many of you, and I would have you give him all the help he needs. May God protect us all.'

He was about to walk up the stairs when Lady Judith put a hand upon his arm, and whispered in his ear. Aislabie frowned, then addressed the room again. 'Some of you may have heard that our guest, young Master Fleet, was also attacked last night. I'm sorry to say that he is in a most grievous condition. I would ask you to pray for his recovery.'

'I won't pray for that devious little shit!' someone shouted, invisible in the crowd.

'Who said that?' Aislabie snapped.

The servants and estate men began to mutter to each other, rumours spreading through the hall.

Simpson shoved himself forward. 'That boy's been creeping about the estate ever since he arrived. Jack caught him and gave him a bloody nose – now he's dead.' He gestured towards the east wing. 'There's your killer, Mr Aislabie – breathing his last up there if we're lucky. May the Devil take his soul.'

'Begging permission, your honour,' Bagby said, growing confident now that Simpson had spoken his mind. His voice rose clear above the room. 'I believe his *guardian* should take the blame.' His eyes flickered towards Lady Judith. 'He's not to be trusted.'

Aislabie frowned at him. 'Mr Hawkins was locked in his room all night.'

'As you well know, Bagby,' Lady Judith scolded. 'You guarded his door. Now let that be an end to rumours—'

'Why was he locked up?' Simpson bellowed. 'Is he dangerous?'

'He's bad luck,' one of the gardeners called out. 'He died on the scaffold, then came back to life. It's not natural.'

'Mr Hawkins was saved by God!' Mr Hallow shouted.

'Or the Devil,' Bagby retaliated.

People began to shout over each other with their opposing theories – on Sneaton's murder and the state of my soul, and whether I might be a killer after all. My heart began to pound hard against my chest. Lies, rumours and accusations. I had heard all this before, when I was arrested for murder. I knew how swiftly a crowd could turn into a mob.

I pulled a pistol from my belt, cocking it beneath my hand to stifle the sound.

'Enough!' A voice cut through the din. Metcalfe raised his hands up over the crowd. 'Enough. Jack Sneaton was a good man and he will have justice. But spreading gossip and accusing men without evidence will not serve our purpose. Mr Sneaton deserves better from us all. Now please, good people – return to your work.'

Aislabie nodded his thanks to his nephew, then put a hand upon his wife's shoulder and guided her up the stairs towards their chambers. Metcalfe remained on the landing, watching the crowd drift away. I lowered my pistol, the sweat trickling down my back. If he had not spoken for me, I might have been facing down a riot. The question was, why had he done so?

He'd known I was watching from the minstrels' gallery. His eyes had searched for mine as he spoke. I could see no malice in them, but there was no warmth either.

The hall was empty now save for Francis Forster, who had waited behind. The two men shook hands, caught in a shaft of sunlight spilling through the window: Forster lean and trim in his fashionable suit, Metcalfe gaunt beneath his fresh clothes. Metcalfe glanced up one more time to where I stood before placing a hand on Forster's shoulder and leading him away towards the drawing room and out of hearing.

I leaned forward, resting on the rail of the balcony. Metcalfe's transformation into a serious-minded inquisitor was unsettling. Just as I'd begun to suspect him, he had seized control of the enquiries into Sneaton's murder. Where was yesterday's shambling, unpredictable, muddle-headed fellow?

The men who'd guarded the house last night had seen him walk out into the deer park, returning just before the fire in Mrs Fairwood's room. He claimed that he despised his uncle – and yet he'd spent the past two or three weeks under his roof. He had ordered three stags from his father's estate, but had seemed shocked by the display of their mutilated corpses upon the steps of the house. His behaviour had been erratic, even wild – causing concern among the servants long before my arrival at Studley. Now, in the face of a brutal murder, he showed restraint and authority.

Whoever killed Sneaton wanted to destroy Aislabie's life – public and private. With the ledger ruined, Aislabie had no bargaining power with Walpole or the queen. He would never return to government. This was something Metcalfe wanted desperately.

He could have started the fire in Mrs Fairwood's chamber, but I had no proof.

He could have killed Sneaton, but I had no proof.

He could be working *with* Elizabeth Fairwood, but ...

Damn it.

One thing I did know – if Sneaton's killer were not discovered soon, the accusations against myself and Sam would only grow stronger. We were strangers from London, and Sneaton had stood between us and the ledger. In the absence of proof, those two facts could be enough to bury us both.

Beneath me, Metcalfe and Forster had returned to the great

hall. They shook hands again. Forster, glancing up to the gallery, offered a hesitant nod and hurried away.

This left Metcalfe alone. He rocked back upon his heels to see me the better.

'You wish to speak with me,' I suggested.

A slight bow. 'I would be obliged to you, sir.'

When I reached the hall, he gestured to the brace of pistols belted at my hips. I unbuckled them and dropped them upon a table nearby.

His eyes flickered to my sword.

I hesitated.

'*I* am unarmed, sir,' Metcalfe said. 'This is not a duel.'

Oh, but it was. I placed the sword next to my pistols. We smiled at each other, polite and full of distrust. It was a shame. I liked Metcalfe, truly. But if I found he had hurt Sam … He might be unarmed, but I still had a dagger, hidden in my coat. One should always be prepared.

We stepped out together into the spring sunshine.

Chapter Nineteen

Metcalfe said that walking helped him to think, and so we strode towards the water gardens. I smoked a pipe, affecting nonchalance. The weather was golden, and I was sorry that Sneaton had not lived to see this morning. Metcalfe walked with his hands in his pockets, and said nothing until we reached the lake, a silver mirror in the sunshine. There were men planting nearby, so we crossed the wooden bridge over the lower cascade, where the roar of the water would cover our voices.

The stone sphinxes confronted one another from opposing banks, locked in an eternal gaze. The one on this side of the bridge was a younger version of her companion, with the same pearl necklace, the same neat blanket of hair spread across her lion's back. As I studied her imperious expression in the bright sunshine, I realised that this was a statue of Queen Caroline as a young princess. She was staring across the cascade at her older self – water rushing between them like the passing of time.

'Is it a fair likeness?' Metcalfe asked.

The queen as a sphinx? A lioness? Yes – I supposed it was.

'My uncle claims they were made in her honour, but there's spite in them, don't you think? The older woman forced to stare for ever at her lost youth and beauty?'

It was true that the queen had grown fat from years of childbirth and a love of sugared confections. But she was still a handsome woman, with one of the sharpest minds in the kingdom. The sculptor had captured this – by chance? – in the sphinxes' determined expression, steady and unchanging from youth to middling age.

'The ledger is destroyed,' Metcalfe observed, running a hand down the sphinx's back, the arrow tip of her tail. 'She will be pleased with you.'

Not pleased enough to release me from her service, I'd wager. 'Mr Gatteker tested your laudanum. He thought the dose of opium might be higher than usual. But you seem quite recovered from it.'

He stopped stroking the sphinx. In profile, I could see the resemblance to his uncle, though his cheeks were hollowed by weeks of poor living. 'Do I?'

'You couldn't possibly recover from such a powerful opiate in one night. You would be shaking and sweating in your coat.'

He shrugged. 'How is Master Fleet? Will he live?'

'You've been playing Hamlet, have you not?' I persisted. 'Pretending madness. Pretending laudanum sickness.'

He gave a half smile, but his soft grey eyes offered no answers. 'Tell me, did you order him to kill Sneaton?'

My heart stopped, just for a beat. Then I punched him hard in the mouth.

It was a perfect strike. Metcalfe flew off his feet, landing with a soft thump at the base of the sphinx. It was only luck that stopped him from dashing his head against the plinth. He lay on his back in a daze, all the breath knocked out of him. A garden boy dropped his rake and rushed over to help. 'I'm well,' Metcalfe said, staggering to his feet. 'Thank you.'

He wasn't well: there was a cut on his lip and he'd grazed his hands in the fall, but if a gentleman refused help, so be it. The boy dipped his head and returned to his work, glaring at me over his shoulder.

I leaned out and washed my bleeding knuckles in the cascade, the cuts stinging in the cold water. My hands were already scratched and bruised from my ride through the hawthorn bushes the day before. They did not look like the hands of an innocent man.

Metcalfe spat the blood from his mouth, then untied his cravat and pressed it to his lip. 'That was uncivil, sir.'

'You accused me of murder.'

'I accused you of plotting murder,' he corrected, 'with Sam Fleet. A boy you insist on calling your *ward*.' He sighed at the notion. '*I know what he is*, sir.'

I frowned at him. Impossible. He couldn't know that Sam was a killer. No one knew. I stared at him in defiance, heart thudding against my chest.

Metcalfe blinked first. 'I knew his uncle. Samuel Fleet.'

My jaw dropped. Sam's uncle, Kitty's guardian, my cellmate – rising up from his grave. What a long shadow he cast, for such a short man. 'How—'

'Our paths crossed when I was a young man. He was a friend to me.' Metcalfe's eyes hardened. 'And then he wasn't.'

Well, that certainly sounded like Fleet. And now I remembered a phrase Metcalfe had used the first night we spoke, sitting on the marble steps of the great hall. *I was sleeping. But now I am awake.* I'd thought it was from a play, or a psalm, but in fact it was something Samuel Fleet had said to me in the Marshalsea, rousing himself from his melancholy and into action.

'It didn't strike me until this morning,' Metcalfe said. 'But then I learned the boy's Christian name. Sam Fleet. Black eyes. Murder.' He laughed, without humour. 'How could it be coincidence? A broken nose would not go unpunished in that family.'

'So, because he is a Fleet, he must have killed Mr Sneaton? And then – what? – carried him to the water trough? Dragged himself halfway through the estate for no good reason, with a broken skull?' I stretched out my arm, pointing downriver towards the distant valley where I'd found Sam this morning. 'It is plain nonsense.'

The truth of this silenced him for a moment. 'Then *you* must have—'

'Don't you dare!' I warned, clenching both my fists. 'I was locked up all night. Sam was attacked because he knew who killed the deer.' I glared at him.

Metcalfe drew back, astonished to be turned from interrogator to suspect. '*Me?*' He began to laugh.

'Do you deny you left the house last night?'

'For a walk. I came here to the cascades, as I do every night. I find them soothing. The rush of water stills my thoughts. I become ... nothing.' He looked wistful.

'There was no one in the park, save for you and Sam.'

This snapped him from his reverie. 'That is not true, sir! The house was guarded by twenty men or more. Any one of them could have left his post without being seen in the dark.'

'Long enough to reach Sneaton's cottage, and kill him? Long enough to carry his body out to the water trough? All this and return without being missed? With no blood upon his clothes?'

'This is madness,' he groaned. 'What of the stags laid out upon the steps? They—'

'—came from your father's estate.'

Metcalfe froze.

'Mr Hallow rode to Baldersby yesterday. The keeper swears he sent them at your request.'

It took him a moment to find his voice. 'He spoke with Malone?'

'If that's the name of your father's gamekeeper – yes.'

Metcalfe swayed upon the spot. 'I think . . .' He swallowed. 'I think I must sit down.' His legs folded beneath him.

'Do you deny—'

'Grant me a moment, I beg you.' He bunched his fists into the grass as if he were gripping the mane of a runaway horse. He took a deep breath, and blew out slowly. 'I swear to you, sir, upon my soul: I sent no such request to Baldersby. I admit most willingly that I am a lamentable figure of a man. But I would never kill anyone. I abhor violence.' He touched his split lip with a reproachful air. 'Mr Hawkins, might I make a tentative observation? If I suspect you of murder, and you suspect me . . . it rather suggests we both consider *ourselves* innocent? In which case . . . well, I wonder if we might both be wrong in our suppositions.' He lifted his grey eyes to mine, brows raised.

He was right – assuming I believed him. I didn't want to. I wanted to grab him by the scruff of the neck, march him back to Studley, and proclaim him the villain. He had every reason to hate his uncle, every opportunity to commit the murder. But looking into his eyes, I knew that this was no act. He was innocent.

I sat down next to him on the riverbank, despondent. The damp seeped into the back of my breeches. A wagtail thrummed into the cascade and out again, ruffling tiny drops of water from its feathers.

'I am sorry that I punched you . . .' I said.

Metcalfe tested his jaw.

'. . . but you did accuse me of murder. And you must admit that your behaviour has been confounding in the extreme. This business with the laudanum. Wandering about the estate at all hours of the night. You *have* been dissembling, have you not? I mean – what *are* you about, Metcalfe?'

He gave a deep, exhausted sigh. 'Lady Judith wrote to me about Mrs Fairwood – asked if I would spend some time here and see what I made of her. In secret, you understand. She knew my uncle would be furious, if he found out. I agreed to a short visit. Rash of me. I was not well, in truth. Not myself.' He paused, fingers working through the mud of the riverbank. So this was how his nails came to be so filthy. 'Seeing you hang . . . it affected me more than I can say. Afraid I rather lost my senses over the matter. *That he should die and I should live . . .*'

'But we were strangers.'

He threw his hands up in a weary gesture, unable to explain the vagaries of his malady. 'I came to Studley to distract myself. Thought I'd spend a few days in pleasant conversation with a beautiful woman before revealing her as a fraud and booting her from the door. Metcalfe the Hero. For once.'

'But why would you help your uncle?'

'Oh, he's dreadful in a hundred ways, I know. It would be *disastrous* if he ever returned to politics . . . But he's not entirely rotten. And he lost his wife and daughter,' he added, his face softening in sympathy. 'I remember Lizzie as a baby. Tiny, merry little thing. Held her in my arms. Can you imagine such a loss? What could be more dreadful? Mrs Fairwood has played upon that grief all these weeks. She has raised his child from the dead. What a wicked, wicked thing to do to a man. What a cruel woman.'

'Perhaps she too has been deceived.'

He frowned. 'How so?'

'Is it not possible that Molly Gaining was indeed Elizabeth Fairwood's mother? She stole enough from your uncle to begin a new life, far away where no one would know her. Perhaps she married and had a daughter of her own. Could she not have grown confused in her final days? Think of the guilt that must have lain upon her all those years. She killed a young woman and her baby daughter. Would it be so strange if her mind shrank from such a terrible truth – most especially upon her deathbed? Perhaps she took solace in a fantastical tale, one where she saw not her own daughter at her bedside, but Lizzie Aislabie, all grown up. Saved from the fire she started.'

Metcalfe rubbed his temple. 'Possible. It would make Mrs Fairwood quite blameless. She certainly has no interest in my uncle's money.'

'No. She's repulsed by the very notion of being his daughter. I can't understand why she has remained at Studley for so long.'

'Ah – I believe I can answer that mystery at least. She is in love with Francis Forster. Do not look so astonished, sir!' he laughed.

'But he is the dullest man on the planet!'

'True enough!' Metcalfe was still laughing. 'My first night at Studley, he sat next to me at supper and never drew breath. Do you know, I felt my brain go numb. A most peculiar feeling.' He lifted his wig and rubbed his scalp. 'The more time I spent in his company, the more I became convinced he must be an impostor. I wrote to all the coaching inns along the Nottingham road, seeking proof about his accident.'

I sat up. 'Did you receive news back?'

'No, but I'm afraid I had become somewhat *erratic* by that point. My letters may not have been entirely sensible. Or legible. I am susceptible to dark thoughts, you see. Suspicions. Things become . . . disproportionate.'

'I understand.'

'Do you?' he wondered. 'I saw Forster with Mrs Fairwood on several occasions, walking around the gardens, deep in conversation. Day and night. Heads bowed close, you know. And instead of thinking, "Aha! Here are two lovers, struck with cupid's arrows", I

decided they were conspiring to destroy my uncle. Then that terrible note came, wrapped around a sheep's heart.' He shuddered. 'I
fell into the abyss, after that. Began to see plots and betrayals
everywhere. Couldn't trust anyone . . .' He glanced about him, and
lowered his voice. 'I've been trying for years to find evidence of my
uncle's South Sea dealings. The depths of his corruption. I thought
perhaps he'd learned of my enquiries and invited me here, through
my aunt, in order to drive me into madness. Set the entire estate
against me.' His eyes had taken on a haunted look.

'That would be . . . elaborate.'

He blinked. 'Yes . . . yes, I suppose you're right. I walk a narrow
path between truth and fancy. I'm afraid I stumbled into the
woods and lost myself for a while.'

'How long?'

'Oh, who counts the days?' he said, vaguely. 'I kept to my
room, in the main. Wandered out at night sometimes. I'd sit
here by the cascade and try to drown out my thoughts in the
roar of the water. Or I'd count the stars. Anything to stop my
mind turning about in endless circles. And in the end, I found
my path again.'

'I'm glad to hear it. So why pretend you were still . . .'

'. . . Mad as a lupin?' He sighed. 'It was a useful conceit. I
might come and go as I pleased without arousing suspicion. And
I knew my uncle would send me away once I was fit enough to
travel. It frightens him, you know. His brother suffered from
melancholic fits. Hanged himself when he was seventeen.'

'Mr Gatteker told me.' I thought of the portrait, banished to
Sam's cupboard room – the young man with the soulful eyes.

'Then you arrived. And the deer was left on the steps, with its
fawn. I feared things were reaching a climax. But I could hardly
spring up the next morning as if nothing had happened. I
thought if I told you I'd been poisoned, it would explain my

somewhat erratic behaviour . . .' He cleared his throat. 'I asked Mr Gatteker to lie about the laudanum. He knew I was pretending to be sick. He was the only one I confided in.'

'Oh! Then Marigold is alive after all? Mr Gatteker's cat,' I prompted.

Metcalfe brightened. 'I suppose she is! If indeed he *has* a cat. Let's say that he does. We deserve some happy news this morning.'

'Marigold is alive. And Mrs Fairwood is in love with Mr Forster.' I shook my head in wonderment.

'*Engaged!* Forster confessed all to me just this morning. Begged me not to tell my uncle. He's determined to secure a position at Studley first, upon his own merit. Poor fellow has no capital to speak of.'

'What a curious match.'

'Indeed! But then love is a curious business, is it not?' He sounded wistful.

I gazed out across the lake. The ducks were gathered close to the bank, dabbing at the water and tipping up to feed with their white tails in the air. The drakes looked proud and handsome, with their glossy green heads and neat white collars. The pheasants pecking at the grass were the same – the hens a dull speckled brown, while the brighter cocks strutted about, trailing their long tails. I thought of Mrs Fairwood in her drab grey gown, and Forster in his bright waistcoat and feather-trimmed hat. I thought of the deep cuffs on his coat, the fashionable pleats and gold wire buttons. And I understood at last.

A curious match, a curious couple, no doubt – but working with a common purpose.

We will seek Revenge.

Chapter Twenty

I leaped up from the riverbank and ran across the footbridge towards the house. Metcalfe caught up with me on the path, panting hard. 'Mr Hawkins?'

I seized a shoulder, thin and bony beneath his coat. 'Find William Hallow. Order him to ride at once to Baldersby. I must know who came to fetch the stags. A clear description, mind – age, bearing, clothes. Every detail.'

'I don't understand . . .'

'Forster and Mrs Fairwood. They plotted this together, with an accomplice. We must find him.'

Metcalfe gave a sharp nod. 'I will ride over to Baldersby myself. Dear God. My poor uncle . . .'

I squeezed his shoulder. Then I turned and raced back towards Studley Hall.

I was almost too late. Aislabie's carriage waited upon the drive, heavy with luggage. Bagby stood sentinel at the carriage steps, sweating in green velvet. Pugh sat above the horses, reins in hand. The grand front doors swung open and Mrs Fairwood hurried out, tiny and determined in a grey riding hood. She looked like a nun, running home to sanctuary. I left the path and took a short-cut across the deer park, boots sucking into the mud. 'Wait!' I cried, as Aislabie and Lady Judith appeared in the doorway.

'Wait!' I cried again, waving my hands in the air. I must have seemed quite wild.

It was enough for Aislabie to hurry down the steps towards Mrs Fairwood. 'What is this?' he snapped, as I reached them.

'She cannot leave,' I said, gathering my breath.

Aislabie bristled. 'I have made my decision. Elizabeth is not safe here – not until we find the killer.'

Mrs Fairwood dipped her head towards him in gratitude.

'If you send her away now, you will never see her again,' I said.

Aislabie ignored me. He led Mrs Fairwood towards the carriage, never once taking his eyes from her face. What a wicked spell she had cast upon him.

I stepped in front of them, blocking the way. 'Madam – I cannot let you leave.'

She scowled at me.

Lady Judith joined us on the drive. 'I do think it best if Mrs Fairwood returns to Lincoln,' she said, and then, more quietly to me, 'for all our sakes.'

'I have pressing news about Mr Sneaton's murder. It concerns Mrs Fairwood directly. Please. We must speak privately.'

The Aislabies exchanged startled glances. 'Very well,' Aislabie said, after a pause.

Mrs Fairwood was defiant. 'I will not be held against my will,' she declared, mounting the carriage steps. 'You have no power to keep me here.'

I stretched my arm across the carriage door.

She leaned towards me. Her hood shielded her face from the Aislabies. 'Please,' she whispered, her dark eyes searching mine. '*Please* let me go.'

I held firm.

Her expression hardened. 'Damn you,' she hissed. She dropped back to the gravel and stalked into the house, shoulders high, cloak billowing in the wind. I followed close behind.

Bagby glared at me as I passed, hands clenched at his side.

The library seemed the most suitable room for an interrogation, the place where Mrs Fairwood felt most at ease. She stepped stiff-backed to the hearth, disdainful and proud, and rested a slim hand upon the mantelpiece.

No one had entered the room this morning. The curtains were drawn, the hearth cold, the candles unlit. Sally was responsible for keeping the rooms in good order, and she was still locked up in the cellar.

Lady Judith drew back the curtains. The library faced north, but at least this allowed some light in from the yard. She stood by the terrace windows, watching Pugh free the carriage horses from their harness and lead them back to the stables. Mrs Fairwood had her books, Lady Judith her horses.

'Well, Hawkins?' Aislabie folded his arms. 'What is this news of yours?'

'Francis Forster.'

'What of him? Has he discovered something?'

'He murdered Jack Sneaton.'

He laughed, incredulous. '*Francis Forster*? He can barely lift his own cutlery.'

But I had kept my eye upon Mrs Fairwood at the fireplace. She had flinched at Forster's name. Now she groped for the nearest chair.

Lady Judith tore her gaze from the horses. 'Why do you suspect Mr Forster?'

'Oh, several reasons. His coat sleeves, for example.'

'What piffle,' Aislabie muttered, pouring himself a glass of brandy.

I held out my arm, tugging at the cuff of my coat. I'm fond of this coat, but the beaux of London would consider it a travesty. They have begun to wear deeper cuffs, ending above the elbow. Mr Forster owns at least two coats in the new style. He wore one last night at supper, do you recall? Sky-blue with gold wire buttons.'

'And this makes him a killer, in your eye? Because his coat sleeves are more fashionable than yours?'

'How can he afford to dress in such a modish way? He makes an inordinate fuss of being poor. That suit must have cost him fifteen pounds at least. More than that – he claims he has been touring Italy these past three years, where the fashions are quite different. He must have been in England for several months at least – and with money in his pocket.'

Aislabie frowned, and sipped his brandy. 'Ridiculous. The fellow's burned brown as a conker. Do you think a winter in England could scorch him to that shade?'

'His complexion is not the work of one season. I believe Mr Forster has been away from England for much longer than that.' I had continued to study Mrs Fairwood closely as we spoke. She was struggling to keep her composure, her eyes set upon her shoes. But she had lifted them once, when I mentioned Italy, her gaze drawn to the globe standing in the corner of the library. I remembered how she had toyed with it two days before, pretending very hard not to listen to my conversation with Sally.

People give themselves away at such moments. I have seen men at the gaming table concentrate so closely upon their opponents' game that they let their own wrists drop, revealing their hand. Mrs Fairwood had been turning the globe upon its stand, her fingers spanning the Atlantic. Back and forth between England and the colonies.

Had Forster truly spent three years on a Grand Tour? Or had it been seven years on a plantation somewhere, labouring under the burning sun? That would give any man a dark complexion. It would make even a short, small-boned gentleman strong enough to carry a stag upon his shoulders for two miles – if it did not kill him first.

'You are speaking in riddles, sir,' Aislabie complained, but he sounded less confident.

'Forster knows the pathways between Studley and Fountains Hall. He has explored and sketched the water gardens. He knows the workings of the house and the estate and may come and go as he wishes. He knows when the servants retire, and when Mr Hallow is ordered up on the moors to hunt for poachers, away from the deer park. And last night, when we retired to our chambers, he rode out into the estate, untroubled by your patrols. What time did he leave, would you say? Past eleven, was it not?'

Aislabie nodded, thinking hard now.

'The ride to Fountains Hall would take no more than a quarter hour, even in the dark. I'll wager my life he didn't return to Fountains until much later. My guess is that he attacked Sam first and left him to die by the river. Then he went to Mr Sneaton's cottage and forced him to give up the ledger.'

'But why would he do such a monstrous thing? I offered him patronage not two days ago. He will be working with Mr Doe on the follies this summer.'

Mrs Fairwood twisted in her seat, her face flooded with dismay. 'Is that true?' she breathed.

'Of course. He's a talented young man.'

Tears sprang in her eyes. She looked away, hurriedly, to the empty grate.

'No, you have it all wrong, Hawkins,' Aislabie said, emphatically. 'Forster's entire future rests upon my goodwill.'

'I don't believe he is thinking very much of the future,' I replied. 'More of the past. He does not want or need your money or your patronage. All he wants, sir, is revenge.'

Aislabie sighed heavily. Even now, he did not want to believe it. 'Then why kill poor Jack?'

'Because last night he learned that the South Sea ledger was in Mr Sneaton's possession. He also knew that Sam could betray his identity at any moment. He forced Sneaton to give him the ledger, and then he killed him. It was the book he wanted, not the man. By destroying the ledger, he destroyed your great dream of returning to power. You are the focus of a burning hatred, Mr Aislabie. He wants to see you suffer. He wants you to lose *everything* that is precious to you.' I glanced at Mrs Fairwood.

Aislabie shook his head, mystified. 'But he is such a gentle soul.'

'An act, I am sure. I believe something terrible happened to him – something connected to the South Sea Scheme. Perhaps his family was ruined.'

'This is not just!' Mrs Fairwood cried. 'You accuse an honest gentleman of murder, without giving him the chance to defend himself. Where is your proof, Mr Hawkins? Burned skin and gold buttons? Fie.'

'Quite so,' Aislabie agreed. 'There are too many "perhapses" and "I'll wagers" to this story for my liking. And how could Forster carry those stags through the park? His arm's broken, for heaven's sake.'

I had grave doubts upon that score. And what a convenient injury, that had left his right hand free for sketching, and every other bone in his body unbroken and unbruised. I had watched him galloping down the drive this morning. Surely he would be more cautious if his wrist and arm were broken? My guess was that he had bound up his arm to make himself appear weak, just as he had hidden his true character behind his dull conversation.

Which suggested he had always planned to commit violence, long before he arrived at Fountains Hall.

But I couldn't prove this, and such speculation would only irritate Aislabie further. 'We don't need proof. The three stags came from Baldersby Park. Mr Hallow investigated the matter on my behalf. I have not been *entirely* indolent,' I said, noting Aislabie's surprise. 'Forster's accomplice collected the stags from the keeper at Baldersby. Metcalfe is riding there now to secure a decent description. Once we have the fellow, we can persuade him to confess. A pistol to the head should do it.'

'Good,' Aislabie nodded, pleased with this at least.

'I'm sure you will be proved wrong,' Mrs Fairwood said, rising from her chair. 'But either way, I cannot see why this should delay my departure any longer. This has nothing to do with me.'

'I must congratulate you, madam,' I said.

This surprised her enough to make her turn, rustling in her grey silk gown. 'What do you mean?'

'On your engagement to Mr Forster.'

It took her a moment to suppress her shock. Then she clapped her hands together, as if it were a tremendous joke. 'Preposterous!'

'What is this?' Aislabie demanded. 'You are engaged to the fellow?'

'Of course not. I have no intention of marrying anyone. Where on earth did you hear such foolish nonsense?'

'From Mr Forster himself.'

She fluttered a hand to her chest. 'Then he has lost all reason. The very notion is repulsive.'

'A strong word for an *honest gentleman*,' Lady Judith observed, drily. 'Though I grant you he is not the most entertaining of supper guests . . .'

'We are not engaged,' Mrs Fairwood snapped. Had she been a child, she would have stamped her foot. 'Oh, this is not to be endured.' She closed her gloved hands about her throat as if she were suffocating. 'This place will kill me, do you not understand?'

I had placed myself at the door. Lady Judith remained at the terrace windows. 'You are in no danger here,' I said, 'not if you confess your part in this. You were coerced, were you not? You love him – but you are frightened of him, too.' She had told me the same, here in this room two days ago. *I am so afraid of him.* Love and fear – how often they were found together in one heart.

'Lizzie,' Aislabie exclaimed in concern. 'My poor child. Come here.'

She drew back. 'Leave me *be*. I am not yours to command. I will not be dictated to, and trapped. I will *not*.' She was breathing heavily in great gulps, chest rising and falling hard. 'I must leave. Why will you not let me leave?'

'Do you like wallflowers, Mrs Fairwood?' I asked.

She laughed frantically, and covered her face with her hands. *'Do you like wallflowers,'* she mimicked. 'Heaven spare me.'

'I notice that you keep a vase in your room.'

She dropped her hands. 'Yes, Mr Hawkins. I keep a vase of wallflowers in my room. I suppose you would see me hanged for it?'

'Did you pick them yourself?'

Her brow crinkled as she sensed a trap. 'I suppose I must have done.'

'Where did you find them?'

A long, careful pause. 'Somewhere out in the gardens.' She began to pace the room, fingers brushing along the spines of the books, groping for comfort.

Lady Judith glanced at her husband, and then at me. 'There are no wallflowers at Studley,' she said, quietly.

Aislabie put down his glass of brandy. 'They were your mother's favourite flowers, Lizzie. Perhaps that's why you are so fond of them. I cannot bear to plant them in the gardens. They remind me of her too much, even now.'

I hadn't realised this was the reason, but I had noticed that there were no wallflowers on the estate. I had only seen them once, since my arrival from Ripon – great patches of them, sprouting from the crumbling walls of a ruined monastery. 'They came from Fountains Abbey, did they not?'

Mrs Fairwood plucked a book from a shelf and began to flick through its pages. 'Oh, very well,' she said, as if it were of no consequence. 'Mr Forster gave them to me as a gift. They grow high upon the walls of my own garden, the same golden orange. I suppose I must have mentioned it to him in passing, and he was kind enough to bring some on his next visit. Is this your grave accusation, sir? Have I ruined my reputation by accepting flowers from a gentleman? Must I marry him now, or be shunned for ever by society?' She slotted the book back on to the shelf. 'Do *you* lecture *me* on dishonour, Mr Hawkins?'

'And when did he bring you the flowers?' I asked, mildly.

Mrs Fairwood opened her mouth, then closed it again, teeth biting her lip. Caught.

I turned to the Aislabies. 'Did you see Mr Forster bringing flowers to your home in the past few days? Did he mention them to you? If we asked the servants, would they remember him riding up to the house with a bunch of bright orange wallflowers in his fist?' I mimed one arm, caught in its sling, the other proffering a bunch of flowers.

Mrs Fairwood continued her tour of the library, the way an animal might test the bars of its cage. Her face was almost as grey as her gown. 'Wallflowers,' she muttered.

One can be undone by such small things.

'I have some sympathy for you, madam,' I said, following her with my eyes as she paced the room. 'You are trapped, and you are afraid. But Mr Sneaton has been murdered, and Sam . . .' I paused, unable to finish that thought. 'You must be honest with me. This must *stop*. You cannot protect him any longer.'

'Hold!' Aislabie exclaimed. 'Hold! What is this? You accuse them of conspiring together against me? Francis Forster *and my own daughter?*'

'You were seen,' I said, addressing my words to Mrs Fairwood. 'Meeting in secret, at night.'

'Impossible!' she cried, then gasped at her mistake. 'We never met,' she added hurriedly.

'Metcalfe saw you.'

She leaned her back against the shelves. She looked as if she would like to fling every book in the library at me. 'Metcalfe is mad. And you are a scoundrel. I have nothing more to say.'

'Very well.' I turned to Mr Aislabie. 'I would ask that you and your wife stay here with Mrs Fairwood until Metcalfe returns. If we release her, she might run and warn her lover.'

Mrs Fairwood curled her lip, disgusted.

'I will not stand guard over my daughter as if she were some low villain!' Aislabie protested. But for all his indignation, I saw uncertainty in his eyes. He was standing upon the precipice and refusing to look down. All his dreams, all his hopes, were about to be destroyed.

Which had been the plan all along, of course.

'Metcalfe will return soon,' I said. 'I ask only that you all wait here, together – and speak with no one else. Now – I must visit my ward. Pray excuse me.' I bowed.

'Of course,' Lady Judith said, crossing the room to take my hand. 'We are grateful to you, sir.' She gave her husband a sharp glance.

'I refuse to think ill of Forster,' Aislabie grumbled. 'You may have convinced my wife, but you have not convinced me.'

I had reached the door of the library when Mrs Fairwood called out to me. 'Mr Hawkins. I would speak with you a moment. In private.'

'As you wish.'

We stood in the narrow passageway and considered each other for a moment without speaking.

'How *clever* you are,' she said, with some venom. 'I should never have guessed.'

'What hold does Forster have upon you, madam? Are you truly in love with him?'

Her nostrils flared at such an abhorrent notion.

'You demanded this audience,' I said, gesturing about the empty corridor. 'What do you wish to say to me?'

She gave a bitter smile. 'I was on my way home. Do you understand? I was on my way home and you prevented me from leaving. So remember this.' She raised herself on tiptoes so she might reach my ear. 'You have killed me, Mr Hawkins. You have killed me.'

Chapter Twenty-one

'Tom no, I'm sorry, it is an interesting thought, but really you are quite wrong, there is no engagement. Come with me.'

I had almost collided with Kitty in the tattered corridors of the east wing. She had been in a desperate hurry to find me – bare-legged, no cap – snatching my hand and pulling me towards our chamber at a terrific pace. I had tried to explain about Forster and Mrs Fairwood – their secret love and plans for marriage – and received the critique relayed above. I should add that when Kitty said she found something *interesting*, she meant *ridiculous*, in the main.

There was no time to tell her about the rest of my ideas: about Forster's clothes, his years away from England, not even that Metcalfe had set out for Baldersby. We were at the ruined door of our chamber before I'd even finished complaining about being called muddleheaded.

Sam lay under a pile of blankets. His eyes were bruised and swollen from his beating the day before. Strange to think that the man who'd beaten him now lay dead. I feared Sam might soon join him.

'Forster is responsible for this, Kitty. I am sure of it.'

'As am I.' She had her back to me, shuffling through a sheaf of papers on the desk. The portraits of Mr Aislabie's lost brothers lay propped against the wall on either side of the hearth – George the debauched rake, and Mallory, the doomed melancholic.

'You agree? Then why am I *muddleheaded*? He confessed to Metcalfe that he was engaged.'

'Of course. Better that than admit the truth. I mean *really*, does Mrs Fairwood strike you as a woman swept away by passion?'

'She said the idea was repulsive.'

'So.' Kitty clapped her hands. 'May I tell you what I have discovered? *All upon my own here, abandoned for hours?*'

I sat down upon the bed. 'I'm not convinced it has been hours, Kitty . . .'

'I suppose not.' She was standing by the casement window, sunlight filtering through the branches of the oak tree. Little strands of her hair glowed bright as hot metal. 'And in truth, Sam helped.'

'He woke again?'

'Briefly. I'm not sure he knew where he was. He kept whispering "brother" – over and over. I thought at first that he was calling for you. But then I thought, Sam isn't prone to bouts of sentiment, is he? So I tried to rouse him again, but he had drifted away. He is very ill, Tom. I fear . . . Even if he recovers, I am not sure he will be the same.'

I touched Sam's hand, refusing to understand the meaning behind her words. He would wake, and he would be Sam again.

'Do you remember what he said earlier, about a picture? Well, then I had a perfectly *devious* idea about those portraits of Aislabie's brothers.' She gestured to the paintings by the hearth. 'I stared at them for *ages*, trying to solve the mystery.' She snatched up one of the paintings. 'Could poor Mallory have feigned his death all those years ago, only to return to claim his inheritance?' She lifted the second painting of the indolent, rakish George. 'What if wicked brother George sired a bastard son, now grown and seeking a *terrible revenge* upon the family? Or a bastard *daughter*, in the shape of Mrs Fairwood? I even tore off the backing paper to see if anything was hidden beneath.'

'And was there?'

'No.' She rested the paintings back against the wall and crossed to the bed, settling upon the other side of Sam. 'So I confess I was a trifle frustrated after that, and really Tom, I don't want to make a *fuss* about it, but I was a *little* cross with you for wandering off again, when I thought we had agreed that we are much better together, especially where *thinking* is concerned?'

I smiled at her, because she wasn't truly cross, and she was also right. We were much better together. I waved at Sam's sketches, strewn across the bed. 'Sam meant *his own* pictures.'

'He did! And if you consider how much Sam hates talking, and how we spend half our lives filling in the missing words for ourselves, then *brother picture* is practically an essay.' She sifted through the pictures, handing one to me. The borders were decorated with detailed sketches of pistols and swords from the great hall. A magnificent pair of antlers stretched along the bottom of the page, points sharp as daggers. The images intertwined like the margins of an illuminated manuscript: a dense thicket of deathly instruments, rendered with precision.

In the centre of the page lay charcoal studies of Mrs Fairwood and Mr Forster side by side. Forster was open-mouthed as if about to speak, his eyes bright with enthusiasm. Sam had caught Mrs Fairwood's imperious beauty with great skill: the frank disdain with which she viewed the world beyond her books.

I studied them both, shifting from face to face. And then the spell broke and I saw it at last: their great secret. I saw it in the shape of the eyes, and the bridge of the nose. The fullness of the top lip, the straight brow. They differed in their colouring, even beyond Forster's bronzed skin. But these subtleties were invisible in a charcoal sketch, allowing the similarities to leap to the fore. Sam, always watching, always noticing what others missed, had captured it with a careful hand.

Francis Forster was Mrs Fairwood's brother.

As an apology for abandoning her, I promised Kitty that she could announce her discovery to the Aislabies. 'But it must be gently done,' I warned. 'Aislabie still believes Mrs Fairwood is his daughter.'

'Why should we care?' she pouted. 'All those mean-spirited things he said to you. He locked us up in here.'

'I know.' I thought of Lady Judith's description of a climbing plant wrapped tightly around her husband's heart. I feared that if we did not remove it carefully, the shock might injure, if not kill him. Aislabie was in many ways an infuriating man, but I did not want his death upon my conscience.

Kitty saw the reason to this. She slipped her blade beneath her stomacher, the jewelled hilt forming a brooch at her breast. 'One must be prepared,' she said, tapping it into place.

Leaving Kitty to put on her stockings and shoes, I hurried down to the kitchens and asked Mrs Mason if she would sit with Sam for a while. She gestured to the meat turning upon the spit, the stew pans simmering on their trivets. She offered to send up one of the footmen, but I wasn't sure I could trust them – not until Metcalfe arrived from Baldersby with a decent description of Forster's accomplice.

'Is Mr Gatteker still here?'

'You've just missed him. He sat with Mr Sneaton until the coroner came. Poor Jack. Who would do such a wicked thing?' She gave me a shrewd look. 'I think you have a notion, don't you sir?'

I hesitated. If Forster knew he was suspected, he might flee the county before we could arrest him. But what if he should come to the house? Better if at least one of the servants were alert to the danger, and Mrs Mason was a trustworthy, sensible woman. I told her some of what I'd learned – enough at least for her to understand that Forster was dangerous.

'Heaven help us,' she whispered. 'Mr *Forster*? He's as thin as a barley stalk.'

'And tough as old mutton. Not your mutton, Mrs Mason,' I added hastily. 'Might Sally sit with Sam? How does she fare?'

Her lips puckered, tightening the deep lines around her mouth. 'She's still locked in the cellar. It's not like his honour. He's not been himself since the grey widow came to Studley.'

'Well it can't be good for her to be locked away, with those burns. Shall we say that I insisted you freed her?' I raised an eyebrow. 'Perhaps I told you that Mr Aislabie ordered it . . .'

Mrs Mason smiled. 'Perhaps you did, sir.'

Sally was so relieved to be released from her storeroom prison that she wept upon Mrs Mason's shoulder, holding her bandaged hands up to protect them. I smuggled her through the east wing, carrying a small tray of food for her, and a pot of hot chocolate. It was almost one o'clock, and she had eaten nothing all day, poor girl. Her face was red and blotchy from crying, and she looked even younger than her fifteen years.

She settled herself on a chair by Sam's bed. We had forgotten to tidy away his charcoal drawings, and, as she sifted through them, she found the portraits of herself, four upon the page. 'He saw me,' she smiled, eyes brightening.

Kitty squeezed her shoulder. 'Send word if he wakes.'

We walked down to the library together, taking a route through one of the horse rooms. There were no servants about, and our footsteps echoed on the boards. I could see a line of dents where Mr Sneaton had taken the same short cut to conserve his strength.

As we reached the back of the house we heard a commotion, and then the library door burst open. Mrs Fairwood ran from the room and out into the corridor. She stumbled in alarm upon seeing us, then jostled her way past us.

We ran after her. As we burst out into the horse room, Kitty leaped upon Mrs Fairwood's back, crashing them both to the ground. Mrs Fairwood took the force of the fall, crying out in pain as she landed upon her wrists. They wrestled for a moment, a little grey figure struggling beneath a girl ten years younger, used to brawling.

'How dare you!' Mrs Fairwood yelled. 'Help! Someone help me!'

Kitty drew the blade from beneath her stomacher and placed it against Mrs Fairwood's throat. 'We know you're his sister.'

Mrs Fairwood went limp. Kitty sat up, pressing a knee into her back to hold her down.

At the same moment Bagby rushed into the room from the great hall, while the Aislabies emerged from the library. Kitty slid her blade quietly back into her dress and got to her feet, pulling Mrs Fairwood by her arm.

'Mr Bagby!' Mrs Fairwood cried, fighting against Kitty's grip. She had lost her pinner in the fight, dark locks tumbling around her face. 'Mr Bagby, you must help me. I am being held against my will. Please, sir!'

Kitty swung her about. Lady Judith seized the other arm, and together they bundled their tiny prisoner back towards the library, while she dragged her feet and shouted to be set free.

Aislabie watched them, as if transfixed. 'I must protest . . .' he began, unsteadily. The last remnants of his dream were dissolving

ANTONIA HODGSON

in front of him. 'She ran from us,' he murmured, as if to himself. 'The first moment she could.' He glanced at Bagby, standing open-mouthed across the room. 'Leave us.'

'Your honour—'

'I said *leave us*, damn you!'

Bagby flinched, then gave a deep bow. As he raised his head, he threw me a look of such unambiguous hatred, I drew back a pace.

Aislabie prowled the room in a troubled silence. He came to rest at a painting of a solid, piebald pony. 'Best Galloway I ever owned,' he said, touching the frame. 'Called him Magpie, for his markings. I could name every one of his descendants. Half of them are dragging quarry stones to the new building today. I could name them all,' he repeated. 'I could look at any horse on my estate and tell you its line – back a hundred years or more.' He turned to look at me. 'Do you think I could not recognise my own child?'

I couldn't answer him.

'Is she my daughter? No, wait. Wait.' He covered his face with his hands. 'A moment.' His shoulders began to shake.

A storm of grief was gathering about him. He was losing his daughter for the second time, here in front of me. A girl brought to life only so she might die again. He dropped his hands, desolate. 'Who is she, if she is not my daughter?' he asked, quietly. 'Why did she come here?'

To break your heart, Mr Aislabie.

I put my hand upon his shoulder and led him back towards the library.

Chapter Twenty-two

Mrs Fairwood sat by the unlit hearth, seething in silence. She had injured her wrist in the fall, and was holding it with a reproachful air. Lady Judith stood with her back to the room, watching a group of men clustered in the yard. Kitty kept guard at the door. The space between the three women simmered with unspoken tension. Or, knowing Kitty, already spoken, at some length.

'They're taking Jack away,' Lady Judith said, in a quiet voice.

Aislabie joined her at the window, and watched his men lift Sneaton's body on to the coroner's cart. 'God rest his soul.' He bowed his head. 'He was a fine man.'

'*He was a liar.*'

The Aislabies turned as one, horrified.

Mrs Fairwood directed her words to me, standing over her at the mantelpiece. 'He swore that he had burned the ledger. He lied on oath.'

'On my behalf,' Aislabie said. 'To protect me and my family.'

'And himself,' she replied primly, still refusing to look at the man she had called Father. 'He must have known about the bribes.'

'They were not bribes. They were legal transactions—'

'Oh, *fie*. If the ledger was harmless, how did you blackmail the Queen of England?'

Aislabie fell silent. He had crossed to the middle of the room and was gazing earnestly upon Mrs Fairwood's profile. Even now, a small part of him clung to the fantasy that she was his daughter. He would not ask her who she was, not directly. While he did not ask, there was still the faintest chance it could be true.

It was time to end this cruel game. I glanced at Lady Judith, who gave a discreet nod. I took Sam's sketch of Forster and Mrs Fairwood from my pocket and handed it to Aislabie.

'What is this?' he frowned.

'They are brother and sister,' Kitty said, from the door.

Aislabie looked at the drawings for a long time without speaking. I heard the catch in his breath, when he saw the truth. I watched the hope drain from his face.

'She is gone,' he said softly. 'My little girl. She is lost to me again.' He took one last look at the picture, then handed it back to me without a word.

At the fireplace, Mrs Fairwood smiled in unashamed triumph.

I poured two glasses of brandy, and passed one to Mr Aislabie. His hand trembled as he brought the glass to his lips.

'Well, madam,' I said quietly. 'You have your victory.'

'Not victory, Mr Hawkins. *Justice*. If you knew what that man did to my family, you would understand.'

'I will not listen to this,' Aislabie muttered. 'I have been injured enough.'

'You *will* listen, sir!' Mrs Fairwood cried, springing from her chair. 'I shall not sit here in silence while you play the martyr. Lord knows I have held my tongue long enough – it is a wonder it is not bit through. Oh!' She threw her hands above her head. 'You dare say that *I* have injured *you*? When you *destroyed* my family?'

Aislabie drew back, silenced by her fury.

Lady Judith turned the handle on the terrace door and opened it with a gentle shove. A fresh breeze spilled into the library, billowing the gold damask curtains.

Her husband sank wearily into the chair by the desk, prodding at Metcalfe's papers. 'What a damned mess,' he muttered, sinking his head in his hands. But it was so much worse than that. Sneaton was dead, and Sam might follow him before the day was through.

Lady Judith stretched against the door frame, casting a wistful glance towards the stables. She was not built for waiting, not in body or mind. Like her husband, she preferred to be *doing*. All of these troubles, all this grief, would be better dealt with on horseback. 'When will Metcalfe return?'

I glanced at the clock upon the mantelpiece. 'Past two, I should think.'

'Well, Mrs Fairwood. We have time to spare. No doubt you wish to tell your story, and I should like to hear it. John?'

Aislabie looked as though he would like nothing less. But Mrs Fairwood's revelations had stripped him of his usual self-assurance. He sighed, and nodded to his wife.

'Very well,' Mrs Fairwood replied, infuriatingly regal. She had been turning her anger upon the fireplace, flinging kindling and coal into the hearth in a haphazard pile. Now she sat down by the fire she'd made – a feeble thing that belched grey smoke into the room. I sat down opposite her, clutching my brandy.

'Much of what I told you is true,' she began. 'My name is Elizabeth Fairwood, and I was brought up on the Lincolnshire coast . . .'

'Would that you had stayed there,' Aislabie muttered from the desk.

'My father was a gentleman – you might have met him at some gathering, or at Court. Sir George Ellory. Do you remember?' Her voice had a yearning note to it.

'I have no memory of him,' Aislabie replied, staring rigidly at the wall. 'But if he was a gentleman, as you say, then you have sullied his name.'

'I shall meet him in Heaven with a clear conscience.'

Kitty – still guarding the door – snorted back a laugh.

'Francis was born two years after me. We shared a tutor until he was sent away to school. After that, my father continued my education himself. My mother blamed him later, when I confessed my desire never to marry. But I have always preferred books to people.' She glanced about her, and allowed herself a brief twist of a smile. 'My brother did not share my preference. When he was nineteen, he fell in love with a girl from a neighbouring family. Maria Castleton. It was an excellent match. Her father had promised a settlement of five hundred pounds a year. But Maria was not yet sixteen. The families agreed it would be prudent to wait a year.

'But Francis was impatient to marry, as you can imagine. He became convinced the delay implied some doubt on the Castletons' side – though in truth they were very fond of him. He was such easy company, so cheerful and generous. I wish you could have known him as he was then.' She smiled at me. 'I believe you might have been friends.'

'Indeed? Was he not interested in architecture at this point?'

'Oh, it was always his great passion,' Mrs Fairwood replied, oblivious. 'He wanted to rebuild the house in Lincolnshire in the new style. He became quite obsessed with the idea.' She looked down at her hands. 'It is our passions that destroy us, is it not? We lose all sense, all perspective. Francis was convinced that the Castletons would respect him if he could show them some great accomplishment, something he had created for himself. He was determined to begin work on the house that summer. He spent every moment on his designs, barely eating, barely sleeping. The servants in our London home would find him slumped over his desk, half-delirious with exhaustion.

'He completed his plans as he had promised, and they were magnificent. The trouble was, he had not considered the *cost*. Francis was never sensible when it came to money. My father had encouraged him at first, but when he saw the designs, he was horrified. They were too elaborate, too ambitious: even with Maria's fortune, the cost was too great. Perhaps in ten or fifteen years, with a simpler design, it might be possible. Francis was furious. He said he would find another way to pay for it, without my father's help.'

'The South Sea Scheme,' I said.

'Yes.' She frowned. 'He was was one of the first to buy shares. He'd stayed in London when we all returned to Lincolnshire. We couldn't understand what kept him in town, when Maria waited for him at home. And then the letters began to arrive. He had invested in the South Sea Company, and had made a vast fortune overnight. And no, we must not fuss, because there was no risk! The Chancellor of the Exchequer himself had said so.'

She glanced over her shoulder. Aislabie kept his gaze upon the wall in front of him, his nails pressed deep into the green leather of the desk.

She turned back, lifting her eyes to mine. 'All through that summer, Francis wrote such feverish letters about his shares and how much he was now worth. It was all he could speak of. My father wrote back begging him to sell out before it was too late. Francis said the world had changed and that cautious old fools should keep their own counsel. And on paper he had amassed an extraordinary fortune. In one summer, he had earned enough to build a *palace*.'

'Then the bubble burst,' I said.

'*Then the bubble burst*,' she mimicked. 'Such a passive phrase, so free of blame. Let us not be delicate, Mr Hawkins. Let us not use *metaphors*. The South Sea Scheme was a fraud played upon the nation, and the men who promoted it are black-hearted thieves.'

Aislabie could endure it no longer. '*Not true!*' he cried, thumping the desk.

'Worse than thieves!' Mrs Fairwood shouted, rising to her feet. 'At least a highwayman has the common decency to admit what he is. You stood upon the floor of the House of Commons and you *swore* that we could trust the company's directors. You encouraged people to invest, even at the very end when you must have known the misery that lay ahead. Do not deny it, sir!'

'What should I have done, *madam*?' Aislabie snarled, defiant. 'How easily you judge me, when you understand so little. I promise you, Mrs Fairwood – if indeed that *is* your name – if I had even *hinted* of my concerns, there would have been a universal panic. It would have been a catastrophe, a hundred times worse than the one we suffered.'

'*We* suffered?' Mrs Fairwood laughed, incredulous.

'I had a duty to maintain order, to search for a safer path.'

'You had a duty to speak the *truth*.'

'And who would have listened? The world had turned mad. Do you know what the king said to me, when I advised him not to invest in more shares? He called me a timorous fool. *The king!* I might as well have shouted into the wind.'

'What specious logic is this?' Mrs Fairwood cried. 'You say you held your tongue to prevent panic – but claim that if you had indeed spoken out, no one would have listened?'

Mr Aislabie began to argue his case again, but I held up my hand to stop him. We might spend the rest of our lives in this room, debating the rights and wrongs of the matter – he would never admit to any fault, and Mrs Fairwood would never grant him any mercy. 'What happened to your brother, madam?'

'He was ruined,' she said, still glowering at Aislabie. 'He'd bought his shares on speculation. When the price collapsed he was left owing thousands of pounds. *Thousands.* My father had to sell most of our estate to pay the debts. Land we had owned for generations.'

'I am sorry,' Aislabie said, though he didn't sound it. 'But how does that give you the right to torment me and my family? Are you insensible to my own trials, madam? Is it not telling that John Aislabie – a commoner – was sacrificed to the fury of public opinion, while my noble colleagues were protected and promoted? I was thrown in the Tower! Stripped of office. Suffered every possible abuse to my reputation—'

'*Oh!*' Mrs Fairwood groaned, collapsing back into her chair.

I understood her frustration. Aislabie's insistence on casting himself as the victim in all of this was excessively tedious. Also – unforgivably – he had referred to himself in the third person. I thought it best to nudge the story along. 'Mrs Fairwood: why was your brother transported?'

She blanched. 'How . . . how did you know?'

It had been eight years since the South Sea calamity. Long enough for a man to be transported and serve his seven years of enforced labour, before returning to England. Seven years, slaving beneath a burning sun.

Mrs Fairwood's hand upon the globe, spanning the Atlantic, had offered me the first clue. After all, if Francis Forster sought revenge upon Aislabie, why wait for so long? But it was the puzzle of his broken arm that had convinced me – the bandage wrapped about his wrist and hand. 'He was branded, was he not?' I touched my left thumb, between the knuckles. 'They mark them here, with a letter. T for theft. M for murder.'

'Dear God,' Lady Judith breathed.

'The bandage was ingenious,' I said. 'Hid the brand and his strength at the same time.'

'Is this true?' Lady Judith snapped. 'Madam! Did you let a murderer into my home?'

Angry tears sprang beneath Mrs Fairwood's lashes. 'You refuse to hear me. I told you, Francis was a gentle, generous boy. That was his undoing. He'd amassed such a great fortune over that summer, but he couldn't persuade my father or Mr Castleton to invest. He decided to buy some shares in Mr Castleton's name. He never intended to keep them. He was going to present the profits to his father-in-law as a gift, at the wedding. Then the whole scheme collapsed and he couldn't sell them. His broker wrote to Mr Castleton, demanding payment.'

'How much was the debt?' I asked.

'Two hundred pounds. He bought them at the height of the summer.'

'And Mr Castleton had him charged for theft?' That seemed cruel. It was a huge debt, but the families could have come to an agreement without involving the courts.

'No . . .' Aislabie said, clicking his fingers '. . . I remember this story. I read about it, or heard it somewhere . . .'

Mrs Fairwood twisted in her chair, so she might seem him the better. 'You remember? Francis Ellory?' She glared at him until he lowered his gaze.

'I don't recall the name,' he muttered.

'Mr Castleton waived the debt, but it made no difference. Francis had bought shares in another man's name, signed legal documents. He was arrested for forgery and fraud. A hanging offence.' She paused. Took a deep breath, and continued. 'My mother collapsed when she heard the news. She was too ill to travel, so I accompanied my father to London. We must not despair, everyone said so. But the law . . . once a thing is set in motion, it can be hard to stop. *You* know this,' she said to me. 'The trial was set for November. My father wrote countless letters, tried every connection. Everyone offered the same advice – we must find someone in the government to support our case. So he wrote to you, Mr Aislabie.'

Aislabie covered his mouth. 'I don't recall . . .' But he did. I'd seen it in his eyes – a flash of guilt, swiftly hidden.

'You were still in office at that time. Imagine – the man who had ruined the country, *still* in power. My father begged you to intercede. You could explain to the judge the hectic madness of that summer. There was a good deal of talk about town, blaming the crash upon foolish young investors. But you knew that wasn't true. *You* knew who was to blame. Not the investors. Not poor Francis. But men like you, Mr Aislabie. Men like *you*.'

Aislabie's lips tightened. Of course he had received the letter, and of course he had not answered. To do so would have been to admit his own culpability.

'Two dozen men stood up in court to defend my brother's character, including Mr Castleton. It made no difference. He was found guilty.' She shook her head, tears in her eyes.

'But he didn't hang,' I said.

'No. How *lucky* we were. Seven years and a branding upon his thumb: an F for Felon.' She drew a deep breath, that turned into a shudder. 'I was there when they burned it into him. My little brother. I will never forget his screams. The smell of his flesh, burning . . . Then they put him in chains and took him away.'

Chapter Twenty-three

Mrs Fairwood insisted on a walk about the yard, to compose herself. She would not continue her story otherwise.

'You may accompany me to the stables,' Lady Judith said, icily polite. 'I wish to see how Athena fares.'

'You care of nothing but your precious horses,' Mrs Fairwood sneered. But she rose and drifted from the room, grey and silent as the shadow that trailed at her feet. Kitty gathered up her skirts and followed at a close distance. If Mrs Fairwood had plans to run, she would find herself stopped with a boot, or a bucket, or whatever else might be lying about the yard.

'How can I have been so deceived?' Aislabie said, watching from the terrace door. 'I never knew a woman could be so wicked.'

I took a sip of brandy. 'She told me she was afraid, the first time we spoke. Afraid of *him*.'

'You think she was coerced?'

'I believe so. More than her pride allows her to confess.'

'Hmm.' He looked at me for a moment, from the corner of his eye. 'You are not entirely without value.'

I clapped my hand to my chest, accepting the compliment.

He laughed, but it soon faded. 'Have you ever lost someone you loved, Hawkins?'

'My mother. A long time ago now.'

'Do you remember her?'

I turned the brandy glass between my fingers. Nodded.

'My children can't remember their mother. They were so young when she died. We never speak of her.' He sighed. 'I thought it best in the beginning. Now they have no memory of a time before the fire, not even Mary, my eldest. Sometimes I think I am the only one who remembers Anne, and Lizzie. Those brief days. When you lose a child, Hawkins . . .' He paused, and swallowed. '. . . it leaves a wound that never heals. The world forgot her, but I never did. I think of them both, every day.'

'Metcalfe remembers Lizzie.'

'He does?'

'He said she was a merry little girl.'

Aislabie's dark eyes lit up. 'She was. She *was*.'

Mrs Fairwood left the stables, heading back through the yard.

'*Look* at her,' Aislabie muttered. 'To think how many hours I wasted, studying the contours of that woman's face.' He returned to the desk, taking the bottle of brandy with him.

Mrs Fairwood arrived at the terrace doors, the bottom of her gown flecked with hay from the stables. She glided past me to the fire and brushed her skirts clean with a fastidious hand, dropping the hay into the flames. Her wrist, when not being observed, seemed to work perfectly well.

Kitty and Lady Judith had also stepped back into the library. The air had grown stifling, so Kitty and I swapped places – she stood by the fire while I guarded the door. Lady Judith was talking with her husband. 'Do you wish to rest for a time?' she murmured, stroking his back. He leaned into her for a moment, then shook his head.

I nodded to Mrs Fairwood to continue. She had left the fireside, drawn to a study of Byzantine coins left open on a table. She traced her fingers down the page. 'We could not stay in

London after the trial. My father brought me up to Lincoln in the hope of arranging a favourable marriage, as if I were some piece of livestock at a country fair. He wanted to secure my future, but I was terrified. Surely no decent gentleman would marry me, not now.

'The months passed and we fell deeper into debt. My father was in despair. My mother had not recovered from her nervous collapse: she lay in her bed at home unable to speak. A living ghost.' She shivered at the memory.

'And then Mr Fairwood proposed.'

'Mr *Fairwood*.' She turned a page on to a new display of coins. Grimaced. 'An *old* friend of my father. I will say this in his favour. He was very rich, and he never once touched me. We married on the third of October, 1721.' She slammed the book closed. 'The next day, my father hanged himself.'

Mr Aislabie turned in his seat, and looked at her. She stood with her knuckles pressed into the table, breathing heavily. Then she pushed back upon her fists, standing straight again. 'My father blamed himself for the family's ruin. He believed he should have ordered Francis back from London and forced him to sell his shares. He took his life out of shame. I pray for him every day. But I know that he is beyond the reach of mercy.'

'No one knows that, Mrs Fairwood,' I said.

She took a deep breath. 'For seven years I lived for one purpose: to see my brother come home. My mother could not travel, so we mourned and suffered alone. Her great wish was to live long enough to see Francis again, but she died two months before he landed at Portsmouth. Perhaps it was for the best.' She hesitated. 'The truth is, my brother never came home. He died the day they branded him. He died on the ship to Virginia. He died in the tobacco fields, when they whipped him like an animal. The man who returned, who wears those fine clothes you admire

– he is a stranger to me. The brother I loved is dead, like my parents.' She lifted her dark eyes to Aislabie. 'Because of you.'

'You are afraid of him,' I said, pulling out my pipe. 'This stranger.'

She clutched her arms. 'Yes.'

'But you agreed to help him.'

She looked down, her black lashes masking her eyes. 'Yes.'

I fixed my pipe, waiting for her to continue.

'Do you believe in Fate, sir?' she asked, at last.

I did not, but said nothing, breathing out a long trail of smoke.

'My brother sailed home last November. On the second day, he met a lady travelling alone. She wore this at her throat.' She touched the diamond and ruby brooch pinned to her gown. And then, pulling off her gloves, she unfastened it, and placed it upon the table. 'They fell into close conversation, the way strangers sometimes do on a long voyage. She told him that she had fled England when she was a young woman. Now she was dying. She had decided to come home and settle certain matters. She said she had done something terrible, many years ago, to a man named John Aislabie. She wanted to see him one more time, and beg his forgiveness.'

'Molly Gaining.' Aislabie's voice cracked as he spoke the name – for the first time in years, most likely.

Lady Judith reached across and plucked the brooch from the table. She handed it to her husband.

'I knew,' he said, long fingers tracing the diamond petals. 'I knew this was Anne's brooch.'

Mrs Fairwood watched him, unmoved. 'Molly died the night before the ship reached England. Francis believed that God had brought them together for a divine purpose: so that he might serve justice upon John Aislabie. The man who had destroyed our family.'

'You dare call this God's work,' Lady Judith breathed.

'Your brother forged Molly's confession?' I asked.

Mrs Fairwood hesitated, then nodded. 'He took some of her papers so he might copy her hand. By the time he reached London he had formed a plan: that I should pretend to be Elizabeth Aislabie, saved from the fire. I refused at first. I could not imagine doing something so bold. Francis swore he would never find peace otherwise. He spoke of nothing else, day after day: I thought I should go mad. In the end he said that if I did not help him, he would disappear and I would never see him again.' She pressed her hands to her chest at the thought.

'I insisted upon one thing: that he would first visit Studley Hall and effect some meeting with the family. I wanted him to be *sure* of the path he was taking. He did as I asked. He secured an invitation to Fountains Hall and he rode up from London. He saw the grand designs for your stables, and the scores of men working on your estate. He sat at your dining table while you spoke of your cruel treatment, and your determination to return to public office. He saw how you closed off the moors and pursued the men who had farmed there for generations. He saw all this, and then he wrote to me. And Mr Aislabie, after I received his letter, I decided that my brother was right. You deserved to be punished.'

Aislabie rose from his chair. 'Enough. I will listen no longer.'

Mrs Fairwood gave a thin smile. 'The truth is a bitter medicine.'

'Insufferable,' Lady Judith muttered.

Aislabie beckoned me to the terrace door. 'I shall ride to Ripon, bring the magistrate and his sergeants back to arrest Forster. Wait here for Metcalfe.' He gripped my arm. 'I want that *woman* guarded at all times, Hawkins.' He strode off towards the stable, boots stamping on the cobbles.

'Oh, what a relief!' Mrs Fairwood sighed, stretching out her arms. 'To be myself again.'

'You have no heart, madam,' Lady Judith said, softly.

Mrs Fairwood tweaked a dark, perfect brow. 'I pity you, Mrs Aislabie. It must be exhausting, defending your indefensible husband. But wives must be loyal, I suppose.' She crossed to the hearth. 'You are very quiet, Mrs Hawkins.'

She was – unnaturally so. Kitty was sitting in a green silk armchair by the fire, her chin propped in her hand. She had not spoken one word since Mrs Fairwood had returned to her confession.

Mrs Fairwood frowned at her. 'D'you know, I am sure I sprained my wrist in my fall.'

Lady Judith had no patience left. Leaving us to stand guard over Mrs Fairwood, she returned to the stables. Perhaps, like Gulliver, she expected to find more reasoned conversation among the horses.

And still, Kitty said nothing. Having finished my pipe, I had nothing to do but pace the room. There were still elements of Mrs Fairwood's tale that did not quite make sense to me. The fire, the threatening notes. I poured myself a fresh glass of brandy.

'*Another* glass,' Mrs Fairwood observed. 'Are you ever sober, Mr Hawkins?' She sat down opposite Kitty. 'Well, madam? What do you think of my story? Has it not stirred your sympathy?'

Kitty lifted her chin from her hand. 'Oh, no. I have just been wondering to myself how you will die.'

Mrs Fairwood gave a little start.

'There's a good chance you will hang, of course. Accessory to murder, that's the phrase is it not? Then there's theft,' Kitty counted this off on a second finger, 'as the deer were stolen. Or would that be termed poaching? The notes threatening murder, well, they are a hanging offence upon their own. And arson, of course,' she held up a fourth finger. 'You would have let poor Sally take the blame for that.'

'The chambermaid?' Mrs Fairwood shrugged.

Kitty glared at her. 'Sally Shutt. Fifteen years old, with no fortune and no family. You would have ruined her to save yourself. Doesn't that *stir your sympathies*, Mrs Fairwood? No, of course not – because *your* tragedy is the only one that matters. As if no one else has ever suffered as you have. I could tell you stories . . .'

'I—'

'What – you would have me weep for your brother? An arrogant prick who gambled away his family's fortune? And *you*. I should feel sorry for *poor little you*? You've preyed upon a father's grief for weeks! Oh! I could stamp on your head I'm so cross.'

Mrs Fairwood was confounded into silence. I doubt she'd been spoken to in such a raging fashion in all her life.

'Why did you start the fire?' I asked, once she had recovered. 'As a distraction?'

'Francis wanted Aislabie to know that he could not protect me – not even here in the house. He wanted to torment him. And he had promised a fire.'

'So you obliged him? You take your sisterly duty a little too seriously, I think.'

'You refuse to understand,' she muttered bitterly. 'Francis has kept me a prisoner here for weeks. He said that if I left Studley, he would tell the world what we had done. He would be hanged and I would be transported. He told me about the ships – how the guards would use my body. He described the vilest things. When I begged him to stop, he laughed at me. He said, begging does not make them stop, sister . . .' She clamped a hand to her mouth, rocking silently in her chair.

'He has lost his reason,' I said.

She nodded. 'I didn't realise at first. Before we came here, he would talk of the future. He said he would come home with me to Lincoln and build me a new house. He talked of Palladio, and Lord Burlington . . . But it was all a pose, a deception. He wanted me to believe he was still the brother I had loved, so that I would help him. But how could he be? The man you have met isn't real. The clothes he wears are a costume. The real Francis is cruel. The light is gone from him – and he cannot bear to see it in others. Worse – he takes pleasure in their suffering. It's the only pleasure he has, now. He feeds upon fear.'

'You're afraid of him.'

'Yes, very afraid. He was fascinated with how swiftly Mr Aislabie accepted me as his daughter. The boundless love of a father. He said, "Imagine if he found you dead. He would be sent mad with grief to lose you again in such a way. Think if I laid your corpse out on the coffin lawn, marked with flaming torches. How I should love to watch him discover you like that."' She gave a shudder. 'You took away my only chance to escape him, sir.'

'Don't you dare blame Tom,' Kitty snapped, still furious. 'You chose to come here and play the part of a dead girl. If you had stayed in Lincoln, we would be safe at home in London, and Mr Sneaton would still be alive. Sam would not be lying upstairs with a broken skull.' She rose and stood over Mrs Fairwood. 'You knew what he planned to do last night, didn't you? You argued with him, while we were playing cards.'

Mrs Fairwood shrank back in her chair. 'I begged him to leave before Sam gave up his name. He refused. He was so angry about the ledger. He said he would take it from Mr Sneaton, and then he would visit everyone on the list. Everyone who had cheated and escaped punishment. I didn't know what to do . . . I stayed up all night, praying to God.'

'Why not *speak* to *us*? We might have protected Sam if we'd known.'

'I thought he was safe with you! You were locked in your chambers.'

'And Mr Sneaton?' I asked.

She tilted her head, defiant. 'He should have told the truth about the ledger, instead of keeping it secret all these years. I'm sure I am sorry that he's dead, but I could not risk warning him. Francis could have killed me.' She drew herself up, discovering again her regal pose. 'I believe that God will understand my actions, and forgive me.'

Kitty raised an eyebrow. 'He might surprise you, Mrs Fairwood.'

There was a tap at the door. Two footmen entered the library, sent by Lady Judith. They looked excited and uncomfortable in equal measure. 'Begging your pardon, madam,' one of them addressed Mrs Fairwood. 'Her ladyship has ordered us to escort you to the cellar. For your protection,' he added.

'I see.' Mrs Fairwood gathered herself. 'I should like to take one last walk about the yard, if I may? Under escort, of course.' She gestured to Kitty and me.

In the courtyard, Mrs Fairwood clasped her hands together as if in prayer, walking slowly across the cobbles. Kitty and I followed close behind.

'She imagines she is Anne Boleyn, bravely facing death,' I muttered.

Kitty snorted. 'And we are her ladies-in-waiting.'

'Mrs Fairwood!' I called out.

She paused, graciously.

'Who aids your brother? He has an accomplice, does he not?'

Her gaze flickered to the back of the house. 'He told me it was one of Aislabie's men, but he wouldn't say which one. If I didn't know, I could never be certain when I was being watched. A footman, a groom ... I must play my part to perfection, at every moment. I cannot express to you the intolerable strain of being spied upon. Of suspecting everyone.' She continued her parade of the yard, chickens squawking at her neat little feet. 'Of course, he *might* be watching us even now.'

'And all he would see is a woman strolling through a yard.'

'Yes ...' She smiled, faintly. 'But if I am locked away in a *cellar* . . . He might decide to warn my brother.'

'Oh!' Kitty grinned without humour at this piece of cunning. '*Bravo*. So we should let you wander about the gardens instead, should we?'

Mrs Fairwood put a hand to her chest. 'I am only trying to help. If Francis escapes, he will take his revenge upon us all, for ruining his plans. You most of all, Mr Hawkins.'

It was impossible to judge. There had been so much deceit, we couldn't know for certain whether she was now telling the truth. Metcalfe would return from Baldersby soon. Could I risk waiting? Now I thought of it, all the servants would know that I had prevented Mrs Fairwood from leaving this morning, and had sat with her in the library in close conference with the Aislabies for over an hour.

If Forster received any warning of this, he would leave Fountains Hall at once. We might never see him again. Or worse, he might disappear for a short while and then hunt us all down in revenge. No – he must be secured as soon as possible.

I called to one of the grooms to bring me a horse, and he waved in understanding. It struck me that he could be Forster's accomplice. It might be any one of these men in the yard. Of course, that assumed Forster had told his sister the truth: that the man was indeed a servant. It might be someone at Fountains Hall. It might be *anyone*. I began to see how unnerving it must have been for Mrs Fairwood all these weeks, always wondering if she were being watched.

'Let me come with you,' Kitty said.

I shook my head. 'One of us must stand guard over her, until we know which servant colludes with her brother.'

'I won't run,' Mrs Fairwood said. 'Where would I go? It makes no difference now.'

The groom approached with Athena, apparently recovered from our adventures. We eyed each other warily for a moment, and then I swung up into the saddle. 'Mrs Fairwood,' I called down, once the groom had left us. 'Your brother's man. You must have your suspicions. Who is it, do you think?'

'I'm not sure,' she said. 'I wouldn't want to accuse someone unfairly . . .'

I frowned down at her, and waited for a better reply.

She sighed. 'Bagby. I believe it's Bagby.'

Chapter Twenty-four

I galloped hard to Fountains Hall, reaching Mr Messenger's home within a few minutes. Abandoning Athena on the carriage-way, I asked the butler to bring me direct to his master as a matter of urgency. God knows my expression, but he led me at once to a room at the back of the house, where Messenger sat with his leg raised on an ottoman, nursing his gout. Mr Gatteker sat with him, drinking a glass of claret.

I was relieved to see that Forster wasn't with them. It gave me the chance to explain myself, and ask for their help.

Messenger greeted me with some surprise, but politely enough through his pain. Gatteker had come to attend him, and to bring the news of Sneaton's death.

'God rest his soul,' Messenger rumbled.

Gatteker raised his glass in memory, then drained it.

'That is why I'm here, sir. Is Mr Forster at home?'

'Forster?' Messenger furrowed his brows. 'I believe he's down at the abbey, sketching again. Not in trouble, is he? I should be very sorry of it. Grown vastly fond of the fellow.'

I took a deep breath, and began.

'Dear God,' Messenger said when I was done. His fingers twirled a furtive cross against his chest. 'Dear God and all the saints.'

Both men looked shocked, but neither had questioned the truth of my accusations. It was as if – once I had given them permission to consider Forster afresh – their instincts confirmed his true nature. There had always been something off about the man.

'We shared breakfast together this morning!' Messenger exclaimed. 'He ate potted venison and sausages – and a jugged pigeon! Blithe as you please. A murderer at my breakfast table . . .' He struggled to his feet, yelping in agony as the weight passed through his knee. 'I must call the house together.'

'No, please – we must not alert Forster. Mr Aislabie will be here presently with enough men to take him. I only wish to confirm that he has not fled. He has an accomplice – one of the Studley servants, I believe. Could he have received warning, within the last hour or so?'

'No, no,' Messenger said, gripping the mantelpiece to hold himself steady.

'Ah – you may be mistaken, sir,' Gatteker interrupted. 'I passed one of Aislabie's men on the road. Thought he must be bringing the news about Sneaton. I said I would take the message myself, but he carried on his way without a word. I thought it strange, but then it has been a very strange morning.'

'And this was a Studley man?'

'Aye – it was Bagby. Aislabie's butler.'

It was a short walk to the abbey. I picked my way through the ruins, the ground a patchwork of high grass and stone flags tangled in weeds. Doves and pigeons fluttered in their nests and along the tops of the old walls, while the jackdaws eyed my approach, curious.

I ventured into the shadowed and cavernous cellarium, every footstep sending echoes to the vaulted ceiling. Lost feathers fluttered in the air, tufts of white and grey. Another turn and I emerged into brilliant sunshine.

Cocking my pistol, I stepped softly through a stone archway into the open square of the cloisters. There was no one there.

The ruins were the size of a small village, and Forster had spent hours sketching them. He could be hiding around any corner. I should leave, draw back until the magistrate arrived with his men. As I crossed the cloisters, I felt as though I were stalking not Forster, but the violence he promised. At the edge of the square lay four great arches. Three were flooded with light, the fourth was almost black with shadow. I hesitated, drawn to the darkest arch. I could hear Kitty calling at me to wait, to draw back. To *think*. My feet pulled me forward.

There was nothing there. The arch led to a short, dank passage, empty even of birds. I laughed at myself, under my breath. Beneath my laughter, I was disappointed. Where was he? Not in sunlight, not in shade.

I stepped through one of the three brighter arches, into a high-walled chapterhouse. The grass had been cropped here to honour the tombstones that covered the ground. Old monks, laid to rest centuries ago. A journal lay on one of the slabs, held down with a rock. I sensed, though I could not know, that it had been left for me to find. The hairs rose on the back of my neck.

I approached cautiously, expecting Forster to appear at any moment. Crouching down, I removed the rock and picked up the journal, flicking through the pages. There were neat sketches of the abbey and of Fountains Hall: scrupulously detailed notes about columns and windows, with measurements and perspectives. I turned to the next page and my stomach dropped.

It was a self-portrait. Forster stared from the page, mouth set hard. The precise lines of the previous sketches were replaced with savage shading and cross-hatching. He had drawn himself without his wig and hat, highlighting the sharp lines of his jaw and cheekbones until he seemed more skull than living man. Where his eyes should be, he had drawn two empty sockets, blood dripping from the wounds. His fingers curled about his head, covered in blood – as if he had seen too much, and ripped his eyes out in horror.

Upon the next page, Forster had drawn a winding riverbank, with a small dark figure lying sprawled upon the grass. Another page, and here was Sneaton, beaten and drowned in the water trough, deer grazing in the distance as if in some country idyll. The next drawing depicted his sister, Elizabeth Fairwood, laid out dead upon the coffin lawn in front of the banqueting house, flaming torches surrounding her. The darkest of fantasies, or worse: preparation.

The following page was blank, save for a message scrawled lightly in pencil at the bottom.

Hawkins – I pray you find this. You have Ruined all my Plans and you will pay for it. You think you are Strong, but I have survived Seven years of hell. I know how to make a Man suffer. You will beg me to end your Life before we are done. E.F.

I took a deep breath and skimmed the rest of the pages. They were filled with sketches of windowsills and door frames, and notes upon classical proportion. He had written that venomous note, then returned to his designs, in the same way he could murder a man, and then sit down for his breakfast, quite untroubled.

I tucked the journal in my pocket and strode back to Fountains Hall, deeply unsettled. Aislabie had just arrived from Ripon with a magistrate and a small band of men.

'He is fled,' I told them, and explained about Bagby.

Aislabie cursed under his breath.

'We should return to Studley and arrange a search party. He is not at the abbey.'

'He might be halfway to Scotland by now.'

'No, he is still here somewhere.' I showed him Forster's message. His body sagged as he read it. 'I'm sorry.'

'He has not killed me yet,' I said, sounding more cheerful than I felt. 'We know who and what he is, and we know his accomplice. We'll hunt him down.'

Aislabie tilted his head and gave me a swift, appraising look, as he had at our first meeting. Then he smiled grimly, and swung up into his saddle.

Back at Studley Hall, Aislabie gathered the house together for the second time that day. I stood with him upon the stairs and looked out across the white caps and gowns, the wigs and liveried suits, the rougher garb of the estate workers. Simpson and his men stood at the back, dusty with quarry powder. Work on the stables did not stop even for murder. Their boots had left muddy trails on the floor. I thought of Sally, scrubbing it clean again, then remembered she would not be able to work for a long time, with her burned hands. I searched for her in the crowd and found her standing with Mrs Mason. She caught my eye and gave a valiant smile, but the day had taken its toll upon her, and Mrs Mason had an arm wrapped about her waist to hold her steady.

Aislabie did not tell his household the full story – only that Mr Forster was suspected of Mr Sneaton's death, and that if anyone should spy him upon the estate, they were to sound the alarm at once.

'*Forster* killed Jack?' Simpson called out, incredulous. He sounded drunk again. 'That foppish prick? I'll bludgeon his brains out if I see him.'

'He is stronger than he seems,' I warned.

Simpson snorted.

'I must share further ill news,' Aislabie said. 'Many of you will have heard about the foul messages sent to me, and the butchered deer. This too was the work of Mr Forster, aided by a member of this household.' Aislabie waited for the room to settle. 'I'm afraid we have all been deceived by Mr Bagby.'

More gasps of astonishment. But I noticed Pugh cup his hand and whisper something to one of the grooms.

'Has anyone seen him in the last hour?' Aislabie asked.

No one had. Like Forster, Bagby had vanished.

Aislabie called upon the men to volunteer for a fresh search party. I offered to join him, but he needed estate workers – men who knew the woods well. 'I hoped you might ride out to meet my nephew. I am worried for him on the road alone.' He looked tired, his eyes rimmed red.

I bowed. 'Of course.'

I asked one of the maids to let Kitty know where I was headed, then hurried to the stables, where Athena was being relieved of her saddle. 'Leave her!' I called out.

Athena snorted at the sound of my voice, and danced against the reins. The groom murmured in her ear and she settled again, enough for me to catch a stirrup and swing into the saddle. Pugh walked over to me, leading his horse. 'You know the road to Baldersby?'

I nodded. 'If you find Forster, don't approach him alone. He'll kill anyone in his way.'

'I'm riding with Mr Hallow.' Pugh tilted his chin towards the head keeper, who was already in the saddle. 'Can't believe Forster would do something so devilish. Seemed such a mild-tempered gent. There's horses like that: good as gold . . . until they kick you in the teeth.'

'Bagby was less of a surprise to you, I think?'

'Bloody fool. He were furious when you stopped Mrs Fairwood from leaving. Took off at a rare old pace to Fountains Hall. Said Mr Forster would know what to do. Said he were the only honourable gentleman around here. Begging your pardon.'

'Not to worry. I had rather gathered that he disapproved of me.'

'He did have some *fanciful* notions . . .' Pugh hesitated. 'He thought that you were, ah . . . That *you and Lady Judith* were . . . Nonsensical o' course,' he added, skating gamely over my disastrous reputation, and her ladyship's shameless flirting.

I rode with Pugh down the path that ran along the east wing, thinking back over my three days at Studley. I could see now – with the eyes of a suspicious servant – how my behaviour might have appeared dishonourable. I had arrived at the estate without my wife, and moved myself at once to an abandoned set of rooms – the ideal place for illicit visits.

We passed the oak tree that grew outside my window. I thought of Sam balancing on its branches on our first day at Studley, barefoot and grinning. I should never have brought him here.

Hallow was waiting for us at the end of the path. He removed his hat and bowed in his saddle. '*Bagby*,' he said, incredulous. 'I'm so sorry your honour, I should have thought to ask for a description yesterday.'

'Peace, Mr Hallow. I doubt it would have made a difference.' Bagby was an unremarkable sort of fellow: middling height, brown eyes, neither handsome nor ill-featured. If he'd worn his liveried suit, that would have given us some clue, but most likely he had changed into rougher clothes to avoid notice. In which case, the description would apply to half the men on the estate.

'He was always a mutton-headed fool,' Pugh said.

'But not a *killer*.' Hallow shuddered. 'You didn't see the body. Devil's work.'

'I don't think Bagby killed Mr Sneaton,' I said, thinking of the sinister drawings in Forster's notebook.

'Maybe he was forced to help,' Hallow suggested. 'Blackmailed, even?'

'Maybe.'

But he had dashed over to Fountains Hall to warn Forster. That was not the act of a man forced against his will.

I turned Athena on to the carriage drive, waving goodbye to Pugh and Hallow. My pistols knocked against my side as I galloped along, and I kept a close eye upon the trees and bushes up ahead. The images I'd seen in Forster's journal flitted through my mind. So much cruelty, so much hatred: and all of it now focused upon me. I prayed to God that the search party found him before nightfall.

*

Francis Forster stands by a window in the east wing and watches the search party ride out, sees Hawkins pass by on his grey mare, deep in conversation. No one thinks to look back at the house. The threat lies out there, somewhere in the dark woods. He laughs softly, thinking of all the men hunting for him while he waits patiently in an abandoned room. Do they not know that he is the hunter?

It is the only decision one can make in this life: to be the hunter or the prey. The deer in Aislabie's park know it, every fox in its den. Man alone has forgotten Nature's greatest law.

Francis Ellory had been prey: on the boat to Virginia, in the tobacco fields. Forster chooses not to remember those first years. They were Ellory's memories, not his – and Ellory died a long time ago. It had been the only way to survive. Once Forster was born beneath

Ellory's skin, nothing could hurt him, because Francis Forster feels nothing. There is only the hunt.

Aislabie had been his prey, and he had come so close to destroying him. Forster closes his eyes, imagining the final scene again, as he has always planned it. Elizabeth, lying dead upon the coffin lawn, surrounded by flaming torches. Transformed from a weak, pathetic woman into a Goddess of Revenge. A death of such magnificent horror, she would be remembered for ever. And the Right Honourable John Aislabie, weeping insensibly over her dead body, sent mad with grief at losing his daughter not once, but twice. Tortured for the rest of his days.

It had been fascinating, watching Aislabie these past few weeks, trapped in his snare. How weak he was, how willing to be deceived. How desperate to protect his beloved daughter. Forster could have spent weeks tormenting him. More threats, more butchery. And a fire. Yes, I would have razed this house to the ground, before the end.

There would have been time enough to find the ledger, too – and to choose his next victim. A long list of the guilty, each one deserving punishment. He could have hunted them all, one after the other.

Hawkins had taken that pleasure from him.

Rage burns in Forster's chest, a pain he had vowed never to feel again. But all is well, all is well – he knows how to rid himself of it.

He has only to wait until nightfall.

A muffled sound brings him back to the room. He turns away from the window to consider the man gagged and bound upon the bed, his face battered and swollen.

'My dear sir.' He crouches in front of his prisoner. 'I am so grateful to you for bringing me here in secret. Your concern for Mrs Fairwood does you credit.'

Beneath his gag, Bagby begins to weep.

Forster frowns, considering. A hunter does not kill indiscriminately. There must always be a purpose to any death. But he made a mistake leaving the boy to die by the riverbank. Even now, he cannot say what stayed his hand. Some remnant of Ellory's weakness, no doubt. And something in the boy's black eyes: watchful and clear, even at the end. Forster had admired that.

He can't afford another mistake.

He pulls a dustsheet from a dressing table and lays it out on the floor. Then he sits down on the bed, shoulder to shoulder with his prisoner. 'This is all Thomas Hawkins' fault. Maddening fellow. I promise you this, Mr Bagby – he will suffer for it.' He reaches in his coat, and takes out a knife. 'I do hope that is a comfort to you.'

He wraps the body in the dustsheet, just as he had wrapped the doe with its fawn. It feels no different. In truth, he had felt more pity for the fawn.

He pulls out his watch. A few more hours yet. A shame there's no way to fetch something from the kitchens. At least he'd breakfasted well.

He lifts a chair and places it by the window, and settles down to wait.

Chapter Twenty-five

I had reached the outskirts of Ripon when I spied Metcalfe on the road ahead. He was travelling with one of his father's servants. Both wore pistols.

I was relieved to see him safe, and told him so. 'Forster has escaped. Your uncle is searching the estate.'

'I have a good description of his man.'

'A wasted journey, I'm afraid. We know it was Bagby.'

Metcalfe frowned, then winced. His top lip was cut and swollen from where I had punched him. 'Is that certain?'

'He ran off to Fountains Hall this morning to warn Forster. Now they are both disappeared.' We turned the horses about and headed for Studley. 'Does that not match your information?'

Metcalfe gestured for his companion to ride alongside us. 'This is Malone, my father's gamekeeper.'

'Fellow rode over two days ago,' Malone said. He was an Irishman of about five and thirty, with colouring close to my own: pale skin, dark brows, and keen blue eyes. 'Carried a note with him, looked enough like Mr Robinson's hand to pass.'

'Blotchy,' Metcalfe explained.

'I'm awful sorry, sir. I should've studied it with more attention.'

'Oh no, it is quite the sort of demented request I would make. You can't blame yourself, Malone. I'm an erratic wretch.'

Malone threw him a kind smile. 'There's no shame in a pinch of spontaneity, sir.'

'Those poor stags,' Metcalfe said, shaking his head. 'Butchered in such a dreadful fashion – and to what end?'

'I think Forster knew you suspected him,' I said. Metcalfe had not – to be fair – been entirely subtle about it. Forster's response had been cunning. Not only had the three stags frightened Metcalfe, they also led back to Baldersby, should anyone think to ask.

'Poor creatures,' Metcalfe said. 'Such a dreadful waste.'

'Oh! Did the meat spoil?' Malone asked.

'Mrs Mason has them hanging up somewhere,' I said.

'Well, then, no waste at all sir!' Malone observed cheerfully to Metcalfe.

I asked him to describe the man who had brought the note.

'He was a handsome devil, that's for sure. Tall as you are, sir, with powerful arms and shoulders. Hard muscles, like a work-horse. I joked with him about it – said he could carry two of those stags across his back at a time.'

I glanced at Metcalfe. 'That doesn't sound like Bagby.'

'Martin Bagby?' Malone laughed so hard it turned into a coughing fit. 'No – this was a young fellow, and strong-looking. An estate man, I'd say. Burned brown from the sun.'

'Was there dust upon his clothes? More than usual?' I asked, my heart sinking.

Malone thought for a moment. 'D'you know, I believe there was. And all under his nails.'

'Quarry dust,' Metcalfe said, catching my eye. 'One of Simpson's men?'

'Maybe.' I rode on in silence. I knew exactly who it was.

John Simpson was prowling about the foundations, watching his men with a narrow eye. From a distance, he always seemed an angry and intemperate master. Now that I ventured closer to the works, I realised that his bellowing was taken with good humour by his men, or at least with a patient roll of the eyes. He pulled a chisel from a mason's hand and worked the stone himself with an astonishing speed and skill. He was so engrossed in his work that he didn't notice me until I stood alongside him.

He gave a start, then removed his hat and gave a shallow bow.

'I'm after one of your men. Thomas Wattson.'

'Sent him home. Found him sobbing to himself in a corner. No use to me in that state. Jack was fond of the lad,' he added, more kindly.

'Where does he live?'

Simpson rubbed his mouth. 'Over near Kirkby Malzeard, I think. Bill!' he shouted out to an older man, tipping stones from a wheelbarrow. 'Where does young Wattson live?'

He scratched his grey stubble. 'Grewelthorpe?'

'Grantley, isn't it?' someone else shouted, while another man called out, 'Inglethorpe.'

Simpson shrugged. 'What do you want him for?'

'Oh, I only wanted to thank him for finding Master Fleet this morning.'

'You can thank him with a few coins. God knows when his lordship'll pay me, now Jack's gone.'

I asked him to send Wattson to me if he should see him – hoping the money might entice him. There was only the vaguest chance I would find him if he did not wish to be discovered – he had given at least three different addresses to his fellow journey-men, and he knew the area far better than I. Most likely he was with Forster – in which case the search party would find him. For now, let him think he was not discovered.

It made me angry, thinking how he'd deceived us. He must have known all along where Sam lay. Had he expected to find a corpse by the riverbank? And what of Jack Sneaton, the man he claimed to admire and respect? The man who'd been teaching him his numbers, helping him to improve himself? What a wicked betrayal.

I was about to take my leave of Simpson when I remembered something I had wanted to ask him. It was of no great matter now, but I was curious.

'Mr Simpson – do you remember your argument with Mr Sneaton? Two days ago, I think it was. When your man broke his leg. You mentioned something about the fire on Red Lion Square.'

Simpson pulled a handkerchief from his pocket and wiped his sweating face. 'No business of yours.'

I stared him down.

'Fuck,' he grumbled, and walked off, away from the building works and down towards the beech tree. He picked up a bottle along the way.

We stood beneath the shade of the tree. The drinking trough had been drained of the bloodied water, but the deer still kept away. I thought of Forster, carrying Sneaton's body out here in the dark. Had Sneaton died in his cottage, or had Forster drowned him in the water trough? Either way, it had been a horrible death.

'Might I trouble you for a drink?' I asked Simpson.

He looked dismayed – as all drunks do when asked to share – but handed over the stone bottle. God knows what it was: some sort of perilous cider, I think. Drinking it was possibly the most dangerous thing I'd done since arriving in Yorkshire, but I took a second swig, nonetheless. It had been a long day. I coughed my appreciation, and returned it to him.

'I promised Jack I'd never tell no one about this,' Simpson said, when I prodded him for his story. 'He only told me because he was drunk. He was ashamed, you see – not that he had need to be.'

'What happened?'

'You know half the story. How he ran into a burning building, and saved young Master William.' He took a long swig of scrumpy, and wiped his mouth. 'It were a terrible thing, the way he described it. He had to fight his way up through all the flames and the smoke. Beams collapsing all about him. Staircase burning out beneath him. But he found them both, up on the second floor. William and Lizzie.' He took another swig. 'They were trapped in different rooms. He only had time to save one and live himself. Had to make a choice between them. Must have been seconds, but he said it felt like the whole world stopped. As if God was watching him, he said – watching to see what he would do. He saved the boy. Maybe because the other two girls were safe. Maybe because William was just a baby. *Ach!*' Simpson waved away the reasons. 'Maybe there was no thought to it, only what he made up to explain it all later. Do you know what I think? I reckon he would have gone back in again and tried to save her. Jack was strong like that. But he fell – and then it were too late.'

That's how Sneaton had known Mrs Fairwood was a fraud. He'd been inside that burning house, and he'd made his choice. 'He was a brave man.'

'Brave as a fucking lion. He had nightmares about it for the rest of his life. Everyone called him a hero, but he never thought that. His leg, his scars, the pain – he saw it all as punishment. Well, he's at peace now, God rest his soul.'

We walked back to the stables. The sun was setting, and members of the search party were riding back across the park. No sign of Forster, devil take him.

'Jack were sweet on that girl, you know,' Simpson said, as we parted. 'The one that started the fire.'

'Molly Gaining?'

'He'd been saving up enough so he could ask for her hand. That's why he never married. She broke his heart.'

I needed warmth and comfort after that tragic story. I trudged up the stairs to our chambers and found Kitty there, waiting for me.

'Sam woke,' she said, rushing over to hug me. 'I told him you would be back soon, and he smiled. He understood me, Tom.'

I hugged her back. 'That's good news.' The first of the day.

'Have they not found Forster?'

'Not yet. And I don't suppose they will, now the light is fading. Kitty: we must be careful.' I took out Forster's journal, and showed her the message he had left me.

'He's turned mad,' she whispered.

'I ruined his great design. He's been building this grand edifice of revenge for months, now I arrive and tear it down in three days. He'll kill me if he has the chance.'

'We should leave, Tom. It's not safe.' She reached for my hand, frowning at my grazed knuckles.

I glanced at the bed. 'As soon as Sam is fit to travel.'

'That could be *days*! We could stand a guard about him until he recovers. Forster doesn't care about Sam any more. It's you he hates.' She pressed her palms together. '*Please*, Tom. Let's find a passage to Holland or France, spend the summer somewhere warm. We can send for Sam when he is recovered, if you wish. Then once Forster is caught and hanged, we can go home.'

Kitty knew how to fight, better than most. But she also knew when to run. And she was right: Forster aimed all his hatred at me now – not Sam. I leaned down and kissed her. 'We'll leave tomorrow.'

'Oh!' she cried, and flung her arms about me.

There was a knock at the door. It was one of the footmen, bringing the bottle of claret I'd ordered from the kitchen. And the spare I'd requested, just in case. Mrs Mason had sent up a large plate of muffins, with butter and damson jam.

'Oh bless you, I am almost collapsed with hunger,' Kitty said, taking the tray and settling it on the dressing table. 'I've never had wine and muffins together before.'

'I could bring you some tea,' the footman offered.

'No!' We both answered in unison.

I asked him to bring supper to our room at nine, along with some broth in case Sam woke up. I couldn't stomach a formal meal with the Aislabies after such a bleak day, and I doubted they would wish to sit stiff-backed in the dining room either.

Kitty opened the window, and we sat on the window seat eating muffins as the light faded to dusk. I told her about Thomas Wattson.

'No!' she cried, dismayed. 'I cannot believe it.'

'Why, because he named flowers for you?'

She rested her chin on her knees. 'He seemed so sorry about Mr Sneaton, and Sam, too.'

'Guilt, I suppose.'

'But why on earth would he help Francis Forster? Was he forced to, do you think?'

'Perhaps. Forster could have killed Sneaton on his own. Wattson was on patrol last night – if he'd stepped away for too long, he would have been missed. And he was certainly angry with Forster this morning.'

'So perhaps he helped with the notes, and the deer, but not the murder. Or did Bagby help him?' She crinkled her brow, confused.

'I don't think Bagby knew what Forster was doing. I think he saw us dragging Mrs Fairwood to the library and went to find a gentleman who would speak for her. Bagby doesn't trust me. He thinks I'm a dangerous influence on Lady Judith.'

'You mean he thinks you're fucking her?'

'Well, yes. For some unfathomable reason.'

Kitty snorted into her wine glass. 'So where *is* Bagby?' And then her smile faded. Because really, there were only two answers to that question. Either he had realised his mistake, and run away . . . Or he was dead.

We sat in silence as the sky turned a deep blue. The day was ended, and Forster was not found. I stoked the fire, studying the painting of Fountains Abbey that hung above the hearth. If I had set off sooner, I might have caught him there, placing his journal on the tombstone.

I crossed the room to sit with Sam. Could I really abandon him here tomorrow? I plumped his pillow, and saw that it was spotted with blood from the wound to his skull, seeping through his bandage. What if the wound festered? He could succumb to some putrid fever while Kitty and I were on the boat to France, all on his own with no family to care for him.

'Tom?' She had been watching me.

'We can't leave him, Kitty. I'm sorry. I know what I said before . . . we just can't.'

She pulled off my wig, and kissed the top of my head. She had always known, in her heart. I could never abandon Sam.

He stirred beneath the blankets, and his eyelids fluttered open. I leaned forward, eagerly. 'Sam. *Sam.* It's me.'

An impatient look came into his eye. *Evidently.*

'Was it Forster who attacked you?'

His breathing turned jagged.

'We'll find him, don't worry. Did Wattson help him?'

'Yes.' Breathed out in a whisper. He winced, and closed his eyes.

We talked to him for a while, telling him that he was safe and that we would take care of him. It was hard to know what he heard, and he soon drifted back into sleep. But seeing him with his eyes open, and able to understand me, gave me hope that he would recover.

The footman brought supper at nine, as promised. There was no fresh news of Forster or Bagby, and the final remnants of the search party had returned at last light. The house would be locked up soon, and men put at every door. There was nothing more to be done tonight.

So we ate supper and finished the last of the wine, speaking softly so as not to wake Sam. Then Kitty slipped a hand into the band of my breeches, and pulled me into the cupboard room, and on to the bed. I took off her gown, and she shivered in the cool air until I covered her, and the heat rose between us. We pushed away the death and horror of the day and lost ourselves in a narrow room, with one candle burning by the bed.

'Tom, you are taking up the whole mattress, you great oaf.'

I propped myself on my elbow, and traced a familiar path of freckles down her porcelain white skin. She was naked, save for the poesy ring she always wore about her neck, and the diamond-studded ring on her finger. She had shifted it to her left hand.

'Mrs Hawkins,' I said.

She yawned, and said nothing.

I lit a pipe and we smoked it together. I told her what Simpson had said about the night of the fire, and how Sneaton had been in love with Molly Gaining.

'What a shame. Just think: if he'd said something, she might never have started the fire.'

'He must have been too shy.'

'I suppose. But to live the rest of his life all alone . . . it seems such a waste.'

I didn't see it that way. Sneaton had lived alone, but people had loved and admired him, and mourned his death. That, surely, was the sign of a life lived well.

The bed was too narrow to lie upon together for very long. So we dressed and looked in on Sam. Kitty found Forster's sketchbook lying on the table and flicked through it, gasping with revulsion when she reached the self-portrait. 'Look how he has drawn his teeth,' she said, holding it up.

I frowned at the image, the black and bloody sockets and blade-sharp cheekbones. His teeth ended in sharp points, like a wolf's. I took the journal from her and threw it on the fire. Bright flames curled about the pages, destroying those terrible images. Elizabeth Fairwood dead upon the coffin lawn. Sneaton's corpse floating in the water trough, surrounded by pages from the ledger.

Paper burned by fire, paper ruined by water. I had pulled the ledger from the water trough and it had disintegrated in my hands. The names of the guilty lost for ever.

And as I thought of it now, I wondered . . .

'Kitty. Why would Forster destroy the ledger?'

She gasped, understanding at once. 'He *wouldn't*.'

I'd seen the pages floating on the water, and thought of them as a flourish – and another act of revenge. With the ledger destroyed, Aislabie could no longer use it to blackmail his way back into power. But Forster had been desperate to find the ledger, for the list of names it contained.

'He must still have it,' Kitty said. 'Unless . . .' Her eyes lit up.

Unless Sneaton had refused to hand it over. I grinned. Of course he'd refused. The book was still hidden somewhere. If I could find it, I might still free myself from the queen's service. Yes – I would have to search one of the largest estates in Europe. Yes, night had fallen. And yes, damn it, there was a distinct chance that Forster was still out there and would murder me while I was poking about the bushes. But what is life, without the odd gamble?

I kicked the wall. Even I could see it was impossible. Sneaton could have buried the ledger anywhere. I could search for years and never find it.

'Never mind,' Kitty said, pouring me a glass of wine. 'At least Mr Aislabie thinks it is destroyed. That should satisfy the queen.'

'Hmm.' I thought of what Sneaton had promised the day before: that the queen would never get her claws on the ledger. True enough ...

I clapped my hands to my head, and laughed at a joke made by a dead man.

The queen's claws.

The ledger was buried with the sphinx.

'It's too dangerous,' Kitty said. 'You can't wander about the estate alone at night, Tom!'

I buttoned my waistcoat. 'If I wait until morning there will be a hundred men out in the gardens. I can hardly dig the damned thing up in front of them. I have to go tonight.'

'No, you don't! For God's sake, wait a few days. Why must you be so *impatient*? It's perfectly safe where it is.'

'We need it now, Kitty. Tonight. What if Sam rallies tomorrow? We must be ready to leave at once.'

'Tom, you can't go out alone, you *can't*. Francis Forster is waiting for you in the woods. He'll *kill* you.'

'Aislabie's men spent half the day searching the estate. I doubt he's within five miles of Studley. And he won't expect me to be wandering about in the dark.'

'No, because only a screaming lunatic would do something so stupid.'

I put my hands on her shoulders and kissed her forehead. 'Enough.' I had to go, and she knew it.

'Fuck, fuck, *fuck*.' She pulled her boots out from a corner. 'We'll go together.'

'We can't. You need to stay with Sam.'

'*Ugh!*' She stamped her booted foot, quite hard. 'Why don't *you* stay with him? And *I'll* go down to the river, as it's so *perfectly safe*. I shall take a basket of cakes and drink tea by the cascade.'

We both laughed. 'At least take Metcalfe with you,' she said.

'D'you know, that's a capital idea. We'll take a sphinx each.'

'*No*. Stay together. One of you on lookout for Forster. Honestly – how much wine have you drunk?' She clomped over, one boot on, one boot off, and kissed me. 'Oh, go, go – then you will be back the sooner. I shall fret *horribly* until you return.'

Metcalfe was in a clean silk nightgown, a crisp white cap on his head. He had been clearing up his room: the window stood open to freshen the air, and the piles of dirty clothes had been sent to the laundry. He drew in his brows as I explained about the ledger and the sphinx.

'Should we not wait a few days?'

'Sneaton must have left instructions for your uncle some-where. It won't be long before he finds them.'

Metcalfe grunted, acknowledging the truth of it. 'Is it safe, do you think – to be gallivanting about the estate at night?'

'Probably not.'

He rubbed his clean-shaven jaw. 'Let me find my boots . . .'

I'd lied to Kitty, up in our chamber. I could have asked one of the servants to stand guard over Sam, while we headed out across the park together. The truth was, I thought there was a strong chance that Forster was waiting for me out in the woods – and I hoped to lure him out. I am a restless soul, and I couldn't bear the thought of sitting trapped indoors for days until Forster was found. Much better to confront him, tonight. I had a brace of pistols, a sword, and a dagger – and for all Forster's strength and cunning, I was a foot taller than him and knew how to fight. Face to face, the odds were in my favour.

Metcalfe roused Malone, who had bedded down in a room above the stables. The horses shuffled and stamped as we lifted a couple of spades from the stalls. In the courtyard, everything was peaceful, the chickens locked up in their coop. Two of Aislabie's men were patrolling the yard with dogs, lanterns swinging on long poles. They hurried towards us as we reached the yard door, which opened on to the woods beyond. It was locked. Metcalfe squeezed my shoulder, and put a finger to his lips.

'Sirs!' one of the guards called out. 'The house is locked up for the night.'

Metcalfe drew himself up tall. 'We are not chickens.'

The guard looked at his companion, then back at us, perplexed.

'*We are not chickens,*' Metcalfe repeated, more slowly. 'We refuse to be cooped up all night.'

'Mr Robinson, sir – it's for your own safety.'

'How dare you!' Metcalfe puffed out his chest. 'Am I to be cosseted and condescended to in such an ignominious fashion? This is not to be endured. Remember your station, you disobedient wretch.'

'Mr Robinson, sir—'

'*Unlock this door at once.*'

The guard did as he was told.

'Malone. We'll need those lanterns.'

Malone was carrying the spades. I took them from him, and he took the lanterns from the guards, who were not at all pleased.

'Should we ask for the dogs?' Metcalfe asked me, from the corner of his mouth.

'Best not press our luck,' I muttered.

We left the courtyard in a procession, Metcalfe leading the way with one lantern and Malone at my back with the other. We kept to the main avenues, our boots crunching on the gravel. Let Forster hear me, if he was hiding out there in the woods. Let him come. I was ready for him.

But he was not in the woods. And he was not waiting for me.

It was past midnight when we returned, jubilant with success. We had found the ledger in an iron strongbox, buried at the foot of the older sphinx. We had worked together under the stars like grave-diggers, Metcalfe quoting *Hamlet* and Malone singing ballads.

I had hoped to encounter Forster on our way back – the three of us together could have caught him easily enough. But I was satisfied at least to hold the ledger in my hands. It felt damp, and the pages were a little foxed – but the writing was legible.

Metcalfe peered over my shoulder, tutting over the names. 'Look at them all,' he said. 'Shameless villains. Tens of thousands of pounds. They robbed the nation dry. Can you imagine such a thing, Malone?'

'D'you know, I think I can, sir.'

Malone went back to the stables, Metcalfe to his rooms, and I carried on up the stairs, holding my freedom in my hands. The *true* accounts of the South Sea Company. The bribes given, the free shares. My Lord this, my Lady that. Right Honourables and Most Reverends. Half the current government was implicated – along with the king himself.

The queen would do anything to keep this from the world. She could never blackmail us again.

'Kitty!' I called, throwing back the ruined door and holding up the ledger in triumph. 'I have it!'

The room was empty, and very still.

Someone had thrown a white sheet over Sam's face.

A chair had been knocked to the ground.

I strode to the cupboard-room door and peered into the gloom. 'Kitty,' I said. As if saying her name would conjure her to me. I stepped back into the chamber. It was not possible, none of this was possible. I had the ledger: we were free. I had *won*.

Where was she?

I lifted the chair by the hearth and my heart lurched. I heard myself say: No.

There was a trail of blood running across the floorboards. A bloody handprint on the wall.

I dropped to my knees, reaching a trembling hand to touch the blood on the floor. Bright red and wet. Gasping for breath, I wiped my hand against the chair to clean it. My head was pounding. I forced myself not to panic. It was only a small patch of blood. She was alive. She had to be.

I caught something glinting in the far corner by the window and crawled towards it. Kitty's brooch-dagger. The blade was smeared with blood. She had fought him – of course she had. I shoved it in my coat pocket and staggered to the bed.

I stood over it for a moment, afraid of what I would find beneath the sheet. And then I cursed myself for a coward, and pulled it back with one swift movement.

Sam lay with his eyes closed, lips parted. White bandage wrapped over his black curls.

I crouched down and put a hand to his chest. He was warm. Thank God in Heaven, he was warm – and breathing.

'Sam.' I shook his shoulder. '*Sam.*'

He groaned, and opened his eyes.

'Where is she?'

A tear slid from his eye.

A hollow feeling opened up inside me. I looked again about the room, and saw a piece of paper nailed to the painting of Fountains Abbey. I tore it free, my hand trembling. It was a sketch Sam had made of Kitty. She smiled out at me from the page, curls loose about her face. Beautiful.

Beneath it, Forster had left a message.

We are waiting for you, Mr Hawkins. Come alone.

Chapter Twenty-six

The abbey was black against the night sky. I held out my lantern, a golden light in the dark. The ruins were quiet now that the birds were gone. I could hear the River Skell somewhere to my left, and feel the west wind pulling at my coat. I groped my way over the broken walls, searching for the tombstones, where Forster had left his journal. He wasn't there.

I turned about me in the silence. If I called out, there would be no hope of surprise. I moved the pole into my left hand, and drew my pistol. Nothing stirred. Where were the old ghosts tonight, the monks who had worshipped here for centuries? Fled into the stones, drifted away upon the wind. I was alone, with nothing to guide me but one candle, and a million stars high in the heavens.

I found myself in the cellarium, beneath its vaulted ceiling. The lantern cast great shadows over the brickwork. It was a long room, full of echoes, with any number of wide pillars to hide behind. I ventured slowly down its length, my feet scuffing against the stone. It felt as if I were walking down the throat of some great beast.

A noise behind me made me turn. 'Who's there?' I hissed, circling blind. Something rustled, and then in one terrible motion, a thousand bodies rose up as one. Bats. I dropped to the ground as they rushed around me, squealing and flapping in a huge cloud. I covered my head with my hands, feeling the beat of their wings like soft breath on the air.

And then they were gone, leaving nothing but silence, and a faint, acrid scent. I rose to my feet, shaken. By some miracle, my lantern was intact. I picked it up and walked down through the nave, alone beneath the towering stones, the open sky.

The aisles were empty. Only the chapel remained unsearched, and the great tower looming up ahead. A perfect half-moon hung above it, silvering the stone.

It will be the tower. The highest point of the abbey. He will want the drama of it.

I stood in the transept, the heart of the old church. This was where the first stones had been laid, and men had worshipped for centuries. I groped for the cross that hung about my neck and sent a swift prayer to the heavens. *Please God. Let her be alive.*

The entrance to the tower stood to my left, black and silent. It must have been magnificent once. Now it was a hollow shell: no stained glass in the windows, no floors, no roof. I raised my lantern and stepped inside. Craning my neck, I glimpsed a flickering light near the top of the tower. There must be a platform running along that wall, though I couldn't see it from the ground.

'Hawkins.' Forster's voice drifted down. 'Join us.'

Us. She lived.

In the far right corner of the tower stood a door, studded with iron. I wrenched it open and took the lantern from its pole, thrusting the light ahead of me up the winding stone steps. In my haste I had forgotten about Wattson until this moment. If he were here, if he were crouched waiting for me on the stairs above, I could do little to defend myself. But what choice did I have?

The staircase ran up the full height of the tower, the steps worn and crumbling. I had run from Studley House all the way to the abbey, and I was soon out of breath. I stopped upon the landing where the second floor had once stood, and which now opened upon a black void. This would have been the place for an ambush: Wattson could have grabbed me and shoved me over the edge before I could even fire my pistol. He was not here. I swallowed hard, gathering my strength, and hurried onwards.

After another fifty steps I reached a narrow wooden door. The light had come from this level. I was almost at the top of the tower, just below the belfry. I turned the ring handle and pushed open the door, shielding myself by the wall. No shots were fired; no one rushed through and kicked me down the stairs. I stepped out with my pistol raised.

I could see two figures huddled together in a dark corner, up ahead to my right. It was too dark to see their faces.

'Forster!' I yelled.

He didn't reply. I held out the lantern to guide my way, then shrank back against the door frame.

There was no floor. All that remained was a wooden platform no more than a foot wide, running along the wall from this door to the opposite corner of the tower. There was no rail or rope at its edge, only a straight drop to the ground a hundred and fifty feet below.

Directly beyond the door lay a small stone landing, leading to the platform. I put one foot upon it, testing my weight. The stone was dry, but there were weeds and moss growing on the surface. I would need both hands for balance. I lowered the lantern and slipped my pistol back in its belt. Tore my wig and hat from my head and threw them back down the stairs. Then I lifted my back foot through the doorway and on to the landing.

This alone was terrifying. The tower was cathedral high, the wind roaring through the empty windows and flapping the edges of my coat.

I took my first step on to the narrow platform. The wooden board bowed and rocked, but held firm. I pressed my back against the wall and stretched out my arms, inching sideways like a crab. Even with my heels to the wall, my feet only just fitted upon the board.

As I drew closer to the belfry window I heard a slight scuffle and then a voice. 'Tom!'

Kitty.

'Tom, go back!'

There was another scuffle, then silence.

It was agony. We were no more than twenty feet apart, but even the slightest misstep could be fatal. The wooden platform rested on a series of stone brackets. If I balanced towards my toes, the board tipped dangerously towards the yawning dark. Twice I thought I would fall, only to slam back hard against the wall, fingers clawing at the stone. There was no time to think of attack or defence, only the next step, and the next.

I reached the belfry window, clinging to the nearest stone mullion with a desperate relief. The wind was wild and bitter up here, howling through the empty window.

'No further,' Forster commanded. I heard the shuffle of footsteps as they moved slowly towards me. Forster had left his own lantern in the far corner, but I could see the white sleeves of Kitty's gown, and flashes of her skirts, and the darker shape of Forster behind her. They walked the platform head on: I could hear the wooden plank lifting and knocking against the stone brackets.

And then they were in front of me, with only the window between us. Kitty's face, lit by starlight.

Forster had a pistol pressed to her temple. His left arm, free of its sling, was wrapped tightly about her waist. I could just make out the brand upon his thumb.

He grinned at me in mad triumph.

'Are you hurt?' I asked Kitty.

She shook her head, then winced. He must have stunned her with a sharp blow. It was the only way he could have brought her all this way without a fierce struggle.

'There was blood.'

'*His*,' she spat. 'I sliced him—'

Forster lowered his lips to Kitty's ear, and bit down hard. She screamed in pain, trying to pull away. I took a step closer and he lifted his head, pressing the pistol harder into her skin. I could see blood trickling down her neck. Blood on his lips.

'Animal!'

He wiped his mouth, and smiled at me, as if I had paid him a compliment. It was the strangest thing, to see the dull gentleman transformed before my eyes. The form was the same, and the features: but the spirit . . . my God. I understood now why he drew himself with vacant holes for eyes. His spirit was as black and desolate as the endless drop below us.

'Throw your pistols over the edge,' he said. 'And your sword.'

I hesitated.

There was a sharp click as he cocked his pistol.

I pulled the weapons from my belt and tossed them away. Drew my sword and let it fall. They were no use to me here.

'You wear a dagger,' he said. 'Take it out.'

I cursed silently, and eased it from my coat pocket. I had to fight the urge to run at him with it: he could fire his pistol before I'd taken a step. I held it up for a moment, then flung it away.

'What happened to you, Forster?'

I was hoping to distract him – beyond that I had no plan. We were trapped together on the narrowest ledge: Kitty could not struggle free without falling, and I couldn't reach her. But Forster had no desire to talk about his past.

'They branded you, I see that. Stole the life you could have had. I know how that might feel. I was sentenced to death for murder—'

'I don't care!' Forster screamed. 'I don't give a damn about you. I had a plan. A beautiful, wonderful plan. And you *ruined* it.'

'Yes, *I* did. *Me*. So let her go.'

'Oh, am I not playing *fair*?' he mocked. 'How rude of me.'

'What is it that you want?'

He gripped Kitty's waist tightly and whispered in her ear. 'I could throw you from this ledge at any moment. Whenever I wish.'

'Then I'll pull you down with me, you fucking arsehole.'

He laughed. 'I like your wife, Hawkins.'

'What do you want?'

He licked his lips. 'I want you to jump.'

My heart lurched.

'No, not jump,' he corrected himself. 'I want you to step off the ledge, slowly, with your eyes open. Facing all of that.' He tilted his chin towards the darkness beyond.

I gripped the window frame.

'Would you do that?' His voice had a hungry, urgent edge to it.

'Of course not.'

'Would you do it *for her*?'

I stared at him, understanding at last.

He grinned. 'Would you die for your wife, Hawkins?'

I glanced up at the moon. One half black, the other half a blazing silver. I loosened my grip on the window.

'Tom, no!' Kitty hissed.

'Let her go. Let her go and I'll do it.'

Forster laughed again, high and wild. 'There is no deal to be made, Mr Hawkins. You must do as I say. You must trust me.

Walk off the platform now, and I will set her free. You have my word.'

'Your word is worthless.'

'So be it.' He twisted on the board and it tilted, rocking them together towards the edge. Kitty screamed.

'No! Wait!'

'Tom, don't!' Kitty lifted her arm, trying to reach me.

'Promise me you'll let her go,' I shouted at Forster. 'Swear it – on your father's soul.'

'I swear.'

'Tom don't, don't,' Kitty sobbed.

I turned upon the ledge, facing the drop below. My heart was beating so hard I could hardly breathe and my legs were trembling. But I was ready. What else could I do? I took a half-step forward, my feet hanging over the edge. Don't look down. Look straight out. Face Death and do not flinch.

Forster began to laugh. A high-pitched, gulping laugh, aimed up at the heavens. 'You would do it!' he marvelled. 'Truly! You would throw yourself from a tower to save her. Without even knowing if I would keep my word. Oh, this is wondrous. Step back sir, step back!'

I didn't understand my reprieve, but I was not about to argue with it. I flung myself back to the wall, fingers grasping the mullion again, my knees almost buckling.

'You don't understand revenge, do you Hawkins? A quick death, what is that? How could that ever satisfy me? I could have killed Aislabie the second I met him. Where would have been the pleasure in it? The justice? I spent seven years in hell because of him. He had to suffer, he *owed me* his suffering. That would have been fair, do you not see? Forster's eyes were full with a wild, desperate longing. 'Imagine the grief, the agony of losing his daughter for the second time. If he had seen her murdered, stretched out upon his coffin lawn. It would have destroyed him. You stole that from me!' he screamed, spit flying from his mouth. 'You stole my revenge! So now you will suffer in his place. You will live, wishing you were dead. You will live, and your wife will die.'

And with that, he pushed Kitty a few inches in front of him, and fired his pistol at the back of her head.

The world stopped. I must have screamed, I suppose. I know that I reached out, and the platform knocked beneath my feet. There was a great, blinding flash, and smoke, and Kitty stood, eyes wide, illuminated in the flare.

I lived a thousand years in that moment, knowing I had lost her. I felt the grief well up inside me before she was even gone, anticipated the life I would live without her, bitter and grey.

And then, as the moment passed, I realised that a pistol did not flash that brightly, nor cause that much smoke – unless it had misfired.

That is the trouble with pistols. They are wayward, unreliable things.

Forster stumbled, blinded by the flash, snatching at Kitty's arm for balance. She staggered backwards with him. In a quick, desperate move I grabbed the front of her gown with my left hand and pulled her into me, locking my right elbow around the stone mullion.

I looked down and saw that Forster had fallen half off the board, his legs dangling over the edge. As he tried to pull himself back up, it lifted and slammed back upon its bracket. Kitty called out in terror. If the board fell, we were lost: we could not cling to the window for ever.

'Go!' I yelled at Kitty. We had to get back to the tower door before he was on his feet. At least there we wouldn't plummet to our deaths.

As Kitty tried to move, Forster reached out blindly and snatched a fistful of her gown, dragging her down. The extra weight wrenched my right arm, still wrapped about the mullion. He would pull us both down with him.

The platform was rocking violently beneath my feet. I put my lips to Kitty's ear. 'Dagger. Inside pocket.'

She groped in my coat and found her own dagger, tucked in the hidden pocket she had sewn for me herself, long months before. She pulled it free and plunged it into Forster's hand where it gripped her gown, grinding the blade back and forth. There was a sickening sound as blade met bone. Forster screamed. Kitty lifted the knife and stabbed again, and again, hacking savagely at his fingers.

He let go.

And in that eternal instant before he fell I saw first astonishment and then rage, pure and terrible as fire.

His howls echoed from the tower walls.

And then, silence.

Afterwards

Chapter Twenty-seven

We limped down the tower steps without a word. When we reached the bottom Kitty sank to the ground, the horror only now catching up with her. I found Forster's body amidst the rubble – a terrible, mangled, bloody sight. This was the death I had been prepared to accept for myself, only a few minutes before – the death Forster had planned for Kitty. This could have been her body lying broken on the ground. But we were breathing and he was not – and in that moment I felt blessed by the privilege of life.

I helped Kitty to her feet. She had a bump on the side of her head, and was grazed and bruised. The wound to her ear looked the most savage – the blood had poured down her neck and stained her gown. The cut would mend, but it would leave a scar, and it made me sick to think that Forster had left his mark upon her.

I found my sword and slotted it in my belt, tucked my dagger into my coat. My pistols were broken. I kicked them into a corner.

Fountains Hall was only a short walk away, but Kitty looked as though she might fold in upon herself. 'Let me carry you.'

She shook her head, then gave a gasp of pain. When the spasm had subsided, she staggered over to Forster's body and stared at it for a moment. Then she spat in his ruined face. 'I can walk,' she said. 'I can walk.'

We headed down the middle of the nave towards the great west window. There we stopped and stared up at the heavens. It was long past midnight. I was – quite by accident – in church on a Sunday. It had been a while.

Kitty touched my hand. 'You would have died for me.' She gazed out through the window into the night beyond, to the glimmering stars and the crisp half-moon. 'I suppose I shall have to marry you now.'

I put my hands in my breeches' pockets. 'Not sure I asked.'

She laughed, and linked her arm in mine. Murmured in my ear. 'If you gamble away my fortune I will shove you off a ledge myself.'

She was jesting, naturally.

I think she was jesting.

'A tragic accident,' John Aislabie said.

'Tragic,' Mr Messenger echoed.

The two men were in agreement for once. The truth, were it widely known, would damage them both. Messenger had invited Forster to Fountains Hall, and Aislabie had given him the freedom of his estate. No one would blame them for what had happened, but no one would forget, either. Fountains Hall and Studley Royal would be for ever associated with an infamous killer.

'A cruel fate for such a holy place,' Messenger said.

'Bad for land values,' Aislabie concurred.

So the truth was replaced with a few pragmatic falsehoods. Aislabie announced that Mr Sneaton had fallen, dashed his head, and drowned. No talk of the bloodstains at his cottage, nor how he might have struggled his way through the park at night without his walking stick. As for the accusations surrounding Mr Forster, and the attendant search – this had all been an unfortunate misunderstanding. He must have slipped and fallen to his death while sketching the old belfry. He should never have ventured on to such a narrow platform – not with his arm in a sling.

I wasn't convinced people would believe there had been two violent accidents within the space of one day, both of them suspicious. But Messenger was respected, and Aislabie was powerful. That same morning, the parson at Kirkby Malzeard and the Dean of Ripon cathedral were leading their congregations in prayers for the two unfortunate gentlemen who had died so tragically, God rest their souls.

I doubted – extremely – that Francis Forster's soul would be making God's acquaintance.

Martin Bagby was not discovered until the following evening, in an obscure corner of the east wing. His body had been wrapped in a dustsheet and shoved under a bed, with a horrible lack of dignity. The blood had pooled beneath him, staining the floorboards and the ceiling below.

It was too late by then to place the blame upon Forster, so to avoid uncomfortable questions, Mr Gatteker was persuaded to declare the death a self-murder. Aislabie arranged matters discreetly so that his ill-starred butler might have a Christian burial. A generous gesture, somewhat marred by his complaints about the ruined floorboards, and the cost and inconvenience of the necessary repairs.

But I have raced ahead of myself.

It was almost dawn by the time we left Fountains Hall. Kitty did not fancy jolting back to Studley in a carriage – she said the thought alone made her head throb twice as hard. So we walked instead, soaked by a sudden rain shower and protected by two of

Aislabie's men, who were by now most confused by all the rumours of murder, and accidents, and injuries. No doubt they suspected something closer to the truth than they were told, but they held their tongues – at least in front of us.

I had been almost dead upon my feet until now, but the pelting rain woke me up. By the time we arrived at Studley I was restored, though a glance at my reflection showed pale cheeks and red eyes, and the hollow stare of a man dragged back from the brink of Hell.

Up in our apartment we found Sam awake, drifting in and out of understanding. His face softened with relief when he saw us. Kitty was so tired that she could scarcely stand, so I helped her into the tiny bed next door, taking off her shoes and loosening her stays so she could free herself from her sodden clothes.

She slipped under the sheets. 'What a night we've had,' she yawned, understating events somewhat. I rolled the blanket up to her chin and kissed her forehead, marvelling at her resilience. She was already asleep.

Back in our chamber, I stoked the fire and laid my head against the wall, grateful for the heat from the chimney. Then I lifted down the painting of the abbey, tore it from its frame, and fed it to the flames.

I could not stop thinking of the moment on the platform, when I was preparing to jump. If I closed my eyes, the floor dropped away and I felt as if I were falling. A fresh scene for future nightmares. But there was a sense of relief too – of joy, almost.

Ever since my hanging I had felt a dull but constant sense of dread that by cheating Death, I had somehow summoned him to my side. If I'd made this dolorous observation to Kitty she would have said it was a natural reaction to being hanged and shoved in a coffin. But was it really so fanciful? Sam – for all his suspicion of metaphysics – had drawn a charcoal shadow about my shoulders.

As I gazed into the fire, I realised that this shadow had now dissolved away. I had offered up my life freely, and Death had not taken it.

The debt was paid. I was free.

'She saved my life,' Sam murmured from the bed, so softly I thought he was dreaming.

He meant Kitty, presumably.

'Sheet.'

This was elliptical, even for him. Later, Kitty told me she had thrown the sheet over him when Forster burst through the door. Sam had lain still, pretending to be dead, while Forster and Kitty fought. He couldn't help her. He couldn't even cry out for help.

'Forster's dead,' I told him. 'He fell from the abbey tower.'

He grunted, pleased. 'Wattson?'

'He wasn't there. But I know where to find him.' I had puzzled it out on my walk from Fountains Hall, who Thomas Wattson really was, and where I would find him. 'I'll deal with him.'

'Wait for me.'

I thought about this. Wattson didn't know I had unmasked him, and if I spoke with Metcalfe no one else would, either. 'As you wish. We'll ride out together when you're strong enough.'

He soon fell asleep again. I sat with him as the sun rose, listening to the crackle of the fire, and marvelling that we were all safe. A blackbird began to sing, sweet and clear in the morning air.

I rose, and stretched, and went to tell Mrs Fairwood that her brother was dead.

The next morning I found Lady Judith sitting alone at breakfast, wearing her distracting breeches. She had already taken a long ride through the estate and said she felt much the better for it.

'How does your wife fare?'

'Well, I think. She is dressing her hair. Your husband?'

She sighed. 'He is in his study, dealing with correspondence. It is best he remains busy. He'll recover, in time. We all will, I suppose.' She glanced at Sneaton's empty chair. 'It will help when that wretched woman has left the county.'

I lowered my fork. 'She's still here?'

'Not at Studley, by God! She stays at the Oak – won't leave until her brother is buried. Can you believe that devil will lie buried in consecrated ground? I should not be surprised if the earth boils around his coffin in protest.' She buttered a piece of toast. 'Speaking of such *grave* matters . . . I spied a great mound of earth by the lake this morning.'

I coughed, and pretended to search for my pipe. 'Indeed?'

'*Indeed*. It looked as though someone had dug a hole, and then filled it in again.'

I fumbled for my pouch of tobacco. 'How curious. By the lake, you say?'

'Yes. Next to the sphinx. Next to the *queen's claws*. Oh, do stop fiddling with your pipe, Mr Hawkins.' She acted displeased, but there was a glint of humour in those wide blue eyes of hers. 'I hear that you and my nephew set out for the gardens last night with a couple of shovels. Tell me, sir – if I searched your rooms, might I find a certain green ledger?'

'Absolutely not!' I cried. Not unless she reached up Kitty's petticoat and found her underpocket.

Lady Judith gave me a sidelong look. 'I don't suppose my husband will ever return to office.'

'He did blackmail the queen.'

'In which case,' she said, her eyes still fixed upon mine, 'I suppose the ledger is of little value to him. And it would present no danger, either, as long as the contents remain secret.'

I inclined my head. I had already decided not to reveal the details of the ledger. Not to save Mr Aislabie's reputation, not for all the world. But to stop a war – for this I would stay silent. While it was tempting to publish and see the government and the royal family destroyed by scandal, the attendant chaos would almost certainly tear the country apart. At the very least it would give France and the Stuarts the spur to attempt another invasion.

If Kitty had died at the abbey, I think I might have done it. In my grief, I would have let England bleed with me. Hundreds would have died, maybe thousands. We might have King James III upon the throne, instead of George II. And Forster – somewhere in the deepest furnace of hell – would have had the most spectacular revenge.

But Kitty lived, and kept the ledger safe. Strange to think that, for a few brief moments, I held the nation's destiny in my hands. I still wonder, sometimes, whether I made the right decision.

Chapter Twenty-eight

Three days later, Francis Forster was buried in the graveyard at Kirkby Malzeard. The parson gave a short sermon, speaking of a young gentleman with a generous heart and prodigious talent, who would now fulfil his promise building palaces in Heaven. I closed my eyes and prayed instead for Jack Sneaton and Martin Bagby.

At the graveside, Mrs Fairwood sobbed with a desperate grief, drawing sympathetic glances from those who stood with her. There were rumours spreading about the neighbourhood that she and Mr Forster had been engaged to marry. Those who knew the truth gritted their teeth and said nothing. The world must think Forster had died through accident, and so his crimes were buried along with his body.

Lady Judith attended the funeral on behalf of the Aislabie family. She wore a gown of orange silk with a black quilted petticoat, and a straw hat trimmed with an orange ribbon. 'Poor Mr Forster did so love his bright clothes,' she said, when people commented upon her gay attire. 'I thought I should honour him. *Do not tell a soul*,' she murmured in my ear as we walked from the grave. 'But I am dressed as the flames of Hell.'

I was helping her into the carriage when Mrs Fairwood rushed forward, holding a note in her grey-gloved hand. 'Lady

Judith,' she cried, loud enough that others would hear. 'I beg you would give this to your husband. *Only to him.* Please, madam.'

Lady Judith had already settled herself into the furthest corner of the carriage, but Mrs Fairwood had placed a foot upon the step, and half the neighbourhood was watching. With a great sigh, she leaned forward and took the note. Then she sat back, staring straight ahead.

I joined her in the carriage and we rode back towards Studley. The note lay upon her knee. 'I should burn it,' she said.

We rode for another mile.

'Damn the woman,' she muttered, and broke the seal.

We passed beneath a tunnel of trees, the air turning cold in the shade. As we burst back out into the glorious sunshine, she handed me the note.

Sir—

Your daughter lives. I shall wait for you at Midnight, at the banqueting house. Come alone and you may learn the Truth.
E.F.

Lady Judith had turned her back to me, her hand gripping the side of the carriage. I could tell from the set of her shoulders that she was crying silently. If she gave her husband the note he would have to meet with Mrs Fairwood, who would doubtless spin more of her insidious lies. But if Lady Judith said nothing, and it were true . . .

We returned to the house in silence. 'Not a word, please sir,' she said, as she stepped from the carriage. 'I beg you. Not even to your wife.'

We spoke no more of it until that evening. We sat together at supper, Mr Aislabie at the other end of the table, trying his best to charm Kitty. There were grey shadows under his eyes, and he had the look of a man recovering from a fever. There were moments when his gaze would flicker to Kitty, and I knew he was thinking of Mrs Fairwood and the dream of his lost daughter. Moments too when the conversation turned to the estate, and although no one dared mention Sneaton, his spirit seemed to weigh upon the room. The meal was not finished when Aislabie made his apologies and left the table, complaining of a headache.

Lady Judith put a hand upon my arm as we left the dining room. She guided me to the snug withdrawing room next door. There were no candles lit, and I could only just glimpse her outline in the gloom. 'I cannot tell him,' she whispered. 'I cannot let her torture him any more.'

I waited in silence, knowing what she would ask, and knowing that I would say yes.

The gardens were spectral and strange in the dark – a thousand shades of black. I could hear the roar of the cascade somewhere to my left, and the rustle of night animals in the bushes. The wind tore through the upper branches of the highest trees, and dense clouds covered the moon. I lifted my lantern and took the high path to the banqueting house.

She stood alone in the middle of the coffin lawn, the grey hood of her riding gown shielding her face, the cape rippling against the wind. Six flaming torches lit the scene, one placed at each corner of the coffin.

It was just as her brother had imagined it, except that she was alive and he was dead.

I stepped forward, holding the lantern high.

Her face fell as she saw me. 'Where's Aislabie?'

'I have come on his behalf.'

She gave a hollow laugh. 'And does he know this? No matter. I will not speak with you.'

'Very well.' I turned and began to walk away.

'Murderer!' she screamed at my back.

I swung the lantern about.

She flung back her hood, her dark hair loose about her face. 'You killed my brother!'

I laughed, incredulous. 'Your brother tried to kill my wife—'

'Liar! You threw him from the tower. And now he is dead, he cannot defend himself against your foul slander. But I know. I *know.*' She tore at her chest, as if she would rip out her heart.

I almost pitied her in that moment – the last surviving member of her family, alone and raging at the world. Defending, in death, the brother she had feared so much in life, and who caused her years of torment. But she had brought this final torture upon herself. 'Two men are dead because you came to Studley. Will you not redeem yourself, madam? Will you not tell the truth at last?'

She threw me a mock-innocent look. 'But Mr Sneaton *fell*. Everyone says so. And poor Mr Bagby killed himself.'

It began to rain, softly.

'Elizabeth Aislabie. Is she alive?' I snapped.

She laughed again, then glanced at the nearest torch, the flame pulling and dancing in the wind. She took a piece of paper from her pocket and touched it to the flame. It caught light at once, turning her face orange in the glow. 'That was Molly Gaining's true confession. She gave it to Francis the night before she died. I would have given it to Aislabie, if he'd come as I asked.'

I watched the last fragments burn, orange embers turning to grey ash. Some floated to the ground, while others spun high into the air, caught in the wind. Was it real? Or another counterfeit?

She brushed the soot from her fingers. 'It was such a *tender* note. Elizabeth has grown into a fine young woman, with two children of her own. Was it a boy and a girl? Two boys?' She gave a little shrug. 'I can't quite recall.'

The rain fell harder, heavy drops hitting the dry grass between us. 'So she lives in one of the colonies. You must remember where.'

'I'm afraid those details weren't in the letter. Francis knew them. Where she lived, her new name. Now, he did mention that to me, once . . . Clara, Catherine?' She gave a sly smile.

'She will come forward herself, no doubt.'

'Oh, the girl knows nothing of her true heritage. And even if she did . . .' Her laugh sent a shiver through me. 'Do you think Mr Aislabie would believe her, without proof? After he believed in *me*? Imagine what a cruel fate that would be – if he rejected his real daughter.'

'I think you know a good deal about cruelty, madam. If any of this is true, you have separated a father and daughter for ever. May God judge you upon it.' I turned to leave.

'I shall write to him!' she called after me. 'You think to protect him, but I shall write to him again. I shall keep writing, and one day, one of my letters will reach him. And he will always wonder, for the rest of his life. It will torment him. It will *kill* him.'

I turned back to face her. The torches were blowing out in the wind and the rain, flames sizzling as they spluttered and died. Her wet hair clung to her face, but she kept her hood down. 'You will not write to him,' I said.

She drew back a pace. 'I have a dagger,' she warned.

I smiled at her. 'I am not Sam's guardian. He has a father: the captain of a gang of thieves.' I folded my arms. 'Someone hurt his wife, once. Many years ago. A gentleman, and a brothel keeper. He bound them together, back to back. And then he set them on fire.' I paused. 'Imagine if he found out that his only son nearly died – because of you.'

Her eyelids fluttered. 'You . . . you would not.'

I stared at her through the rain.

She shivered, pulling her drenched cloak about her shoulders. The last of the torches fizzled out, leaving only my lantern alight.

'Go home, Mrs Fairwood,' I said.

Chapter Twenty-nine

It was another week before Sam was well enough to ride out to Kirkby moors. In all this time, Thomas Wattson had not once come to work on the stables. Simpson said he'd given him up as a lost cause. 'Shame. Worked hard, that one. And he had a talent with a chisel. Worth ten of these bloody wastrels.' His men exchanged amused, unspoken thoughts about this, over his head. Simpson was the sort of master who never praised a man until he was out of hearing, or dead.

As Sam recovered, Kitty and I watched for signs of any permanent damage to his mind or his body. At the very least, I expected him to be more cautious, and less given to jumping out of windows. Whether this was the case was hard to tell, as he was not yet strong enough to leap about in his usual way. A direct enquiry about his health was rewarded with a shrug, or – if he were feeling voluble – an irritable grunt.

Kitty would have joined us on our visit to the moors, but she had already promised to take a ride about the estate with Lady Judith. It transpired that Mrs Aislabie had several pairs of *riding breeches for ladies*, as she termed them. An etiquette had formed around these garments, in consultation with Mr Aislabie: they were not to be worn about the house, and were designed solely for the benefit of touring the estate to some specific purpose. Lady Judith had become expert at finding a new *specific purpose* each morning just after breakfast, and had given Kitty two pairs of breeches as a gift, not that she could ever wear them in public without being arrested as some sort of *hermaphroditic invert.**

So I rode out with Sam. I need not trouble you with our conversation, as there was none. I was content to let Athena set the pace, and as we did not encounter any burst deer guts, or murderous architects, we muddled along very well. I patted her flank. 'I shall miss you, when I go home.'

Athena pricked up her ears, and gave a soft snort.

'D'you see that, Sam?' I said. '*Conversation.*'

Sam curved his lips. We continued on in silence, until we reached the Gills' cottage.

'*Remember who you are.*' That had been Sneaton's warning to Wattson, when he had dared to ask about Simpson's bill. I'd assumed Sneaton was reminding Wattson of his lowly position as a journeyman, but the warning had been more precise than that. *Remember who you are, Thomas Gill. Annie Gill's boy.*

Sneaton had told me the Gills had nine children. I'd counted eight when I'd visited the cottage. Of course the ninth might have been anywhere, and there had been no reason to think he had been sitting at the table, dangling his baby sister on his knee. Should I have noticed how easy she seemed with him? She'd giggled with joy when he bounced her up and down, and screamed when he set her on the floor.

---

* Aislabie sent me a bill for this *gift* a few months later. I ignored it. It now hangs upon the wall above my desk, next to the order banning my entrance to the Marshalsea prison, and the royal pardon exonerating me of murder. Aislabie also claimed he was missing a fork, but in faith I have not the slightest notion what he meant by that.

I suppose I should at least have been suspicious when he turned his horse about and rode back to the cottage, presumably to give a warmer farewell to his family. He'd claimed that little Janey had stolen the coins from his pocket, but he had not been paid a farthing since Christmas. And even if there had been a single coin left to steal, would he have been so easy about its theft?

Once I had begun to consider the idea, other thoughts struck me. How he had volunteered to ride out with us, and had seemed so pleased by the journey. How he shared Annie Gill's high cheekbones, and her tall frame. How he'd known about the poachers' track beneath Gillet Hill, where we had found Sam. Not that the Gills were poachers, *no indeed*.

The dogs began barking before we saw the cottage. 'It's hidden in that copse,' I said, pointing towards a cluster of oaks and elms ahead. 'Won't see it until we're hard upon it.'

Sam snuffed in approval. His father's den was buried deep in a maze of streets, surrounded by a square of taller houses. No one reached it without being seen by at least a half-dozen of Fleet's men.

By the time we entered the copse, three of the younger Gills had climbed into the branches. They whispered over our heads as we passed beneath them. The oldest one – a boy of about nine or ten – made a hissing sound between his teeth. Sam twisted in his saddle, and with impressive aim threw a stone through the branches, hitting the boy squarely on his forehead. He gave a yelp, then began to cry.

'*Sam!*'

'Lesson.' He lifted his voice, so the boy could hear. 'You going to hiss, keep out of range.'

'They're only children, Sam.'

He gave me his *How have you survived this long?* look, and slid from his saddle.

330

Annie Gill stood in the doorway, pinning up her grey hair in honour of our arrival. Little Janey clung to her skirts, sucking her thumb. 'Gentlemen,' Annie said, warily, as we approached.

'Mistress Gill. I'm here to speak with your son Thomas.'

She opened her mouth to protest, then thought better of it. 'He's not here.'

'Then fetch him, please. We'll wait.' I put my hand lightly upon the hilt of my sword.

She drew herself up tall. 'I'm not afraid of you, sir.'

'Then you'll see no harm in sending for him, will you?'

The cottage was quieter today: the baby was fast asleep, and the rest of the Gills were outside somewhere, including Jeb. We sat at the rough table to wait. Janey toddled up to Sam and gazed at him with the unconditional adoration tiny children give to older ones. She raised up her arms. 'Lift.'

Sam pulled her on to his lap, so that she was facing him. 'My name's Sam,' he said, bumping her on his knees with each word. 'What's your name?'

'Janey.'

'How many sisters you got, Janey? Can you count them?'

'Three.'

'Only three?' Sam held out his hand, stretched his fingers wide. 'I got five. One, two, three, four five.' He counted off each finger in turn, and tapped his thumb to her nose for the fifth.

Janey giggled.

'I've a sister your age. She's called Bea.'

'Bea!' Janey yelled at the top of her lungs, then started buzzing.

The two of them chattered away happily, while I watched in astonishment. By the time Wattson had arrived (for that is how I still thought of him), Sam was tilting his head forward so that Janey could poke her finger into his curls. Wattson frowned, and plucked her from Sam's lap. After much wailing, she was persuaded to toddle outside and find her siblings.

Wattson joined us at the table while his mother sewed by the fire, listening to every word.

'Glad to see you well, Master Fleet,' Wattson said, gruffly.

'No thanks to you,' I said.

He rubbed his thumb across his palm. At least he had the decency to look ashamed.

'Do you think he had a choice?' Annie said, without looking up from her stitching. 'It's not *his* fault.'

'Yes it is, Mother,' Wattson muttered.

Annie didn't hear him. 'If you're looking to blame someone, start with John Aislabie. Painting us all as thieves and ruining our name. *Never trust a Gill.* How was Thom supposed to find honest work?'

'So you changed your name.'

'Didn't want to,' Wattson said. 'But all the best work's up at Studley. Mr Sneaton said I could work on the stables if I took a different name. Said a man should be judged by what he does, not who he is.' He looked away.

'How did Forster find out?'

'That devil!' Annie stabbed her needle into the cloth. 'May he burn in hell for ever.'

'There's a few fellows that know I'm a Gill,' Wattson said. 'Them that grew up hereabouts. And there's a girl, works up at Fountains Hall. We were close, for a time.'

Annie snorted something under her breath.

'Forster threatened to reveal who you were.'

Wattson nodded. 'I would have been thrown off the estate on the spot. But it weren't just that—'

'And he's still owed his last quarter pay,' Annie said loudly, trying to cover his words. 'Wouldn't have seen a farthing.'

'Mother—'

'No more, love,' she warned. 'It's not your fault—'

'Will you rest?' His voice boomed through the cramped cottage. 'It's *my* story and I shall tell it true – here if nowhere else.' He glanced at Sam. 'I owe him that.' He took a deep breath. 'I wrote the letters.'

Even Sam was surprised by this. 'First two?'

'I was angry. Kirkby moor has been common land since . . .' he gestured helplessly.

'Since God created it,' Annie finished.

'All Mr Aislabie does is ride about, pretending he's king of the bloody place. It's not right. He's made poachers of us folk for doing what our families have done for hundreds of years. I shouldn't have made all them threats, but I wanted him to take us seriously . . .'

'Well.' I pulled out my pipe and tobacco. 'He certainly did that.'

'They was good threats,' Sam nodded approvingly.

I lit my pipe. 'And Forster found out? How? The girl at Fountains, again?' Heaven save us from vengeful lovers.

He stared at his scarred stonemason's hands. 'We were set to marry. But when I told her I was a Gill she said she weren't marrying into a den of thieves.'

'I shall have words with Jenny Flynn, the next time we meet,' Annie promised. '*More than words.*'

That sounded fair to me, though Wattson looked pained about it. Still in love with her, poor devil. 'Forster came up to me one morning, out by Mr Sneaton's cottage, said his horse were lame and would I help him. I'd seen him about the estate so I thought nothing of it. We went into the woods and he drew his pistol, aimed it square at my chest. He said he knew I were a Gill, and that I wrote the letters. And if I didn't do what he asked, he'd see me punished for it.'

333

'Worse than that,' Annie said. She rose and joined us at the table. 'Tell them the rest, love.'

He curled his fists at the memory. 'He thought I was like him, that I was after revenge. But all I wanted was for Mr Aislabie to *listen*. I said I wouldn't help him. And he says, *That's your choice, Gill.* Then he says: *Your parents must have known – I'll see them thrown in gaol for it. And how will your brothers and sisters survive then? They'll starve to death if they don't sell themselves, won't they?* He said he'd make sure Jenny was punished too, for not coming forward about the letters. She could be transported for it, he said. Then he told me what they did to young maids on the boats. Boys too . . .' He shuddered. 'If it were just me, I would have stood my ground. But he would have ripped this family apart, without a thought.'

Worse than that, I thought. He would have enjoyed it.

'It don't make it right, what I did. I know that. But he didn't ask for much, not at first. Just to keep an eye on Mrs Fairwood and let him know when she left the house. He liked her to know he was watching her. And I left the sheep's heart, with the note. I never thought . . .'

'And the deer, with its fawn?'

He sank his head into his hands. 'I don't want to think of it. Makes me sick.'

'Forster killed them, I suppose? And the stags?'

Wattson groaned, without dropping his hands. 'He gave them names, as he slit their throats. He said: *This one's Aislabie. This one's Metcalfe. This one's Mrs Fairwood.* He hated them all.'

'Did you know Mrs Fairwood was his sister?'

He looked up, stupefied with horror. His mother poured him a mug of beer without a word. He wrapped his hands about it, but didn't drink.

I took a long draw from my pipe. There seemed no point in asking him if he had helped carry the stags – no doubt he did.

Three stags laid out to match the Robinson coat of arms, to sow confusion and to frighten Metcalfe. 'And this was what you saw, Sam? Up at the banqueting house?'

'I never saw you, Master Fleet,' Wattson said. 'And I'm very sorry. I should never have let him hurt you.'

'No,' I said, because here was the crux of the matter. 'You should not. You let him lie there for hours.'

'I thought he were dead. God help me. I didn't know what to do. I had to go back to my post, guarding the house. I stood there in the dark . . . Dear Lord in Heaven, may I never know another night like it. Standing there with the rest of the men, all of 'em laughing because they thought it were some great joke, and they would be paid for it. And all the time I knew Forster had killed a boy, and I'd stood by and let him do it. God forgive me . . .'

'Worse,' Sam corrected. 'You held me.'

Wattson hung his head. 'I decided I would go to Mr Sneaton at dawn, and tell him everything. I was so ashamed. He'd taken a chance with me, and this was how I repaid him. But then I came to the cottage and you were there, sir, and there was blood . . . When I saw Forster, I knew he'd killed Mr Sneaton. And he just stood there on the steps, smirking. *Bastard.* I thought the least I could do was lead you to Gillet hill – and let God decide the rest.'

I sat back, drawing deep on my pipe. Annie was watching me closely, picking at her long fingers. If her son had told the truth, Forster would have been arrested. Kitty and I would have been spared that terrible night at the abbey, and Bagby would be alive. But as far as the world was concerned, Forster and Sneaton had died through accident, and Bagby was a suicide. Wattson couldn't stand trial unless we unravelled an entire web of lies, and in the end, what good would it serve? He would be transported, if he were lucky. More likely hanged. The Gills would be driven from their home.

In any case, this was not for me to decide.

'I could kill you,' Sam said, softly.

Wattson raised his head. His mother snatched up a knife, holding it ready.

'Not now,' Sam expanded. 'Somewhere quiet. When you wasn't expecting it.' He skewered Wattson with a black-eyed stare. One heartbeat. Two. 'But you was protecting your family.'

He rose swiftly, taking us all by surprise. 'I ever need you, you're mine. You ever cross me, you're dead.'

He held out his hand.

Wattson – after a moment's hesitation – reached out and took it. 'Thank you, sir.'

Sam nodded, satisfied. He looked just like his father.

Chapter Thirty

I wanted to see the moors one last time before we left: I doubted I would ever return to Studley again. I guided Athena up the cottage path and out towards the open wild.

'Hall's that way,' Sam said, hoicking his thumb down the hill.

'I want to show you something. Thank you for not killing Wattson.'

'No profit in it. You're welcome,' he added.

The weather had turned warm. It was almost May, and there was a feel of summer to the air. The grouse were less timid this time: I spotted a few heads poking up from the heather. A black and white bird with a long black crest darted across our path. 'Look.' I tapped Sam's arm. 'A lapwing.'

'What did you want to show me?'

'All this.' I gestured about me. 'The moors.'

'Waste of land. No cover. Where's the houses? Rubbish.'

I gave up. 'There might be some carrion up here. New bones to add to your collection. Rabbit, grouse. Maybe even a fox or a sheep's head.'

He dropped from his horse and hurried out into the heather.

We spent a good hour rambling across the moors in search of bones. For once, Sam forgave the country for being *empty* and *worthless* and became almost a boy again, hunting eagerly through the bracken for dead animals. We collected his finds in a sack and started back to Studley Hall.

'I've spoken with Kitty,' I said, bowing across Athena's neck to avoid a low branch reaching across the road. 'You're welcome to return home with us to the Cocked Pistol.' We had decided to delay our trip to the Continent, now that it was not needed. Home shone like a beacon in both our minds: the shop, Moll's coffeehouse, our own bed. 'Kitty will put some money aside for your studies. Do you still wish to become a surgeon?'

Sam was silent for a long time, even for him. He wouldn't look at me, staring off down the valley instead. 'I'm a Fleet,' he said, at last.

I was surprised. I'd been sure this would please him, that it was what he wanted more than anything. 'Why not think about it on the ride home? That's five days to consider the matter.'

And so we left it at that.

We spent one last night at Studley House. Metcalfe had already returned home to Baldersby to spend time with his father, but with a promise to visit the shop the first moment he arrived in London. 'Late September,' he said, 'if I'm well.' And then he put in an order for a couple of whores' dialogues from the shop, which Kitty promised to send up in some discreet fashion.

Mr Gatteker cared nothing for discretion, and spent a good half hour asking about our *curious* titles over supper. 'Mrs Gatteker is excessively voracious.' A pause. '*For books.*'*

Mr Aislabie was less appalled by this conversation than one might expect, and I'm convinced he ordered a few items for himself, under Gatteker's name. He was glad to see us go though:

---

* We never did meet Mr Gatteker's wife. Or his cat. It's possible that both were phantasms.

we were too much of a reminder of Mrs Fairwood, long returned to Lincoln but still haunting his thoughts. In truth we would have left days before if Sam had been strong enough to travel.

We played cards, and I lifted a further thirty pounds from the Aislabies. I'd earned it, and they could afford it. I distributed some of it about the servants and in particular Sally Shutt, Francis Pugh, William Hallow, and Mrs Mason. Hallow said I would dance with the angels in heaven, which sounded agreeable. Mrs Mason packed some extra bottles of claret in with our baggage.

Sam slunk off on his own to say goodbye to Sally. He'd bought her a ribbon, or to be more precise, he had stolen one of Kitty's. Sally must have liked it, as he came back an hour later with a certain swagger in his step.

There was a quiet moment that final evening when I stepped out into the park to smoke a pipe and watch the deer grazing beneath the beech tree. The sun was setting, the sky a glorious red. The air was fresh and warm, and, as I stood upon the steps, I felt a promise of better days ahead. The water trough stood on its hillock, looking for ever like a tomb. But it felt as though Jack Sneaton's spirit had moved on: God willing to a happier place.

A rustle of skirts behind me. Lady Judith, in a cornflower blue gown that matched her clever eyes. 'What a splendid evening.' She put a gloved hand upon my arm. 'My husband is too proud to thank you. I wish I could tell him *all* you have done on his behalf.' We had said nothing to him of my midnight rendezvous with Mrs Fairwood.

'Does he still hunt for the ledger?'

A half smile.

I lowered my voice. 'Did you speak with Metcalfe?' I'd suggested that he might be able to make a few discreet enquiries about Elizabeth Aislabie. Most likely Mrs Fairwood had been lying, but there were one or two paths he might explore.

'He has promised to investigate, quietly. He blames himself for all of this, you know.'

'Metcalfe?'

'It's his nature.'

Three words, and a depth of sadness beneath them.

'We are lucky, are we not?' I said. 'To be blessed with sanguine temperaments.'

'We are, Thomas.' She leaned closer, brought her lips to my ear. 'We *are*.'

We left just before dawn, Kitty at my side, Sam upon the opposite bench with his back to the horses. Pugh took us as far as Ripon, where we'd hired a coach, paid for by the queen, who was – at present – feeling generous. I'd written to let her know that the ledger was in my possession and that Aislabie would trouble her no longer. I had not added that I intended to keep the ledger to ensure she did not force me on another mission, or threaten to hang Kitty for murder. So for now she was grateful, and I intended to make the most of her largesse.

The roads were improved with the good weather, and we travelled with open windows, the scent of fresh grass and cow dung wafting through the carriage.

'Stinks,' Sam muttered, the boy from St Giles, where weaker men fainted from the noisome air. A magnificent pair of antlers rested on the seat next to him – an eccentric memento from his trip. I was certain I'd seen them last hanging in the great hall at Studley. I whiled away a good half hour wondering how he'd smuggled them out.

Kitty and I drank a bottle of wine and made each other laugh all the way to Blyth, where we planned to rest for the night.

'You are yourself again,' she said, as I helped her from the carriage.

I kissed her, not sure if this were true, or even what it meant.

The innkeeper sent boys out to collect our baggage. Sam watched them with the suspicious eyes of a thief. 'I know everything in them bags,' he called after them. He snatched his sack of carrion treasures from the hands of a younger boy, eyes burning like a demon. He had boiled down the bones and planned to display them when he returned home – wherever that might be – a grouse, two rabbits, a badger's skull, and the antlers. I could pretend this was simply his inquisitive mind at play; the questing, questioning spirit that made him want to become a surgeon. But there was more to Sam Fleet than that. Dark and light, with no promise of which would triumph, in the end.

The innkeeper was offended. 'My boys are honest, sir. Please tell your valet not to worry.'

'He's not my valet,' I said, following Sam inside. 'He's my brother.'

Epilogue

June, 1728
Charles Towne, in the Province of Carolina

Charlotte d'Arfay walks down the cobbled path to the harbour, holding her son James by the hand. They have come to see the great ship arrived from England. She walks slowly in the heat, sweat glistening on her brow, skirts clinging to her long legs. There will be a thunderstorm later, she can feel it in the air. She puts a hand to her stomach and wonders about her baby. She would like a daughter this time, after two boys, but will not tempt fate with wishes.

If she could wish for anything, she would ask for her mother to return home safely from England. She knows in her heart this won't happen. She has received no word in over six months. The trip remains a mystery. Charlotte's mother has always been a private woman, not given to dramatic gestures or impulsive acts. What could be so important that she must leave her home and head for England, abandoning her family and her friends? Why would she travel so far, in such poor health?

Charlotte suspects she will never see her mother again, not in this life. But still she comes down to the harbour whenever a ship arrives, and watches the passengers as they clamber on to dry land.

It is too hot for holding hands. James runs ahead along the path, so like his father it makes her smile. She's glad Christopher has decided to sell his commission and leave the army. Now the family can settle permanently in Charles Towne. She has designs upon a plot of land on Chalmers Street. Christopher will need persuading: he lost the d'Arfay fortune to the South Sea Scheme, and it has made him cautious with money. Charlotte teases her husband, but in truth she loves his steadiness and his good sense. Better a careful man than some feckless gambler, over fond of liquor and low company. Thank God she did not marry one of those devils.

The passengers are being rowed to shore in small boats. She is close enough now to see the relief on their faces. Dry land at last. James waves to them as they stagger up the harbour steps, bodies used to the sway of the sea. Her heart lifts when she spies a woman of middling age wearing a green hood. But it's not her mother.

'Can we go there, Mama?' James is pointing at the ship – an English galley with a red ensign drooping in the humid air.

She smiles, indulging him. 'You wish to go aboard?'

'Aye, and sail to England!'

She laughs, and ruffles his hair. They have no reason to go to England. Christopher's family disowned him when he lost his estate. And she has no relations there.

Charlotte's gaze skims over the ship. For a moment she feels the world tilt about her, as if she were on the ocean. She is very small, younger even than James. A white sail soars like a cliff above her head. The boards creak beneath her feet, and the wind tugs at her hair. Her clothes are damp and smell of salt water. She sees her own tiny fist stretched out in front of her, clutching on to a rope. Her mother is there, guiding her steps.

She shakes her head, and the vision is gone. Charlotte has never sailed on a galley. She has never crossed the ocean. She was born here in Virginia.

But sometimes she dreams of water, and sometimes she dreams of fire.

The baby stirs and kicks. She draws James's head to her belly so he can feel it. He giggles, then pulls away and races back up the path, away from the harbour. Charlotte follows him, fanning herself in the heat.

Historical Note

I'm happy to report that there were no murders at Fountains Abbey or Studley Hall in 1728 – at least, not to my knowledge. However, the story is based in part on real characters, incidents, and situations. Most of this information came from fascinating estate records held in the West Yorkshire Archives. It was here that I discovered the wonderful and tragic Metcalfe Robinson, John Simpson's desperate demands for payment, and Mrs Mason's kitchen accounts. I also encountered John Aislabie himself through his letters – complaining about John Messenger, voicing suspicions about the Gill family, obsessing over his horses, and arguing over the price of everything. ('The prices of the yeiws were most extravagante and I do not know what you mean by four pounds for Garden Seeds'.)

So, for those who are curious about the facts and stories behind the novel, here are some notes, followed by a list of the real characters in the book, and a description where possible of what happened to them next.

'Elizabeth' Aislabie and the fire on Red Lion Square

In January 1701 a fire tore through John Aislabie's London home. His wife Anne died in the blaze. Their baby son William was saved when a servant threw him from a high window. Sisters Jane and Mary also survived. A third and youngest daughter died in the fire with her mother. Sadly, I could find no reference to her name. She's not mentioned in the family tree that now hangs in Fountains Hall, or on the plaque above the family vault in Ripon cathedral. I chose to call her Elizabeth as Aislabie had both an aunt and a sister of that name.

Molly Gaining is my invention – but it was believed that the fire was indeed started to conceal a theft.

The green ledger

Following the South Sea crash, Aislabie was thrown in the Tower. When asked to produce his accounts, he swore that his secretary had burned them, as was usual for his tallied books. (I've seen his accounts from his time as Treasurer to the Navy. Somewhat tragically, I even have pictures. So, you know ... *lying.*)

Aislabie bought South Sea stock on behalf of King George I, set at eye–wateringly corrupt discount prices. He also advised the Prince and Princess of Wales. The king invested tens of thousands of pounds from the Civil List into the scheme. Aislabie would have noted all this down in his private accounts. If they'd been published, even eight years later, it would have been catastrophic for the monarchy and the government. So while the story of Aislabie's blackmail is an invention, it's quite possible that he kept that ledger. Aislabie knew the price of everything, after all.

In fact, a similar accounts book was smuggled abroad just after the crash by the South Sea Company's cashier, Robert Knight. What happened next is too convoluted to recount here, but in order to keep the contents secret, the government agreed *in writing* to support the Holy Roman Empire in a potential war against Spain.

Fountains Abbey and Studley Royal

Studley Hall burned down in 1946. If you search for images, all but one show it after its grand Palladian remodelling by Aislabie's son William. Aislabie's water gardens are now a World Heritage site, owned and looked after by the National Trust, along with Fountains Abbey and Fountains Hall. The stables were completed in 1732. They survived the fire and are now a private home.

Aislabie never managed to purchase the abbey. In October 1720 – right in the middle of the South Sea debacle – John Messenger suddenly demanded more money, surely knowing Aislabie would refuse. Had he decided that he didn't want the abbey going to the now notorious chancellor? Aislabie declared, peevishly, '[Messenger] cou'd never induce me to give a farthing more for Fountains since I can do as well without it, and if I coud buy it to'morrow I shou'd not want it.' William Aislabie bought the abbey almost fifty years later, when the Messengers were short of funds again.

If you visit today – and you must! today! – you will see John Doe's follies, the deer park, the moon ponds, and the cascades. The banqueting house is still there with its rusticated icicle ornamentations, but before I turn into Mr Forster, let me wake you up with the news that by 1730 there was a statue of Priapus lurking behind it. It was later destroyed, but there are now three separate places to buy scones at Studley Royal, so that is some consolation.

Fountains Hall and Fountains Abbey remain much as they were. There are tombstones laid out on the floor of the chapter house, and the door to the tower steps is still there. Locked, of course.

The riddle of the sphinx(es)

There are four sphinxes in the water gardens. They've been moved around at various times, but one pair now sits by the footbridge on the lower cascade as they did in 1728. I have no proof that they were meant to represent Queen Caroline, but the resemblance is uncanny, right down to the golden locks, pearl necklace, and enormous bosom. Garden statuary was often invested with allegorical and political meaning in the eighteenth century, so it's feasible. And Queen Caroline was definitely sphinxy.

Anonymous notes and butchered deer

Anonymous threats were common throughout this period. E. P. Thompson includes numerous examples in his essay, 'The Crime of Anonymity'. I borrowed some phrases from them. Thompson also recounts how notes were sometimes smeared with blood, or left on a doorstep 'with a dead bird or beast . . . or even the heart of a slaughtered beast'.

Arson was by far the most popular threat. Studley Hall itself was damaged by fire at Christmas 1716 – Aislabie blamed Anne Gill for it. Someone also attacked and killed several of his deer around this time, to the point where he even considered getting rid of the herd.

Aislabie was zealous when it came to punishing poachers. When his steward caught a man stealing, Aislabie wrote: 'I wou'd have you proceed against Hodgson with all the vigour imaginable by bringing actions against him and lay him up in Goal [sic] for ever'. Then again – never trust a Hodgson.

Real people in the novel

John Aislabie

Aislabie never returned to power. He spent the rest of his days pouring all his ambitions into his family, his gardens, his horses, and his land. (I like to call this his extended gardening leave.) He died in 1742.

Judith Aislabie

Lady Judith was born in 1676, so Tom was right, she was over fifty when they met, not that this would have stopped him. Judith's son Edmund married Aislabie's daughter Jane, so they were quite the blended family.

Like her husband, Judith was very keen on horses and horse racing. In 1723 she was responsible for the first ever women's race, which took place at Ripon: 'Mrs Aislabie gave a plate to be run for by women, and nine of that sex mounted their steeds, rid astride, were dressed in drawers, waistcoats, and jockey caps, their shapes transparent, and a vast concourse of people to see them.'

Judith died in May 1740. In her will, she mentioned her granddaughters before her grandsons, and left them all an equal sum of £500. She bequeathed £500 to her daughter-in-law as well, along with much of her jewellery, noting twice that the money was 'for her own separate use ... to be put out by her direction'.

Metcalfe Robinson

I discovered Metcalfe Robinson through his lively if somewhat blotchy letters to his brother Thomas. He was funny, self–doubting, loyal, confessional, and loving. He also suffered from very serious bouts of depression. There were self-loathing comments

('I cannot but incommode you', 'I shall make a ridiculous figure') and worrying insights into his fragile state of mind ('After all my irresolutions which you was in the right to think might kill me').

Tragically, Metcalfe committed suicide in 1736. A legal document describes how he was deeply affected by his father's death, 'having laboured Severall years under a great disorder of mind'. Four days later, on 26 December 1736, Metcalfe 'shott himself through the head, and died instantly'. I can't help but think that his grief, coupled with the pressure of taking over as baronet, was simply too much to bear.

John Simpson

In autumn 1728, Simpson wrote a desperate letter to Aislabie regarding unpaid bills: 'I made bold to write to you to Studley on the 30th of Octo; but did not meet with the favour of an answer ... above is copy of my former to you of which I never had the least answer'. These were brave words, and Simpson quickly returned to the customary (and necessary) deference: 'Hoping your honour will not take this boldness in me amiss being on all occasions with the humblest respect honoured sir your most obedient humble servant.'

Nowadays, we would probably refer to Aislabie as a 'nightmare client' – changing his mind, haggling over costs, delaying payment, redesigning in the midst of construction. In the end, it seems to have broken Simpson – financially and physically. In December 1728, Aislabie's steward wrote to him: 'Last night Mr Simpson died, he only got his Bills made up last Friday night.' William Fisher, the head gardener, was even more blunt: 'I suppose you no that Mr Simpson is Dead and Died very poor and his work men all Ruined by him.'

The Gills

'I am not at all surpris'd at the accident that has happned; I know that Anne Gill is so devilish a woman that there is no mischief she cou'd invent, that she wou'd not execute. Is there no way to find it out? Let the reward for the discovery be never so great, I will pay it.' So wrote John Aislabie on 1 January 1716, following a mysterious fire at Studley Hall on Christmas day.

In April the same year, Aislabie writes about 'those rogues that kill'd the Deer'. He hopes that a reward might help break 'this gang' or '[drive] them out of the country'. Once again, he suspects the Gills: 'I wou'd give any money to fix it upon Gill or any of his companions'.

Perhaps the Gills were the leaders of a local gang – but no one was convicted for either crime. Something certainly seems to have happened between Anne Gill and Aislabie – he is still muttering darkly about her in a later letter.

Thomas Wattson

(Also spelled Watson.) When Simpson died in December 1728, William Fisher wrote at once to Aislabie: 'Theair is on of his men Thomas Watson a good work man and worked at the Canal Last Summer he Desiers me to write to yr Honor in his be halfe if you pleas to Employ him'. Aislabie replies: 'as to Thomas Watson, I know he is a good workman, and I shou'd give him what encouragement I can'. Shortly after that, Wattson appears regularly in lists of Robert Doe's men.

Mrs Mason

Mrs Mason's scrupulous accounts were an invaluable resource, revealing what would be ordered for the table in April, for example. The Aislabies, being astoundingly rich, ate well. In fact theirs was a model of a balanced diet – lots of fresh vegetables, fish and 'sallet'. Mrs Mason seems to have been given responsibilities beyond the kitchens – in one month alone she pays bills totalling £340 to (among others) bricklayers, gilders, masons, and plumbers.

Francis Pugh and William Hallow
Pugh turns up in a list of bills as a coachman, earning a monthly wage of fifteen shillings. (Aislabie's bill for wine at Studley in 1733 came to £182.) He also took trips to London, presumably driving members of the family, and/or belongings between the Aislabies' several houses. The head groom at Studley in 1728 was called Mr Benson – I amalgamated the roles for the purpose of the story. Hallow was unmarried when he came to Studley, and lived in a cottage on the estate.

John Messenger
Messenger would have been fifty-two in 1728. He was protective of the abbey as both a religious and historical site. At the same time, it was overgrown with ivy and there were several trees growing inside the ruins. There are no surviving estate papers for the Messenger family. However, the rivalry and animosity between the two families were of long standing, evident in border disputes and litigation spanning decades. Messenger died in 1749 aged seventy-three.

Mr Gatteker
There is a reference to an apothecary called Mr Gatteker in a set of bills for April 1734. He was paid just over £5. I liked his name so I stole it, and turned him into a physician. He may, or may not, have owned a cat.

Select bibliography

I would like to thank David Barnard for kindly sharing his own notes and illustrations, and for being so generous with his time. I met David in summer 2014, when he was training National Trust guides at Fountains Abbey. He gave me a fascinating and incredibly helpful tour in torrential rain. His research and his advice were invaluable as I began my own tentative studies.

For anyone looking for a comprehensive, beautifully illustrated book by the leading expert on Fountains and Studley, I recommend Mark Newman's *The Wonder of the North: Fountains Abbey and Studley Royal*. Unfortunately for me, it came out after I'd begun writing, but it was a very useful resource when I came to go through the final edits.

Needless to say any embellishments within the novel are mine alone.

Contemporary sources
Archival material
West Yorkshire Archives, Leeds

WYL150 (Vyner collection) and WYL5013 (Newby Hall) – a mixture of family letters, accounts, estate correspondence and legal documents, including letters by John Aislabie and Metcalfe Robinson, Simpson's bills, Mrs Mason's accounts, etc.

Centre for Buckinghamshire Studies, Aylesbury

The Diary of John Baker of Cornhill, linen draper, 25 May–13 July 1728. Baker wrote an entertaining diary of his tour of the north. He visited Studley Royal in June and was given a guided tour by John Aislabie. He also visited Baldersby, where the deer came right up to the window.

Speeches and commentary

'Mr Aislabie's Second Speech on his Defence in the House of Lords', 20 July 1721; 'Mr Aislabie's two Speeches Considered', 1721; 'The Speech of the Right Honourable John Aislabie, Esq, Upon his Defence made in the House of Lords', 19 July 1721; 'A Speech Upon the Consolidated Bill', 1721; 'A Vindication of the Honour and Justice of Parliament against a Most Scandalous Libel, Entitled, The Speech of John Aislabie, Esq.', 1721.

Secondary Sources

—*Dinner at Lacock in 1729* (Wiltshire Folklife Society)

—*Mr Aislabie's Gardens* (New Arcadians)

—*Studley Royal: A Celebratory Tour Occasioned by the Rejuvenation of the Pleasure Grounds* (New Arcadians)

Bates, Malcolm, *A Very English Deceit: The Secret History of the South Sea Bubble and the First Great Financial Scandal*

Hay, Douglas, 'Poaching and the Game Laws on Cannock Chase' (essay in *Albion's Fatal Tree*)

Horn, Pamela, *Flunkeys and Scullions: Life Below Stairs in Georgian England*

Parker, George, *Studley Royal and Fountains Abbey*

Paul, Helen Julia, *Politicians' and Public Reaction to the South Sea Bubble: Preaching to the Converted?*

Thompson, E. P., 'The Crime of Anonymity' (essay in *Albion's Fatal Tree*)

Willett Cunnington, C. & Cunnington, Phillis, *Handbook of English Costume in the 18th Century*

Acknowledgements

Thanks to my agent Clare Conville for her constant support and for being such an inspiring woman. To my amazing editor Nick Sayers for his encouragement and – once again – for some exceptionally good editorial notes. (And the inevitable request for more horses.) And to Kerry Hood at Hodder – look, I know you still hate a fuss, but thank you. Again.

To the whole team at Hodder – I take off my hat and execute a low, grateful bow. Particular thanks to Richard Peters and Alice Morley, to Lucy Hale for her dedication and enthusiasm, and to Cicely Aspinall for all her speedy and generous help. And to Charlotte Webb for a thoughtful and thorough copy-edit.

Much thanks to everyone at Conville & Walsh, especially Jake Smith-Bosanquet, Matt Marland, and Alexandra McNicoll.

Thanks to Sarah Sykes, Miranda Carter, Imogen Robertson, and Robyn Young. You fine, fine women, you. And to Maria Campbell for her kind support. Much love and thanks to David Shelley, Chris Gardner, Mark Billingham, Rowena Webb, Ian Lindsay–Hickman, Val Hudson, Lance Fitzgerald, PJ Mark, Gordon Wise, and Michael McCoy. And to my brilliant friends at Little, Brown, especially Cath Burke, Ursula Doyle, Clare Smith, Hannah Boursnell, Adam Strange, Richard Beswick, and Sean Garrehy.

Finally to my sisters in friendship: Justine Willett, Victoria Burns, and Joanna Krupa. And to Kay, Michelle, and Debbie, my sisters in blood, who are therefore stuck with me, the poor devils.

7